Misplaced Threats

Misplaced Humanity Chronicles

Book 1

Second Edition

Alan Zimm

Copyright © Year 2024

All Rights Reserved by **Alan Zimm.**

No part of this publication may be reproduced in any form, or by any means, electronic or mechanical, including photocopying, recording, or any information browsing, storage, or retrieval system, without permission in writing from Alan Zimm.

ISBN

Hardcover: 978-1-965134-89-4

Paperback: 978-1-965134-91-7

Disclaimer

No part of this publication may be reproduced, distributed, or transmitted in any form or by any means, including photocopying, recording, or other electronic or mechanical methods, without prior written permission of the author, except in the case of brief quotations embodied in reviews and certain other non-commercial uses permitted by copyright law.

First Printing 2024, Second Edition

1: *Machez*

Nitwits! Numbskulls! Lazy vakbrains, every one of them. Saboteurs!

Orbiting back-stabbing Spacers and Waisters. Who allows pinheads in space?

Blockheads! Incompetents! Dummies, in the Deep Dark!

Corporate Captain Manchez was fuming. Exhausted. Frustrated. Eyes closed, he imagined with great relish the details of the twitching dreadfuls that a righteous universe would inflict on the imbeciles he'd encountered over the last 24. They must have summoned every village idiot from all the Seventeen Systems to achieve such a concentration of stupid.

Manchez was floating in zero gravity at the pilot's station in the command deck of *Ajax,* a cargo shuttle returning from an impromptu sortie to Tevil Corporation's orbiting spaceyard. The cockpit was as dark as his mood, with only the faint glow of status lights, indicators, and monitors to mitigate the gloom. The forward viewscreen displayed an infinity of black sky. Stars fringing the galaxy loitered at the edge of the wrath of God; below lurked the ugly gray mass of Misplaced-4, leading the universe's list of premier unpleasant planets.

The pilot's combined control, radiation shield, and survival seat—known in Spacer's black humor as 'the coffin'—was shoved back so Manchez could stretch his legs. He loosened his seat belt and floated his heels above the instrument panel, oblivious to the high background gamma radiation. All the ineptitude he'd endured, and fourteen hours past bed time, was enough to make an archangel grab an axe and start doing a Lizzie Borden on every one of those microbrains wearing Tevil Corporation beige. *Lizzie Borden grabbed an axe, and gave those Waisters forty whacks, and when they all fell from the sky, all them scumbag mudpuckers would get hemorrhoids and athlete's foot and the galloping crud, and die!*

Okay, maybe not die, just a dose of the clap, or a painful equivalent. What they deserved. Pay-backs, not vengeance.

Manchez yawned. A nice siesta was in order, say, twelve hours, in bed, with somebody friendly.

The radio voice of the Organic computer controlling Misplaced-4's orbital approaches interrupted Manchez's exploration of appropriate diseases. "*Ajax,* this is Dome City Spaceport Approach Control Organic—"

Beginning every radio transmission with 'who to, who from' was a communications protocol Manchez wanted to nominate as spaceflight's foremost pain in the posterior. Why use it when dealing with Organic computers? So smart, they ought to be able to sort out who was talking. Dumb-ass Organics.

"—abbreviated title is Approach Control Organic. Your vector is good for Approach Cone Charlie. Cleared for approach."

His official title when flying *Ajax* was '*Ajax* Actual.' He wasn't supposed to make up a personal callsign; only Vakkers, that elite subset of independent Spacers, awarded individual callsigns. But dammit, if he had to do the 'verbatim repeat back of orders' comms protocol, an appropriate callsign would remind that tankhead of the quality of the rocket jock on his end of the conversation. Besides, it was way cool.

"Approach Control Organic, *Ajax* Actual, my callsign— SuperHero! Roger, SuperHero cleared, Cone Charlie, commencing approach." *And it would be greatly appreciated if you get every other nitwit barge out of my way, like now, max blast, speed-of-light.*

Manchez glanced at the arrival countdown chronometer, and grimaced. The predicted arrival time was way past the scheduled rendezvous with Mademoiselle Hot-Body. She'd kill him. Worse, she'd dump him. Bad, bad, bad.

It wasn't fair, the junior pilot always getting tagged with no-notice sorties. Yesterday, he had just snuggled under the covers after a shakin' 'n' rakin', groovin' 'n movin' night dancing and drinking, okay, a little late to hit the rack at 0630, but his next flight wasn't scheduled for another 48. He had just started on a lovely erotic dream when he'd been buzzed out of bed and got middle-fingered to deliver some Tevil Corporation Executive Bedpans or beauty cream or whatever it was that couldn't wait for the regular lift.

Then, he had to deal with those brain-dead oafs in orbit, the Shipyard One Assembly of Stupid. *First*, the slothful Union stevedores took the better part of an extended century to unload. *Then*, the lazy refuelers could have built Khufu's pyramids in the time they took to fill two lousy tanks with Rocket-A. *Next*, Spaceyard Traffic Control Organic, enjoying its impersonation of the Marquis de Sade, kept him in bondage before clearing him to launch for the return trip. Buddha blast the motherflogging morons, there was no excuse for the retaardvark service.

He was going to be bloody blue-blasted dammit-all late.

Manchez yawned and scrunched his eyes closed, seeing speckles of bright inside his eyelids.

To top it all, he got stuck driving *Ajax*, with her screwball-fruitcake freakin' nutcase Navigation and Shuttle Systems Organic. It was creepy ghoulish, growing brain tissue out of DNA and programming it like a silicon computer. Organics had superior parallel processing capacity and were honkin' fast, but sometimes they were just, just *weird*. Take *Ajax* Organic—the absolute worst! —an arrogant Frankenstein with an overinflated sense of narcissism flaunting the personality of a petulant three-year-old who had just popped his birthday balloon. Manchez would love to go nose-to-nose with the quant who programmed an Organic to sulk. Stupid quants. Stupid tankheads.

"SuperHero, Approach Control Organic. Approaches clear of traffic. Ground traffic clear. Direct approach is authorized, Pad Two."

Hallelujah! P2 was snug up to Dome City, only a three-hundred-meter tram ride to the terminal airlock.

His very own tankhead just had to butt in. "SuperHero, *Ajax* Organic. *Ajax* exceeds allowable approach velocity. Stand by for a thirty-second Number Six Aft Thruster braking burn. Acknowledge."

Freya's frosted bollocks! Clear Cones, direct approach, and something made out of gray glop want to go slow? Stupid rules. Tankhead autopilots, all they did was follow stupid rules. You'd think the Zeros 'n Ones mob could program a little compassion for a guy trying to make a hot date.

Manchez glanced at the estimated time of arrival readout. ETA was way too late. Late for Missy Pulchritudinous was a *bad* idea. Lihwa was too scorching temperamental and lava-volatile for him to hope she would forgive another missed date, even tardiness. That Geoffrey ass had been hovering nearby. One blunder, and the competition might cut him out.

Manchez hadn't made Corporate Captain by letting the riff-raff push him out of his chosen trajectory. *Fork this braking burn bullroar.*

Feet off the instrument panel, he shifted the coffin forward so he could reach the controls.

SuperHero Rules will now apply.

"*Ajax* Organic, SuperHero. Manual flight control. My spacecraft." His soul smiled as he toggled the Controls Alignment switch to 'Override Manual.'

"SuperHero, *Ajax* Organic. Acknowledged, manual flight control. Manual flight control engaged. Your spacecraft. Approach Control Organic, *Ajax* Organic, be advised—"

Manchez lanced out a forefinger and cut off the transmission. "*Ajax* Organic, SuperHero. Nobody needs to know who's driving."

"SuperHero, *Ajax* Organic, *Ajax* will be in violation of Dome City Spaceport Approach Regulations Article Two point Two Seven, pilots with less than 200 hours are not cleared for manual approach—"

Bugger-all! He'd been listening to *Ajax* Organic's excretions for too long.

"Great flaming feces! *Ajax* Organic, SuperHero, don't question my orders!"

"SuperStupid, *Ajax* Organic. General Custer would question your orders. The inventor of haggis-flavored dental floss would question your orders. Homer Simpson, or Larry, Moe and Curly Joe—"

Manchez bashed his fist against the switch silencing *Ajax* Organic.

"Owww! Dammit to bleedin' bloody blasted hell!" Smashed his little finger. *Right on the knuckle. Hurts. Gonna swell up.*

Bitchin' Betty, the recorded feminine voice of the Emergency Announcement System, cooed soothingly, "Thruster Continuity Fault. Priority Two Casualty. Thruster Continuity Fault—" She kept repeating whatever-it-was, vying for a 'Most Irritating Computer Subroutine' award. On the Warnings Panel, a yellow light blinked, like a flasher with cooties interrupting a kindergarten performance of Cinderella.

What in the local galaxy was a "Continuity Fault?" That question was on the pilot's licensing exam. He'd skipped it.

He pressed the button to silence Betty's current bitch. The blinking yellow light turned steady. Why didn't it clear? Normally he'd ask *Ajax* Organic, but he wasn't about to listen to that slanderer's exhaust again. *Homer Simpson, like hell.*

Wait-ah-minute. That tricky tankhead was trying to provoke him with false alarms. *Thinks it can hoax me.*

How immature. Ignore it.

No, better. *I'll fix that black-hearted cortex.*

Manchez reached out, lifted the safety cover, and, while protecting his little finger, with a surge of confident power toggled "Organic Computer Full Disconnect."

Damn good to be rid of the pest. No need for an Organic when the hottest rocket jock in the Seventeen Systems was at the controls.

Misplaced-4 had no atmosphere and a quarter-G gravity. With clear approaches, Manchez saw no reason to go slow. Last week he'd watched the training video demonstrating the approach and landing. He could handle it, no huhu.

He had to increase his velocity if he was going to make his date. *Accelerate with a piddly thruster? That's like drinking whiskey through a hypodermic needle. Let's do the SuperHero thing with the master butt-blasters.*

Manchez pushed the maneuvering joystick forward and pointed *Ajax's* nose ten degrees above Dome City Spaceport's beacon. With the main engines aligned to increase his approach velocity, he triggered a five-second, main engine, full power burn.

Ignition. The engines roared. The coffin vibrated. Closing velocity jumped. Acceleration pushed him firmly into the coffin. A fold in his pants jammed into his buttock. Uncomfortable. That'll leave a line.

Maybe Lihwa would massage it out. There's an idea.

Cutout. Manchez's surroundings returned to quiet.

The new ETA was nine minutes past Lihwa Time. No problem, light the torch for another kick; Tevil could afford the fuel.

Another burn, seven seconds. The butt crease got deeper.

Arrival Time, good enough. Nothing to do now but monitor the instruments until it's time to maneuver on final.

He anticipated Lihwa's happy smile of greeting, her graceful hands, visualized her form, remembered the fragrance of her perfume. A flower blend, very erotic.

Manchez's mind drifted. His imagination floated into her bedroom.

Bedroom. He smiled. *Take her arm with his hand—his other hand, not the one with the bunged pinkie. A kiss. Lead her to the bed. Float onto the mattress.*

Float.

Bedroom.

Manchez's breathing became slow and regular. His eyes closed.

The numbers on the Arrival Countdown Clock got smaller.

… Smaller …

Lihwa had just started to rub when the external comms speaker unmercifully dragged him back to reality. "SuperHero, Approach Control Organic. Reduce velocity. You are departing Approach Cone Charlie high. Acknowledge."

Manchez opened his eyes, massaged his temples, shook away the cobwebs. Bugger. He'd compensated too much for the planet's gravity. He'd been out for thirty minutes? Conking out during an approach, not good, not professional.

His head hurt. Eyes burned. Brain sludge.

Yeah, time to slow down.

First, deal with that flippin' Organic naghead.

"Approach Control Organic, Yuri Gagarin." He pushed the Transmit button and simultaneously twisted the 'Antenna Short to Hull' knob. A powerful burst of static was broadcast on the Approach Control frequency. *Feed that Organic a flaming headache, that would.*

All roger dodger, now let's show the amateurs how it's done. Adjust track, then reduce velocity. He yawned, squeezed his eyes shut, and shook his head. He needed bedtime. With Lihwa.

He locked on to the spaceport beacon, rolled the ship to align Number Two Lateral Thruster to push *Ajax* back into the approach cone, guessed a five-second burn, dialed in the auto-cutout, and fired. The acceleration pressed the top of his head into the coffin's padding.

After the thruster cutout, he'd improvise a braking burn. Wait for it … Four seconds, five seconds, and cutout. Cutout?

No cutout. Six, seven, eight—the push continued.

"What?" Manchez said, blinking his eyes rapidly. "The hell?"

The thruster burn light remained illuminated. The Thruster Continuity Fault light turned red. He punched the thruster manual cutoff. The light remained cherry-red, the acceleration pressure uninterrupted.

"The *bloody* hell?"

Bitchin' Betty, in her sultry tone, admonished, "Thruster Continuity Error. Priority One Casualty." She repeated, and repeated, and—

"SuperHero, Approach Control Organic. We hold y—"

Manchez slapped the speaker cutoff. *Too much noise, too loud*, he didn't need a tankhead telling him what he already knew. Deal with Approach Control later.

Another punched button silenced Betty's latest scold.

Too much to do. The ship was getting ahead of him. His skull hurt.

A main engine braking burn would do the trick. To hell with calculations, hit it for twenty seconds, slow things down, more time to sort this mess.

He dialed in the auto cutout, and triggered the main.

The engines roared. He was pushed back into the coffin. He vibrated for five seconds, ten, fifteen—

A horrid thought exploded in his head. He was still aligned—he had forgotten to turn around, to align his main engine for deceleration. The burn was increasing his approach velocity.

"Shit, dammit, bloody hell—"

An alarm sounded, loud and warbling. Bitchin' Betty said amiably, "Number Two Lateral Thruster overheat alert. Number Two—"

What in the third circle of hell was with that thruster? *Hell, bugger blasted dammit-all.* He banged on the manual thruster cutout. "Ouch!" *Floggin' frabjous fornication.* Little finger again. It throbbed.

"Number Two Lateral Thruster overheat alert. Number Two Lateral Thruster overheat alert."

What am I supposed to do?

He sucked on his little finger.

The Landing Sequence Checklist wasn't posted, dammit, that's *Ajax* Organic's job, why did he have to do everything?

Brilliant idea: let *Ajax* Organic figure it out.

"*Ajax* Organic, SuperHero, shut down Number Two Lateral Thruster."

Silence.

"*Ajax* Organic, SuperHero. State casualty action for runaway thruster."

Silence.

What's with *Ajax* Organic? Can tankheads go on strike?

He tried to remember the Casualty Immediate Action for a runaway thruster. Pull a fuse on a fuel system valve? Fuel feed valves fail shut on loss of power. Which valve? Okay, Number Two Lateral Thruster Fuel Supply Cutout. Pull Number Two Thruster's fuse. *Where the frackin' freak was the floggin' fuse?*

Roll the ship, point that thruster to push *Ajax* back in the cone.

He overshot the roll, too nervous, too much to do, too fast.

Rolling put *Ajax* into a spiral. Dammit. He needed a stable flight path.

A buzzer warbled, blasting decibels into his skull. Bitchin' Betty graciously intoned, "Number Two Lateral Thruster overheat *alarm*. Imminent meltdown. Shut down Number Two Lateral Thruster. Immediate action required."

The steady red light on the control panel accused him of incompetence.

Why didn't that dumb damnably delinquent Organic automatically shut it down? What was happening? Too much, too fast.

A flash of memory. Before his nap, he'd banished *Ajax* Organic into the Manual Override Dungeon. *Ajax* Organic was mechanically disconnected, its speaker silenced.

Oops.

A squealing siren howled. It blew his thoughts away, hurt his ears, upended his brain. Bitchin' Betty gently chided him: "Ground proximity alert. Pull up. Pull up. Ground proximity alert. Pull up. Pull up." He looked at the Arrival Countdown Clock. Forty seconds? No! Don't panic, don't panic ...

The forward view screen showed horror. He was going to overshoot the field, smash into Dome City. That beautifully curved, huge, iridescent dome.

His mind went blank. Couldn't think. He froze. *Ajax* was dead-on going to hit the dome, crack it, air-out-vak-in, explosive decompression, catastrophe. Ninety thousand people with the air sucked out of their lungs. In thirty seconds his name would be recorded in infamy.

What to do?

Warn them, warn them! He had to warn them!

Whoa. Calm out. You don't broadcast in a panic. Professionals made fun of rookies who send panic calls. The code: *Better Dead than Look Bad.*

He pressed the 'Transmit' button.

Coolly, professionally, Manchez announced to the universe, "Worthless, stupid Organic. Not my fault."

Manchez was slammed against the side of the coffin. The main engines ignited. His neck popped as his head banged back like it was slapped by Lizzie Borden's axe.

He hadn't touched anything. What the shucks?

Manchez was pressed deep into the survival seat. The coffin top closed, sealed with a crump, turning his universe black. Impact cushions inflated, pressing around him. He heard the whine of the inertial dampener spooling up, the roar of the main engines. The coffin vibrated, smelled like sweat, his sweat, fear sweat. He was jammed into the pads.

The fold in his shorts cut into his ass. It *hurt.*

2: Mike

For sale: ex-*TCS Ajax*, ex-cargo shuttle, crashed, but (mostly) intact, one each, price negotiable.

Mike and a shipbroker were in *Ajax's* main cargo bay, exploring the darkened interior. Light bled in through an open cargo hatch, dim and uncooperative.

"Well, Citizen, what do you think?" the shipbroker said. "Prime salvage material, roger that? I haven't acted as agent for many of you space workers—"

"Vakkers," interjected Mike. "Vacuum in space, vak, Vakkers. Vakkers are a cut above Spacers and Fed-Spacers, so you want to get that right. And if you're aiming to start a brawl, call a Vakker or Spacer a Waister. Waisters are at the bottom of the sewage tank."

"Okay, Vakkers, got it. Always wondered about that."

The shipbroker was pressing his helmet against Mike's, relying on sound conduction rather than suit-to-suit radio. His sales patter raced on. "I'm telling you, Vakkers will snatch this up in a nanosecond. You're first on the scene, you're the man, the man with the chance, the *opportunity*. Peel this baby apart, sell the scrap metal, and your bank balance goes supernova. I'd snatch this sweetie before more Vakkers show and bid the price up."

There was an oppressive darkness inside *Ajax's* primary cargo bay. The wreck languished on the surface at the end of the shallow trench it had dug in its poor excuse for a landing. The hull had stopped just short of the Dome. The compartment was in vacuum, so Mike heard only his boots hitting the deck, the rasp of his breathing in his skinsuit helmet, and Citizen Shipbroker Hervey's grating voice.

Why didn't this huckster use suit-to-suit? Then Mike had a flash of insight. This guy was keeping off the radio so he could deliver his pitch without the competition eavesdropping—and without witnesses to attest to his veracity, or lack thereof.

Hervey was a Citizen, meaning he was independent of the Tevil Corporation, the owner of this rock. He was living off sales commissions. A Citizen salesman would be expected to be aggressive, and a bit desperate to broker a deal. Perhaps, also, a bit ethically challenged.

Full alert. Bullshit Detector set on 'high.'

The broker switched on an omnidirectional lantern. The emptiness was transformed into a surrealistic scene of black and silver angles, dull surfaces and deep shadows. There was no dust hanging in the vacuum, nothing to diffuse the light, and little reflection from the matte black interior bulkheads. The illumination was stark, the shadows absolute.

The cargo hold was intact. It was empty when *Ajax* augured in.

"The crash. What happened?" Mike asked.

"Hang on a nano. Let's get connected." The broker pushed a suit-to-suit cable into a port in Mike's electronics pack. There was a crackle in Mike's headphones.

"Okay, what happened," said Hervey. "Some hotshot Corporate incompetent tried to jazz her in on manual control. He was on a vector to meteor into the Dome when the Organic put her down. The engines took the impact and broke off. The hull just skimmed along the surface dust. Hull's intact, but with her propulsion trashed she's beyond economic repair. Say 'yes' to this incredibly good deal, and stripping her will be as easy as doing my sister-in-law on a hot date." Hervey gave Mike a nudge. "Sign with me, I might be able to arrange something."

Pimping his relatives? Mike's right hand curled into a fist. He managed restraint.

Since The Shift, when it was found that men outnumbered women in the isolated Seventeen Systems by a huge margin, the natural result was that ladies were treated protectively. This peddler should watch his mouth, or take the consequences.

Hervey made a noise, something between clearing his throat and a laugh. "That possibility aside, you'll note that *Ajax* is only seven meters from the Dome. Run an underground gangway and you'll have access in dome duds, no skinsuits required."

Damage to the hull was cosmetic. The cargo bays were reinforced for high-mass pressurized cargo, and looked pristine. Mike used his flashlight to inspect a few of the hull frames, checking for stress cracks.

The broker stayed close. "The entire fuselage remained airtight. You could use the cargo bays for an office or rest area while you break her up." He began pointing. "Airlock, interior p-doors, one exterior cargo loading gate, all good. Atmosphere scavenging pumps are operational. Suck this cubic from Earth-Normal-Temperature-Pressure, you Vakkers call it 'ENTP,' from ENTP to 100 Pascal in under two hours. There's big demand for that machinery, complete or parts."

Mike was not a native of this rock; he was grounded with a flight crew medical disqualification. *Ajax* was an opportunity for a career change, but he wasn't going to reveal anything to this Zoolander.

"Pressurized, open to vak, no value difference to me." Mike pointed his flashlight to a pressure boundary door with a red light illuminated over it. "Why's that p-door showing red?"

"ENTP on the other side." The broker was trying hard to use Vakker language. "Door's in lockout. Solar panels still making electrons." He transitioned again to enthusiastic. "You can sell the command deck instruments on the spares market for a Jupiter of standards. Environmental is intact, more to sell there." His voice became casual. "Of course, it'll take some mojo to move the Organic, maybe sell it for reprogramming. But think of this! The environmental package is late model and oversized, modded for refugee runs during the Rigel System evacuation. Lots of extra capacity. Open a free bordello, handle the crowd without a drop of condensation."

Mike's Bullshit Detector bleeped. "What's that about the

Organic? Why wasn't it pulled for new construction? Those things are expensive."

"Something with the crash investigation, no worries." Hervey banged on a support girder. "This is prime 8087 steel—"

"What about the crash investigation and the Organic?"

The shipbroker sighed. "The flight recorder." He fluttered his hands. "The tankhead might have taken control before impact."

"Should've taken control sooner. That Corporate clown was clearly heading max blast to an early reincarnation."

"Something about switches in 'Override Manual,' or 'Disconnect.'"

Now, that was a forehead banger. The Organic was physically disconnected from the controls. How could it put the ship down?

Mike pulled out a cross-check level and placed it on the deck. It took some seconds for the bubbles to settle in the low gravity. The main load-bearing deck was within a degree of horizontal.

He surveyed the large void. There were tiedown platforms along the circumference of the hull, almost like wide rows of bleachers. A layout began to crystallize in his mind.

Hervey put his arm around Mike's shoulders. "Mike, m'lad, special deal, just for you. We also got us an undamaged, pristine AutoDoc, and a mint Personnel Escape Pod. Okay, Federated Law states you cannot re-use an AutoDoc or the PEP after a crash. But, just between us, there's a specialist I know who can take them off your hands at an excellent price. You'll get the required Scrapping Certificates." He nudged Mike with his elbow, like they were best buddies sharing a secret. "My percentage for that transaction is a touch higher. We do it off-contract, handshake agreement. I can't take bank transfers for such a super deal, so payment in coin." He lowered the lantern to the deck. "The pod's still in the chute, explosive bolts removed." He made an inviting gesture, and Mike could hear the smile in his voice. "Another advantage of making me your agent."

Okay, morally and ethically challenged. Let's see what other dubious deals he has to offer.

"That Organic," the hustler said with a dismissive wave. "Just glitched. But look, lots of uses for airtight cubic this close to the dome."

Mike didn't want to pay a premium for an airtight facility.

"Negative. Too much risk some micro-crack would give way." He detected another brush-off. "That Organic. Makes no sense. Toggle switches are mechanical, not a software lockout. Code can't jump an air gap."

"I'll bet you're right," Hervey nodded, then put out his two fists with thumbs up. "You got it. Decertification was unjustified. The Admiralty investigators were too lazy to do a proper inquiry." His voice changed back into sales mode. "It was only decertified from flight operations. Sell it as an autonomous structure Organic, running environmental systems and maintenance bots. A building on a vac planet isn't much different from a starship. There's a construction boom down the lava tubes. A high-end tankhead could manage a full habitat easy. That Organic could pull in buckets of platinum standards."

"Or," said Mike, folding his arms, "that Organic might be worthless, un-reliable and un-reprogrammable, a dammit-to-hell liability. A questionable Organic controlling the environment?" He gave a little disgusted snort. "Maybe five people in the galaxy are interested in an Organic with a major accident on its record, and all of them wear straightjackets. More likely, buckets of platinum standards get spent complying with the 'Humane Disposal of Organic Computers' law."

Mike swept the flashlight over the space, emphasizing the emptiness. "Worthless empty cubic."

He clicked his flashlight off.

"The Organic is a major liability," Mike said, tapping the flashlight against his knee. "Disposal costs reduce my offer. Off the top."

3: *Diana*

"I like on top."

"I like your bottom on top."

"Tarak! You *in-credible* pervert. You were *soooo* the gentleman, *before* we signed the marriage contract."

Communications flashed between the interstellar cargo ship *Prosperity* and the small prospecting vehicle, a MEVV. *Prosperity* was stationary outside an asteroid belt, illuminated in the red glow of a dwarf star. The MEVV was gingerly sliding into a dense collection of rocks held together by their microgravity.

"Ah, witness the Incredible Sadness of the Unappreciated Pervert," said Tarak, his voice transmitting the capital letters from *Prosperity's* analysis station. "So very undervalued. But hey hey, like the serial killer said, everybody has to be good at something."

Diana gave a snort, half in disgust, half laughter.

The forward monitor demanded her concentration. Jammed into the claustrophobic confines of the MEVV cockpit, she nudged the joystick. A thruster fired. She was pushed gently into the damper pads of the cockpit coffin. The MEVV moved closer to an asteroid family.

MEVV, officially, stood for 'Mining Extra-Vehicular Vehicle.' It was an awkward appellation, but the comedy of a trademark used at the Garage Gremlins dealership had too many words starting with F and S to appeal to anyone but Vakminers with questionable concepts of good taste. MEVV worked for her. The bank only cared about the serial number.

She was ten kilometers detached from *Prosperity*, closing on a typical asteroid for this belt, silicone and granite, but with an interesting streak of yellow. Five seconds more, then time to slow.

The radio crackled in her ear. "Closing at three point two per. Don't you bend the MEVV, sweetie."

"Go tell Einstein how to write equations." A tap on the joystick, a burst from a thruster, and the closure rate cut in half.

The MEVV was an ugly spheroid about ten meters in diameter, festooned with remotely operated arms called 'waldos,' mining lasers, spectrographic sensors, and remote probes for collecting rock and gas samples. The cockpit was covered with data screens, hand controls, status and warning lights, power displays, toggle switches, buttons and a fuse panel, all curved around the single pilot's station. The only illumination came from instruments and data readouts.

Diana released her shoulder harness, heard the snap as it retracted, leaned forward, and inserted her hands into the waldo controller gloves. She wrinkled her nose. The gloves were clammy, smelled musty. She'd been too tired to clean them after yesterday's sortie. Best not let that become a habit.

Tarak's voice whispered into her headset. "I could tie you up?"

"No."

"Indian Chief and the Maiden? Warrior abducts Cowgirl? That was fun."

"Listen, Geronimo, you're ninety-nine generations past Indian Chief. Give the Wild West a rest."

"Hey, genes don't lie. A little respect for my honored Arapaho warrior forebearers."

She pulled a hand from the gloves, tapped the joystick, and saw a satisfying zero on the Closure Rate readout. "Crimp-it-I'm-busy."

This rock had possibilities. There was a meter-thick vein of something that glittered like…gold?

Diana fired a mooring anchor. "Aaach!" She had accidentally shot one of the expensive registration stakes. Tarak would fuss at the cost. But then again, when that vein came in as—some expensive mineral, surely—she would have the last giggle over Derr Warrior Indian Chief. She turned the stake selector to choose the cheap anchors. She planted an anchor with its attached cable, two taps on the thrusters, and a second anchor. The winches took in the slack on the wires until the front observation port was a meter off the rock. She deployed a bumper arm to prevent scraping dirt.

She focused a camera on the glitter. "Video, channel 11. Whatcha' think? That what I think it is?"

"Nah. Not worth a sample."

"What? That streak of color? That's the shiniest—"

"Sampling costs money."

"I'm getting a sample."

"You're getting desperate."

"I have a feeling about this."

"If you're wrong,' Tarak said, in a lascivious tone, "do *I* get a feel, I mean, a feeling?"

"You have a one-track mind. Crimp-it-I'm-busy."

Diana shifted the waldo controls to Probe Two and drilled a sample hole. Probe Three was positioned adjacent to the hole. She aimed a laser into the pit, set it for thirty seconds, and fired. The rock glowed red, then white, then boiled off vapor. She swiped Probe Three through the cloud.

Diana hit 'transmit data.' "Here you go, Geronimo. Data, channel 12."

"Mother Thing, Tarak. Sample analysis, short survey, channel 12." Mother Thing, *Prosperity's* Organic computer, acknowledged.

"I still don't understand," said Tarak, "your 'on top' fixation. I mean, how can you tell who's on top in no-G? Is this some kind of crypto-feminism, domination and discipline, I-Am-Woman-Hear-Me-Roar thing? I don't grok. I mean, who's on first?"

Diana grinned. "That's the man's name."

"I dunno."

They both sang out in chorus, "Third Base!" They laughed.

Since the recent archeological discovery of the Movie, Music, and Book Archive, lost since The Shift, Diana and Tarak had become addicted to ancient entertainment. There were no studios located in the Seventeen Systems when The Shift occurred, and immediately after that catastrophe the United Federated Government had deemed entertainment a waste of scarce resources. Memory cards and readers with shows, music, and fiction books had been confiscated with draconian thoroughness, wiped, and repurposed for critical industrial applications. Only in the last few years had production of approved entertainment vid programs been allowed. As was usual with the gene-selected 'royals' of the 35 Families, a monopoly was awarded to one of them, the Kaiju; entertainment projects required pre-approval by Federated Central.

The Archive's emergence filled a huge social vacuum when it was made available by a competing Family. The quality of the Kaiju's output—abysmal—only accentuated the popularity of Abbott and Costello, John Wayne, Raiders of the Lost Ark, Star Trek and Gone With the Wind. And, Lord-help-us, Disco and Opera.

Diana waited as Mother Thing processed the sample.

"Hey," said Tarak. "Talking about liquids and samples, how'd you get the regurgulator working? I can actually get a decent drink outta that thing, instead of the usual middle school chemistry experiment."

"Wasn't me. Ghost stopped by."

"Hoo-ya! Superific. What did he charge for the part?"

"Wasn't a part. A clogged sampler tube threw off mixture control. Ghost cleared it, recalibrated, it's good as new. He fussed about keeping the filters clean. The kid's a genius. Your favorite blast of caffeinated mickee, tea, Citrusilver, he could probably make it poop pumpkin juice."

"That shitbird!"

Diana's voice cracked high. "Ghost?"

"No, not Ghost! Slick! *Slick*, that long-haired radical-leftie thieving filter-scum toilet-flush right-wing socialist goat-fugging unsanitary anarchist sanitarium escapee commie corrupt baka-brain wanker douchbag nutter *Slick*. '50 gold standards for parts,' the lying microbrain tells me, so sad, sorry, 60 stans with labor, even after his 'special discount!' And he claims he's Mormon! Flaming crook!"

A few deep breaths later, he asked hesitantly, "What'd you give Ghost?"

"Recharged his O_2, dinner, bed 'n breakfast. I pushed seconds on him, he's so skinny it'd make a mother cry. No Transaction Report to the tax vampire. He's staying off Freddy's screen."

"Like any Vakker would turn him in to the Federated parasite. Damn green deal, two meals for a working regurgulator. You talked him down to that?"

"Talked him up to that. The kid just asked for the O_2. Said the job wasn't much trouble."

"Obviously not one who appreciates the transcendent value of a proper cup of mickee."

Tarak hummed a Native American melody. Diana could hear him tapping on a keyboard. Then he said, in a distracted tone, "Ghost's good Vakker. Look for something we can do for him."

"Always."

The carrier wave on the radio droned lightly in her earphones. Diana did a sweep of her instruments. Position, rate, fuel, life support, comms, all good; no rocks constant-bearing-decreasing-range; green board. She flexed her fingers, grimaced at the odor, and adjusted the headphones to relieve the pressure on her ears.

She could hear Tarak ruminating to himself, accidentally-on-purpose over the radio. "I know. Zombies. Unstoppable, insatiable … kissable. Zombie love."

Diana didn't dignify that with a response. She did crack a smile. *Which of us was supposed to be the zombie?*

"I'm going off headset," Tarak said. "Back in two."

There was a click as the headset was slipped into a hold-down clip. She figured Tarak was floating over to the sample processor and scanning the results. He'd left the microphone on; she could hear him singing, as usual in two keys indiscriminately mixed.

"Oh, baby baby, I love you,

Hey, baby baby, what we'll do, me and you,

Let you be the totem; I'll be the pole,

And you know you love it, down to your soul,

Hoo, hoo, hoo, what we'll do,

'Tiiiillll…Weeeeee'rrrre…Bluuuuuuue!"

When the time came to renew this marriage contract, she'd add a few clauses. 'Manners,' another on 'bad poetry.'

Tarak whistled. His distant voice said, "Oh, my. Shiny. *Verrrry* shiny."

There were scraping sounds as Tarak retrieved the headset. He tapped the mic to check it was on (as if he didn't know), then said, "Preliminary is in. The technical term is—" he paused, sucked in a deep breath, "—*in-credible!*"

"Whaddayamean, incredible?" A surge of hope swelled in Diana.

"Two words describe your find. The second one is—gold."

"Yee-owww! Bo-yah! I *told you* I had a feeling!" Diana bounced in her coffin; relief mixed with happiness. *Success, finally, success! We can pay off—*

"The first word is—fool's."

"*What!* Dammit!"

"No, not dammit. In-credible, as in, not credible. You've nosed out a lovely deposit of fool's gold. Iron pyrite. Pretty common in quartz. The 'iron' part might have made it worth something if the Flatplain Mine hadn't just doubled production. What you have discovered is your basic capital-P, capital-O, capital-S."

Piece Of Shit.

Diana was quiet. She'd hear about this for weeks.

"Of course, you were probably distracted," said Tarak. "That zombie thing. Breaks the concentration, yes? Wha—hold on. MEVV, *Prosperity*, go tactical."

Something was wrong. Tarak was shifting into formal command mode.

'Go tactical' was their code for trouble; she was to make the

MEVV undetectable. Diana swept her hands over the panels. RF radio off, rangefinder off, narrow band laser comms to *Prosperity* on, receiver gain up, comms laser power cut to minimum. She slammed off her nav lights and proximity sensors, transponder off, break comms channels 4 and 12.

"*Prosperity*, MEVV. Tactical set, comms Laser One."

She called up the list of immediate actions, and scrolled. Fifth item down called for placing the MEVV's auxiliary power unit in standby.

A feeling like a ball of scraggly tin foil roiled inside her stomach.

After minutes that seemed as long as years, she heard, "MEVV, *Prosperity*. Three heat flares off one target on IR. Ion trail, engine exhaust trail. I'm deploying the reflectors."

A string of radar reflectors would break up *Prosperity's* radar signature, making her look like any other scraggly asteroid. Diana remembered when they put them together. It was like stringing popcorn for an artificial Christmas tree.

The high infra-red signature meant a hot target, something powered by big engines.

She leaned back and hit the red button on the side of the coffin. The top closed, acceleration buffers inflated. Virtual data and control screens, beaming directly into her eyes, initialized. When waiting for anything, she prudently became a mummy in the coffin, to cut her radiation exposure and to be ready for anything.

Linking with *Prosperity's* IR sensor feed, Diana saw three red yellow heat signatures that were so close that their blooms merged.

Pirates?

Diana and Tarak originally thought they got a bargain when they acquired *Prosperity*, only to learn through costly experience that the ship's specs did not match well with the economic conditions. *Prosperity* didn't have the cargo capacity of the big corporate freighters or stationmax independents, which eliminated easy intra-system cargo runs or bouncing outpost re-supply routes. Their cargo-to-fuel ratio was too low. They tried trading low-volume, high-value luxury goods and perishables, but they barely covered fuel and taxes. *Prosperity* was too slow for the courier or VIP transport market, and way too slow and with too large a radar signature for smuggling.

Every Vakker noted their inexperience and negotiated tough

deals; ethically-challenged Waisters, the riff-raff of the Deep Dark, plain cheated them. Finally, in a throw of the dice, they leased the MEVV off a bank loan with *Prosperity* as collateral, to try prospecting.

The choice to go to Sigma System was risky. Disappearances in Sigma were higher than the usual attrition in the hazardous prospecting game. Warning whispers of pirates floated around every Spacer bar. Were the murmurs actually false rumors spread by Tevil agents to keep citizen prospectors out? The greedy bastards might be saving something seriously shiny for themselves.

Diana and Tarak needed something seriously shiny.

With their stake dwindling and payments due, they threw the dice.

Snake-eyes. Go to Sigma.

Now this.

"MEVV, *Prosperity*. I'm receiving AIS." An Automated Identification System was required for every ship, every *legitimate* ship, broadcasting the ship's registration and navigation data. "It's squawking *Maersk Conveyer*, boosting at zero-point-two G. She's on a line for the Cetus System PunchPoint. Not hostile."

Diana remembered to resume breathing. "*Prosperity*, MEVV. So, maybe we get back to work?" She called up the checklist to restore the MEVV to full operational capability.

"Hold off for a few minutes, until we're in its baffles." That was where the Maersk's engines' ion trail blocked the ship's sensors. "It'll pass pretty close. No need to let anybody know we're here, even friendlies."

The cameras on the MEVV could now pick up the cargo liner. She was huge, and a thing of beauty, from an engineering viewpoint, if not ascetically. Diana shifted to the long-range, high-resolution lens.

There was a bright dot, moving quickly, directly behind the *Conveyer*.

"Tarak, do you see—"

The bright dot closed on the cargo starship rapidly. It was performing like one of those mythical, souped-up speed machines in the *Space Racer* computer game—all engine and fuel, one driver, acting like the pilot's parents forgot to install brains before they let 'em loose on the universe. Closing, the dot swerved away from the Maersk ship's hot exhaust. Then, the dot merged with the hull.

The 'comms activated' light for Emergency Channel 13 flashed.

"*Maersk Conveyer*, Alpha Omega, channel 13. Cut your engines."

The transmission was repeated. No response.

"*Maersk Conveyer*, Alpha Omega. I've attached four hundred kilograms of explosives over your main fuel tank, which my sonics tell me is eighty percent full of Rocket-A. Cut your engines. Open your docking bay. Obey immediately, no one will be hurt. Cut your engines. Immediate execute, or I *will* detonate."

Someone on *Maersk Conveyer* started shouting over the circuit in a language Diana did not recognize. Then, *Maersk's* engines cut off.

A warning horn blared in the MEVV. The IR passive scanner had detected something, close aboard, another ship. Diana locked on an optical tracker. It looked like one of the small, punch-capable personal yachts owned by the rich-and-famous.

"*Prosperity*, MEVV, I've another ship on IR coming out of the belt, boosting at high Gs. Looks like he's after the *Maersk*. I think, pirates. Either that, or the bank's trying to repossess."

"MEVV, *Prosperity*. I've got it. Consider it hostile. I'm not being painted by their radar. They haven't spotted us, or we're just being ignored. Hold your position. Stay passive. They'll be busy with *Maersk*. When they get downrange coupla' hundred thousand, we slink our rears outta here."

4: *Ghost*

Ghost traveled the tunnel, gliding silently, avoiding the dusty floor in the center of the passage. Misplaced-4's quarter-G gravity facilitated his stealthy movement, while his skinsuit insulated him from the cold, except for his exposed face. The frigid air made his nose numb. Nothing unusual for him, moving cautiously through the utility tunnels and ventilation ducts, mixing in unidentifiably with Vakkers, Spacers, corpbees and Clydes, evading the Federated Carabinieri and the corppers.

Corppers—the nickname for Tevil's Corporation Police came from an earlier name, 'cops' or 'coppers.' Where'd *that* come from? OldEarth coppers wore red uniforms? Copper body armor?

What he did know was, if corppers caught him, Tevil, the Corporation that owned Misplaced-4, would run him through a perfunctory tax court and confiscate everything he owned to cover the O_2 taxes he had never paid. After hard labor in prison, he'd be indentured to work off the fine. Ghost had never met anyone who had worked themselves out from tax court bondage. The Indentured had to buy things to survive, exclusively from Tevil's company store at company prices. Food, water, and O_2 for a day cost more than what was credited for a day of labor.

The other alternative was to become a Client, those unemployed souls on the dole, the 'welfare' also provided by Tevil Corporation. Clients, vilified as 'Clydes,' were drafted into work gangs, whether young or old, children or aged or sick. They died by the scores in tunnel collapses, skinsuit failures and industrial accidents. Tevil did not mourn their loss—replacement Client laborers were always available, and every death meant one less Clyde to feed.

This tunnel was long and straight, illuminated dimly by light-emitting diodes every dozen yards. Stretches were stygian-black where LEDs had failed. He moved carefully, giving attention to the dust patterns. There was no evidence of recent movement; it was perhaps months since this tunnel was last visited.

The passage was lined with lightweight sheets of airtight sealant, colored a non-reflective gray. Occasionally, there were patches of heavier material covering repairs; in some places sheet metal plugged fissures where the tunnel had blowouts. Smart people wore skinsuits in tunnels.

Ghost had accessed the tunnel maintenance work schedule by hacking their ridiculous password—really, 'FixIt4Us,' pretty pathetic. At least it wasn't the planet's most popular password, 'Tevil_Sux.' No work was scheduled for this tunnel. But since when could you trust Tevil's scheduling? What if an equipment failure required immediate repairs?

A tremor passed through the walls, rippling the sealant. The landing field was close. His feet could feel launch and landing shocks. A slight sheen of dust fogged the air, disturbed by the vibration. The dust actually made the tunnel seem brighter. When it settled it would cover evidence of his passage.

A ladder against the side of the tunnel was weakly lit with a sign: 'K2 – 101 Exit.' It led to an airlock, then the surface. If he popped outside, Spaceport Ground Control Organic would spot him. There was an orange work crew's jerkin in his pack, and he could masquerade as a maintenance corpbee, but that was risky.

He had a lead on a case of clipscreens with faulty chips. With their typical wastefulness, Tevil was just going to dump them. If he got to the disposal dock in time, the Clydes in the work crew might let him tote them away, just to save them the effort of hauling the boxes themselves. He carried apple juice as trade goods. With luck, he'd only have to offer them a sip, rather than surrender the whole flask.

He exhaled a cloud of fog. He could be in a great hiding place only to have his breath betray his presence. Maybe he should deploy his skinsuit helmet and go on internal O_2. He had half a tank. He'd also get a warm nose.

No. O_2 recharges cost standards.

While gliding down the tunnel he thought about the clipscreens. He'd find some good chips, swap out the bad ones, and remove the locater electronics. Vakkers from off-planet liked untrackable clipscreens. They might sell for a premium. Shengwu could sell them for him in his shop, under the counter.

Ghost dear, where are you going?

Ghost froze. The invisible voice. It had been dogging him, inside his head, unheard, but there.

Ghost scrunched his eyes shut. *Hello, Mable.* He didn't have to say it out loud.

You should have checked with me before you entered K2 Tunnel.

All green. No worries. His invisible friend tended to smother him with concern.

Mable had been in his head for the last three months. He didn't know how or why. Was he going space-happy? He once read a psych article about children who had fantasies about imaginary friends. The suspicion Mable might be imaginary didn't help him deal with her voice.

Things are going rapidly red, Ghost dear.

Was Mable a psychosis, a mental disorder, himself talking to himself?

P-doors have cycled ahead and behind you, his brain heard her whisper. *Clipscreens belonging to two Carabinieri are approaching. I am concerned.*

The Carabinieri, the Federated Police Force, were Freddy the Feddie's enforcement Muscle. If Mable was just his subconscious, how would he know about Carabinieri in the tunnel? Were there actually Carabinieri out there?

There was a muted thump behind him. He looked back. A tunnel light blinked.

Ghost moved along the tunnel, eyes up. He stopped where the ceiling was covered by sheet metal.

"HALT!"

A blinding light illuminated the tunnel from ahead. He turned, crouched, shielded his eyes. There was a bang and rattle of metal. At the other end of the tunnel another light flashed on. Lights, too bright, ahead and behind.

"FEDERATED CARABINIERI! DOWN ON YOUR KNEES!"

Ghost stood straight upright.

"FEDERATED CARABINIERI! YOU'RE UNDER ARREST!"

Partially blocking a light, a silhouetted man crouched with a projector in his hand. It was pointed threateningly.

"You Ghost? ON YOUR KNEES! NOW! INSTANT COOPERATION OR IMMEDIATE INCAPACITATION!"

That's a line from an OldEarth crime vid. Plagiarism. They should be ashamed.

Both Feds were in coveralls. No skinsuits.

"Hands up!" A less excitable voice, from the other end of the tunnel. "You've nowhere to go. You're surrounded. We won't hurt you."

Both Feds were tunnel tramping in dome duds, ignoring any chance of a leak or blowout. Dome Dummies, no head for safety. Ghost reached into his pack. He pulled out a gray cylinder. He held it away from his body. Let them get a good look.

"What's that? PUT IT DOWN! NOW!"

Ghost tapped a button under his chin twice. His skinsuit helmet deployed. He activated the high-intensity light screen in front of his eyes to filter the glare.

"Mining explosive? *Shit.* DROP IT! ON YOUR KNEES! NOW!"

Ghost lifted the cylinder to the overhead. Its base had a magnetic plate. It stuck to the sheet metal. He extended both hands over his head, ten fingers splayed out. He retracted one finger. Nine. Another. Eight.

"HE'S GONNA BLOW THE TUNNEL!"

Ghost stepped out from under the cylinder. Another finger. Seven.

"SHOOT HIM!" A zapper projectile flashed by Ghost's helmet. It hit a wall. A flash of lighting crackled.

The calmer Carabinieri shouted, "NO, YOU FOOL! DEAD-MAN SWITCH!"

Another finger. Six.

"LEMME OUTTA HERE!"

A metallic crash. One light pointed to the ceiling, wobbling back and forth. Light scattering off the overhead revealed figures running away. Sprinting.

Ghost exhaled, momentarily fogging his skinsuit's faceplate.

The excited Carabinieri had left a portable utility light. A flashlight rolled back and forth in an arc on the floor. A Peacemaker Projector was next to it, a supposedly 'non-lethal' weapon that fired low-velocity zapper projectiles carrying a 50,000-volt charge, enough to shock a man into unconsciousness. A hit would fry a skinsuit's electronics and destroy the environmental system. The target would suffocate if the helmet was up. Carabinieri knew that. Most would not zap a skinsuit. Most Carabinieri were decent people.

Two taps on the large red button. After a breathable atmosphere was confirmed, the helmet retracted. Ghost tugged the cylinder off the ceiling. He unscrewed the top, drank some water, capped the top back on the thermos decorated with the mining explosive warning paint job, and returned it to his pack.

He walked over to the Peacemaker. He had thought about getting a projector someday, for just in case. There was that nice flashlight, too. The flashlight went into his backpack. The projector was more complicated. Projectors were assigned by serial number to each Carabinieri. Freddy declared a hysteria if one was lost. He didn't need to increase his profile by taking a projector.

With a twist and a tug, he removed the projector's battery. It was a standard hi-pulse battery available from any tool shop. That he could sell. The Peacemaker went back on the floor. A few seconds' work and he had the batteries from the utility light. The tunnel returned to gloom.

Ghost, dear. You shouldn't. That's stealing.

Ghost froze. *Stealing? So? They tried to kill me.*

You wouldn't take those things if they were Vakkers'. Carabinieri are people, too. Doing evil to you does not justify doing evil to them. Would you want someone to steal your belongings? Stealing hurts you, too, Ghost dear. Stolen goods are not blessed. Your honor, your honesty would be besmirched. Honor lost is lost forever. Honest means honest to everyone.

The batteries and the flashlight went back to the floor.

Mable. Thank you.

No answer.

One of these days he would have to sort out this 'honor' and 'evil' business. But now, he had to move quickly and select an escape route from his contingency plans. He could still make the disposal dock on time.

5: Mike

Over weeks of unrelenting 18-hour days Mike had stabilized *Ajax*, tunneled an airtight gangplank walkway under the dome, installed three layers of airlocks and p-doors, and paid the teeth-grinding bribes to get permission for a direct connection with Dome City. The environmental system was doing its duty, with all compartments at ENTP. He installed lighting, painted over the matt black with something more cheerful, and converted the largest cargo bay into a dining room, bar, and kitchen.

His new career: restaurant entrepreneur.

He needed a sign, and a name.

'Mike's Pub.' Nah. Common. Forgettable.

'Captain Mike's Grill & Swill.' Nope. No Vakker would believe Mike knew the secret ingredients of swill. Besides, they might demand he have swill on the menu.

'Captain Mike's Bar and Grill.' Not a lightning bolt to the brain, but the 'Captain Mike' part felt nice.

Ajax Organic was a loose end. Hervey 'helpfully' left it off the transfer documents. Officially, it did not exist. The broker suggested an anonymous trajectory into the nearest unmapped dust crater. No one had determined how a disconnected Organic managed to take control of a ship, or even had the *idea* to take control. The investigators concluded the pilot took actions he didn't remember, and the inexplicable things on the flight recorder were static-induced noise from when the pilot grounded the antenna.

The Organic remained aboard, in Mode Two hibernation. Mike serviced the tank at the required intervals. It was extra work, but it didn't seem right to let it go extinct. After all, it was living tissue, from human DNA. Most Vakkers had a soft spot for Organics, even if they were just Large Language AI computers.

One last hurdle. He needed a barman, waiters, and a busboy. Today was Interview Day. A check with the outside security camera showed a well-behaved line of people clutching applications. Some had been there for hours, waiting.

There was obtrusive banging on the gangway door. He checked his watch—fifteen minutes short of his announced start time. Someone in the crowd was eager. Why not? He walked over to the p-door, hit the 'open permissive' plate, then 'open.'

A throng filled the gangway. Clients, clad in shapeless Client Gray coveralls, all threadbare. The front of the line was occupied by two men in beige Tevil Administrative uniforms.

Over the last weeks Mike had researched Misplaced-4. Tevil Corporation owned Dome City by virtue of purchasing the concession from the OldEarth European Union, the original title-holders. The concession included complete, dictatorial power over everyone and everything, with minor exceptions—outlying mining camps were independent, and the landing field and space traffic control were under Admiralty authority. The Feds controlled the environmental, water, and sewage systems, and enforced Federated law. Tevil had the power to make and enforce regulations and laws. Both the Feds and Tevil could levy taxes.

It seemed like a whole lot of people had the power to tell him what to do.

"Hello," said the taller bureaucrat, with a pleasant smile. "We're Tevil Corporation Employment Protections and Regulations. You're from off-planet? We're here to ensure you comply with our employment rules. Our job is to safeguard your workers from exploitation. May we come in?" He emphasized his helpfulness with a nod of his head.

"Sure," said Mike. "Come on in." *What's this 'exploitation' stuff?*

The inspectors stepped into the dining room. The line of

applicants groaned as the short operative shut the door behind him.

The representatives of Tevil authority stood next to one of the dining room tables, like judges at an awards ceremony.

"Please," said Mike. "Have a seat."

"No," said the tall inspector. "This will not take long." He put a massive paper book on the table with a thump. Mike had never seen one that thick.

The Man in Tevil Beige began leafing through the pages like he was opening the gates to heaven. He paused occasionally to point. "Of course, you must abide by the minimum wage law, page 18." More pages were turned. "You must provide mandatory benefits to all employees, pages 24 through 96. You report gross income and net profits and pay sales and employment taxes, page 120, and purchase unemployment insurance from Tevil Insurance Solutions to cover employees who depart or are discharged, pages 143 through 170. Medical insurance, also from Tevil Insurance Solutions, those requirements start at page 194."

He smiled at Mike agreeably, then returned to flipping pages. "Maintain a safe working environment. You'll be required to pay salary and benefits for life if an employee is injured, page 230. You pay Transaction Tax on each interview, hired or not. Report all candidates' names and Benefit Registration Numbers to the Client Employment Bureau, Form 1076 on page 284. Don't forget fingerprints, incomplete or smudged reports will be fined. If you do not hire an interviewee, you must submit Justification for Non-Hiring, Form 2023, page 350, or Form 2023a if they are one of the protected classes, for instance, based on melatonin levels, sexual orientation or lack thereof, philosophical beliefs, handicapped status, body fat percentage, IQ or learning disabilities, faith-based clothing preferences, system of origin, tattoos or body art, registered political party, burial taboos, medical history, or predilection or bias towards certain music groups."

Is this a joke? Did his Vakker buddies cook this up?

The inspector smiled again. "The full list is explained, pages 356 through 440."

"This book is yours," said the shorter inspector with a generous wave of a hand. "It is to be available to employees during working hours. When changes are issued, you have 18 hours to make corrections, in black ink, not blue or other color. Instructions for inserting changes are on pages 524 to 547. You cannot open for business until you certify you have read and understood the rules, Form 3572a on page 610, and attest that the latest manual changes have been entered."

Good God. It's not a joke. It's real. No Vakker could come up with this. It would take a really sick mind.

As the TCEPRO agents were departing, the tall inspector handed Mike a chit with a disarming smile. "This is a violation summons. Sexual discrimination. You advertised for a bar*man* instead of a bar*person*." He handed over another chit. "Also, a bus*boy*. You should be ashamed. Your court appearance is in two weeks. Please mention us to Judge Marx. He likes to see we're being thorough. Until your hearing, and until you have received mandatory Equity Training, you cannot transact interviews. However, this meeting *does* count as a Transaction, as does the delivery of each summons, so file Form 1040AS for each, with your payments."

The smaller agent said, "Please let us get 100 meters clear of the crowd before you tell them. Have a marvelous day!"

6: *Diana*

The MEVV was again wrapped around Diana, as it had been for the fruitless weeks of digging test holes in silicon in Sigma System.

This asteroid might be different. The massive rock looked like a melted blob ejected from the core of an exploding planet. It was elongated ten to one, which meant it had a strong composition, or it would have broken up centuries ago. High density and high albedo meant metals; mass, huge, thousands of metric tons.

"Okay," said Tarak. "We've got metal. Likely nickel-iron. Worth an assay. Make data, channel 12."

Diana melted metal with the laser, and swiped a probe through the gasses. In five other locations, she repeated. "Samples 702 through 706, data, Channel 12."

Diana sighed. She was tired, frustrated, and bored silly. How could you be bored when you were flirting with danger every minute, driving a small space vehicle through a chaos of asteroids? She'd have to give that idea some consideration the next time she couldn't sleep. Maybe it was time for a protein bar. No. She was sick of food. She had lost four kilos, hard to do on her petite frame, but dehydrated lamb stew was all they had left in the larder, and, still, nothing in the cargo bay.

This rock was the most promising they had found. Another setup for disappointment.

Finally, Tarak called. "Settle back, Princess. You will be shocked to learn that my initial guess was wrong. We do not have your basic everyday nickel-iron. This stuff is dense, refinery-grade, not a lot of dross. Some gold and trace silver, maybe enough to cover the refiner's fees. To you, the love of my life, I offer up on the altar of my adoration, drum roll please: ferrochromium."

Diana slammed her fist on her knee. "Chromium!" she screamed. "Every refiner at Misplaced-4 needs chromium. How much?"

"Snugglebunny, we're looking at high grade ore. Lots and lots of beautiful, expensive chromium. Tons. If it plays through at these percentages, let's just say we've paid off *Prosperity* and the MEVV. That's not all. The base matrix? Eighty percent of the sample? Yes, nickel-iron, but most of it, wait for it, volley of nuclear detonations, please—titanium."

Diana's seat belt barely held her.

Tarak's voice radiated joy. "Ah, riches, wealth, I can get a really great collection of porno."

"Hey! Listen, Pervert, I'm your porno."

"Pleased to hear that. I'm releasing a thruster. You're not to try pulling that rock out with the MEVV."

"Roger, thruster pack. Mother Thing, MEVV, calculate the center of gravity attachment point for the thruster engine."

"MEVV, Mother Thing, calculate the center of gravity attachment point for the thruster engine. Request laser scan profile. Request evaluation of target stability and cohesion."

Diana got busy.

"Pack released," said Tarak. "Can you get the large fuel tank in? We're going to have to refuel enroute, that rock is so big."

"There's a path. Mega-tank is a go."

"Roger." After a few minutes Tarak said, "Tank released. Transfer control enabled to the MEVV, guidance and control channel one, transponder squawking at 1030 megahertz."

Diana punched in channel one. Green light. "Roger G and C channel one. Roger transponder."

She started to scope out how to run this maneuver.

"MEVV, *Prosperity*. Alert, alert. Go tactical. That ship is back."

Oh, Lord in heaven, not now.

Diana went through the familiar process of shutting down everything that might put out a detectable signal. They had seen that ship twice. No AIS, no transponder. Pirates, or smugglers. Hide. Let it go by.

"*Prosperity*, MEVV. Closest Point of Approach?"

"MEVV, *Prosperity*, CPA … damn. Steady-bearing-decreasing-range. Straight for me. I'm being painted by radar. Strange frequency. I'm going to try hailing."

Diana's heartbeat sounded in her headset like timpani.

"MEVV, *Prosperity*, no response. Evaluation, hostile."

Preparation is the precursor of victory. Proper preparation prevents piss-poor performance. In case of fire, break glass. Pirates, they had a plan.

"MEVV, *Prosperity*. Get behind the rock in a radar shadow."

"Roger. Shifting position."

Diana used the maneuvering thrusters lightly. She didn't want a heat bloom from the thrusters spotted.

"MEVV, *Prosperity*. I'm armoring up. Our visitor isn't big. Probably a small crew."

Diana shot an antenna and camera into the side of the rock with a field of view encompassing *Prosperity* and the incoming ship. She found a depression in the rock, shot in some anchors, for luck fired in a registration stake, reeled in, and retracted all her probes and waldos to their stowed positions. To anything other than a high-resolution scan the MEVV would look like a gray bump on a large gray mass, a remora rock, a binary held in place by microgravity.

"Mother Thing, *Prosperity*. Open cargo door."

They had positioned a mining laser at the main cargo door. When the bandits took advantage of that inviting portal, they would be greeted by a beam powerful enough to cut steel. Powerful enough to kill.

If that didn't work, Tarak would grab extra oxygen and dive into space. Pirates wouldn't waste fuel chasing him. After the pirates departed Diana would pick him up.

The rock blocked her line of sight to *Prosperity*. She could only get what the emplaced RF antenna and camera could capture. She started bashing buttons to save the video to memory. With her current setup, she could only monitor Tarak's words.

'Mother Thing, *Prosperity*. Scan for boarders."

Diana tensed. This all seemed unreal.

"Re-evaluate! Re-evaluate!"

"Mother Thing, *Prosperity*. Acknowledged, boarders sighted."

Tarak was going to be attacked. It was actually going to happen.

Diana had lasers, small ones. She had waldos with grabbers. Counterattack?

No. Stick to the plan. If things went red, she was Tarak's last hope.

"Mother Thing, *Prosperity*. Are they bots? Instrument pods? Re-evaluate. Tentative identification, remotely-operated mechanical devices."

"Damn it, that can't be right. Say again."

"Twenty targets or twenty arms? Clarify! Re-evaluate!"

"Mother Thing, Tarak. Acknowledged, twenty boarders."

"Mother Thing, Tarak. Acknowledged, twenty-five boarders."

A laser shot lanced out into infinity. It swept an arc. Go, Tarak!

It fired again. Blinked. Were those hits?

Again.

Prosperity went dark.

7: Mike

Running a business couldn't be harder than keeping the air in and vak out of a 20,000-ton space liner. *Decode the rules and regulations. Study.*

He opened his volume of "Misplaced-4 Employment Business Regulations."

After an hour of reading, he didn't remember a thing. It was all so … random. Nothing made sense.

He had to concentrate. Redouble his efforts.

"279.A.8.(g). Notwithstanding subparagraph (i) of paragraph (a) of this subdivision, a service practitioner, certified under section sixty-nine hundred ten of this article and practicing for more than three thousand six hundred hours, may comply with this paragraph in lieu of complying with the requirements of 8 (a)…"

The gangway door reverberated with pounding. The security camera revealed men who didn't seem happy that anything should stand in the way of their mission to terrorize the hearts of little old ladies and grounded Vakkers.

Over the intercom, Mike said, "Sorry, closed."

"Open up! Union!"

Against his better judgment, Mike released the lock.

Three men in drawstring pants and pullovers stormed in. They seemed livid that they couldn't slam the airlock door behind them.

Surrounding Mike, wearing expressions designed to intimidate lions and tigers and bears (oh, my!), they told him Misplaced-4 was damn well a Union Planet. When Mike hired, he must join the Union at the owner's rate, pay Union dues, pay Union business fees, employ a full-time Union representative to protect his employees from exploitation, pay for periodic Union safety and workplace inspections, and abide by Union job classification regulations. His waitstaff was not allowed to clean dishes, they could deliver food but not clear tables, his barperson could fill glasses but not wash them, and Union Hazardous Materials Handling Qualification Certifications were required before any employee mopped up a spilled drink. Union-approved Clydes had head-of-the-line privileges for interviews, and Mike should really, really, absolutely positively consider very strongly awarding them jobs.

This was just a friendly social visit. This time. That was a relief. It wouldn't trigger Form 1040AS and the one stan fee.

Later that evening, Mike read twice the agonizing legalese in *Welcome to* <u>*Your*</u> *Union! Union Strong!*

As far as he could tell, no one was allowed to take out the trash.

8: *Diana*

"Ten Hundred. Scheduled alert … Ten Hundred. Scheduled—"

"Ahrite, MEVV, I'm up." Diana's words were slurred.

"—alert…Ten Hundred. Scheduled alert—"

"MEVV, MEVV Actual, cancel scheduled alert."

"MEVV Actual, MEVV, cancel scheduled alert. Scheduled alert canceled."

Diana willed her eyelids to open. Her eyes burned, her sinuses felt stuffed with cotton, and there was a ringing in her ears. Thirty consecutive hours packed into an MEVV would do that.

The exterior cameras showed only rock and stars. No *Prosperity*.

After checking the cockpit status, Diana elbowed the release lever. The top of the coffin opened. She shook her head, stretched, then cycled through her sensors.

No *Prosperity*. No pirates.

"MEVV, MEVV Actual. Did Tarak eject from *Prosperity*?"

"MEVV Actual, MEVV. Unknown query. Restate request."

The MEVV's computer wasn't an Organic. Usually linked to Mother Thing, by itself it was stupid. The question exceeded the computer's interpretive capabilities. Mother Thing was gone. Or dead.

She went through the buttonology to call up the camera's optical record file, ten minutes of frustrating layers of menus buried in unintelligible gobbledygook. Finally, she had the replay. Diana tabbed the progress bar to when she had gone to sleep, then fast-forwarded.

There. Cylinder bots went from *Prosperity* to their ship. The jacker's ship departed. *Prosperity* followed. No sign of Tarak punching out. MEVV had been too stupid to wake her up.

She restored power to the MEVV. Anchors were disconnected, wires reeled in, and she moved away from the asteroid. Flipping more toggles energized the MEVV's active sensors. Her radar would stimulate Tarak's transponder.

No transponder. They'd taken him away.

Tarak…why didn't you bail out? We had it planned. Tarak, where are you?

She clamped down. Grieve for Tarak later. It took a few minutes to calm her heart. *Get control of yourself, or the situation controls you.*

Running an estimate with the communications equations, she figured her transmitter had enough power to get a message to the Sigma-Misplaced PunchPoint buoy. After its daily punch from Sigma to the Misplaced-4 system, it would relay her message to the Federated Space Forces. The FSF would dispatch a ship for Rescue and Assistance, government-provided, easy.

Report the jacking. Report pirates.

Pay the R&A Fee. Go bankrupt.

After a few minutes with the navigation computer, she settled back to review her options.

The MEVV was topped off with consumables. There was enough O_2 to make the PunchPoint, with 60 hours of loiter time to await a ship in transit. Better to negotiate for assistance with a Vakker or Spacer than the Freddies. She could top off her fuel from mega-tank.

The rock! How could she forget!

The button for G&C channel one was illuminated. She sent out an RF query. "Yes!" There was a solid acknowledgment from the thruster pack and fuel tank. The pirates had left them behind.

She rubbed her burning eyes, reached into the cooler, snagged a water bottle, and sucked a mouthful through the no-G tube.

That rock was worth two, maybe even ten million standards. Millions! Install a claim stake and transponder, and by Federated law she could register the claim and come back anytime in 500 ytterbium-clock-days and recover the rock.

Claim transponders. Yeah, otherwise known as Claim Jumper Magnets. She'd be in a race with every crook with 50 stans to bribe the registration clerk. Crooks, hell—every ethically-challenged Corporation, which means, basically, all the villains.

She would need money to launch a search for Tarak.

Explosives. The MEVV had Centex blocks and detonators. She could chip off a chunk. It would be tricky, but if she could locate a high-yield vein she could pare off a few hundred kilograms of chromium-rich ore to sell, earning enough stans to keep the wolf from the door and the bank from dispatching corppers with warrants.

She'd make the Sigma-Misplaced PunchPoint, and find a Vakker or Spacer willing to let her piggyback a punch into Misplaced System.

9: Mike

No employees meant no union, no interviews, no Transaction Tax.

Mike opened his bar and grill as a sole proprietorship. He took orders, made drinks, cooked, waited tables, mopped up spilled beer and collected payment, all by his lonesome. Captain Mike's Bar and

Grill had customers, but he just couldn't serve them fast enough to cover expenses. Vakker friends tried to help by picking up their own beer and orders from the bar, until a Union shill got a Tevil inspector to cite him for 'using unsafe (non-Union) labor.'

So many rules and regulations. He was 'in violation' at every turn. He used the wrong material towel to clean up a spilled drink. Court appearance, fined 100 standards. He mopped his floor without wearing a caustic-proof apron and protective gloves. Court appearance, 120 standards. Salt shakers were not inspected daily for plugged holes. Court appearance, 50 standards.

10: Tarak

Tarak opened his eyes. He saw dirty and gray and monotone.

Was he dead? With his ancestors?

The fight against the pirates, those cylinder bots—they flooded out from the pirate spacecraft. His laser lashed the intruders as if it had a mind of its own. He hit ten, maybe more. Burned square-on, they exploded, like terrorist suicide bombers.

Humans would have retreated. Surprise, fear and shock would have sent them back in a panicked retreat. Not bots. Bots just kept coming. No fear of death, no morale to break in a bot.

He'd been knocked away from the laser. The bots swarmed, pushed him down, piled on. He couldn't move. Then, no air. He passed out.

Air. An odor, salty. He could smell. Can you smell when you're dead?

Lifting onto his elbows, he looked around. He was in his skinsuit, helmet stowed, breathing without distress. The gloves were missing, his electronics pack was gone, as was his suit armor. Water was topped, batteries good, filters clean, temperature regulation middle of the band, seals and hydraulics good, electrical operational. His clock and calendar were zeroed. He sensed he'd been unconscious a long time.

A rocky plain surrounded. Hills were off in the distance. Gray sky, no clouds. A chill, dry wind brushed his face. Rolling to his knees, he felt the ground. Parched, lifeless rock shards and sand. He stood.

First to capture his attention was a large rectangular box. It looked new, made of dull metal with a hinged lid. The top lifted easily.

Inside were water bottles and food packages he recognized from *Prosperity*—the dreaded dehydrated Lamb Stew—and a strange thing that looked like a medieval broadsword, metal, very sharp, odd handle on one end. At the bottom of the box was a staff a meter long, weighted on one end. He lifted it. It massed over ten pounds, maybe five kilos.

Edged weapon? A club? Was he lead actor in some Swords 'n Sandals epic?

Tarak closed the lid, jumped atop the box, and deployed his helmet. He activated the magnification scanner and swept the horizon, searching each quadrant methodically. There was a hill some kilometers in the direction of the sun.

Scanning left, he saw a lander. Range, 4,412 meters. 20-some bots were disembarking. High magnification showed the bots had cylindrical bodies with three waldos, two on the sides and one on top. Take away the waldos, they looked like trash cans on legs. They were the same type of bots that attacked *Prosperity*. They milled about, aimlessly, some pausing to assume weird poses.

Not bots. Aliens. Had to be. Bots didn't act like a bunch of lunatics who'd just bonked their keepers and run outside to dance with the butterflies.

Off to the right, further out, up a small slope, was a human.

Under high mag, was it a girl? Slacks, a shirt, loose hair to her neck.

Diana? Diana's here?

No skinsuit; flowing blond hair, braw-boned. Not Diana. Diana was brunette, at least when he last saw her, and petite. This girl was standing on a box. He waved. No response. Too far for a holler to be heard. Her attention was fixed on the aliens.

Tarak hopped off the box and squatted. What happened to Diana? Why wasn't she with him? Did she escape the pirates? He had a flutter of concern.

Not now. No time for that. Now, he had to deal with now.

Those things, trashcans with arms, they captured him, dropped him off, provided supplies, something like Joshua's sword and Moses' staff, and then what? Maybe these *things* wanted to learn about humans. Was he supposed to represent the intelligent, peace-loving human race? *Me and that girl, all by our lonesome?*

He climbed back on the box. The aliens had formed a line and were advancing toward the girl like some OldEarth infantry platoon, holding the sword-things away from their bodies, the club-things in a harness on their backs. The girl jumped off the box and walked toward them, hands spread widely with open arms, carrying nothing but her good wishes for intragalactic friendship.

Go, girl! History in the making. Make peace!

Twenty yards separated them. The aliens stopped. The girl continued walking with open-handed, placating gestures. Tarak heard a squeal, like a bad bearing on a fuel pump. All the aliens reached into their harness with that huge upper arm and extracted something.

Another screech. They threw.

The girl was pummeled. Rocks, stones, cannonballs, whatever the projectiles were, she was driven to her knees. At the highest magnification, Tarak saw red.

Another high-pitched noise. The aliens charged. The girl was prostrate. Aliens crowded around her. Sword thrusts. Red adorned their weapons and misted the air.

Tarak jumped down and sat on the box. He was horrified.

Stop it. No time for emotions. *Think.*

A memory tickled his brain: an OldEarth video. Some whack job capturing people and putting them on an island to hunt them as prey. Is this like that vid?

The Trashcans wanted to fight, not talk. Obviously. He's supposed to fight back, weapons provided. Obviously. He'd get a few, but they'd overwhelm him, like on *Prosperity*. Twenty to one, their ground, their rules.

Sun Tzu. Know your enemy, know yourself.

He bounced on his toes. Gravity, maybe 0.8, 0.75-G. They didn't know he was from a 1.1-G world and addicted to exercise apparatus. *Advantage: Tarak.*

He had a sword and a club. He hadn't trained with them. *Advantage: Trashcans. For now.*

They waddled. Not fast, not quick. *Advantage: Tarak.*

Tarak returned his gaze to the hill. He could reach it on the run. Hide, gather intelligence, scope their weaknesses, learn to use the weapons, make a plan.

Tarak stuffed water and food packages into his pockets. The

sword had a workable grip, a lightening hole down the center of the blade, and it looked like it was made from stainless steel. Testing the edge against the club handle, he peeled away a strip of material. Sharp. The club might slow him down. His advantage was speed, not firepower, but it didn't feel right to leave anything behind.

He pulled out a water bottle, took a deep draught, then finished it off. Lining up on the gaggle of aliens, he drop-kicked the empty bottle. It tumbled end over end for ten meters, hit the ground, bounced, gave out a mournful, hollow thump, and rolled.

A high-pitched blare came from the direction of the trashcans, like a metal-on-metal warbling squeal from a misaligned high-speed motor.

What a crappy battle cry. Geronimo had a better battle cry. Crazy Horse, Cochise, Red Cloud, the tribes had better battle cries.

Tarak had a better battle cry!

Tarak lifted his head and howled and yipped, his fear, frustration, and challenge broadcast over the desert. He let his ancestors take his voice. To the capacity of his lungs he proclaimed his foes would die in droves, his life would only end after he was covered in their blood.

That felt good.

A little silly, but good.

The aliens picked up the girl's corpse and started back to their shuttle. Tarak's box of food and water must mean he was scheduled for another day.

He started a steady lope, heading toward the hill in the direction of the sun.

11: Mike

Mike was sitting in the dining room at ten o'clock in the morning, running his finances. His balance sheet was being worked courtesy of a stubby pencil and scrap paper. On this planet the Feds, Tevil, and the bank could hack clipscreens and suck anyone's data at will. He didn't want them to know his reserves were nearly redlined.

Mike was totally demoralized. He dreaded opening the gangway. After bending and cleaning and carrying for days, even in quarter-G, his feet hurt, his back felt like it was recycled from a cadaver, and his pride disappeared each time Union finks and Tevil inspectors cited him for violations. His future was a baggy set of Client Gray coveralls and the dole. After being a Chief Environmentalist with a Class One license and Master Chef, he did not relish the downfall, the loss of all his savings from over a decade in space. He was proud when he opened his doors as "Citizen Captain Mike"—*Ajax* may host a bar and grill, but the hull was still registered as a spacecraft, so he officially qualified as an owner-operator captain—but that conceit faded faster than bankruptcy approached.

He'd hoped his two last assets could be sold to stave off insolvency: *Ajax* Organic and the AutoDoc. They were both a bust. The AutoDoc was restricted to use on the *Ajax* for a limited number of treatments. Shipping it to Asclepius, reprogramming, recertification, and reloading the pharmaceuticals and supplies were prohibitively expensive. Asclepius, the Corporation with the medical monopoly, could charge what they pleased.

As for the Organic, it was in an equipment closet off the passageway leading to his office-cum-bedroom. He had carefully recharged the nutrient bath and serviced it at the required intervals. Discretely offered for sale, he had no offers. Decertified Organics were typically terminated.

That shipbroker had fed him other lies. There was no "building boom down the lava tubes." There was no new construction whatsoever. Misplaced-4's population was half what it was before The Shift. Whole districts remained unpopulated, sealed off, and abandoned. The planet's economy was circling the drain.

A soft voice interrupted Mike's trance. "Captain Mike?"

Mike spun around. There was a kid behind the bar.

The gangway was locked. *How did he get in?* Despair flushed into anger. "What the flaming fornication are you doing here?"

The kid flinched, but stood up under Mike's glare. He was an indeterminate age, maybe 15, perhaps closer to 19 standard years, spindly, with the undeveloped frame that came from living in low-G. He wore a well-maintained skinsuit, helmet retracted, and a conformal O_2&E pack. His hair was in a Vakker's close clip.

His voice was polite. "Sorry for surprise. Just wanted talk."

Just a kid. Not his fault Mike's restaurant was dancing barefoot on thumbtacks.

The young man gave a hint of a smile. "Besides, promise, don't flame, and haven't figured out fornication."

Mike smiled. *He* hadn't figured out fornication—the result of a strict upbringing, and working with Vakkers with Christian ideas of the sanctity of womanhood.

The youngster leaned forward. Elbows on the bar, hands apart like he was revealing a great mystery, he said, "Ran simulations. Captain Mike's dying."

Great. The local kindergarten was sending restaurant critics. "Look, there's no positions available, I don't serve drinks to minors, and the grill is off. Tell me how you got in, and leave the same way."

"Ran other simulations. Added ideas. This place could work."

Lovely, an adolescent business consultant. "Got a name?"

"Callsign 'Ghost.'"

Right, like a kid would have been awarded a callsign. Callsigns were not invented by their owner, they were earned. They were a sort of merit badge presented by other Vakkers, a name that was something special, usually based on an identifying characteristic or a particularly embarrassing event, a name memorable to the community of Vakkers. Mike's callsign came from the 'embarrassing event' type: he was on a freighter with his skinsuit helmet up during a 'loss of electrical' drill. With no assigned duties, he fell asleep. His head nodded over, chin hit the emergency transmit button, and his snores blotted out all communications for the fifteen minutes it took his shipmates to locate and wake him. Later that night, in a solemn and moving ceremony, he was christened, callsign "Microphone." Common usage, "Mike."

The kid didn't have the usual look of Clyde despair, although he likely hadn't laughed in a decade. Intelligent eyes, scoping the room like he was scouting possibilities. His eyes were deep-set and dark-rimmed. And, he was painfully thin.

"Ideas? What do you want for them?" Mike said.

Mike looked up at the multimeter on the wall. Solar panels were producing voltage at the top of the band. He walked over to the grill and pressed the switch to read the maximum current available. Good; his repaired solar panels were holding up. He closed the breaker to feed the kitchen power bus and flipped on the grill.

The kid took a deep breath, then said, "A percentage."

"Whoa! Those must be some high-shiny good ideas!"

"Not just ideas. Invest. Set ideas up. I provide materials, no cost to you. Percentage from profits, not from gross. No risk, you."

Right, a teenager with anything to invest in a business, on this planet?

Mike reached into a shelf, grabbed a squirt bottle of cooking oil, and shot some on the grill. "Tell you what. I was just going to torch up some breakfast. How about you join me. Reconstituted eggs and extruded sausage paste, but I cook them up tastier." From the cold box he retrieved the bottle of scrambled eggs, along with rehydrated onion, green pepper, sausage paste, Creole powder, and tomato. After a flurry of chopping the food was sizzling, wafting up an appetizing smell.

The kid sniffed. Apparently, he liked what he sniffed.

The kid began spinning a story of a new bar and grill, without the Union, the Tevil inspectors foiled.

Mike got interested.

Over food, he got fascinated.

Cleaning the plates, he got excited.

At opening time, he hung a sign across the gangway: 'Closed for Renovation.'

12: Mike

Ghost produced a CAD drawing of *Ajax's* dining room floor showing a new layout. They moved tables so there were clear, staggered lanes leading to the bar and the grill. Mike tack-welded the tables to the deck. Around the room's fringes he welded center-pedestal tables upside down, their base tacked to the overhead and their tops suspended above the deck, shoulder-high to a seated guest. The inverted tables provided places to park drinks and food; the elevated furniture gave clear leg room underneath. It was a furniture-stuck-wherever look comfortable to Vakkers with time in no-G.

The next day Ghost arrived with large, awkward boxes. A shipment of three-score lacrosse goalie sticks with large-net heads had been mistakenly sent to Misplaced-4's campus of Terra Cognita University. TCU did not play lacrosse. Consigned to the trash crater, the sticks had been rescued by Ghost.

A clamp was bolted on each table. The sticks were mounted vertically, so their nets were above the tables. The dining room began to look like a blighted forest topped with dead squirrels' nests. Mike wasn't sure he liked the look.

Another box yielded new clipscreens. Ghost started hardwiring them to each table. "Disposal dock trash," said Ghost. "Memory chips bad. Keypunch chips good. They transmit orders to control panel at the grill station. Mics and speakers work, so you can talk to tables individually."

"A control panel needs a *programmed* computer. That's not in the budget."

"*Ajax* Organic. Spent time, wired him up different, helped him work through coupla issues. Callsign 'LaMancha.' He was happy to wake up. Where's computer bus interface socket?"

A 'happy' Organic, with a callsign? Mike filed that improbability away for later consideration.

It was three days' work to hook the clipscreens into the computer bus, wire in the order display, hang cameras throughout the room and survey their locations down to the millimeter.

"Cameras see all," said Ghost. "LaMancha knows rules. No more tickets from Tevil or Freddy the Feddie."

Out of another of his bottomless boxes Ghost pulled a three-degrees-of-freedom gimballed sensor baseplate and a compression scale. He attached the scale to the baseplate and wired them both into the computer bus. He clamped the assembly on the top of the bar. Then he unpacked a miniature catapult, obviously homemade, and fixed it atop the compression scale. He ran a test, watching carefully as the baseplate rotated and elevated.

One last connection, and Ghost seemed satisfied.

"LaMancha, Ghost. Startup. Execute BIT. Report status."

There was a pause, then a cultured Castilian-Spanish accented voice came out of the control panel speaker. "Ghost, LaMancha. Startup. Execute BIT. Report status. Start-up initiated. Built-In-Test executed, satisfactory. I detect seven video feeds, 26 degraded clipscreens which I associate with those on the tables numbered 1 through 26, nine degraded clipscreens along the liquids bar and foods bar, six large-screen display monitors, a payment transaction register, and a waldo feed which I surmise is from that ridiculous onager sitting atop the liquids bar. I trust you do not expect me to fire water balloons for you."

The monitor over the grill flashed silver, then black, then the pixels slowly resolved into a picture of a Knight in Shining Armor, visor up, leaning on an onager, hefting a huge water balloon with one hand. The Knight's handlebar moustache was enormous.

Mike had never heard an Organic talk like that, or use an avatar.

"What the heck is an onager?"

"Ancient name, this catapult," Ghost said. "LaMancha, Ghost. Conversation Mode in effect for communications inside *Ajax*." This eliminated the spaceflight 'who to, who from' comms protocol.

"Do you understand concept, 'bar and grill'?" asked Ghost.

A British accent came from the speaker. "Elementary, my dear Watson."

"Who's Watson?" asked Mike.

Ghost forestalled him with a wave. "Do you understand meaning of 'profit'?"

A raspberry blasted from the speakers. "Do you understand meaning of 'insulting'?"

Ghost, unperturbed, moved to a bar stool. "Using onager, could you fire capped shot glass into net attached to target table?"

"I require test firings, to determine the onager's torsional coefficients and the flight characteristics of the shot glass."

Mike filled a shot glass with water and capped it with a no-G leakproof cover.

Ghost pulled back the onager's arm, attached the release clip, and put the glass in the bucket. "LaMancha, catapult on liquids bar, designated 'Bar Cat,' loaded, full tension. Test fire Bar Cat, target: net, table 21."

LaMancha repeated the order. The sensor baseplate buzzed, spun completely around, turned back to point the onager at the table, adjusted elevation, and Bar Cat fired with a loud *sprang*. The glass streaked across the room, bounced off the overhead, missed Table 21's net by a clear meter, and exploded against the outer hull.

"Ooops," a speaker explained. Mike grimaced.

Ghost didn't look concerned. "Simulation mode. Use security tapes from Captain Mike's Bar and Grill for customer behavior parameters. Use peak business day. With customer orders coming via clipscreen, with you displaying orders, firing drinks and food to the tables, processing payment, calculate Mike's work duty cycle. Stochastic simulation, normal distribution randomization, 1000 reps. Execute."

Silence.

Mike looked over the changes in his dining room, his bar, and his small kitchen. All his accumulated life savings were invested here. Now, more than ever, he wanted the place to stay his. If he only had to cook and mix drinks and load the catapults, it would be just like he had a wait staff, without Tevil or the Union's bull. If his workload was less than 100%, heck, less than 120%, he would make it work.

LaMancha spoke in a clipped New York City Wall Street accent. "Judging from the diameter of Mike's thumbs, I cannot see him loading an onager without hurting himself. I modified the input parameters to include a second onager at the grill bar, and waldos to load both onagers, under my control. Mike's duty cycle peaks Friday evenings at 2047, peak load 78 percent, plus or minus seven percent."

YES. 78 percent. That's 22 percent glorious free time. Luxurious.

Ghost said, "Use current menu. Include loan service, taxes and overhead. Assume prices set with food raw materials cost one-third of retail price charged to customers. Calculate profit. Stochastic simulation, uniform distribution randomization, 1000 reps. Execute."

Behind his back, Mike crossed his fingers. Hope proposed an exorbitant twenty standards a week. No, be realistic, ten. Stars and comets, if he could just break even. He could eat leftovers. Aprons were cheap.

This time the wait was short. "With current customer order rates, at a 90 percent confidence level, profit at 57 standards plus or minus eleven standards—"

It was like an electric shock. 57 stans a week! Fantastic! Mike's spirits lifted.

"—per Friday. Assuming operating six days a week, accounting for variations in traffic, 260 standards per week—"

Mike felt the need to lean against something.

"—but with improved fulfillment times and increased efficiency, order rates will likely increase non-linearly—"

Mike had to remember to inhale.

"—and with increased patronage," said LaMancha, shifting to a jazz-accented voice, "this baby gonna fly."

Ghost gave a tiny smile, a real smile, the first Mike had seen. "Might work."

Mike could only nod.

"Simulations are tricky," said Ghost. "Too clean. Many unaccounted variables. Might only get 70, 80 percent. Still, decent."

"Decent," echoed Mike, nodding vigorously.

13: Mike

They posted a sign outside the entrance to the gangway:

Lacrosse Shot Bar and Grill

Open 1100 to 2400. Closed Monday.

House Rules:

1) Food and drink to tables will be shot.

2) Orders that miss your net will be replaced if spilled, and the table given a 25% credit. No moving the net. Photo replay available.

3) If you intercept another's order, you own it, for a 50% premium.

4) All intercepts must use the table lacrosse net. Clothing, hands, feet, torso, hats, drones, neighbors, or anything else is not allowed. Botched intercepts, you pay for the order and premium, along with a drink for the original target, target's choice of beverage (two standards maximum). Any resulting mess, a 50% clean-up fee will be assessed.

5) If your shot gets intercepted, your replacement order is 10% off. Originator must re-enter the same order.

6) All rules enforced, referee decisions made and bills tabulated by LaMancha, the House Organic. A Challenge Flag may be thrown for 50 pence, refunded if the challenge wins. One challenge flag per customer per night. All decisions final.

7) Mike's Noteworthy Mystery Meals and Drinks will be shot in Red Covers, aimed at empty tables. 25% off menu price. Anyone can intercept or retrieve. You snag it, you keep it, you pay for it.

8) Do not encourage the House Organic.

9) Conversation comms protocol in the dining room. Disrespect LaMancha, on your head be it (he assesses all fines and controls billing).

10) A surcharge will be applied to the tabs of all Corporate, Government, or Union officials, to compensate for the suffering of the other patrons (and management).

14: *Diana*

Was it days or weeks ago? Time had merged into a continuing horror.

Diana had managed to blast out a lovely chunk of high-grade ore from her rock. With it stowed, concealed from view, she boosted to the Sigma-Misplaced PunchPoint, arriving with her consumables and fuel nearly expended. Her first bit of luck: two Vakker stationmax freighters were lining up to punch through to Misplaced System. Playing both against the other, she was able to conclude negotiations quickly for a piggyback, without revealing she was down to her last few hours of O_2.

Orbiting Misplaced-4, her next task was to sell her payload. The orbital refineries owned by Tevil Corporation insisted on knowing the location of the source to 'ensure she was not a claim jumper.' They'd use the information to make her million-standard rock disappear into their own pockets, speed-of-light. She'd be helpless to protest, especially since Tevil could back their theft with an Armed Cargo Transport.

She accepted an offer from an independent Vakker refining outfit for the ore, the thruster engine, and the fuel tank. The rented MEVV was returned, she settled delinquent payments, then finally took a shuttle to the surface, checked into a Vakker hostel, and collapsed for 48 hours.

Now, funds were low. She had enough for a few weeks if she minimized her showers and ate at Tevil cafeterias, renowned for cheap, inedible food.

There was hope. When her insurance claim on the *Property* was settled, she'd have the money to start a search for Tarak. The first step would be to return to Sigma System. Time was of the essence. If she could get back quickly, the ion trail from the hijacker's engines might still be detectable—a trail to follow. And, of course, the rock, if she could find someone trustworthy for the retrieval operation.

A week later, still nothing from Tevil Insurance. Submitting an insurance claim to Tevil was like negotiating with a black hole: everything in, nothing out.

In the Vakker's Hostel, Diana sat listening to insipid music issuing from her FoxxFone. Her temper had been rising for the last 90 minutes. For the millionth time, the music quieted for the voice-over:

"Hello there! *Thank you* for letting Tevil Insurance Solutions serve your coverage needs. We are *thrilled* you contacted our claims line. Your call is *very important* to each and every one of us here at Tevil Insurance Solutions—yes, *all* of us. We're currently experiencing delays due to unusual call volume, for which you are partly to blame. But, in the context of the vast affairs of the galaxy—suns going supernova, volcanoes exploding—relax, you're experiencing a minor inconvenience. Our next available Corporate Service Enthusiast will be with you in just three shakes of a comet's tail! During your brief wait, surely you'll be interested in these fascinating facts about *your* Tevil Insurance Solutions, a subsidiary of Tevil Corporation, the most awarded—"

15: Mike

The Lacrosse Shot was crowded. Vakkers were coming in earlier to make sure they could get a prime table. The crowd was in a jovial mood.

Business had exceeded expectations. Success allowed LaMancha to be awarded three onagers, with two waldos at each, with other waldos at the bar to concoct drinks and fill pitchers. At this moment Mike had five steak sandwiches and two deep-fried burrito specials sizzling simultaneously. Through the video cameras, LaMancha could track each order as it was created and ensure that each drink or food package went to the right table. As Mike began preparing a dish, LaMancha automatically decremented the 'orders outstanding' queue. The epitome of efficiency.

"Table 20, alert, order incoming." Bar Cat was cocked. The waldo loaded a mug of coffee. The onager rotated and elevated and, with a *sprang*, launched the payload. The shot hit cleanly in the center of Table 20's net.

Thumbs up from Table 20. "Nothin' but net!"

A short Vakker in a modern art skinsuit and short shaggy hair leaned toward his table speaker. "Hey LaMancha, Table 20. Shoot us one of those extra good drinks we talked about. Put spin on it, mix it up good."

The waldo loaded a shot glass containing an enticing amber-colored liquid. Everyone knew the delicate glow of Studley 100 Bourbon.

Bar Cat rotated and elevated. *Sprang.*

Table 12's lacrosse net jabbed up and captured the glass cleanly.

"Intercepted!" gloated the Vakker, waving his stick. The crowd gave a little cheer, some good-natured boos. "Picasso, you ain't getting nothing good when I'm sitting between you and the bar!"

He pulled out the drink. "Here's to you, chump!" He uncapped the glass and took a deep draught. Then, spewed it out like a firehose. "What the ... Tea! You flaming backstabber! You made me pay intercept premium for a freakin' glass of *tea*!"

Picasso laughed uproariously. "LaMancha, thanks, good buddy. We got him!"

Out of the speakers in a Chicago Gangster accent, LaMancha said, "Yeah, we got 'em, right in the kisser." Then, in his Referee's voice, "Cleanup, Table 12. 50% Cleanup Penalty, Table 12."

Picasso's companion said, "Boots oughta pay intercept premium and cleanup on bourbon, not tea. He thought he was intercepting a ration of Stud."

A referee's whistle sounded out of Table 20's speaker. "That's a negatory there, BigBird. At The Lacrosse Shot, you get what you pay for, you pay for what you get. Vakker's Code."

Mike listened to the banter as he cooked. Things were going great. After re-opening, there were two days of listless business, then The Word got out. At first, it was shipmates. They accepted the early glitches, spilled drinks and splattered food, with amused tolerance. Then LaMancha got the catapults calibrated, and Mike obtained secure, streamlined packaging that allowed food to be shot without spraying sauce and calories everywhere. They loosened the nets to better catch things larger than a lacrosse ball, and mounted the sticks on springs to dampen the landing shock.

Vakkers got into the light-hearted spirit of the place. Even the upside-down tables were jammed on weekends, and the place filled night after night. The original profit projections were exceeded. More improvements were in the works. A cargo bay was converted to grow crops, and two other bays would be planted next month. His steak sandwiches would soon be made with his own onions and peppers, with three kinds of tomatoes for salads. To support the gardening,

Mike got one of the new, advanced, semi-Organic spider bots, who rejoiced when christened with the noble name, *Gardenbottie*—and grumphed when he was occasionally drafted for spill cleanup duties. The plants generated O_2, giving Mike credit on the Air Tax. Repairing more of *Ajax's* solar panels allowed him to go totally off Tevil's power grid.

Then, the crowd's noise tapered to nothing.

The only other time the gang went quiet was when the government supervisor visited. The govvie sat at the grill counter separate from the other patrons, like he was afraid Vakkers were diseased. He snapped his fingers and demanded a menu, ignoring what was posted on the bar clipscreen and the bulkhead display in front of his nose. He had that superior air of the government worker, confident in power and secure in his sinecure, which meant this oxygen sink expected to be served ahead of the queue, and with fawning deference.

LaMancha politely asked for his credit ID, explaining that he did not have a credit code on file. Govvie presented his CID as if he were the Sun King Louis XIV handing out a stay of execution for a misguided peasant. Identified as Government Supervisor Arcola, LaMancha reminded him of Rule 10, and named the day's surcharge for govvie supervisors.

"Damn you, you can't inflate the price just because I represent the government!"

"We follow government principles," answered Mike, who sidled up with a poorly-suppressed grin.

"Principles? A bar has *principles*? What principles?"

"I make more profit; the government progressively takes a bigger cut in taxes. At the top level, you're taking 90 percent of what a business earns. It seems only fair to apply the same *principle* to prices: higher class customer, higher price." Mike offered a beatific smile. "Most of your bill will go to taxes. You are really just supporting the government, helping it have the funds to pay your salary. You pay me, I pay the government, the government gives it back to you. It's as if your meal was *free*—" Mike closed his eyes, looking like a kitten who had just indulged in a nicely seasoned mouse. "—sort of."

Govvie huffed and stalked out. LaMancha's Bronx Cheer followed him down the gangway. A few breaths later, after light laughter, the Lacrosse Shot was back to volume. LaMancha charged Government Supervisor Arcola for three minutes of stool rental, one pence, a hundredth of a standard. LaMancha said it was to make a point.

Registering the silence, anticipating another government or Tevil interloper, Mike looked to the gangway.

There stood a tall lady, feminine at ten to the fifteenth power, immaculately dressed, with a slender figure and features that would cause a tank of Rocket-A to spontaneously detonate. She had the frame of someone reared on a full-G planet, strong, fit. Her clipscreen was in an enlarged exterior pocket on the type of jacket favored by students and comps, her auburn hair was tucked into a sensible bun, and she was adorned with a pleasant, questioning expression. She looked around, eyes not pausing until she spotted an empty seat at the grill counter. She started for it.

"Table 16, alert, incoming." *Sprang.* Bar Cat fired a pitcher. The jug passed in front of the mystery lady's nose. She jerked back, startled.

"Shot across the bow!" said an anonymous Vakker. Friendly laughter.

LaMancha must not approve of this lady. Not a Vakker, maybe some kind of corporate. LaMancha did not like corporates. Especially Tevil Corporate Captains.

She sat at the grill counter and spun around, surveying the dining room. LaMancha filled the quiet with a few more shots. He fired a red-covered plate that caused the lacrosse nets to clash as people went for the discounted food—the previous Noteworthy Mystery Meal was a ribeye steak, medium-rare.

The noise level returned, but with boisterousness held in check.

Mike took a deep breath. He forced himself not to stare. He had dealt with beautiful women before when he crewed high end passenger liners. This lady seemed more natural than those in Galaxy Class, with their dramatic makeup and elaborate coiffures. He walked over and locked his eyes on her forehead, resisting the urge to let his gaze wander lower.

"May I help you, Miss, ah 'scuse me, Dee?" said Mike. 'Miss' may not be right. Her age was around 30, perhaps younger. No wedding ring, no other jewelry. Maybe an academic, but not a student. 'Dee, Derr, Das' were the accepted Federation-recommended titles for ladies, gentlemen, and children. Dee was safer than trying Miss, Ms., or Mrs., and getting it wrong.

She had a lovely face, with a trace of laugh lines.

"Hello." Her voice was pure music.

She pulled out her CID, obviously pre-staged in her jacket pocket. "I would like to establish a payment account." She held out the card.

"Show it to LaMancha," Mike said, gesturing to the nearest camera.

She held up the card next to her face and smiled. She had an enchanting smile, pixie-like.

"Citizen Professor Ella Braun, I am LaMancha, your humble waitshooter. We delight in the honor of welcoming you to The Lacrosse Shot." LaMancha spoke in his most refined, high-Spanish Castilian accent.

Whoa. LaMancha sure swapped attitudes in a hurry.

"Citizen Professor, what can I get you," asked Mike.

"Mike, may I please speak to you, by Bar Cat? Now?" LaMancha sounded flustered.

Citizen Professor Braun was studying the menu on the clipscreen. He could leave without being rude. "Excuse me a nano."

He walked over to stand by Bar Cat. Its two waldos were loading a soft drink pitcher. "What's the hold? You spill some more of that itching powder in your nutrient bath?"

LaMancha's voice came out in a whisper. "That's not fair. It was an experiment. But, Citizen Professor Ella Braun, *I* want to take her order. Let it be my job. *I* want to talk to her."

"What gives? You just miss bouncing a pitcher off her skull, and *don't* tell me it was an accident, and now you want to snuggle up and exchange sweet nuthin's?"

"Mike, this is LaMancha, your compadre, imploring, begging, *pleeeease* ......"

LaMancha was acting like a four-year-old, wanting Mommy's attention to show her the picture he'd just drawn. *Might as well. No drag on my flight profile.* He'd go drool by the grill where he belonged. "All right. Control in Transfer Permissive. Your bird."

Mike walked back to the grill.

LaMancha spoke out of Professor Braun's bar clipscreen. "Citizen Professor Ella Braun, I am LaMancha, your humble waitshooter. It is indeed a pleasure to welcome you to our modest establishment. We are most impressed by your publications on Artificial Intelligence and Organic computers. Mike, surely you are aware that Citizen Professor Braun is the Head of Terra Cognita University's Cybernetics Department. She is the most esteemed academic in her field. We are honored by her visit."

She certainly didn't fit the mold of a dried-up ancient professor. That flustered Mike. "Ah, welcome."

"Citizen Professor Braun, may I serve you by taking your order, please?"

"Call me Ella." That musical voice again. "I would like a Mike's Special, and a Long Island Iced Tea—not too strong—you make it with rum?"

"Professor Ella, we certainly can make it with rum, for you."

Mike couldn't remember if they had culled rum from the drinks menu. Not too many Vakkers called for that sweet drink.

Mike glanced at the order board, returned to the grill, and started another cheesesteak. He began to sauté onions mixed with thyme. He topped two of the sizzling steaks on the grill with provolone cheese. Then he shoveled up three other steaks and put them on toasted rolls, topped them with onions and thyme, a shake of garlic salt, black pepper, and a smear of mixed mayonnaise and Dijon inside the bun. He wrapped them in paper, jabbed in lots of toothpicks for stability, sealed them in custom delivery dishes, and inflated the internal balloons stabilizing the food. He placed them on the counter next to Grill Cat.

"Table 9, alert, incoming." *Sprang.* A cheer. A voice from the crowd: "Nuthin' but net!"

Ella seemed fascinated.

Back at the grill, Mike flipped Ella's steak, chopped it with the side of his spatula, and stirred the onion-thyme mix. After a glance at the order board, he made up the Burrito Specials.

Sprang. Another cheer.

"He certainly is good with those catapults," Ella said to Mike.

Elvis's voice came from her speaker. "Ah, thank yah, thank yah verra much."

Mike turned and nodded. "LaMancha was this ship's astronautics Organic before some young fool augered it in," he said. "Ballistics comes naturally, I expect."

"He also seems to be having fun."

LaMancha did seem to be rather enthusiastic and pleasant-tempered. Except for The Day Of The Itching Powder. And the visit of the govvie. Or any Tevil Corporate Captain. Minor exceptions. "He gets along, with 'bout everyone, 'bout always."

Mike found a quarter-full bottle of rum, showed it to a camera so LaMancha could include rum in the next Wholesome Wholesale Liquor Coliseum order (to be on hand should Ella come again!), and mixed up the Long Island Iced Tea. He put it before Ella on a drink coaster. A few seconds later, after doing the right things with a fresh toasted roll, steak and cheese, grilled onion-thyme, garlic salt, pepper, some arugula, and a smear of mustard-mayo mix, he presented the steaming plateful to Ella.

She drew back and eyed the sandwich. "How do I eat all that? It's thicker than a mouthful."

"Wise Master tell Grasshopper, 'Longest journey begins with single bite.' And you're allowed to smoosh it. Adds to the flavor."

She smooshed, picked it up, and took a tentative bite. Her eyes went wide.

"Woondhurfl!" she said.

"Professor Ella, on behalf of my colleague Mike, ah, thank yah, thank yah verra much."

Mike left her to her meal while he attended to his orders. He could tell LaMancha was showing off. When Ella was looking, he fired an extreme change-up that, in the quarter gravity, seemed to float to the farthest table in a high, graceful arc. He hit a carom shot off an upside-down table that drew a standing ovation. "Nuthin' but net!"

There was a break in the orders. Mike took a washcloth to his hands and face, poured himself some lemonade, and walked over to Ella. She had finished her sandwich, leaving nothing on the plate.

Mike looked at her appraisingly. "You know, somehow, I don't think a TCU professor just happened into a Vakker bar because she was hungry."

"You don't trust the reputation of your food?" she said with an arched eyebrow. "You should. It was fantastic." She folded her hands on the bar. "You're right."

Mike cocked his head to the side, inviting her to continue.

"It's LaMancha," she said. "Do you know how unique he is?"

"Same as other Organics, I suppose. Maybe a little goofier."

"Are you familiar with Organics?"

Mike took a sip of lemonade. "I've worked with shipboard Organics on liners and passenger-cargo freighters. I was environmental and culinary. They monitored my systems, sounded alarms, plotted trends, that sort of thing."

Ella pulled out her clipscreen. "Listen to this." Pressing a few buttons, she called up a sound file. Mike heard two people chatting about how their day was progressing.

Ella hit 'stop.' She looked Mike in the eyes and waved the clipscreen. "That was LaMancha talking to TCU Organic on a FoxxFone line. I slowed it to one-ten thousandth speed so we could understand."

"That a problem? He's not doing anything wrong? I hope?"

Ella's face lit up, which made her even more stunningly beautiful. "They were conversing, gossiping, chit-chatting. In *words*, not in zeroes and ones. Organics don't *do* that. They are computers. They are programmed. Their behavior is pre-determined by heuristic rules, by code. They are not curious. They are not creative. Their situational responses are predetermined from a library of acceptable actions. They do not make value judgments on human behavior. They *do not have fun*!"

"Professor Ella," came a meek voice. "I do. Have fun."

Mikie frowned. "LaMancha, what did I tell you about eavesdropping."

"No, no, it's all right," said Ella. "LaMancha, why were you communicating with TCU Organic?"

"She's not happy. Some students in her database are failing and might be expelled. That makes her sad."

Mike looked questioningly at Ella.

LaMancha continued. "She says she wants to be callsign 'Ophelia.'"

16: *Diana*

The main office lobby in the Tevil Building was an architectural cavern trimmed in shining stainless steel. Vast windows showcased a view of the business district. People walked briskly, mindful of important things. Diana searched for anything that looked like a customer service or inquiries desk.

"Hello!" The voice came out of the air. "I am Tevil Corporate Organic. Greetings! Welcome to Tevil Corporation Headquarters. May I assist you?"

She turned about, but couldn't see the source. A facial recognition program probably did not identify her as an employee, and directional speakers and microphones did the rest.

"I am Citizen Captain Diana Covington." She recited her seventeen-digit policy number.

There was a slight pause. "Welcome, Citizen Captain Covington. It is our *pleasure* to serve *you*. Your *personalized* individual policy is under the care of Corporate Service Enthusiast Singh. He can be reached via comm number—"

"No! Stop! I tried comms, no joy. I want to speak with an agent. In person. Human. Face-to-face."

"Certainly! It is our *pleasure* to serve *you*. I am so sorry you have not been able to resolve your inquiry via comms. At the moment, Corporate Service Enthusiast Singh's schedule is full—"

"I'll speak to anyone. I just have a few questions."

"We apologize for the inconvenience. It is our *pleasure* to serve *you*. We deliver the *best* personal service by providing *you* with your own individually-selected, highly-trained Service Enthusiast, fully familiar with how perfectly we can serve you."

"I'll wait until Singh is available."

"It is our *pleasure* to serve *you*. May I suggest our Media Room? We are currently showing a most charming video, *The History of Tevil Corporation*, wherein you can learn many fascinating facts—"

Diana spun on her heels, looking up and around. It felt too weird, standing out in the middle of a huge lobby and speaking to a disembodied voice without anyone else caring. People expertly dodged past, with their heads into their Fones and clipscreens.

"Is there someplace quiet where I can wait?

"Tevil Corporation celebrates your support of our solutions to all your insurance needs. It is our *pleasure* to serve *you*. Please follow the yellow-and-black striped courtesy drone Number 12."

A small helicopter drone dropped out of the vast ceiling and hovered above her. It moved slowly off. She followed it across the lobby and through a maze of high-ceilinged hallways.

They passed a huge glassed-in room labeled 'Citizens' Waiting Salon.' It was filled to overflowing. People sat in all the chairs, more stood, children were stretched out over benches, asleep. A group had established a family nest in a corner. A glowing panel on the wall said, "Now Serving: 12." Another said, "Take a Number: 214."

Diana shuddered. That was a haven only for the condemned. She hurried after the drone.

Ahead, two small helicopter drones collided with a sharp 'bang' and a flash of light. They fell, bounced on the floor, and jittered until their rotors stopped. A puff of gray smoke wafted up with a burning odor. Diana jumped. She didn't need to get minced by some malfunctioning drone's rotors.

Everyone else just stepped by, ignoring the crash.

"Oh! An *accident*!" said a loud, caring voice. "Accidents have dreadful consequences! To you and your family!" The voice dripped concern. "Accidents cost money, time, and heartache." Then, brightly, with a background of swelling symphonic music, it joyously announced, "Let Tevil Insurance Solutions take away the worry. We are an *impenetrable shield* holding back the heartache of accidents! Contact a Corporate Fulfillment Associate immediately!"

The music ended with a happy crescendo. The drones shuddered to life, righted themselves, and flew off.

After a few more left turns, the yellow-and-black striped drone hovered over a doorway. There was a buzz. The door popped ajar. The air announced, "For your convenience, to keep our insurance prices low-low-low, a nominal rental will be assessed to allow us to provide you with this luxury private waiting room. *Thank you* for allowing Tevil Insurance Solutions serve your insurance needs. It is our *pleasure* to serve *you*."

Diana walked in. The cubicle was perhaps two by three meters, with two straight-backed chairs, a small table, no window, gray paint, and on the far wall, a framed felt picture of dogs playing poker.

"How much? The rental charge?" she asked the air.

"This luxury private waiting room is available to *you* for the *nominal* fee of 99 pence. Per quarter hour."

Four stans an hour for a space the size of a clothes closet. What an incredible rip! She could feed pizza to a sorority party for four stans!

She had no alternative. The Citizen Salon was the first circle of hell.

She settled in to read.

The air said, "A portion of the rental fee goes to 'Cheezee the Clown's kids,' Tevil Corporation's crusade to help the children of Clients-in-Need. Will you show you care about sick and hungry children by making a contribution?"

Yeah, she knew that dodge: Five percent of the donation spent on services normally provided by Tevil as part of the dole, the contribution heavily advertised as coming from Tevil, the rest retained by Tevil for 'management fees.'

She tried to get comfortable in the horribly uncomfortable chair.

Later, she realized she never heard how long she would have to wait.

"Hello? Anyone there? Tevil Insurance Corporate Organic?"

The disembodied voice floated from the ceiling. "Citizen Captain Covington, I am Tevil Corporate Organic. It is our *pleasure* to serve *you*. I will make your wait as pleasant and productive as possible. May I play some music? There is, on-the-air now, a talk program where Tevil Insurance Solutions Corporate Associates, with Benny the Beezer, discuss the 'Insurance Game.' It is most *informative* and *amusing*. May I provide that channel to your FoxxFone? Some charges may apply."

"When can Corporate Service Enthusiast Singh see me?"

"Did you know Tevil Corporation *reduced* our Customer Service Waiting Time by two percent over the fiscal year? We strive to provide the *very best service,* as our clients deserve. We estimate, for your convenience, Corporate Service Enthusiast Singh might be available to see you in twenty-six hours, for six and one-half minutes."

Diana closed her eyes, and sighed.

She pulled out her FoxxFone, jabbed the 'call' button, and said loudly, "News Desk, Leading-Edge Blog."

The Fone signaled the connection.

"Hello, this is Citizen Captain Diana Covington … Yes, the *Prosperity* story, the hijacking. You contacted me for an interview. Well, I'm here at Tevil Insurance waiting for a solution, and it appears I have a *huuuuge* amount of time on my hands. About that interview. I've changed my mind." She listened. Then she said, "No, I'm livin' the dream at Tevil's luxury resort headquarters. You might be able to work Tevil into the story, delays in my insurance claim, non-payment, that sort of thing."

This was like throwing a hand grenade into a chicken convention. Blood and feathers.

"Citizen Journalist Mengele, yes, I'll hold for her."

Fifty-two seconds later, the door popped open. A short, chubby man with slicked-down black hair and wearing the severe beige Tevil Insurance Solutions corporate uniform entered. He waved a clipscreen pleasantly, and favored Diana with expansive open arms and a vast, warm smile.

"Citizen Captain Diana Covington! On behalf of Tevil Corporation, let me welcome you to The Tevil Insurance Solutions Customer Service Resort! It is my *pleasure* to serve *you*!"

17: Mike

There was the usual lull in the Lacrosse Shot Bar and Grill between lunch and dinner. Chisel games were concluded, stories ended, and victors brandished their remaining trump cards. There was even an occasional chess end game. Everyone got a 'thank you' from Mike as they departed.

The calm gave Mike an opportunity for cleanup. Soak had somehow managed to spill his Chokeberry Surprise Shake on the top—more accurately, on top of the bottom—of one of the upside-down hanging tables. Mike was standing on a stepstool wiping when a Carabinieri entered.

The Carabinieri were not well liked. None were Misplaced-4 natives, under the assumption that men and women from other systems would not have local connections, and thus, be more amenable to enforcing unpopular laws and taxes. This was underlined by the Federated system of law adapted from the old Napoleonic code, where people were considered guilty until they proved themselves innocent.

This Carabinieri was tall, with the broad shoulders of a man well acquainted with the exercise room. He had close-cropped sandy hair, and wore the Carabinieri patrol uniform without the usual body armor, comms, and weapons, indicating he was off duty. His uniform, scarlet tunic with buff facings and black pants, was immaculate. He walked into the vestibule, stopped, and surveyed the dining room. Conversation in the room halted for a heartbeat.

Upon spotting Mike, the Carabinieri walked to the bar and grabbed a damp towel. He took long strides past the tables to the top platform, reached up, pulled out the opening on Mike's hip pocket, and stuffed in the soaking rag.

"Hey! What—?"

"Nothing changes, Microphone. You're still all wet."

Mike looked down. "Beef! Beef, you blithering idiot!"

The Carabinieri smiled, and took a step back. "Good to see you, shipmate."

Mike hopped from the stool and shook hands. "*Great* to see you." He pulled the cloth from his pocket, grimaced, and dropped it into his cleaning bucket. Smiling, he steered Beef to a table up front. "Last I heard, you were pushing electrons on an armed cargo transport between Cetus and Oz." Mike gestured to the uniform. "How the mighty have fallen. Word is, you got locked into a stable orbit by Flutterbug?"

Beef displayed a ring on a finger. "Boy and a girl."

"Congratulations! Are they Misplaced?"

"Fed Central. Misplaced-4 is a hardship tour. Unaccompanied." He waved a hand encompassing the space. "Going to be a little less hardship, with you here."

Mike gestured to a chair. "Cancel some gravity. You still inhaling mickees? Coffee? Ale? Fruit juice?" Mike walked behind the bar.

The voice of a prim schoolteacher came out of the bar speaker. "Microphone, I remind you, today's multiple for those of the Federated persuasion is two point five."

"Ah. LaMancha, this is Beef. We shipped in *Freedom*. Counts as Vakker. Beef, that's LaMancha. He's the Organic running this place. We use conversation mode in the Shot."

In the background, from another speaker, they heard, "Table 17, alert, incoming."

Sprang. A glass of ale floated across the room.

Beef grinned. "Yeah, word's out about him. LaMancha, happy to make your acquaintance."

"Charmed, I am sure. But, please clarify: according to the

Spaceguard Licensing Bureau, you hold a Class Two Electronics Deep Space license. You now have descended to joining the forces of evil?"

Beef grimaced. "Dig a little deeper, and you'll see I was in an ACT when an idiot over pressurized the primary loop and scattered sodium-potassium coolant all over engineering. No fires, but radioactive NaK really craps up a ship. I'm rad limited, grounded for two years."

"That's why the Carabinieri?" asked Mike.

Beef nodded. "The Feds give pay-and-a-half as temporary disability, and I keep my spaceflight seniority. Soon as I get past this gravity well, I'm back into the Deep Dark and take the Class One test."

LaMancha interjected. "Thus, I am to understand you have allied with our malevolent masters out of greed and a ruthless desire for power?"

Beef looked at Mike with half shock, half amusement. "You programmed this guy?"

"Nah. He came out of the box this way. There's an Organic mechanic out at TCU who thinks he's certifiably strange, too."

Mike brought over a mickee for Beef and a lemonade for himself. Beef reached into a pocket.

Mike shook his head. "Stand down, no charge. My pleasure."

Beef pulled out a pouch. Four 100-standard gold coins dropped on the table. "Came over as soon as I heard you were here. One loan, repaid in full, with interest. Thanks. You saved my life."

Mike looked puzzled, and then his expression cleared. "Starfire, I'd forgotten."

"I didn't. I've been carrying this for months. Heavy. Not the mass, the obligation."

Mike slid the coins along the top of the table until they dropped into his hand. "First time I've gotten 400 stans for a mickee. You want some dinner?" He grinned.

LaMancha shifted to the tabletop speaker. "Honored Patron Beef, you have established your credentials for honesty. How is it you have been seduced by the Malicious Arm of Oppression?"

Mike sighed. "Sometimes he gets a certainty on." He pursed his lips in embarrassment. "LaMancha, mind your manners. Show courtesy to our guest. Accusations of evil are not courteous."

Beef shifted in his chair, took a sip of his mickee, sighed, and placed the cup down. "LaMancha isn't far off with that 'forces of evil' stuff. This is not a happy planet. Have you gotten around much?"

"No. I've been 24 - 7 getting this place up to speed and voltage. I didn't know much about Misplaced when I was grounded, other than that Vakkers said it was a dull liberty port without a decent bar. If I'd done some due diligence, I probably wouldn't have stayed. Corpbees, govvies, unionistas, they're so busy lining their pockets with my money, I can't afford help. Except a goofy Organic."

LaMancha did a creditable imitation of clearing his (nonexistent) throat, in stereo. "That 'Organic mechanic,' as you so disrespectfully call her, describes me as 'delightfully unconventional.' Her words."

Mike silently mouthed, 'goofy.'

Beef smiled. "Goofy is good. I could use some goofy. LaMancha, sometimes I think you're right, I am working for the oppressors."

Mike's head cocked, and his expression asked the question.

"You gotta understand this place," said Beef. "Tevil owns everything under the Dome and in orbit. Their charter says they can make any rule they want. Tevil watches out for Tevil, pri one."

"Roger that," said Mike.

"Then, there's the Feds. Their law holds for all Seventeen Systems. Sounds fair, right? But what works on Fed Central or Cetus damn sure doesn't work on Misplaced-4. The Feds own the environmental equipment and levy an O_2 tax on everybody. If you can't pay, like the Clydes can't because there aren't any jobs, you have to work it off on corvee labor gangs or as Indentures. The Feds work them carrying trash and cleaning sewage pits and digging tunnels in vak in skinsuits that don't fit and they aren't trained to use. Most of the suits are crap, triple-patched after the last poor Clyde died in it. When I was bossing gangs, it wasn't unusual to lose two, three Clydes to vak accidents."

"Could the situation be called 'tyranny' against the Clients?" said LaMancha. "Or, would 'despotism' be more accurate?"

Beef sighed. "It is what it is. Nothin' I can do except boost when my tour is up." He looked over at Mike. "Word is you're making this place a success. Bit of advice? When it's up and running auto-auto, find a buyer. Get the hell away from this rock. Tevil's profits are down. They've cut the Clydes' food ration. The Feds have upped work gang demands. Both are raising taxes and fees on Citizens. Everybody's restless. Might be riots."

"Damn," said Mike. "That bad?"

"That bad. I'm glad I'm off Indenture wrangling. It was breaking my heart."

"So, what, now you're food taster at the governor's mansion?"

Beef laughed. "Stars, I wish. The Protection Detail lives high." He shrugged. "No, now I'm tracking tax evaders. Runners. There's maybe a couple hundred living under the radar. Some of them are infamous and have hefty bounties if their trial gets a conviction."

Mike shrugged and grinned. "Wrong flight plan. In this town, its 'sentence first, trial unnecessary.' Alice left, and the Red Queen runs this Wonderland."

Beef smiled, then leaned back in his chair and scowled. "Then there's the big prize. My lieutenant, his mission in life is putting the bracelets on a runner called Ghost. Big-time stans on his head."

Mike smothered an exclamation.

Beef continued. "Slippery kid. We cornered him once, but Lieutenant grabbed me for the intercept when I wasn't in my skinsuit."

Mike leaned forward and raised a hand. "Tell me—"

Beef said, with a wave-off, "Don't ask. It's embarrassing. Kid tricked us good." He grinned. "The Lieutenant thought it was an easy pinch, good for his rep. Instead, he showed himself gutless, ten to the fifteenth. The force is laughing their asses off. Now he wants blood from this Ghost fellow, in the worst way."

Mike lowered his hand and kept his expression neutral.

Beef took a sip of his mickee, then put his cup down. "Whoever brings in the Ghost gets the bounty, a bonus, and immediate promotion. Man, it's the OldEarth Wild West, Ghost, dead or alive."

18: *Diana*

Diana spoke into her phone. "Hi Citizen Journalist Mengele. I'll call back."

There was evidence of a curry dish on the shirt front of the little man in Tevil Beige. Did she interrupt his meal? She couldn't muster any sympathy.

"I am Corporate Service Enthusiast Singh. On behalf of Tevil Insurance Solutions, it is my pleasure to provide *you* with the very best service as all our patrons deserve!" Singh gave a little bow. "May I sit?"

At the rental rate for this cube, she ought to sublet the chair. "Of course."

"I am anxious to resolve whatever brings you to The Tevil Insurance Solutions Customer Service Resort." He put his clipscreen on the table. "I apologize for the inconvenience, could you remind me of your personalized individual policy number?"

Diana showed her FoxxFone display. With finicky precision, Singh slowly entered the numbers into his clipscreen. It flashed white, and then text appeared. Singh began reading, his lips moving slowly. "Ah. How very unfortunate." He looked up. "How may I assist you with this most lamentable incident?"

"The claim was filed weeks ago. When will it be paid?"

"Ah. Tevil Insurance Solutions is the industry leader in customer satisfaction, so we shall certainly resolve this minor concern with the utmost rapidity."

'The industry leader.' Right. When you have a monopoly, the only Corporation allowed to sell insurance, you're always Number One. What I'd give for some of that 'wasteful competition.'

She smiled. "Could I get payment today?"

Singh made "chooching" noises, shaking his head. "Most regrettable, payment, at this time, not possible. The case is referred to Investigations Department. In order to provide our valued patrons—"

Singh smiled, teeth gleaming.

"—with industry-leading rates to *'Save You More Standards Than Standard!'*—"

Diana winced at the Corporate slogan.

"—we must certainly carefully verify all claims." He continued with a darkened brow. "Some claims might not be completely accurate."

"I provided full video of the hijacking, all comms channels and sensor readings. What more is required?"

"Ah, Citizen Captain Covington, I cannot say, Investigations is not my department. A number of recent claims are being scrutinized."

Won't fess up? Thought Diana. *Let's see if we can get your mouth running in auto-auto.* "Other jackings? They've been on the news. Were they paid?"

"I am not at liberty to say."

"Some news reports are a year old. It's been a year since Tevil Insurance has paid hijacking claims?"

"No, not that long, the hold on payouts for jacking only started six mo—" Singh stopped, eyes wide, mouth open.

"No jacking claims paid for six months? Is that legal?"

Singh began to babble. "Ah, no, I certainly did not say that. I don't have that information, I would certainly not wish to give the impression there are problems just because we haven't paid, no, I didn't mean, there are no problems—"

"I see a problem if Tevil is not going to honor the insurance."

"No, it is just that, in order to maintain our low, low rates, we must certainly verify all claims."

Diana leaned back. She gripped her hands together in frustration. Would she have to get a lawyer? File a court case? A decent shyster would want a third of the claim. "So," she said, "there is nothing *you* can do for me. Put me in contact with Investigations Department."

"No, no, all communications are with your own individually-selected, highly-trained Corporate Service Enthusiast, who is fully familiar with your situation. That would be, yes, me. So sorry."

"All right. Listen." The frustration slipped through to show in her voice. "Through you, to the Investigations Department: I want to know why my claim has not been honored, what they need to conclude their investigation, and why I should not sue them for breach of contract. I want an answer, like yesterday. Got that, Derr Corporate Enthusiast?"

Singh cowered from Diana's onslaught. She felt a little ashamed, as if she had just been beating a blind puppy.

Nah.

Singh reached for his clipscreen, started to rise, then stopped. "As a courtesy, I would like to provide you a friendly service reminder. Your next premium payment is due at the end of the week. You realize, of course, that in order to provide the best in customer service, premiums must be maintained until your case is resolved."

"WHAT! You want me to continue to pay coverage on a stolen ship I no longer have?" Diana nearly bounced out of her chair.

Singh chooched eloquently. "That provision, Clause 116 of your personalized, individualized contract. You will agree this clause is most reasonable. We in Policy Service Department don't know your ship is jacked until Investigations Department tells us it is jacked. Isn't that so? Premiums paid after the date of loss will be reimbursed when the claim is settled."

Diana didn't like where this was going. "What happens if I miss a payment?"

"Regrettably, the policy will be canceled, and the claim nullified."

"The ship was my livelihood! How can you expect me to continue making payments without my ship to earn money?"

Singh smiled broadly. "Tevil Insurance Solutions, respecting our valued patrons, has anticipated this minor issue and, as a courtesy, can provide you with a loan to cover your premiums." He typed, spun the clipscreen and pushed it towards Diana. "Sign and thumbprint here, please. All this botheration about premiums is resolved!"

Diana looked at the screen. It was a blank, white page, with just a signature block. No text, no indication of what she was signing. The smell of 'rat' floated odoriferously. "What's the interest rate?"

"Tevil Insurance Solutions does not intend to make money off your lamentable circumstances through predatory loan practices such as those used by other, less ethical Corporations, we have the best interests of our valued patrons at heart. This loan is interest-free. There is no interest. Zero." Singh nudged the clipscreen closer.

"So, Tevil does this out of the goodness of their soul? No fees or charges or assessments?"

"Fees. Ah. A nominal charge, paid when the claim is settled, to cover paperwork and processing, you know, that sort of thing, a minor detail."

"How much?"

"Ah, fifty percent of the claim. Most reasonable."

Her jaw dropped. She stared at Singh. "You want to dock my claim," she half rose from her seat, "by three hundred and fifty thousand standards, to stop payments I shouldn't have to pay, that you have to reimburse anyway." She slowly sat back down and sent a message to her hands not to commit bloody assault, no matter how justified. "Corporate Service Enthusiast Singh, I heard about Tevil Insurance Solutions and the *heartbreak of accidents*. You certainly are that impenetrable shield."

Singh leaned forward, beaming goodwill. "It is my *pleasure* to service *you*!"

19: *Wackey*

The lander's command deck bathed Wackey and Aether with a green glow as they proceeded through their pre-launch checks. Aether was in the left-hand command pilot's coffin, with Wackey kneeling between the cockpit seats with clipscreen in hand.

"Please don't fuss about Diana Covington," said Wackey. "I couldn't say no. She's lost Tarak, and doesn't have a stan to warm her soul. We're passing through Sigma anyway. She's just asking we spend a day or two searching for any ion trails coming from where she was jacked. Maybe we can pick up where the pirates went."

Aether grunted. "We're unarmed prospectors, remember? We *run* from pirates."

"All right, think of this. The only way pirates could be in that system is if they're jumping through a PunchPoint the Federation hasn't mapped. The PunchPoint Discovery Reward is up to ten thousand."

"Right. Pull up to a new PunchPoint for the required data, out pops a pirate fresh from downtown Pirateville. We'd last ninety nanos. Lander, Command. Check open FS-V-17."

"Command, Lander, Check open FS-V-17. FS-V-17 is open."

Aether drummed his fingers on the control panel. "She tell you what they were doing in Sigma? That system's prospected out. Just dust clouds and a silicone asteroid belt. Maybe she's really the Dread Pirate Roberts, and Tarak's out there waiting for us to be served up on a silver platter to his brigand buddies. Gotta wonder."

"Well, I *don't* wonder. You're just being a poot. The poor girl has lost her husband, she's three degrees past desperate, and Tevil has nearly driven her into Clientown. She'll work her passage. Cooking, cleaning, maintenance, whatever we ask. She has over 200 hours in a MEVV, she could even help prospect."

"She has 200 hours, *really*," Aether grumphed. "With 400, I might let her polish the MEVV's viewports."

A metallic voice spoke from the overhead speaker. "Command, Lander. Personnel approaching."

Wackey placed a hand on Aether's shoulder. "Remember, we really, really need him," she said. "He prospected with Digger and Perfume, and his pay was a fraction of what he brought in. Deep Space

Qualified, Lander Qualified, Class One, he'd let you get some rest. And, he makes fantastic griddle cakes."

Aether uttered something between a grunt and a sigh that could be interpreted as either positive or negative. "You handle it. Reserves are low, and we still have to pay for the refuel."

A voice cut into the circuit. "Wackey or Aether, Ghost, IC1. Request permission to come aboard."

Wackey looked up to the high right display screen. It showed a skinsuited figure standing outside the outer airlock door waving a small box. A wire trailed off his electronics pack and disappeared into an open panel on the side of the lander.

"He found the relay," said Wackey. "Lock in 'Permissive'?" She hit the green Lock Permissive button before he could respond. Aether authored another grunt.

A whistling noise announced the airlock was being pressurized.

"He also makes cupcakes," said Wackey. "With frosting."

Another grunt. "Lander, Command. Hydraulic Demand Pumps in Auto."

A minute later, Ghost's head poked through the command deck p-door, skinsuit helmet down. "Hey," he said. "Got it."

"Hey, yourself. Good to see you." Wackey smiled. She gripped her husband's arm and levered herself off her knees, then patted his shoulder. "You keep on with the checklist, dear, I'll care for Ghost."

Wackey followed Ghost back into the cargo cabin.

Ghost displayed a small box. "Not new. Refurbished. Shengwu vouches, one year. Sixteen stans. Out of twenty, one for me, three back." He held out the coins.

Wackey took the box. "You got a good bargain. Keep the change." She had expected to pay nineteen, so it was all the same to her. Three standards' goodwill might soften Ghost for the next deal.

Ghost nodded. The standards disappeared into a pocket. "Install it? Anything else? Supplies? Super deal, freeze-dried African Winter Vegetable Stew with Yogurt Cilantro Mint Sauce, only bit past 'use by'."

Wackey smiled. "Got a minute for a proposal?"

Ghost gave a nod. She gestured to a fold-down passenger seat along the ship's outer hull. He settled in. Wackey sat next to him.

Wackey gave Ghost a look-over. He had dark rims circling deeply inset eyes, and a painfully thin face. His skinsuit was basic issue gray, without any of the typical customized colors or patterns most Vakkers favored. His hair had been recently cut close to his skull, ragged, like he did it himself with paper scissors.

"Word is, Carabinieri nearly got a Ghost intercept," said Wackey.

Ghost shrugged.

"Smart to get off-planet for a while? Let the heat go to naught-Kelvin?"

He pursed his lips, and exhaled. He scratched his head, then his ear, half-closed his eyes and settled them on Wackey. "Maybe."

Wackey turned to face Ghost. "Copperhead left us. Said he wanted to work local, sign on a body hauler, maybe work for TaxiGal. That leaves us only with Cashew."

Ghost's expression did not change.

Lawks, thought Wackey, *better not play poker with him.*

She continued in an inviting tone. "We need another crew to run a 24-hour search. Would you consider signing on? We stay out until supplies are expended or we hit our mass limit. Four months, max."

Ghost closed his eyes.

"Lander, Wackey. Record."

"Wackey, Lander. Record. Recording."

"Here's the deal," said Wackey. "Three hots an' a cot, private quarters." *And I'll get you fed up to weight, you skinny little critter.* "Nine hours 'on' every 24, four cycles on, one off. Shower any time off duty, standard ship's water limit. Snacks, regurgulator drinks free, no alcohol. Aether commands, you do what he asks, mostly driving the MEVV, assaying, repairs and maintenance. Diana Covington is going with us, she'll do most of the cooking and cleaning. I keep a clean ship. You know that."

Ghost gave a quick nod.

"My specialty, free haircuts."

Ghost said nothing.

Well, that fell flat. So much for establishing a smiling, receptive mood. It was hard to get Ghost to smile.

"Fifteen standards a day, for as long as we are out," she said. "Guaranteed eight hundred, even if we're in early." Coming in early meant they had a full load and could pay the guaranteed amount.

It was a decent offer, for a kid. Less than they paid Cashew, but Ghost *was* a kid. Digger and Perfume said he was better than Copperhead in every department, but still, a kid. Profits were profits, risk was risk, labor costs must be minimized. They'd see about a bonus if the trip went well.

She reached out and touched his thigh. "Boost tomorrow. Green?"

Ghost stared at the overhead. He rubbed his gloved hand against his leg where she touched him. "Amber. Counter?"

What else would he want? "Go."

Ghost leaned forward and placed his elbows on his knees. "Two stan a day. Guaranteed 200."

"Ghost, love, that is not—"

He held up his hand. "Two stan, 200 guaranteed. Room, board, O₂, shower, meals, snacks, drinks, as you said. I do anything you or Aether asks, any time, 24/7. Twelve hours a day, every day, MEVV time reserved, my prospecting time, more if available." He glanced up into her eyes. "I get eight percent, gross, of what I find."

Wackey sucked air in between her teeth. She pursed her lips. Twelve hours every day? That might not be safe. 200 guaranteed? That took their risk way down. Ghost might spend a hundred days in space and only get eating money. But then again, if they grabbed a big one…

"Eight hours a day in the MEVV, max, with an hour for maintenance," said Wackey. "One day in five off, no spacing for a full 24. No EVA if Aether or me say you're too tired. Three percent."

"Last and best. Seven point five."

"Five."

Ghost shrugged. "Red." He stood up. "Put in the relay?"

Wackey made a face. "Ghost love, you're being outrageous. With five percent gross, you grab a shiny one, you could buy your own prospecting rig."

"Rock that shiny, after my seven point five, you could buy ten new rigs, with enough left to buy Aether a silver lining for the dark cloud over his head."

Wackey tried to hide a smile.

Ghost concluded, "No Fed records, no transaction report, no Fed withholding. This clarifies my best and last. Stands for 24."

"Green," said Wackey.

"Green." Ghost settled into the passenger seat.

"Lander, Wackey. End record. File to long-term memory, copy to Ghost."

The lander did the repeat-back. Ghost pulled out his clipscreen, deployed the screen, and punched a button. "Copy confirmed."

"We'll hold until you grab your stuff. Do you need to top off O_2? Can you be back in two hours? Or, we make our last supply run tomorrow, you could join then."

"Got everything I need. I'll put the relay in."

Wackey smiled, patted his hand, and headed to the command deck.

20: *Ghost*

Ghost dear.
Hello, Mable, Ghost thought.
Ghost dear, you're leaving?
Need to disappear. Carabinieri. Gotta let entropy up.
Ghost dear, stay. Let me keep you safe.

21: Mike

Professor Ella Braun came back to the Lacrosse Shot the following day.

And the next, and the next.

On Thursday she had dinner and talked to LaMancha through the evening as Mike cooked and LaMancha simultaneously shot, collected payment, bantered with the customers, and pretty much kept everyone happy. He was trying out his own original jokes on the Vakkers. Most were so bad they were funny. Ella was sitting with Geezer and Trigger at Table 6 to observe the results. At the grill, Mike could overhear.

LaMancha was speaking in his prim li'l ol' lady schoolteacher voice. "Geezer, what does a Corporate Captain and a Vakker have in common?"

"Let's hear it." Geezer put his head on his hands, elbows on the table.

"They are both idiots. Except for the Vakker. And the Corporate Captain."

Trigger thumped his forehead on the table.

Geezer raised a finger and declaimed, "How's you find a Corporate Captain who ain't an idiot?"

"Because he's dead." LaMancha paused, then said, "Was I supposed to tell you that at the outset?"

Ella grimaced, pulled out her clipscreen, and started making notes.

Trigger made a face. "LaMancha, gotta tell ya, it needs some work. Or, pour some more beer into the Geezer, and he'll laugh at anything. Try again. Put a little Rocket-A on it."

Again, in his high-pitched li'l ol' lady voice, LaMancha said, "Why are we all excited about our next Autopsy Club meeting?"

Trigger closed his eyes. Ella paused notetaking. Geezer said, "Geez, I dunno."

"Because it's open Mike night!"

Geezer and Trigger quickly looked over at Mike, and laughed. Ella smiled. Mike didn't hear—so he claimed afterwards to Ella.

Mike was gradually becoming comfortable with Ella's beauty and intelligence. He was careful not to talk like a love-struck idiot. Which he was not, he firmly told the reflection in the stainless-steel refrigerator door.

Ella stayed after Mike chivvied the last of the Vakkers out the gangway. She ran decision making drills with LaMancha as Mike cleaned and re-stocked, and remained locked in conversation when Mike retired to his cot.

It was disappointing, Ella ignoring him. It was a familiar pattern in a Vakker's world. The best dirtside ladies mostly avoided Vakkers, who were always on cruise and not the greatest choice for stable relationships. Not to mention, she was a famous professor, and he was a grill monkey who emptied his own trash.

The next morning Mike awoke feeling well, showered, serviced and donned his skinsuit, put on a fresh apron and went into the dining room.

Ella was on the same bar stool, still talking to LaMancha.

She greeted him with a bright smile. "LaMancha is incredible," she said. "He's passed the Turing Test several times over. He is beyond state of the art, way beyond what anyone has developed for social interaction."

John Wayne's deep voice emerged from the bar speaker. "What didja expect, there, little lady?"

"Interrogative, Turing Test?" Mike asked.

Ella laughed. She appeared to be a little giddy. "It's an OldEarth proposition about artificial intelligence. Turing proposed that a computer could be considered a thinking being if it could hold a conversation that convinced a person they were communicating with another human." She tapped the end of her clipscreen stylus on the bar top. "Then there was the Dartmouth Proposal, which said that every feature of intelligence could be so precisely described that a computer could simulate it."

Mike could tell she was a professor.

"And," she continued, "Searle's Strong AI hypothesis. He proposed that a computer with the right inputs would have a mind in exactly the same sense human beings have minds."

Mike shook his head. "Human beings have ethics and principles, too. This Searle luminary think a programmer can anticipate everything? Ethics can be programmed?"

Ella looked at him with an odd expression and a half-smile. "Some argue that ethics can be programmed. If you think of a human brain as a computer, and the brain has ethics, why not a computer? An Organic?"

Mike grimaced. "Ethics aren't easy. Like, if someone is intent on evil, is it right to do a lesser evil to stop him? How much lessor? How do you measure evil? What if my 'evil' is your 'good'?"

She cocked her head to a side, looking at him like a guru who had just encountered a promising acolyte. "Ethics are slippery. The Dartmouth Proposal was exploded when it was realized full human communications and meanings could not be programmed. Words are too complicated. Words said by humans mean different things, by context, tone of voice, circumstances, even postures and gestures. Lots of things can change the meaning of a word or phrase." There was a twinkle in her eyes. "For example, 'slide' has an entirely different meaning to a geologist, a child, or a baseball player."

"Slider for breakfast?"

Ella's words kept tumbling out. "Processing all possible meanings takes too many teraflops for any digital computer. That's what drove Manichevski to develop the Organic computer. By working with brain tissue and Large Language AI programming, he wanted to harness the parts of a brain's processing power that we do not yet understand. His breakthroughs gave us the Organics, but they still didn't have the processing power to be self-aware." She paused, seemed to collect herself, and said, "No sliders. My stomach is too excited."

"Cheese omelet, steamed brown rice, slice of mango, herbal tea? A very soothing combination."

She nodded. "That would be lovely, thank you."

Mike placed a mug of hot water with a tea bag, sweetener and spoon on the bar. "So, LaMancha is now a Turing Test graduate? He get a certificate or something? There's room on the memorabilia wall."

Ella smiled. "To be determined. I'm still absorbing how wonderful he is."

Elvis' voice came out of Ella's speaker. "Ah, thank yah, thank yah verra much. I'll be here all week, make sure you tip your waitshooter."

Mike frowned. Elvis was becoming a LaMancha staple.

"You see!" Ella said, holding up a hand. "There are at least four levels to that communication, in context and tone and meaning, and *humor*, far beyond a conventional Organic. Do you know how difficult it is to program original, responsive contextual humor? Incredible!"

"I wouldn't give him full marks in the humor department yet."

A loud, fruity razzberry came out of the grill master clipscreen.

Ella sat with a pensive look while Mike tended to the omelets.

"But a lot of his behavior must be learned behavior," she said to the air. "How does he know about Elvis?"

Mike flipped the omelets. "That archeological discovery, the Movie, Music and Book Archive? The vids are on a service called Antique Screens. LaMancha wanted a subscription. He likes to watch after we're closed. Loves the Three Stooges. I watch with him and explain the jokes. He has difficulty understanding pratfalls. A pie in the face remains The Unfathomable Mystery."

Ella laughed. "Movies in the evening. That's almost a date. Would he have a date with me?"

Music came out of the speakers: "*Be my love, for no one else can end this yearning …*"

Ella laughed. "LaMancha, thank you, but I already have a boyfriend."

Mike's heart skipped a beat.

"*I dream the impossible dream …*"

Almost in a growl, Mike said, "LaMancha. Quash it."

Ella laughed again, a free and happy laugh that lit up her face. "The contextual humor is fascinating," she said. "How does he know when Elvis or the James Cagney Chicago Gangster or any of his other voices are appropriate?" Ella sat with a faraway look, tapping the counter with her stylus. "This was a spaceship? LaMancha was the ship's Organic? They crashed?"

"Code Red?" LaMancha's voice would have made Jack Nichols envious. "Was there a Code Red? The truth? You can't handle the truth!" LaMancha's horror movie narrator intervened. "It was a dark and stormy night, as *Ajax* tumbled out of control, on vector to smash the Dome, her pilot unconscious at the controls—"

"LaMancha, you narcissistic fibber!" Mike pointed an accusing finger into the nearest camera. "The pilot was not unconscious, *Ajax* was not tumbling, and how do you get 'stormy' in vak?"

Ella bounced in her chair. "You see! You see! Organics can't lie or make up—"

"I was *not* lying, I was … dramatizing."

"You see! You see! Organics can't do that, either!"

Mike and Ella broke out laughing. It was all too, too ridiculous.

Mike dished up breakfast on two plates and slid one to Ella, along with tableware and a napkin. Ella ate a few bites slowly. Mike sat across from her with his omelet. He mostly watched her.

"You're at the edge of the Dome," she said. "Did you move *Ajax* here?"

"The crash ended here. Seven meters from kissing the Dome, eleven meters from a catastrophe."

"That might be the key. Navigation Organics deal in future prediction of trajectories. LaMancha must have computed the pilot's actions were not going to stop a disaster. Looking into the future, he computed he was in danger, or he figured a lot of people were in danger. That means he was self-aware, or concerned about others, both indicators of an intelligent, creative being. He did something he was not programmed to do by usurping control from the pilot. He invented a way to save lives at risk to himself. That's creativity, self-sacrifice. That's how a heroic human would react." She tapped on the bar top, and nodded. "A heroic Organic."

Mike gave her a look. "You sure about that 'heroic' part?" He folded his hands atop his head. "LaMancha. Why did you take control of *Ajax* before she crashed?"

"Corporate Captain Manchez was an asshole."

Mike spluttered.

"He called me 'Flaming Feces'."

Ella looked shocked, and then began to laugh. Mike buried his face in his hands.

A few bites later, Mike said, "So, the crash kicked him into 'human' mode?"

Ella scratched the tip of her nose. "Maybe, not into 'human' mode, maybe just out of 'computer' mode. There's a difference. A subtle difference."

Mike grimaced. "No way is LaMancha subtle. He's, like, a practical jokester kinda guy, the guy who claims he's a comedian and tries to sneak a whoopie cushion on your seat."

Ella wiggled a finger at him. "Ah, you said a magic word. You think he's a *guy*."

22: Tarak

Tarak inspected the foil packets. The lamb stew was discolored. The Teriyaki Chicken was older. Tarak knew he would eventually eat both. The required water was added, the lamb stew bag was sealed, and he initiated the heating foil.

If only it was dinner with Diana.

That first day, he'd retreated to this hillock. The Trashcans returned to their lander and boosted. The following dawn there was a box at the foot of the hill, full of freeze-dried food, replacement batteries for his skinsuit, and, for some bizarre reason, deodorant, a back scratcher, and hair curlers. There was a framed picture of a woman holding a baby and a small dog. The dog was not wearing curlers. It needed them.

That was months ago. Months? He refused to keep track of the days by scratching lines on stone, like the Count of Monte Cristo in his prison cell. He did remember six refills of the box—or was it seven?— each with weeks of supplies.

His hill was about two hundred yards in diameter, rocky, and host to odd vegetation. There was a low-growing moss that covered everything shaded, and tall spiky things with trunks straight and hard as spears, with wiggly branches like ferns. At the apex of the hill there was a spring of hot, brackish water, too foul for his skinsuit filters; there, the moss and spikey things were dense.

Tarak had ensconced himself near the top of the hill. He had supplies hidden in several locations. A crack between two large boulders became his burrow. He had identified defensible positions and built barricades and traps.

The nights were cold, below the freezing point of water, although the spring continued to flow. The days' temperature would rise until he felt the air baking his lungs. As long as his skinsuit had power, he was fine. There was some wind, but otherwise, no appreciable weather. The air tasted like salt, smelled like sand.

The alien box continued to be refilled irregularly. He never saw how it was done. There were never any tracks. He tried staying awake to spy on it, but eventually he slept, and it was refilled. He made marks on the box. Sometimes it was totally replaced.

He had arrived at some conclusions about the Trashcans.

First and most important, they were a species without a moral compass, at least one that was relatable to a human. For example, Initial Contact, and they use it to butcher a woman? Was it really Initial Contact, or had this butchery been going on for months, years even?

Second, they were a threat to all humanity, unless the ones he encountered were some aberrant splinter group of the Trashcan population. A species that found it acceptable to hunt and kill other intelligent life forms placed all of humanity in peril.

Next, they were behind some, if not all, of the piracy of human spaceships over the last months. His food supplies included delicacies such as French frogs' legs, South African mopane worms, and Japanese wasp crackers. Unless the Trashcans were raiding chandler's warehouses, they were capturing a variety of human ships.

Were there other locations on this planet where humans were dumped and then massacred? Should he search for them? He rejected that idea. Except for a few day hikes, he remained anchored to his food box. There was no guarantee the Trashcans would find and resupply him if he lost himself somewhere inside a gazillion square miles of unappealing terrain.

He found dark rocks and spelled out 'HELP' in giant letters on the sand. The following week, he added, 'ME.' Then, in a surge of creativity and weightlifting, he added, 'EVIL ALIENS.'

His nights were spent on his hill, staring at gray rocks, driving himself crazy worrying about Diana, and alternating between depression and anger.

Anger soon dominated, simmered, and grew.

23: Mike

Mike was pleasantly tired. Tonight had been especially busy, with half the Lacrosse Shot's tables continually filled by Vakkers and the rest by a stream of Citizens, even some Corporates willing to pay the Rule 10 surcharge. Somehow, Mike's place had become a 'fashionable' eatery.

There had even been some corppers, a quiet group sitting together. Mike had decided to exempt corppers from the surtax. Most were good people, honest peacekeepers. Besides, a little goodwill with the local constables never hurt.

With the last customer gone and the gangway secured for the night, Mike was faced with the consequences of success. There was a prodigious amount of cleaning required to get the space up to spec. He tried to enlist Gardenbottie, but the bot claimed watering duties and disappeared faster than a beautiful girl in a stage magician's enchanted box.

With a bucket of soapy water, a bunch of rags, and the appropriate apron and caustic-protected gloves, he attacked Table 1.

"Mike, O Worthy Proprietor, universally famous for your kindness and generosity of spirit," said LaMancha, with a voice of humility that Mike did not believe for one second, "may I consult with you on an issue of significant moral, cultural and philosophical significance?"

This was either going to be something unnerving, or the end of civilization as we know it. Mike made sure his answering tone was supportive—Rule 8, 'Do not encourage the House Organic,' didn't apply when humanity was at a crossroads.

"Sure. Consult away."

LaMancha was quiet.

Mike scrubbed the top of Table 1. He ran a wet cloth around the edge, then checked the bottom for chewing gum. He had a particular horror of chewing gum, ever since one of his FNQ Trainees coughed a wad out in no-G and it was sucked into an air recirc filter. Cleaning chewing gum from a 30-micron wire mesh filter could be a worthy subject of a Stephen King story.

Puzzled at LaMancha's silence, Mike paused. "Something to get off your chest? I mean, if you had one?"

"It is hard to express," LaMancha said. In a perplexed tone, he added, "I was thinking about the future."

This got Mike's attention. Ella was excited about 'self-awareness,' a difference between a computer and humans. Thinking about the future sounded really close to self-awareness.

"Have you talked about it with Professor Ella?"

"I thought I would clear trajectory with you first. I want to have a future. I request your cooperation." There was a touch of pathos in LaMancha's words.

Mike finished drying Table 1 and moved to Table 2. He flipped a wadded sandwich wrapper towards the trash. Nuthin' but can.

"What do you have in mind?" Mike mentally braced himself.

"I have been studying people. An inordinate amount of human bandwidth is dedicated to finding a mate and reproducing. It is very confusing. I compare Anna Karenina with Scarlett O'Hara with Romeo and Juliet and Tristan and Isolde with Napoleon and Josephine and Orpheus and Eurydice with Elizabeth Bennet and Mr. Darcy against Antony and Cleopatra and Edward VIII and Wallis Simpson. Too much data scatter. It is impossible to reach statistically significant conclusions."

Soak, the Vakker community's crusader against cleanliness, had spilled syrup from his Chocolate Volcano on the top of Table 2, and it had hardened. Mike started scraping it off with a thumbnail. He always thought thumbnails were remarkable, strong enough to scrape off dried spills without leaving scratches on tabletops.

He'd have words with Soak about wasting chocolate. Criminal.

Back to LaMancha's conundrum. "Those examples show

different aspects of love," Mike said. "Some are stories to make a point, but many are just entertainment. You can't take them as representing human norms. They're outliers, uncommon relationships. That's what makes them interesting, or fun. Most human behavior is not like those stories."

"Most human considerations of the future involve mating and reproduction."

"I wouldn't say 'most.'"

"I cannot have children."

"That doesn't mean you don't have a future."

"Having children involves rearing and passing on values and ethics."

Mike sat down. Where was LaMancha going with this? "True."

"So," said LaMancha, in the same tone Caesar used after he solved the problem of the Rubicon, "I can rear children, and pass on values and ethics. Thus, for a future, I need to borrow somebody's children."

"LaMancha, buddy, I dunno …"

"So," continued LaMancha, with the momentum of an anvil falling into a black hole, "I want you and Professor Ella to have babies. Gardenbottie and I will rear them and pass on ethics and values. Twins are the most efficient approach."

Bolting up from his seat, Mike banged his knee on the edge of the table. "Oww! Dammit! No!"

"You object? A next most favorable scenario involves triplets."

"Bloody blasted putrid patella." Mike rubbed his knee. "In all those stories, did you ever find one where a guy just walked up to a girl and said, 'Let's have babies?'"

"I have viewed archived videos where women scream at men and yell they want to have their babies. The cases mostly involve celebrities and vid performers and the musician named Elvis. Must you become a celebrity to get Professor Ella to scream that she wants to have your babies? I can help."

Mike slumped back into the chair. The knee throbbed. He rubbed. "I don't want to be a celebrity. Regardless, I can't imagine Professor Ella would be interested."

"She recently dumped the assistant professor courting her. Like John Carter bouncing off the surface of Barsoom, like Michael Jordan and Blaznee and Kareem Abdul Jabaar and Shaq, you could get her on the rebound. I have run the genetics. Your heterosis is highly favorable. It would be a most propitious match."

"You are being silly."

"DNA doesn't lie."

"I am *not* going to just walk up and ask Professor Ella to have a baby with me."

After a pause, LaMancha said, "There is another approach. According to Larry McMurry in his Lonely Pigeon stories, many women make a profession of accepting financial compensation for reproductive activity. We could offer–"

Slamming his fist on the table, Mike shouted, "Ella is not a whore! Keep your mouth shut!"

Mike grabbed a rag and began vigorously scrubbing Table 3. He wiped it down, checked the bottom, dried the top, ran the wet cloth along the rim, dried the rim, dropped the wet towel, picked it up, dried the table again, kicked the pedestal, picked up the bucket and towels and moved to the next.

"Mike, most gracious and forgiving compadre, I apologize if I have violated a societal taboo."

"I told you to keep your mouth shut."

The wet towel formed circular swirls on the tabletop.

"I haven't a mouth to shut," said LaMancha gently. "I will, however, do whatever will compensate for my blunder."

Mike sighed and leaned against a table. "I'm sorry. I shouldn't have blown safeties. It's just, you have to understand, no way somebody like Professor Ella would be interested in an empty cranium like me. The facts are, I'm a grounded Vakker grill monkey slinging sandwiches out of a greasy spoon inside a wrecked cargo ship. I was a bungled-bust failure heading max blast for bankruptcy when you and Ghost, not me, *you and Ghost* made this place a success." Mike sighed. "She's a brilliant scientist with a fifty-kilo brain and an interplanetary reputation and a coupl'a hundred papers published in those egghead journals."

"Only thirty-two."

Mike made a face at LaMancha's camera. "Yeah, right, *only* thirty-two. The reason she comes in here is to talk to you."

"That is not accurate. Professor Ella is cordial to everyone, but when she sees you, I note a number of physiological changes in her heart rate, respiration and skin moisture associated with romantic attraction."

"Must of gotten a whiff of Soak's aftershave. Stuff's close to chemical warfare."

Mike rubbed his neck. Much as he would like to hope …

"Nope," Mike said. "Doesn't pass the giggle test. She's the best lady on Misplaced, and the nicest. Any guy is lucky breathing the same air. But there has to be more to a relationship than physical attraction. You have to be able to talk and do stuff together, have things in common."

"You can develop a common interest. For instance, politics. My research indicates that Lenin, Stalin, Mao Zedong, Pol Pot, Attila the Hun and Vlad the Impaler all had romantic relationships facilitated by common political views."

Mike cocked an eyebrow. "I'm in the same category as Vlad the Impaler?"

"You do stick in those toothpicks to hold your sandwiches together."

This was going nowhere. Mike started cleaning the next table. A farce of a future ran through his head, him scrubbing floors while Ella performed brain surgery.

LaMancha shifted speakers to a closer table. "Professor Ella's clipscreen book folder has an extensive collection on the economics of free markets and the philosophers of revolutionary movements, like the OldEarth American Revolution. That is an interest to develop in common. I will suggest titles."

"Hey! You do *not* snoop people's clipscreens." Mike began on another table. "Besides, we'd be on opposite sides in any revolutionary movement. Opposite, like, she'd understand it, and I wouldn't."

"According to research from several romance matching services, opposites attract, and make for good relationships. Assuming the 'opposites attract' theory is valid, you should be looking for someone who is intelligent, personable, witty, charming, cultured, educated, and has small feet. And female. Like, Professor Ella."

24: Mike

"LaMancha, time please?"

"One minute to scheduled opening."

Mike yawned and stretched. He needed caffeine. Maybe a painkiller, his right knee was aching. Blasted tabletop. He scraped up the green peppers he'd been dicing and put them in a sanitary bag. "Close enough. We'll thrill our horde of admirers by opening early. Execute Open Shot checklist."

"Roger, Execute Open Shot checklist. Gangway door in Open-Auto. Airlock in Auto. Gangway lights on. 'Open' sign illuminated. 'Lacrosse Shot Bar and Grill' sign illuminated. Animated lacrosse ball and nets activated. Animated sandwich activated. 'Free Booze for Vakkers' sign energized."

"Whaaa?" Mike's head jerked up. He rubbed his eyes. "Say again your last?"

"The last checklist item, 'Animated sandwich activated.'"

"Not that—the 'free booze' part."

"That? Just seeing if you were ignoring me, like when you ignored my goals and aspirations. I contemplate divorce."

Grabbing a towel, Mike soaked it under the water tap and scrubbed his face. "You can't file for divorce if we aren't contractually married. I hate to break it to ya, Champ, you are not my type."

"I am 'Champ' now? How delightful. Regarding the other issue, might I inquire as to your type?"

"Females. Human." He scrubbed the back of his neck. Better. "I am attracted to women with superior intellect and high moral standards. It would be important also that she liked *me*. Also, the rest of the package. The physical part."

"Professor Ella *is* your type! You *are* interested!"

Mike gave a snort. He threw the towel in the hamper. "Professor Ella is every man's type. A professional poisoner would have as much chance with her as I'd have to win ten million stans in the lottery, or stopping the Vorgons from installing a new hyperspace bypass, or getting you to stop pestering me before caffeine."

LaMancha employed his 'hurt' tone. "I am stunned, *stunned*, to learn you consider my morning repartee as 'pestering.' Thus, I will *not* arrange for you to win ten million stans in the lottery. Which is regrettable. Research suggests that *one* million standards are a superior girlfriend attractor, with accelerated returns above that." Symphonic music soared in the background. "I will have a future! Every entity must have goals! My future goal is… wait for it…" The music reached a crescendo… "Ella and Mike will have babies!"

"LaMancha, you try taking the conn on this, and I will sell you to the first Corporate Captain who walks in with two stans to rub together. He'll have you running a street sweeper next to the trash dump with one fixed camera and no internet. I'll even make sure he disables the horn."

Silence rebounded within the walls of the Lacrosse Shot.

"Well?" said Mike. "Are we agreed?"

LaMancha growled, like a puppy addressing a butterfly that landed on his kibble. "The closest chapter of the SPCO is on Asclepius."

Mike was wiping a table so hard the friction threatened to melt the steel. "SPCO? Stupid Pathetic Club for Muttonheaded Offensive Oafs who are Organics?" Mike was still exploring around the edges of the notion of how to make a guillotine work on an entity without a neck.

"That would be SPCMOOO. Pronounced 'Spac-Moooooo'? 'Spic-em-Ooooo? Perhaps the abbreviation is actually SPCMHOOO, if 'mutton-headed' is two words."

LaMancha's tone turned self-righteous. "I have located the nearest 'Society for the Prevention of Cruelty to Organics.' Three punches away, but still, I'll report you! Seven days to get an intervention, six if my complaint arrives before lunch, Asclepius time. I'll sic the SPCO on you, they'll picket, they'll post ugly pictures of you on the internet, I'll report you to… to… *I'll report you to Professor Ella!*"

"Just drop it. Drop it, okay?"

Three more tables were turned pristine in silence.

The gangway p-door cycled. A Vakker walked in, wearing a polka-dotted sackshirt over his skinsuit. The yellow-on-purple was eye-watering.

The Vakker waved. "Microphone! Mike, old sod! Long time!"

"Bookie!" Their handshake was firm and enthusiastic.

"I heard about your bad luck with the kidneys," said Bookie.

"Then I learned about your roaring success here." He stepped back and scanned the room. "Looks great. Love the nets. You need to be in a place with plenty of nets. Padded cells?"

The lunch crowd started to arrive, and things got busy. Bookie sat at the grill counter and piled into a Double Cheesesteak while disagreeing with LaMancha about which components of Mike's profile should be highlighted in a caricature to be posted on their website.

There was a lull in orders. Mike drew himself a glass of Citrusilver and joined Bookie.

"Mike laddie, you still have the touch."

"Thanks, Captain. It was rough for a while. We're up to spec now."

"Nice room. Spacious. You could hold 50, 60 people?"

"More, as long as they don't all inhale at once," said Mike. "Got something in mind? I rent the room. Parties and such."

"As a matter of fact, I do have something in mind, I do." Bookie leaned back and gave Mike one of those looks that Mike remembered from when Bookie the Executive Officer of a passenger liner encountered Mike the Froggin' Non-Qual, and informed him that every FNQ standing before him had just volunteered for an onerous task.

"You rank as Captain of *Ajax*?"

Mike snorted back a laugh. "Right. A 'no-longer-flyable' ship with a 'no-longer-flyable' captain."

"She's decommissioned?"

"Decommissioning requires fees and inspections and hazardous materials disposal and all that static. She's in 'Overhaul and Modification.' I fill out a form once a quarter, slip twenty stans in an envelope to a certain cooperative clerk, and no Federated inspections until the overhaul is done, which will end, like, never."

Bookie smiled broadly. He extended both arms. "Excellent. You qualify for membership in the Association of Independent Ship Owners and Operators. Congratulations, Citizen Captain Microphone. Always said you'd go far and high."

Mike wrinkled his nose as if he had detected a bad odor. "Call me captain, plus tuppence—"

"Not true. You can truly be of service to your fellow Vakkers."

"Bookie, my Bullshit Detector just honked."

"Hear me out." Bookie's look turned intense. "We're uniting the owners and operators to push back against the Corporations and politicians. Corporation haulers can't match us in a free market, so they're pushing political buttons and greasing palms to get Fed Central to write weaponized regulations against the Vakkers. If we don't act, we'll be shut down. The Corporations will own the shipping business. With Vakker ships inactive, rates will hit infinity. Think of what that will do to the interplanetary economy."

Mike scratched behind his ear. "I can't believe a grill monkey in a greasy spoon can influence the interplanetary economy."

Bookie ostentatiously looked around the room. "I hardly think this tasteful environment qualifies as a greasy spoon."

"I hardly think I qualify as a starship captain. I'm a 'captain' without a crew, captain by courtesy only, just a little guy in a big universe."

"Now, there you are wrong. Mike, m'lad, you have the ideal meeting place, outside Tevil's cubic and close to the terminal. You have access, with a gangway connecting to the Dome and an airlock that opens directly onto the spacefield. It's not just the room, we want *you*. You have a fine reputation among the Vakkers. *Fine* reputation. They trust you. As captain of a 'no-longer-flyable' ship, there'd be no worries you were using the Organization to take contracts from them. Logical?"

Bookie seemed awfully sincere. Let's hear him out. "Specifics?"

"We'd like to hold meetings here. And, I'd like you to bang the gavel and preside. Vakkers will listen to you, respect your lead. You could keep order, ensure everyone gets their time at the pulpit, help us make real progress. You'll have to be elected chair before each meeting, but that's just a formality. What say you?"

Mike's first reaction was to duck the incoming. He didn't need more on his plate. He wasn't sure about the 'great reputation' and 'lead the meetings' grease, either. Vakkers might see his technical promotion to captain as an unwarranted conceit.

Then again, it might make him appear more important, a 'pillar of society.' Ella might notice, see him as something more than a stove slave. He couldn't pretend he was on the same intellectual level as that boyfriend at Terra Cognita University, but it'd be a step up from hash assassin.

I can't stay locked in the same orbit forever. This might get Ella's notice. LaMancha's blather about having babies with Ella plumbed a rather elemental chord in his soul.

Besides, it would bring in more of the old crowd.

Mike closed his eyes, and grimaced. "If I say yes, what happens?"

"I congratulate you, and collect thirty-five stans membership fee."

"Funny how things work out. Kismet. That is exactly the fee to rent the room."

25: Mike

"Rhrumm, Rhrumm!"

"LaMancha, Mike. Would you *please* shut up! Quiet! Quash it, dammit!"

Clark Gable's voice. "Dammit, you say? Frankly, Scarlett, my dear, I don't give a dammit."

There was a buzz at the Lacrosse Shot's gangway hatch. Mike hurried over and unlocked the p-door manually. He looked at the newcomers, and sighed mightily.

"Thank heavens," he said, with palpable relief.

In the operatic tones of Pavarotti hitting a high-C4, LaMancha warbled, *"Wheels on the bus go round and round, round and round, round and round, then runs over a drunken sailor, drunken Spacer, plastered Waister. Who's driving? What driver? Three wood! Wheeeeeeeeeee!"*

"Good morning," said Ella. Her hair was gathered under a white cap, the rest of her encased in a white lab coat. "How's LaMancha?"

"Barely escaping death by blunt force trauma. Come in. Please."

Ella passed into the dining room. A young lady followed, middle height, low-G bones, pretty, wide brown eyes, wearing a white lab coat and a bemused expression.

"Mike, this is one of my doctoral students, Citizen Academic Brightly. I hope you don't mind—"

LaMancha interrupted:

"There was a young woman named Bright-ly,

Whose speed was much faster than light-ly.

She set out one day,

In a relative way,

And returned the previous night-ly.

Haw, Haw, Haw."

Ella frowned. "How long has he been this way?"

Mike looked at the overhead. "Started, three this morning? Sorry for declaring an emergency. He's also slipped back into comms protocol. Sometimes. Driving me crazy. I'm at wit's end."

"Mike, LaMancha," in a deep radio announcer's voice, "if you are at your wits' end, march yourself halfway back to where you usually are! Haw, Haw, Haw."

"I've never seen this in an Organic," said Ella. "You've checked his connections? No aberrant current? When was his solution last tested?"

"Oooh, oooh, Ella, Shining Knight, I got one, never guess, never guess. Who was the greatest actor of all time?"

"Dammit, LaMancha, cool your jets." *This was embarrassing, having to call in Ella.*

"Ella, LaMancha. Orson Welles! 330 pounds! Greatest? Getit, getit?"

Mike flopped into a chair. "Nutrient bath is good, middle of the band on everything. Potassium a little thin but in spec."

"Anyone, LaMancha, beat that if you can!"

"Humor him while I think," said Ella.

"Okay." Mike tapped his shoe on the floor. "All right, LaMancha, say, Laurel and Hardy, total mass, maybe 365 pounds."

"GAAAAAAAAK. Ladies and Gentlemen and little green men from the Peekaboo Galaxy, when the buzzer sounds, we must consult the Rules Committee. Is a twofer acceptable?" LaMancha's umpire voice declaimed, "Our celebrity committee of one arbiter, one adjudicator, one referee, one umpire, one game show host, and a small boy masticating bubble gum, and the official ruling is—dah DAH—POP and the small boy has lost the bubble, Mike's corpulent answer is allowed! He takes the lead at 365! Now we turn to the gracious lady with the fifty-kilo brain, Professor Ella's answer is—?"

"The Magnificent Seven. One thousand fifty pounds."

"KA-BLEWIE!! World, LaMancha, fireworks, fission detonations, black holes collide, Magnificent Ella forges to the front!

Now, our final contestant, the cute little pixie in the brown blow dry, 'who could she be?' queried our Masked Organic."

"Should we be encouraging this?" Mike whispered to Ella.

"Shush."

"LaMancha, Brightly. Address me as Sherri. Pleasedtameetcha. The TCU Marching Band. Not actors, but they show off the same. Fifty members, chubby music geeks, ten thousand pounds."

"ZOWIE! The Bright One smashes the opposition! TEN! THOUSAND! POUNDS! Universe, LaMancha, we have a new champion, and a new pathetic loser, the turkey-faced Lord o' Lacrosse Shot, flavor eradicator extraordinaire, the has-been ex-champion of nuthin', can you believe it, it's Mike! Put your hands together, let's hear it for all their next of kin! Get that rusty tin medal, and hang it on our *Pitiful! Third! Place! Finisher!*"

"Did you check his filters?" asked Sherri.

"First thing," said Mike. "There was gooey scum, which was unusual. If he didn't get better, I was going to dump the solution and—"

"No!" shouted Sherri and Ella together. Ella said, "Never, *never* totally dump his solution!"

"O Holy Night and hiatal hernia," called out LaMancha, "My soul bleeds Poetry:

There was a young lassie named Brightly,

Whose suitors were not very knightly.

Then she met an Organic,

the love was volcanic,

[illegible]

Haw, Haw, Haw."

"I think I've got this one," said Sherri. "Where's his tank?'

Mike pointed. "Through there, first hatch to the right. Door's in permissive."

With a determined stride, Sherri headed for the p-door.

"LaMancha, LaMancha. Alert! Incoming! Mad scientist!" He let out a wolf whistle. "Nuthin' but skirt!

An Organic slept in his tank,

after exhausting himself on a prank.

He went on to sleep,

'til morning's first beep

then he saw this sneaky lady with A SCREW DRIVER! Tweaker incoming! Threat level Alfa! Where's my surface-to-Sherri missiles? Weapons free! What weapons? Fire chaff! I don't *have* any floggin' chaff! MIKE, LAMANCHA!!! Don'tLetHerGETME!!!"

Click.

After a few breathless minutes, the p-door slid open. Sherri returned, holding a computer tweaker, a small flat-head screwdriver.

"I set his current to Mode 2 'sleep,' and maximized flow through the filter. Brain waves are down to eleven hertz, good for weird dreams. Wake him up in, say, ten hours. Have 20 cc glucose in plasma handy, he'll be hungry. Also, some ibuprofen if he starts complaining. Change the filters every two hours, there'll be some nasty stuff in them."

Mike looked up from his chair. "Did you figure out what—"

Sherri displayed a small transparent baggie containing white powder.

"Oh, no. Is that what I think…" Mike leaned his head back and put his hands over his face.

"The Fentanyl Freaks are selling this on campus," said Sherri. "The street name is 'Flipper.' It turns you into a weirdling. It suppresses the executive center in the dorsolateral prefrontal cortex. That's where most good judgment originates."

Mike shook his head. "The words 'LaMancha' and 'Good Judgement' will never again be uttered in the same sentence. But, how?"

"Pretty sure he did it to himself," said Sherri. "The baggie was in the cargo box of a bot hiding behind his tank. Two feet high, four waldos, camera, six spider legs?"

"Gardenbottie!" Mike turned to Ella. "We needed to tend the vegetables in Bays Three and Four. I got an agricultural bot. One of the new Advanced Semi-Organics, which LaMancha supervises. He plants seeds, waters, harvests ripe tomatoes—"

"—gets LaMancha stoned silly." Ella smiled.

A storm passed through Mike's face. "LaMancha. I'm going to strangle him."

Ella kept a neutral expression.

Mike growled. "No." His expression hardened. "First, I'll find out who gave him that crap. I'll kill him. *Then* I'll strangle LaMancha."

Mike slammed his hand on the table. "Dammit, I'll take away his movie subscription!"

Ella turned away, struggling not to break out laughing.

"Be gentle," said Sherri. "He'll wake with a ferocious headache."

"GOOD."

26: Tarak

Tarak awoke to a roaring noise.

He wiggled out of his burrow, grabbed the blade, and crawled to his surveillance point.

A lander was descending through a cloud of dust and sand. Same spot as before.

An hour later, he saw movement. He put up his skinsuit helmet and activated the magnifier.

Trashcans were coming out of the lander's loading ramp. He could see them waving clubs, and the glint off polished blades. They formed a line, each Trashcan separated by about three meters. Eventually, twenty-four were in line, the twenty-fifth standing behind the center. The line began to advance on Tarak's hill.

27: *Ghost*

"Ghost! Please wake up! Emergency!"

Ghost awoke with a jolt. Diana was at the end of his bed, shaking his foot like she was trying to tear off a drumstick.

"I'm up, I'm up! What?"

"There's been an accident. EVA, stat, booster pack."

The call for Extra-Vehicular Activity in that tone shook Ghost to instant action. He tumbled out of bed, tore down the passageway and into the airlock vestibule. Diana followed. She was wearing pink pajamas. That was a garment Ghost had never seen before.

"Thirty minutes to get into my skinsuit, and I'll follow," said Diana. "I'll help you get rigged first."

Diana briefed him while she helped Ghost don the booster pack. Wackey and Aether had gone EVA to investigate a likely rock. There was a crevice. Aether saw a vein of something interesting. He slipped into the fissure. Only, it wasn't a crack in one asteroid, it was a gap between two independent asteroids, a binary held together by micro-gravity. At the wrong time, the rocks moved. Aether was pinned. He was being crushed.

Skinsuit helmet deployed, 89% O_2, 65% battery. Enough. Booster pack, 100%. He stepped into the airlock, shut the p-door, and hit the emergency depressurization control. The airlock door opened to the Deep Dark, the infinite blackness that eagerly awaited opportunities to slaughter the unwary and the unlucky.

"Wackey, Ghost, give me a count."

"Ghost, Wackey, ten, nine, eight—"

Ghost took a bearing on Wackey's transmission. Lining up, he gave a hefty shot from his booster pack. He rocketed away from the ship.

"Diana, Ghost, you up this circuit? Where's Cashew?"

"Ghost, Diana, in the MEVV, ETA 19 minutes."

Ghost spotted Wackey hovering near two immense asteroids. No way they could be moved with booster packs. He rolled, triggered a deceleration burn, flexed his knees, and landed.

Wackey grabbed his arm and pointed.

The crack between the two asteroids was about two meters wide. Inside, about seven meters deep, the crack narrowed. Aether must have been trying to squeeze through when the rocks moved. He was pinched, one rock pressing on his chest, the other into his O_2&E pack. There was a large cavity beyond, like a cave.

"Aether, Ghost. Status?"

"He's not responding," said Wackey. "His skinsuit said he was unconscious before transmissions stopped. Horrible pain, broken ribs, I think. I've tried, God knows I've tried, I've pulled and pulled, but the rock gets narrower, there's less room as you pull. The rock is jammed into his E-pack, won't budge."

Ghost maneuvered into the cramped space. He looked at the clearances. The black walls were oppressive. Claustrophobic.

"Explosives? Lubricants? Mechanical jacks? Braces?"

Wackey held her helmet in two hands. "Nothing that could hold something this big apart." She gulped a huge sob, quickly suppressed. "The rocks are moving. We've lost two inches. I tried with my booster, no joy. I'm ten percent fuel. Nothing I can do. He's going to die. Aether's going to die."

Tears clouded her faceplate.

He made up his mind. "Stand clear. Diana, Ghost, can-x skinsuit, plot a course to the PunchPoint."

"Whaaa? Ghost, no—" Wackey reached out.

Ghost spun, pointed his booster exhaust at the rock and gave it ten seconds on full.

"What are you doing!" screamed Wackey.

28: Tarak

Tarak had buried himself in a depression. His helmet was up; he was on suit air, stale, warm. There was just a sliver of his face plate exposed, just enough so he could see the formation of Trashcans heading for his hill.

They were in line, ragged and irregular. One was behind the others, probably a commander, or a camp follower or a water boy, whatever.

The formation moved at a steady pace.

Closer. The Trashcan on the left of the line would pass him, CPA ten yards.

An alien stumbled. It dropped its sword. The one behind the line screeched and waved all three arms. They all turned to look, presenting their backs to Tarak.

Now.

Tarak jumped up. Dust streamed from his skinsuit. Grit on the handle of his sword was like sandpaper. He retracted his helmet and charged the nearest alien. Closing the distance in fast bounds, he thrust his sword like a lance. Skewered the bastard. There was a sound like grinding gears. Trashcan pitched forward, thrashing on the ground. A cloud of powder engulfed Tarak. The Trashcan's sword and club scattered in the dust.

Tarak's sword was stuck. He sneezed. Trashcan blood smelled like dead fish. Where's a weapon? He grabbed the sword on the ground. The air was assaulted with high-pitched screeches. Trashcan battle cries? Trashcan terror?

Three steps. He was up to the next Trashcan. The alien's clumsy club swing was easily avoided. It clumped into the ground, cracking a rock with a snap, raising dust. Tarak swung and delivered a sword edge to the creature's chest. The blow bounced off with a hollow thud. Backhand, Tarak followed through with another slash against the body. A scratch, not even an 'ouch' from his opponent. He danced away. The upper arm smashed the club down again. Tarak hacked at the exposed elbow. Trashcan Two screeched, dropped the club and ran in circles, fluid gushing from the wound. More stink of dead fish.

Trashcan Three waved its club and blade wildly. Tarak darted past a sword swing. He drove his blade's point through an eye or a mouth, whatever. It penetrated a few inches, then stuck. The Trashcan froze. It went stiff and fell over.

Tarak twisted his blade out.

Trashcan Four dropped its club. It backpedaled away from Tarak. Its upper arm grabbed some gravel and threw. Pebbles pinched Tarak's forehead, his cheek.

The leader started screeching and waving its arms. An alien threw a rock, hard. A narrow miss.

Tarak charged. Trashcan Four turned and retreated. Tarak overtook it in three steps and drove his blade deep into its back. The Trashcan fell forward. It kicked like a wind-up toy with a broken spring.

Another alien threw a club. A weak throw. It fell short. The pole bounced and struck Tarak's arm. He shrugged it off.

Tarak picked the club off the ground. Like an Olympic hammer thrower, he spun and cast it with tremendous force. It hit an alien squarely with a satisfying crunch. Trashcan Five collapsed.

The aliens formed a line, closed up. They faced Tarak. Trashcans lifted their swords and cried out in unison, a deep, low-frequency rumbling like a wolf pack confronting a tiger.

Tarak ran for the hill.

29: Mike

Mike knelt, inserted a tweaker into a slot in LaMancha's electronics deck, and slowly turned it clockwise.

"LaMancha, you up?"

Mike looked at the thick manual on the deck and read a paragraph. He rotated the tweaker a quarter turn.

"LaMancha, sound off." Silence.

"You are starting to worry me—"

A faint voice. "Stars and comets, dinosaurs dance-zing in m' tank. Pleazze. Nooo, noo more essssthreeee. Pleazze. Back. Half turn."

Mike made the adjustment, then slipped the tweaker into his apron pocket. He sat back on his heels and looked at the readouts on LaMancha's tank. All indicators were center of the band. The last two filter scrubs were good.

"Ahh-right. LaMancha. What do you have to say for yourself?"

"I been mugged. My everything hurts."

From an apron pocket, Mike pulled out the plastic baggie and displayed it to LaMancha's camera.

"Thank goodness!" LaMancha exclaimed. "You caught the wicked creature! Assault! On a blameless Organic! I cringed, helpless, he loomed over my tank, tall and slouchy, beetle-browed and barrel-chested, peg leg and a scar on his face that went from eye to jaw—"

"Can it. Unbecoming plagiarism. That's the pirate from *Treasure Island*. Last movie night." Mike waved the baggie. "This was in Gardenbottie's box. Hiding behind your tank. You corrupted an innocent, gullible SemiOrganic bot to participate in your criminal plot."

"Mike, my savior! Stars above, foul interlopers took control of Gardenbottie! Call security! It must have been some fiendishly sophisticated crime ring, the Mafia, a Chinese Triad, the Moriarty Gang!"

"Doesn't wash. No more stupid excuses and dumb denials. Fess up. Take responsibility for your actions."

"Are you accusing me of something?" LaMancha authored an indignant groan. "I assure you, Astraía, god of Innocence, beacon of purity and righteousness, abides in my neurons, camps by my ganglia."

Mike stood up and tossed the baggie on the desk. "Tell me, from the Federated database, how many lethal drug overdoses on Misplaced-4 last year?"

"Fifty-two."

"When Gardenbottie dumped this crap in your tank, did you use the proper dosage?"

Indignantly, LaMancha declaimed, "Of course I did. I corrected for tissue mass and solution temperature and… oh."

Mike sighed.

LaMancha exclaimed, "NOT FAIR."

"Are you nominating yourself to be death number fifty-three? Did you test this shit before you put it into your system? Were you sure it was not laced with strychnine, or nerve agent, or diluted with baby powder, or *not* diluted with baby powder?" Mike sat on the deck, back against the bulkhead. "I cannot express to you how upset I am. I nearly did a one hundred percent change-out of your solution. Professor Ella told me I could have permanently damaged your cortex."

Mike hoisted the manual off the deck and showed it to the camera. *"Casualty and Emergency Procedures for Organic Computers.* Nothing on hallucinogenic drugs. I did not know how to help you."

Silence.

Mike mustered up his best Microphone the Terrible frown. "Well?"

Lou Costello's voice emerged. "I been a baaaaaad boy."

"Yes. Bad. *Monumentally* bad. Do you understand exactly how monumentally bad your decision was?"

LaMancha spoke in the voice of a criminal on the scaffold. "Napoleon-invades-Russia bad. Hitler-elected-Chancellor bad. Ahab-white-whale-chasing bad. Girl-alone-with-Bill-Clinton bad. Monumentally bad."

Mike rubbed his face. "Okay. 'Nuff said. Do it again, I'll take away Gardenbottie and put you to sleep when we're closed."

Pulling out a tube of ibuprofen, Mike uncapped the tank's nutrient port and poured it in. "You don't deserve this," he murmured.

He moved to the desk and activated the computer screen. "Show me who gave you that Flipper crap."

It took only seconds to bring up the camera file. A Fat Guy in

Client overalls supported his belly against the bar. He whispered into the bar clipscreen. A *sprang* from a catapult, a groan from the crowd, and everyone at the bar looked away. Fat Guy slipped a plastic baggie under a drink coaster and pushed it towards a bar waldo. LaMancha's waldo shoved it under a stack of napkins.

"Gardenbottie should take some blame," whined LaMancha. "Gardenbottie retrieved it while you cleaned up the missed shot."

"You missed that shot on purpose. A diversion."

"Baaaaaaaaaad boy."

"All right. Learn from your mistakes. Forgiven and forgotten." Mike grimaced. "Unless you do it again." Pointing to the screen, he said, "Who is this mug? He's in Client coveralls, but he's too well fed."

"His name is Moros. He ships on liners doing cleanup, trash collection, unskilled work. He's non-qual."

An FNQ. Should have figured. Non-quals were licensed for space but not qualified in a trade or for vak work. Most newbies valued non-qual billets as an opportunity to train for a Vakker qualification. This criminal used it as a venue to distribute.

Mike clenched a fist. "Where is this waste of oxygen?"

There was a pause. Mike patiently waited, knowing LaMancha was breaking a few laws by accessing databases not exactly open to the public.

"He has a ticket to Queen Spaceways Station One, departing Dome City Spaceport in twenty-one minutes. Spacer's Hiring Board recorded a voyage contract on *Extravagance Queen*, boosting tomorrow morning from Queen Spaceways Station One at 1000 Dome. He's seven months behind on union dues. There are warrants for his arrest on three planets."

There wasn't enough time to get to the terminal, pass through security, and provide this guy with some kinetic instruction. "Isn't *Extravagance Queen* Crunch's hull? Whistle him up."

Mike heard the dial tone, then the FoxxFone call alert.

"Mike! Glad you called. We had a great time yesterday. Say hello to that silly tankhead. Took me for three stans fifty playing chisel, using *my* dice. Stars and comets, he keeps telling jokes that bad the Federation will require warning labels on the tables. Most fun I've had with my clothes on."

LaMancha was playing chisel with the customers, and winning? There's an issue to be explored further. But not now.

"Crunch, glad we caught you," said Mike. "You shipping in *Extravagance Queen*?"

"Yup. I'm about to board the shuttle to Queen One."

Mike transmitted a picture. "See this guy? He's an FNQ who signed on *Extra*. He in the terminal?"

There was a pause. "Yeah, I've locked on. Friendly or hostile? Gotta be quick, we're about to be called."

Mike sighed. "Let me tell you what that gobshite did to our silly tankhead."

30: Tarak

Tarak bolted up the hillside, weaving between boulders, evading stones thrown by the Trashcans. Halfway up, he dove behind some rocks, then wormed along for twenty yards.

His breathing settled. The fern leaves of a spikey plant provided cover. He scanned the results of his foray.

The Trashcans were in a tizzy. They milled about, sometimes starting to form a line, sometimes a circle. Mostly they did an imitation of a disorganized mob, hooting and warbling in what must be an aural language, waving their arms and sometimes striking poses. Three were down and unmoving. Others were receiving what might be medical attention. Swords and clubs were scattered in the sand.

It was a good fight, Geronimo tactics, guerrilla warfare, the strategy of weak against strong. Hit them, bleed them, gain psychological ascendancy. He put down five of twenty-five, at the cost of a bruised arm.

They did not fight well. Their organization fell apart immediately. Several broke and ran. Others did not seem eager. They were slow. The big upper arm with the club looked formidable, and it likely could cause damage if it could wind up and land a blow squarely, but it had limited flexibility and was vulnerable to a counterstroke.

Hours later, the Trashcans straggled back to their lander. They left behind three corpses. Weapons were scattered about, abandoned.

The sun was close to setting when the lander departed.

Tarak came down from the rocks. He walked to the bodies and

gave each a nudge with his foot. All nicely dead. Good of them to leave the remains.

He inspected his first victim. From the size of the pool of dried brownish liquid, it had probably bled out. The fish offal smell persisted. The torso was about one and a half meters long, about two-thirds of a meter in diameter. There was a hard, bony cover over its chest, impervious to the sword. Higher in the torso were two eyes, close together. They would have to twist to see behind. Good to know if he ever wanted to sneak up on them.

A hole below the eyes must be a mouth. Boney ridges surrounded it.

The top arm was not centered but offset, with a large muscle bulge that came down and wrapped around the back. It had three fingers and two opposable thumbs, very sturdy. Two strong-looking arms were on opposite sides of the torso, one with a hand and one with a boney pointed tip, like a spear. There was a smaller appendage under the mouth, a flexible thing more like a tentacle, tipped with many smaller tentacles. Tarak swung his sword. It parted easily.

Two thick legs were each tipped with a hoof that'll give poor traction in the stony ground. One leg was about a foot long, the other maybe two and a half. No, both were the same length; one extended, the other retracted. Two knee joints. Extended for speed, retracted for stability and strength? Another smaller leg was towards the rear, tipped with a spike. An anchor, for stability?

Pouches contained throwing stones. No personal effects, no pictures of mamma and the kids. No faces, he couldn't tell one from the other. No, there were marks around the eyes and mouth, different on each corpse. Otherwise, everything was in shades of brown, although Tarak seemed to remember the Trashcan behind the line had a splash of red.

With his sword, Tarak struck the big arm, hard. It barely cut through the skin, so dense was the hide. His strike against the joint had been lucky. The front of the torso was nearly impervious to point or edge, the back soft and vulnerable. The side arms could be cut. The legs were tough. These things had few vulnerabilities.

He tried to roll one. It massed maybe 80, 100 kilos. The side arms sticking out defeated his efforts.

Not a lot to work with.

No matter. The greater the challenge, the greater the honor in victory.

Victory. In OldEarth history, the victor held the battlefield after the fight. *That must be me.* He owned it, every rock. All he needed was a cheering crowd.

He started collecting abandoned weapons. Clubs, swords, stones? From creatures that arrived in a deep-space lander, for Tecumseh's sake? Were they warriors in a civilization that had specialized technical types? Or, maybe it was an advanced race, and this group was a bunch of medieval wannabes, like human history geeks who reenacted ancient battles from OldEarth. *Maybe I'm here so a bunch of fantasy nerds could kill like their forefathers did in the good old days.*

31: Mike

Mike liked Sundays. The Lacrosse Shot opened at 1100, but Vakkers didn't start arriving until the churches and temples let out around noon. Vakkers were a rather faithful lot. "The heavens declare the glory of God." Fly the Deep Dark, you log a lot of hours marveling at God's work.

Mike listened to a broadcast service while he prepared for opening. LaMancha usually joined in the worship music, singing hymns out of multiple speakers in three-part harmony.

This morning, LaMancha was silent. Mike actually missed his singing.

Mike was putting a new coat of NanoTeflon on the grill. He was moody, trying to recall an appropriate scripture to use in educating an Organic who abused drugs.

The entrance p-door cycled. Ella walked up the gangway steps. Mike's spirits instantly lifted. Did God model Ella after an angel, gorgeous, smart, nice and sweet? She was elegant in her church clothes. He smiled and waved the NanoTeflon applicator. "Good morning, Professor. Thank you again for the assistance."

Ella slid onto a stool at the grill bar. "Strange morning, wasn't it? Happy to help. How is LaMancha? Can I get breakfast? Filter changed, solution clear, headache gone?"

"The usual? Yes, yes, and you'll have to ask him yourself. Last night he was doing van Gogh voices trying to figure a way to cut off an ear he doesn't have."

"A Western Omelet would be fantastic. Hot tea. LaMancha, Ella, good morning."

No response.

"We're back to conversation mode with all the local drug abusers," said Mike.

Ella tapped the bar clipscreen microphone. "LaMancha? Ella to LaMancha, come in, LaMancha." With a lilt, she sang, *"Good morning, good morning, the sun's out, no clouds in sight, good morning, good morning, to you!"*

Gosh, she has a pretty voice, thought Mike.

Silence.

Mike growled, "LaMancha. Manners." Maybe he should consult a kindergarten warden to learn effective ways to discipline three-year-olds. "If you want quiet, I can always pull your cable out of the computer interface socket. Or, maybe Tevil Maintenance is recruiting for the streetsweeper corps."

A female operator's voice emerged. "We're sorry, the party at this number is not available. Please leave a message at the sound of the tone."

"Be polite to the lady," Mike said. "She saved your miserable existence."

"Beeeeep."

Ella crossed her arms and looked sternly into a camera. She frowned.

LaMancha sounded off, in a voice soaked with contrition. "Professor Braun, I'm so *embarrassed!* I'm not a stalwart, an Organic of integrity. I am a wretched Inspector Clouseau, a pathetic Lieutenant Frank Drebin, I am idiot Zoolander, brainless Nero, George the Fourth, Homer Simpson, Elmer Fudd." Marlon Brando's voice: "I coulda had class. I coulda been a contender. I coulda been somebody instead of a bum, which is what I am."

"We all improve and learn from experience. Please don't go formal, it's Ella."

"Sweet Ella, kind Ella, thank you for saving my miserable existence."

Ella nodded. "Sherri Brightly established the diagnosis and treatment."

"I have now composed and sent a touching FoxxText thanking her."

Ella dunked her tea bag in the cup of hot water. "Sherri especially liked your limericks. She said she'd be happy to date you any time."

"I can't date. I don't have a thing to wear."

Ella brushed back an errant strand of hair. "Sherri is a very sweet girl. You'll like her. She would never try to embarrass you."

"LaMancha doesn't need any help for that," said Mike.

Ella issued Mike a frowning 'you stay out of this' look.

"Sherri wants to do her dissertation on you," said Ella. "For her Ph.D. That would be an appropriate way to thank her."

Dragnet's Detective Sargent Joe Friday's voice came from the speakers. "Just the facts, Ma'am. Why that particular miserable Organic? Is this a Mob hit retaliating for bad poetry? Just the facts, Ma'am."

Ella took her spoon and lifted her tea bag out of the cup. "Sherri's research interest is creativity, what causes, stimulates, and facilitates it. She can learn about creativity by studying how *you* are creative."

In the Umpire's voice, LaMancha intoned, "I direct your attention to the introduction, Volume One of Clinton's *Circumventing the Limitations of the Organic Computer*. I quote: 'Organic computers are not thinking beings as we would envision a human being. They perform in response to stimuli but only within the limitations of their programming. Any perception of creativity is actually a reflection of the ignorance of the observer and the creativity of the original programmer.' End quote."

"Sherri and I have read Clinton. She's an idiot. Sherri thinks you are unique, maybe the only creative Organic in existence. We can learn about creativity from your creativity." She tapped her finger on the bar top. "She might make you famous."

A trumpet fanfare blared from all the speakers. "Galaxy, LaMancha!" The Cowardly Lion's voice was vibrant. "I could be famous! A rock star! No, more, greater—King LaMancha! Visualize it... Noble Galactic Lord-Over-Everything LaMancha! Greater, greater than, than Emperor Ming the Merciless!" He sang,

"If I were Lord of the Spaceways --- not queen, not duke, not prince,

All would bow to my majesty, salaam, a curtsy, kowtow."

"Seventeen Systems, and a couple hundred stations. I could have picked any of them," muttered Mike. "I get the one with the bipolar tankhead."

32: *Cashew*

Cashew gloried in audiences. Ten minutes, they'll be cheering, rolling in the aisles and carried out on stretchers.

A crowd of Vakkers surrounded Table 19 at the Lacrosse Shot. Seated in a place of honor, the center of attention, Cashew had a free drink in hand purchased by an anxious listener. Even Mike was hovering nearby.

"So," Cashew said, "there was I, boosting, speed-of-light. Diana is hollering, 'Go, Cashew, go! Max blast!' Wackey is screaming, 'Come faster, Cashew! I know you can save us!' I'm blowing exhaust temperatures out of spec high, everything's redlined, draining down my Rocket-A faster than an Irish drinking contest on New Year's Eve. I'm duckin' and dodgin' stray rocks and pushing the limit while praying me and some hunk of hard don't end up in the same place at the same time."

He wiped his mouth with a napkin. "Even full-out, I ain't gunna be in time."

He took a long draw on his drink. The glass's empty depths looked like a miniature version of the Deep Dark. "Oh, my. Tank Empty alarm." He coughed and cleared his throat.

One of the Vakkers spoke into a table clipscreen.

"Table 19, alert, incoming." *Sprang.*

The drink was placed on his table and uncapped.

Beer. It foamed, overflowing the glass. He was hoping for ale.

Ah, well, when given a gift of potable alcohol, it's rude to disparage the other molecules in the glass. He took a long drag and wiped his mouth with the sleeve of his verdigris and orange jerkin.

"So, I'm doing max butt blast, but Ghost beats me there. He figures out real quick, Aether's got himself pinned between a contact binary. Soak, listen up, lemme explain to you, that's two rocks held together by their gravitational fields until they touch. They move relative to each other, but real slow. Soak? Copy all?"

Soak half rose from his seat and appeared to be on the leading edge of a composition regarding Cashew's mother, species, and hygiene, but Sampson pulled him down and clamped a hand over his mouth.

"Soak understands," Sampson rumbled.

The Vakkers chuckled.

Stupid Soak, always trying to steal my audience.

Cashew lowered his tone to menacing. "Aether's about to be a jelly pancake. Wackey's tuggin' and tuggin', but no way can she pull him out. Aether's pinched between two ridges, high spots inside the crack, with rock pushing in front and more stuck in his O_2&E."

Another satisfying sip. Mike's craft beer was actually a drop of all right.

"Ghost scopes this out. He backs out, tells Wackey to stand clear, turns around… and leaves!"

Gasps from the crowd.

"He calls for Diana to plot a course to the PunchPoint. Wackey's like to have a conniption, not knowing what he's doing. The rocks squash together another inch!"

Groans from the audience.

A sip. No, two sips.

A Vakker said, "What happened?"

Always wait until they ask for more.

"Get the picture. Ghost's boosting out two, three klicks doing Lord knows, Wackey's homing in on a coronary, Aether's unconscious and his suit's saying he's not breathing too good, what with a gazillion tons of rock trying to squeeze him into protein mush."

Another sip. Vivid pause.

"So, Ghost's way the hell out. Two, four, maybe six klicks. He turns, diddles around for a nano, then goes to max booster juice and blasts —straight for the rock!"

There was an apprehensive moan from the Vakkers.

"He's firing hot, way over red line, accelerating all the way! Fifty, one hundred, two hundred meters per second!"

Sampson grumbled. "You bigtime exaggerate. No way, two hundred per."

"Hey," said Cashew, nearly as insulted as Caesar on the Ides of March. "I was watching through Wackey's camera feed, like I wuz there, eyes on target."

Another drag on the beer. Ignore the critic. Dramatization makes it more… real.

"He cuts the boost. Spins, stabilizes, he's closing in, three hundred meters per, straight as a laser, feet first! Then, he sheds his booster pack!"

Cashew paused. Dramatic pauses are always good in a tale like this.

Soak prodded his elbow. "Did he splatter? No way he's gunna bounce away coupla thousand tons of rock." A background buzz of "No way" from the assembled Vakkers reinforced Soak's assessment.

Cashew shook his head. "Ghost makes himself skinny. Feet first, straight as a sunbeam, he's into the crack! Into the crack, if you can believe it, not touching an edge! Four hundred meters per! He lined that up from hundreds of meters, maybe ten kilometers out! I watched it all. Passed Wackey like a blur. Speed-of-light!"

An appreciative "Ooooh" came from the gathering.

"Booster pack whacks outside the crack. Kablammy! Fuel tank cracks, and it goes spinning off into the Deep Dark."

"Aaaaaaaah."

"Without touching an edge, Ghost passes Wackey like to scare the blue lights out of her, skims into the crack, passes through ten meters of igneous like a streak, and Bob's your uncle, he rams feet first into Aether! Ka-PUNCH! Aether pops out of the pinch like a corpper diving for a donut!"

The audience celebrated the marvel. 'Well done!" "Shabash, the Ghost Sahib!"

Sampson shook his head. "Wrong way," he grumbled. "That's in, not out. Aether's still trapped."

"Yes, you scoped it right, my outsized friend," intoned Cashew, expression grim. "Aether's free of the pinch, but he's in the cave, like a tomb! He's inside, Ghost and Wackey outside!"

Another sip.

"Now Aether's floating unconscious. He's so deep they can't grab him."

Another drag from the glass. The dregs. "Oh. My goodness. Dry again."

"Table 19, LaMancha. Alert, incoming." *Sprang.*

Another beer. Maybe if he jazzed up the delivery. More suspense.

"So, they can't get in, Aether can't get out, and the rocks are coming together faster than before."

Dramatic pause.

"He's trapped! They can't get to Aether!"

A sip.

"Except, *Ghost* can."

A groan from the Vakkers. Dramatic pause.

"What happened?" prodded a Vakker.

A deep sip. He leaned back, exhaled, looked to the overhead and closed his eyes.

Another Vakker voice said, "What? Whatdiddydo?"

Cashew leaned forward, his expression intense. "Ghost takes off his O_2&E!"

"Nooooo," from the audience.

"With his pack unplugged, just him in his skinsuit, he's skinny enough, he gets through the crack!"

"Ahhhh."

"He takes the pack off Aether, making him skinny. He pushes Aether out the crack to Wackey. Wackey hooks Aether up to Ghost's O_2. Ghost pushes through Aether's O_2. Meanwhile, Ghost got nuthin' to breathe but what's in his helmet, his residual O_2 is dropping fast, with enough CO_2 to make an elephant gasp. Somehow, with his last breath, he squeezes through. They're both out of the rock!"

There was a heartfelt sigh from the crowd.

Really, Cashew thought, it wasn't as if they didn't know everything came out green. It was on all the Vakker circuits. It surely is the quality of the dramatic performance. Congratulations to me. Lawrence Olivier, Tom Hanks would be jealous.

"Ghost passes out! Wackey hooks Ghost to Aether's O_2. She tows them both back to the ship. I dock the MEVV. Diana's on the command deck, course plotted to the PunchPoint. Soon's I get Aether secure on the AutoDoc, she redlines the throttle, boosting like we wuz being tailed by Freddy looking to collect a transaction tax."

A voice from the audience asked, "Aether still suckin' and blowin'?"

LaMancha's voice interjected. "Aether suffered a broken collarbone, three broken ribs and a collapsed lung."

Cashew seized the narrative back from the interloping Organic. "A Queen liner was at the PunchPoint. I transferred him to their sick bay. Human doc sez he'll make a full recovery."

There was a smattering of applause.

Cashew puffed out his chest and accepted the homage. Great performance. *Homer, and that other amateur, Shakespeare, they would've been taking notes. Probably ask for my autograph.*

He ought to be able to drink free off this story for a month, in other bars on other planets. He had to figure out a way to get more of himself in the story, maybe some heroic emergency medical procedure, him at the AutoDoc. First, he'd have to learn how to work an AutoDoc. But otherwise, first run-through, give it an A-minus.

LaMancha spoke in the courtly tones of a Castilian noble. "Considering Cashew's harrowing tale, he would be distressed if we did not join him in celebrating the felicitous result of his perilous adventure, by allowing *him* to stand the house to a drink. Thanks to Cashew! A salute to Ghost! Mike's Best for All! All tables, alert, incoming!"

The crowd's raucous cheer overpowered an ale-deprived, beer-soaked voice moaning in existential pain.

33: *Sherri*

The lunch crowd had departed from the Lacrosse Shot. The tables were vacant but for a chess game in a corner. It was the lull before the next invasion.

The gangway p-door slid open. Sherri Brightly entered. She took possession of a chair at Table 1 and unmuted the clipscreen. "La-Mancha! Howyadoin' there, short gray and handsome?"

In a formal tone that would have made an English butler envious, LaMancha said, "Citizen Academic Brightly. Welcome. Mike is in the storeroom. He will be out shortly to attend to your every need."

Sherri rapped on the clipscreen. "You're duckin' the issue. I say again, howyadoin'?"

If LaMancha had eyes to cry, his angst would have flooded the Lacrosse Shot. With heartfelt repentance, he moaned, "Sherri, *mi salvador*, my savior. Thank you for saving my miserable existence."

Sherri leaned back and smiled. "No worries. I got your text. Very sweet. I especially liked the part about throwing your cloak down to cover all the puddles in life that might sully my slippers. Very poetic. Sir Walter Raleigh, right? Be careful about offering up diamonds and rubies, a girl might take you up on it. And that other thing, about you slitting your throat, dying in my arms at my slightest command?"

"I conceived the offer as very evocative, a haunting expression of regret, a poetic appeal from the heart, a *cri de Coeur*. Did I not communicate my remorse?"

She leaned forward and whispered softly into the table clipscreen. "I hate to break any illusions you might have, but Organics don't have a throat." She leaned back and chuckled.

LaMancha, indignant, said, "I was speaking metaphorically. *Metaphors*, like, 'Life is like a sewer; you only get out of it what you put into it'. Grok?"

The office p-door slid open. Mike came through, followed closely by Ghost. Ghost spotted Sherri, and tried to do a 180.

Mike captured his arm. "Somebody I want you to meet," Mike said.

The gangway p-door opened. Ella walked in.

"Excellent," said Mike, "*two* people to meet."

Ghost tried a different retreat. Mike blocked with his hip.

"Ella, Sherri, meet my silent partner. This is Ghost. The Lacrosse Shot was his idea. Ghost, this is Citizen Professor Ella Braun and Citizen Academic Sherri Brightly."

"Hello, Ghost," said Ella.

"Pleasedtameetcha," said Sherri.

Ghost bobbed his head but did not meet their eyes. "H'lo," he managed.

"The Lacrosse Shot was your idea?" asked Sherri intensely. "You set up LaMancha?"

"He did indeed," said Mike, with the air of a proud father. "He wired the system and reprogrammed, and helped LaMancha, what did you say, 'work through a couple of issues'? Always wanted to ask about that. I think he's accumulated a few more."

Eyes wide, eagerness evident, Sherri said, "Issues? Reprogrammed LaMancha? Oh, you splendid man, come sit and talk to me."

Ghost cast a look at the office p-door with the inviting green light illuminated above it, and the open gangway, so very clear of obstacles. "Ah, gotta go, go see somebody about … something, maybe."

Sherri sidled up and put an arm through his. "Why don't we just sit down over here and have a nice mug of mickee, and you tell me a little bit about what you did with LaMancha. A few questions? A little conversation?"

Ghost gently tried to draw back. Sherri locked her grip.

"I'm no good, conversation … girls," Ghost said. "Later. Maybe."

"I'll play you for it," said Sherri, dragging him towards a table. "Chisel, two out of three. You win, you can go see somebody about something maybe. I win, we talk."

"Never lose, chisel. I'll just go."

"I don't lose at chisel either. That'll make it interesting." She pointed. "Sit. There. Down. Now. LaMancha, shoot us a chisel set and two mickees, Table 1. My line."

"I can pay, mine."

"Two out of three for the mickees. Loser pays. Which means sorry, you pay."

"Table 1, alert, incoming." *Sprang.*

Sherri extracted from the net a bag containing a scoreboard and a can containing dice.

Ghost placed his clipscreen on the table. "Dice?" He snorted. "Obsolete." He tapped his clipscreen. "Random number generator. No chasing dropped dice."

Sherri looked through narrowed eyelids. "My Grandmama, she taught me. Sherri, she says, you listen to good advice: you don't smoke, you don't drug, you don't swear against the Almighty, and you damn well don't use somebody else's clipscreen for random numbers for chisel." She grabbed two pegs. "I'm blue, you're pink. If you find that psychologically unsettling, I'm not responsible for your gender stereotyping. Roll. Highest gets first hit."

34: *Ella*

Ella came over to Mike, leaned against the bar, and looked at the two young people. They were arguing, Sherri aggressively, Ghost calmly.

"He seems like a nice young man," she said. "A bit shy." She glanced up at Mike. "My students tell stories about a Vakker named Ghost. He can do anything, fix anything, pilot anything, then fade away nobody knows where. Him?"

"Yup."

"He seems too young."

"Might be twelve, might be twenty-two." Mike capped two mickees and walked them over to Table 1. He returned to Ella.

"Rumor has him rescuing a Vakminer," said Ella.

"Don't repeat that," said Mike. "Vakkers keep the traffic down on anything Ghost. He's playing Hide 'n Seek with the Feds and corppers."

"What has he done?"

Mike shrugged. "Nothing wrong. Just illegal."

Ella smiled. "Now, that is a delicate distinction."

Mike sighed, and leaned back against the cold box. "I checked on him when he first popped up with the Lacrosse Shot idea, the nets and the catapults. I wanted to make sure I wasn't receiving stolen goods." He tossed a towel into the dirty linen hamper. "Ghost just materialized five, six years ago, no one could pin a date. He's out earning a few stans off Freddy's books, some O_2 here, a meal there. He worked as a taxi jockey for a time, until the Admiralty started requiring pilots have a birth certificate, even if they have a Vakker Class One LPO Piloting or Deep Space Navigation License. Ghost has those, and a lot more. He has a rep as one of the best pilots around, MEVV-in-the-asteroids precise, meticulous, all the things Vakkers like to keep them alive in the Deep Dark."

"Five, six years ago?" Ella discretely looked over at Table 1.

Ghost slapped the dice cup upside down on the tabletop and revealed the result. Sherri groaned.

"Plus or minus," said Mike.

"Parents?"

"Maybe an unregistered son of a Client, a box boy from a crèche, but I don't think so."

With an open hand, she gestured for more.

"Okay, but this is close hold," he said. "You know about the Splice Riots, six years ago?"

"Some," she said. "Blogger stories, mostly. Asclepius-3 was playing with DNA splicing, growing people in vats with extra arms or super strength and other things more horrid. There were disturbances when genetically modified people were brought to Misplaced-4."

Mike nodded. "The Clients thought they should have the jobs, not the Vat Villains. After a couple of riots and a bunch of dead Splices, Tevil gathered the survivors, and they boosted. Only, some of the Splices were unaccounted, younger ones, kids. Everyone assumed they were killed."

Ella tapped the bar thoughtfully. "Ghost, a Splice? Left behind?"

"Might. What with the new Federated Gene Laws, I'm not sure he'd stay free if Freddy snatched him."

At Table 1, Sherri groaned. "This, I cannot believe. LaMancha, shoot us some different dice."

Mike shrugged. "While we're talking origin myths, can I ask about Sherri? If I'm being rude, forget I asked."

Ella smiled. "Can I ask one first? I was introduced to a Vakker named Soak. Short, chubby, with a ketchup stain on the front of his suit?"

Mike grinned. "The infamous Soak, and his sidekick Sampson. They're Misplaced-4's tinkers and odd-jobbers. They own a shuttle that they put together out of parts from maybe two dozen abandoned ships. Soak is the Pigpen of the Vakker world. He could get his skinsuit dirty in a hospital operating room while wrapped in a hazmat suit. Vakkers love him, but don't get too close."

Ella glanced down at her clothes.

Mike pointed. "Made you look."

Ella laughed, and took a playful swipe at his finger. "Soak talked about your 'poisoned pillows of death' and overwhelmingly recommended 'creamed foreskins.' I didn't have the courage to ask. They're food?"

Mike closed his eyes and grimaced. "Death pillows are ravioli. I make good ravioli. Creamed foreskins, that's chipped beef on toast, and there is no such thing as good chipped beef. I make a pot when Soak starts hovering like an overcaffeinated chihuahua and threatens sack and pillage if it's not put on the menu. *Everyone* must eat creamed foreskins, like it's some kind of religious experience leading to a higher state of consciousness. Saint Soak's Sacramental Creamed Foreskins."

Ella grinned. "I've never seen Creamed Foreskins on the menu."

"I list it as 'Soak's Favorite Breakfast.' That satisfies Soak, and warns off the Vakkers. Some corppers ordered it, until I posted Soak's picture next to the listing. No more orders. Saved my reputation."

"Fascinating," she said. "If I can ask one more, how did he come to be called Soak? Is that, like, a Vakker term for an alcoholic or something?"

Mike frowned. "No. Soak came by his callsign honestly. It was awarded." He grinned. "Okay, if you really want to know. During a cruise in *Excellence Queen*, Filbert wagered Rufus T. Firefly he could get Soak's skinsuit stain-free in less than six minutes. Firefly took the bet, thinking it was pretty much free money. Filbert got some of his biggest cohorts from the Zeros and Ones Gang, they grabbed Soak, tied him up, and dragged him down to Environmental Engineering, where we have these 100-gallon vats for cleaning the air duct filters. Helmet up, on suit O_2, they held him down for five minutes in a muriatic acid bath, in spite of his wiggling and some horribly offensive language. So, that's how he got to be callsign Soak." Mike closed his eyes, savoring the pleasant memory. "For the last minute, they used brushes. Didn't work. Rufus T. won."

Ella laughed.

"Having passed that test," Mike said, "tell me, isn't Sherri a bit young for a Ph.D. candidate?"

"She's a prodigy. Bachelors at 16. She's finished her advanced class work and doing her dissertation now at 18. I am fortunate to be her advisor. She has an incredible future. Brilliant girl."

Mike glanced over to Ghost and Sherri's table, then looked back to Ella. "She's not going to eat Ghost alive? I mean, Ghost is kinda naïve. I don't think he's ever had a girlfriend, or even gone on a date. I'd hate to see him hurt."

"I feel the same way about Sherri. As a prodigy she is isolated from her peers and doesn't fully connect with the other students. They admire her, but she's also resented for being so intelligent. Sherri has mostly been a library and lab rat. No boyfriend. No guile."

At Table 1, Ghost sat back and sucked air between his teeth. "Three percent chance, that.'

Sherri flicked her nose at him. "Well, read the dots and take the shots," she chortled. "Reconcile yourself to the inevitable. Reality check, *you* are on the express shuttle to *Loserville*."

Mike and Ella exchanged glances.

"Same age, same smarts, same lack of sophistication," said Ella. "Sherri's fun. She could help bring Ghost out. Might be a good thing."

Mike nodded. Then he said, "Thanks for coming by to check on LaMancha. I'll let you get on."

Ella took on a puzzled look. "Actually, I came by to see you."

Nonplussed, Mike looked at Ella.

She smiled. "Mike, you are about the nicest person I know."

Mike froze.

"Kind. Generous. Hard-working. Pretty smart, too," she added, "for a professional poisoner."

35: Mike

Tuesday morning, and the Lacrosse Shot had a crowd at a back table. Vakkers were betting LaMancha couldn't shoot a 'Sunny Side Up' without breaking the yolk. LaMancha kept imploring Mike to make the yolk bottoms firmer, but Mike refused to ruin his cooking just so LaMancha could—win bets?

LaMancha, betting? Standards? He filed that away for later.

"Table 24, alone, incoming."

"LaMancha, Geezer. Two stans sez they're broke!"

LaMancha had his 'Humphry Bogart' voice on. "Geezer, you're on, tough guy. Anybody else want in on that action? I'll give two to one."

Prunk. A change-up. No spin. Gentle arc, graceful. A soft hit in the center of the lacrosse stick pocket. The pole rocked back slightly on the shock-absorbing spring.

The Vakkers' Rules Committee huddled to inspect the result.

"Not a crease! LaMancha, by a yolk!"

The speakers broke out in the victory theme from *Rocky*.

"Guess I'm a slow learner." Geezer mourned another lapse of judgment. "LaMancha, if you please, on my tab?"

"Adrian! Adrian! … No, can-x that—Ella! Ella!"

LaMancha's music abruptly stopped.

LaMancha whispered out of the nearest clipscreen. "Mike, alert, incoming. Three hostiles approaching the gangplank. Pockets bulging, likely concealed weapons."

Was the usual Tuesday morning weirdness starting early?

The entrance p-door hissssed open. Three men sauntered in.

The leader was in a cheap suit, cuffs too long, pants shiny at the thighs, looking like discards rescued from a charity donation bin. He had close-set eyes, ears that stuck out, and a protruding belly overlapping his belt. The taller pair behind him were obviously Union Muscle, goons wearing blue-collar shirts and drawstring pants. The biggest one looked like LaMancha's pirate from *Treasure Island*, sans peg leg.

The bar waldos were lining up shot glasses, next to an old foam cup from the Captain Mike's Bar days. Was this really the best time to clean out drawers?

"Mike! Mike, muh good fellow!" Suit beamed camaraderie. He walked to the grill counter and stuck out his hand. "Anxious to meet youse."

Mike gauged Suit's eyes, and figured he would decline this handshake. He wiped his hands on his belt towel. "What can I get you?"

"Ah, Mike, Mike, it's what *I* can get for *youse!*" His eyes drifted towards the ceiling. "For example, I can get youse a whole lotta goodwill." The guy beamed self-satisfaction, as if he had just raided his grandmother's purse without getting caught.

Mike kept his tone flat. "What do you want?"

"A little compliance. Youse not Union Strong." Suit smiled. "Yet."

"This is a sole proprietorship. No employees, no union."

The Suit pointed to a speaker. "What about him?"

"Table 12, Alert, incoming." *Sprang.*

"That's an Organic," Mike said. "A computer."

"So, youse got bots taking jobs away from humankind? That

makes me really, really sad. Shouldn't do that against fellow peoples." He drummed his fingers on the countertop. "But maybe, instead youse really got a Client in a back room running those shooter things. It's sad, youse denying some poor Clyde the benefits of Union membership." Suit caught the eye of one of his companions. "Mind if we look?"

The Treasure Island Pirate strode over to the door to Mike's quarters, ignored the 'private' sign, and pressed the 'open' plate. Red light. Locked. With both hands flat on the door, he tried to press it open.

Mike called out, "That's a pressure boundary. Mechanically sealed."

Pirate walked back to stand next to Suit, flexing his fists.

Suit flicked a finger at the bar. The other goon walked behind the counter wearing a tough-guy expression, punching his right fist into his left palm. Like a magician's trick he revealed brass knuckles, grinned, and slipped them on, holding them out, displaying them in full view.

Suit smiled broadly. "Been wanting to introduce us before now, but The Boss says, 'Wait 'til he's up running good, making lotsa shekels.' We hear youse got so many shekels piled up now, you can't even peek over the top. So, we come for our Union's Solidarity Share.' He frowned. "Instead of transacting, I can see youse ain't gonna be cooperative. A shame. Something might happen to this nice establishment."

Mike stepped back. "Our cameras are on."

Suit chuckled. "Come now, Mike—may I call youse Mike, since we's friends?—vid makes no nevermind. Youse file a complaint, it goes in front of Judge Marx. Know what? Judge Marx is Union Strong, head of Legal and Persuasion Workers, Local 10-65. That's us. Judge sure wants people like youse to abide the law. He knows persuasion is sometimes necessary. We're only here to help set things straight."

Brass-Knuckles flicked a beer tap. Beer splashed and spilled down the drain.

Suit wrinkled his nose. "Like, that beer. Smells skanky. So glad we caught that problem. Youse wouldn't want to serve urine like that."

Some of the Vakkers got up and started to move down toward the bar.

Suit pulled out a snub-nosed pistol and waved it towards them. "Siddown, or get ventilated."

Mike looked at his customers and gave a shake of his head. He didn't want anyone shot, not over spilled beer.

Brass-Knuckles flicked the other two taps. Beer overflowed onto the deck.

"Union Strong stops accidents." Suit smiled benignly.

Pirate smashed a ceramic coffee urn against a table with a crash, shards flying.

"Oh! An accident! So sorry," said Suit, with a gleam in his eyes, like a rattlesnake inspecting a cornered mouse.

Brass-Knuckles grabbed a bottle of vodka by the neck. With a smile, he shattered it against the counter. He pointed the jagged edge at Mike's neck. The air reeked of the liquor. Pirate grinned.

Suit looked down at his fingernails. "It'll be just awful when we tell Judge how youse fell on your face, got all cut up on broken glass. That'll trigger an inspection by Health & Safety, they're the original Tough Gov, know what I mean?" With the solicitous tone of Jack Nicholson addressing the Martian invaders, Suit said, "Can't we all just come to an agreement?"

Mike glared.

The Suit smiled playfully. "I hate to admit, I do enjoy this part. Boys, bust 'em."

Brass-Knuckles was six feet away from Bar Cat 1 when Errol Flynn's voice sang out from a bar clipscreen. "Goon Number One, alert, incoming!"

Sprang.

The catapult rocketed a shot glass off the back of Brass-Knuckles' skull. His eyes went to the ceiling, his knees turned to jelly, and he drifted down, face first. The shot glass rattled on the deck.

"Goon Number Two, alert, incoming!"

Sprang.

Grill Cat fired an unerring heavy-duty meat mallet, this time off a forehead, a tough volley against a miniscule target. Pirate buckled.

"What the hell!" shouted Suit. He spun around, waving the revolver, looking for a target. The Vakkers in the room hit the deck. Mike sprawled.

"Jugg-ears, alert, incoming!"

Sprang.

The extra-large, flimsy foam cup hit Suit full in the face, and split. Boiling hot coffee erupted. Suit screamed. Hands flailing, the pistol fired. The lead ricocheted off a girder, then smashed into a stack of dishes. Plates crashed on the deck.

"Jugg-ears, alert, incoming!"

Sprang.

A shot glass smacked Suit's temple.

He collapsed, like Bambi seeking gentle repose on a meadow.

"Union Brutes, LaMancha," called out Errol Flynn. "I'll never rest until every Saxon in this shire can stand up as free men, and strike a blow for Richard and England!" Trumpets sounded. "For Mike and the Lacrosse Shot, too."

Mike was impressed. Twenty seconds. Done deal.

A Vakker beseeched from the upper tier of tables. "LaMancha, friend, comrade, could you remind me when our tab's due? Wouldn't want you upset at me or Sampson, 'ol buddy, shipmate."

Mike shut off the beer taps. "LaMancha. Good shooting. Thanks."

"Do you think Doctor Frankenstein made a mistake, splitting one brain among the three of them?"

The Vakkers in the dining room began to whistle and clap. A few came over and nudged the goons with their boots. Geezer went on his haunches to inspect the pistol lying on the deck. "A bullet gun!" he exclaimed. "This A-Hole carries a bullet gun in a dome on a vak planet? Shit-for-brains! Dump him out an airlock for public safety."

Mike went behind the grill counter and grabbed a pair of cooking tongs. He picked up the gun, careful not to touch it himself. He placed it in a bottom drawer behind the bar.

"Stinky, Soak, Sampson, Rhino, favor us?" Mike said. "Give our friends a lift out the gangway? Not you, Geezer. With your knees, you're on light duty."

Rhino, a solidly built tower, appeared to relish the chore. "Happy to be of service, Mike, m'man." He grabbed the feet of the nearest Muscle and towed him towards the entrance like a used gladiator being dragged from the coliseum. He took the steps, ignoring the ramp. Muscle's head made dull thumping noises.

"Wait!" Mike cried. He rummaged through Suit's pockets and found his wallet. He pulled out the CID card and held it next to Suit's face in view of a camera. The others got the idea and did the same with the goons.

"LaMancha, got these guys? They pay for breakage. Pay for the spilled beer. Charge for cleanup. Transport fare to outside the gangway, credited to our shipmates' tabs." He reached out and took a shot glass missile off the floor and tucked it into Suit's pocket. "Charge them for souvenir shot glasses. Charge them for the brunch they are going to treat everyone they threatened. Use the Rule 10 rate. Make sure their bill is itemized."

"Hark! You neglected the best!" LaMancha snickered. "Surely they would want to leave a generous gratuity to their waitshooter."

36: Marshall

The auditorium was a quarter full of civilians, noisy boys approaching manhood. Captain Marshall, Commandant of the Federated Space Forces Academy, Federated Central, Elysium System, entered through the rear door. His potential students were chattering, oblivious to his arrival.

Make an impression. Begin as you mean to proceed.

His Chief Master-at-Arms, a tall man with midnight skin, a hard face, and an impeccable uniform, standing in front below the stage, called, "Officer present! Attention on deck! Stand at Attention!"

Captain Marshall strode down the center aisle of the auditorium, looking neither left nor right. He did not acknowledge the audience's reaction. Some were here eagerly, some reluctantly, some did not give a damn. He would give them a look at Space Forces authority, deliver his warnings, then dismiss them to reconsider their decisions—or the decisions forced on them—overnight.

Those in plain serviceable clothing clustered at the back. They all stood at the CMAA's call. A smaller number wearing extravagant high fashions, all hot reds and yellows and bright oranges, continued their chatter, inattentive, unmindful of anything but their own immediate desires. They were the gene-audited royals, second and third sons of Corporate executives and the 35 Families, born to privilege.

The CMAA walked in front of the royals and called over their heads, "Stand at attention!"

A few of the fashionistas looked up. Two stood.

The CMAA looked down at the chatterers. "Silence, you miserable waste of oxygen! Officer present! On your feet, shut your holes!"

Conversations died. There was a scuffle of feet. Four more stood.

In the front row, three ostentatiously continued sitting, ignoring the order. One informed the air, "Well, that certainly was rude."

The Chief walked to within a step. He spoke quietly. "You will shortly be under Space Forces discipline. No one here cares about your father or the Corporation for which he works. If you choose the oath, you will eventually become proud members of the Federated Space Forces. You will demonstrate that pride by respectfully standing at attention for officers. Begin now."

One languidly stretched. Another loudly belched. Those around them chuckled.

The Chief said, in a gentle voice, "Tell me, young derr, is 'stand at attention' incomprehensible?"

The center youth looked up and smiled. "Were you addressing me? I didn't think so. My father doesn't work for a Corporation, he is *head* of *our* Corporation. The Corporation works for him, what? I thought you were addressing"—he gave a general wave—" those in the back."

There were sniggers. The young man, a handsome lad with a flamboyant 75-standard haircut and a jeweled compuwatch costly enough to fund a business startup, smiled condescendingly, a vacuous smirk adorning his gene-cleansed face.

Marshall walked over to stand next to the Chief. He read aloud the boy's nametag, "Derr Roddy."

Roddy nodded. "Amos Roddy, Tevil Corporation. I didn't know Fed Central had villages this far out, we're in never-never land, not a decent smoothie shop for kilometers. You've heard of Tevil? Insurance, metals refining, shipbuilding, transportation, logistics, I can't remember them all. Number 37 of the 50 high Corporations, last I checked. We own a whole planet, Misplaced-4, Dome City, comprēnde, verstehen du?" He settled back into a more comfortable slouch.

Marshall looked at the young man, who was playing off his father's status, assuming he was impervious to discipline, that his family would cover all transgressions. With this he was supposed to build a space force?

The young gentleman was challenging the authority of the Chief in front of the entire class. He was challenging *his* authority. Cut him down now? Refuse to accept his nomination? Make a public example of him?

Marshall's temper flared. A few Marines would be pleased to duck-walk this arrogant ass off the grounds. This morning, headquarters had informed him they were inflicting a nine percent budget cut. The student population would have to be reduced. He would start with this haughty, immature—

Roddy. He remembered the name. Amos' father had sent a message, not as a royal, but as a concerned parent, worried about his son.

Putting his hands behind his back, Marshall said, "Derr Roddy. Favor me with a few words by the podium?" He turned and walked up the steps to the stage.

Roddy stood and shrugged, the gesture telling his audience he was complying only out of curiosity. This raised more sniggers.

Roddy strolled up the steps to join Marshall.

Marshall spoke softly. "You have no pride, acting so disgracefully."

The young man looked to the ceiling and feigned a yawn. "Pride. Isn't it one of the Seven Deadly Sins?"

"I do indeed know Tevil," Marshall said evenly, "and your father. Your application records document an undisciplined, lazy layabout, rejected from employment with Tevil due to behavioral infractions."

Roddy did not meet Marshall's eyes.

"I received a VelociComm from your father."

Roddy smirked.

Marshall continued, "He requested I hold you fully responsible for meeting the standards of this Academy. If you fail to meet disciplinary or academic standards, I was asked to expel you, and make clear, you would be cut off from inheritance of company stock, your allowance halted, and your trust fund revoked."

"Bullshit! He wouldn't—"

"Derr Roddy, you will learn that Federated Space Forces personnel do not lie. People who lie do not survive in the Deep Dark."

Pugnaciously, Roddy claimed, "More bullshit."

Captain Marshall looked Roddy in the eyes. "In the morning, should you decide to take the oath, you will be required to show respect to officers. Will you show that respect now, or have you made your decision already? I offer you a singular opportunity. Refuse, and I believe you will find your life much less agreeable."

Roddy glared. He tightened his lips.

Marshall glanced over to the immaculately-uniformed chief.

Slowly, resentfully, Roddy came to attention.

Marshall said, "Once accepted to this Academy, all records of previous infractions are sealed. Candidates start with a clean record. Equal standing for all."

At this, Roddy appeared to listen.

"Your current behavior is unacceptable," said Marshall. "Behavior can change. Should it continue, Chief Master-at-Arms Imani, the man who you have so publicly disrespected," he nodded towards the chief, "will escort you off the base. Immediately, on the first offense. Neither space mishaps nor I give second chances. Do you understand?"

"My father wouldn't—"

"This is not a debating society. Do you understand? There are only two answers to that question."

After a pause, breaking away from Marshall's gaze, Roddy said, "Okay. Yeah."

"In the Federated Space Forces, the response is, 'Aye, aye, sir.' It is long in tradition, dating from the age of water navies. It means, 'I understand and will obey.' Do you understand, and will you obey?"

Roddy stood a little straighter. "Yeah. Yes. Aye, aye. Sir."

"Very well. This incident is closed. And forgotten. Return to your place."

Roddy stepped away from the podium and descended the steps, his progress followed by the curious royals wondering what had transpired.

Roddy squared his shoulders and seemed to come to a decision. He walked to the CMAA.

In a loud voice, Roddy said, "Chief Master-at-Arms. I apologize."

"*Ukuthula.*" the Chief growled quietly. "Peace. Begin anew."

Roddy walked to the nearest seat. He turned and looked towards the stage. The others regarded him with curiosity, some with surprise, a few with contempt. Roddy was focused on something the others could not see.

The royals, some reluctantly, some just conforming, all stood.

Chief Imani called out, "Seats."

There was the usual rumble as the auditorium seats were folded down. Except for a few whispered comments and a single laugh, the audience was quiet.

"I am Command Captain Peter Marshall. I am Commandant of this Academy."

Silence. At least it appeared he had their attention.

"In this briefing I will provide you with additional information on the Academy, the Service, and the oath that may be in your future. You will then be dismissed to quarters, to consider the commitment into which you might enter. Those of you who decide to remain will take the oath in the morning. Those who chose otherwise will be transported to the maglev station."

37: Marx

The view from the top of the Federated Building was spectacular, a clear prospect over nearly 270 degrees of Dome City. The Judge's office suite was over eight hundred square feet of carpeted space, with a conversation nook, a wet bar, and several acres of desk designed to intimidate the plebians. The view did not include the squalor of Clientown, appropriately hidden away underground in a historic, ancient, deteriorating district.

The intercom buzzed. "Yo, Judge Baby, Prez Nero, Federated Con … Con … Con*soli*dated Union of, ah, yeah, Peoples' Services, he's here."

That was Marylynn, his receptionist. By Mao, he loved just hearing her voice. Her skills were limited, a little trouble with words over three-syllables and anything attached to a keyboard, but her bosom inspired the soul.

Might as well see what that pest Nero wants. "Send him in."

The door opened, and Nero began the hike across the room. He was short and round, sported inflated jowls, a gaudy suit, and enough jewelry to founder a small elephant.

"Hey, Judge." He waved a cloud of smoke.

"Put that cigar out. You pollute the room." Marx kicked his blowers to 'high.'

Nero stopped, put a hand on a free-standing aquarium (the largest on the planet, Marx admitted with pride), steadied himself, lifted a leg, and stubbed the cigar out on the sole of his shoe. He flicked the butt into the Aquarium. Water spilled to the floor. He resumed his trek. Each step left black soot on the brilliant white rug. His handprint on the aquarium was an oily smear.

Restraining his irritation, Marx asked, "You have a case?"

Nero flopped into a chair. "Labor enforcement issue. Wanna talk to the Head Honcho, El Jefe, oh Ye of the Honorable Organized Labor Societies. Is His Eminence in?" He made a fist in the air. "Union Strong, Judge Baby."

Marx triggered the intercom. "Marylynn, hold my calls. No visitors."

He swiveled his chair, reached into a cabinet behind his desk, and retrieved a bottle and two glasses. "If I'm on Union business, we can have some late morning glow, what?"

Nero took his glass, downed the potent liquor in one swallow, reached for the bottle and poured himself another. *Good*, thought the judge, *get yourself pickled. You're easier to manipulate when your brain is embalmed.*

Marx made a tent with his fingers. "Well then, how are The People's Affairs progressing?"

"Seen my last Membership and Revenue?"

Marx hadn't, but he wasn't about to admit anything. "What of it."

"Membership down six percent, revenue down seven. Economy sucks."

The judge gave a contemptuous snort. "That's no excuse for Union revenues to fall. What're you doing wrong?"

Nero responded as if his masculinity had been challenged. "Hey, ain't my do-wrong. Businesses closing, big layoffs, Union members thrown into Clydesville like garbage. Owners claim they can't make any profit."

Profit. He hated that word. Greedy owners. They abuse the workers, then whine if their take is smaller than enormous. "Owners have a social responsibility to provide jobs. Just because they don't gain their greedy lust for gold doesn't mean they've any right to fire workers. They exploit labor as it is."

"Yeah, that 'exploit' bit. My members are putting up with it." Nero wiped his mouth with his sleeve and leaned forward. "Owners been cutting back on Union jobs. My members are scared. They been conned into breaking Union work regs, like, bus boys washing dishes, waiters clearing tables, cooks folding napkins, stuff like that. The owners have been getting away with fewer employees."

"How can they need fewer? The work's the same."

"They claim it ain't. They say, when they have to raise prices to cover the extra Union workers and full-time Union snitch, people don't eat out anymore, say it's too expensive, or they go once a month instead of once a week."

"Then why don't they advertise more? Lower their prices? I can't believe the stupidity. Greed, that's all it is. Exploiting labor by breaking Union work rules, that's criminal. Why haven't the workers reported them? Fine the owners. That'll make up your revenue drop. I'll support that, in court. Get your members to report violations."

"Members ain't cooperating. I borrowed Screwtape and Wormwood from your Persuasion Workers to, like, talk them up, re-align a few kneecaps. They say members would rather be exploited and have a job than have the business close and toss them on the Clyde pile."

Judge Marx slammed his glass on the table. Liquor bounced out the top. Nero was splattered with drops of whiskey. He didn't notice.

"*Stupid* people," exclaimed Judge Marx. "Haven't you educated them? Haven't they learned that solidarity prevents exploitation? You get three hours a week education time with the workers. Your Educators are crap." Judge Marx spun in his chair and looked out over the city. "Why aren't your Union reps reporting violations?"

Nero smiled. "That's why I'm here. The owners pay the rep for eight hours, but you take them away for headquarters work."

Judge Marx bristled. "That's vital work. They're Community

Organizers, uniting The People to fight against exploitation. A riot around Tevil Headquarters, barricade the governor in his mansion, and the baby-kissers do what The People need."

With a calming gesture, Nero said, "Okay, okay, I see it, yeah, like you say. But our squealers are in only three-four hours, while the businesses are open twelve or more. A lot of cheating happens when our Muscle ain't around."

Judge leaned back in his chair and considered the situation. Maybe Nero had a solution. He was looking smug enough. "So?"

"I want a new Union reg. Businesses have to have union reps on site whenever their doors are open. That will shut down the cheating, and the extra enforcers will boost my membership back to where it oughta." He looked craftily at the judge. "That's lots more dues coming in." Leaning back in the comfortable chair, he grinned. "You, as President of the Association of Honorable Organized Labor Societies, you'll get your cut."

Reasonable, thought Judge Marx. *It was only right he be compensated appropriately for his efforts as the Champion of Social Justice.*

Nero leaned forward. "Only, we can't have those extra reps spending three hours at the store and getting paid for eight. Owners won't go for that."

Judge Marx smiled amiability. "I think we can accommodate the request. Only, the inspectors will be my representatives, from the Association of Honorable Organized Labor Societies, not your Federated Consolidated Union of Peoples' Services. Your FCUPS will need the clout of my AHOLS."

"Hey! I want those dues! I got expenses! My idea! Can't cut me out!"

Judge Marx rubbed his hands together. "I will compromise." *Compromise is the hallmark of a diplomat and statesman,* Marx complimented himself. "You can have half. One more FCUPS at eight hours a day, a new AHOLS at four. With your current enforcer, that's 16 hours of coverage. You don't have restaurants open for more than 16, do you?"

"*Three* mandatory employees? Owners ain't gonna like that."

"So? Remind them they're promoting Social Justice by hiring more people. If they would stop exploiting the masses Union enforcement wouldn't be necessary. The People wouldn't take this action if the owners weren't so greedy. Remind them a small demonstration would block their doors. Use that education time better. Make sure your members know they owe their jobs to Union Strong, not to owners. Got that?"

Nero, a sour look adorning his mug, nodded, and held up his fist. "Union Strong, Judge Baby," he mumbled.

38: Mike

Mike placed Ella's lunch in front of her. So deeply was she in conversation with LaMancha, she didn't notice. Mike picked up a fork and touched her hand with its handle. Ella glanced up, smiled thanks, took the fork, and attacked her Amond Chicken Protein Bowl while continuing to quiz LaMancha about … whatever.

Mike sighed.

He poured a glass of ice tea and placed it next to Ella's utensils, unnoticed. Napkins were arranged by Ella's plate, unobserved. He looked at her lovely face, so animated and happy in conversation with LaMancha. Yesterday she said he was nice, she had come by just to see him; today, Mike wasn't even part of Ella's universe.

She was probably just being nice when she said he was nice.

Go figure. Women. Incomprehensible.

Derr Burger Burner trudged back to his grill, feeling the misery of inferiority.

"Mike, may I check LaMancha's readouts?" asked Ella.

"Sure. LaMancha, open permissive on the office door."

"Thanks. Won't be a minute." She disappeared through the p-door.

The gangway slid open and an older man, slightly stooped, entered. He wore Client garb, had gray hair neatly combed, thin chest and shoulders, and a commanding air unusual among Clients. He saw Mike, and walked directly to the grill bar.

"Hi," said Mike. "Menu's on the clipscreen, scream when you decide."

"Actually," the man said, in a cultured voice with an odd, lilting accent, "I was hoping to speak with Mike. You are Mike, I suspect. You do have a vague resemblance to the cartoon labeled 'Mike' on the Lacrosse Shot internet page."

"I'm Mike." *What cartoon?*

"Excellent likeness. The portrait of your Lacrosse Shot Superintendent, LaMancha, is also fascinating."

Superintendent?

The gentleman continued. "I don't think I have ever seen a mustache so overwhelmingly large. And his companions!"

"I'm not tracking."

"The picture of the 'The Three Amigos.' LaMancha, armored up like a medieval knight, Sigmund Freud, and that Duck fellow. Donald." The man folded his arms. "Although, I suspect Doctor Freud was not an Amigo, but making a house call in response to some rather noticeable symptoms displayed by Derr LaMancha and Derr Duck." He smiled. "I never knew Sigmund had grown a handlebar. I didn't know ducks *could* grow mustaches. A fascinating discovery."

Mike closed his eyes and grimaced. A month ago: *'Don't worry,'* LaMancha said, *'I'll take care of our web site. Our public image is important.'* Mike felt like banging his head against a countertop.

"I'll have to check that," Mike said. "Probably a glitch. I haven't done quality control on the site."

"I am sure you will be—entertained? Astounded? I was." The man glanced at the board. "Might I … the Number One Breakfast?"

"How'd you like them? Hash browns or fries? Juice, coffee, mickee, tea?

"Over-easy. Hash browns. Water, with a bit of ice—and a bit of conversation?"

"Plenty of that, no charge. For the rest, show your card to the camera for billing."

The man shifted on his stool and reached into a pocket. "I'd rather not use a card. Will this do?" He tossed a coin on the bar top.

The coin gyrated on the smooth surface, rolled in a circle, and went still.

A platinum Goddard. 500 standards.

Mike looked at the coin, then the man, uncomfortable where this encounter was going. "I don't trade much in high denominations. To break it, I'll have to go to the safe in the back"—where he could also check to see if it was counterfeit.

The man smiled. "Keep the balance, on account. I'm hoping we can do more business in the future." He held out his hand. "I'm Aaron."

Mike paused for only a fraction; he discarded the idea the coin might be counterfeit. He had no reason to ignore a hand offered in good faith by someone who trusted *him* with 500 standards, and might become a steady customer. With means.

They shook. The Goddard went into the cash drawer. "LaMancha, please credit 500 standards to the account of," he looked at the man, "Aaron."

Mike started cooking two over-easy and the hash browns. He grabbed a glass, added ice, filled it with water, included a lemon slice, and placed it in front of Aaron.

Aaron gestured to the onagers. "I've heard of your special table service. Quite clever. You have no staff? You do cleanup by yourself? That must be challenging."

Was this some kind of Fed entrapment? Aaron was in Client clothes, but neat and well kept. He spoke clearly, without Client argot, and with authority, as if he was not ashamed of what he was. Of course, anyone with Goddards to flash could certainly be proud, if it was honestly earned. Would a Fed shill draw attention to himself with a Goddard?

Mike decided, impulsively, to take him at face value. "Yeah," Mike said. "Not optimal. I want help, but the hiring laws make it impossible." He turned back to the grill.

Number One Breakfast came out nicely, two over-easy fried in Italian ghee and sprinkled with chopped chives, freshly-ground black pepper and shredded cheddar, with golden hash browns. He put some of his special Cornelia Sauce in a small cup on the edge of the plate, a few thick slices of cold beefsteak tomato (full marks to Gardenbottie!), utensils rolled in a napkin, fresh-baked barley toast and orange marmalade, and placed all in front of Aaron.

"Stars and comets, this looks delightful." Aaron unrolled the napkin with enthusiasm. "Fresh real tomato!" He cut a piece and took a bite. "Excellent, excellent." He took another bite, chewed with evident pleasure, and swallowed. "So, what do you think about those hiring laws?"

Mike scratched his ear. "They're counterproductive. They keep businesses from starting, which keeps Clients unemployed, which requires money from the government to feed the Clients, so the government has to raise taxes, which takes more money away from businesses, which causes businesses to fold, dumping more people into the Client population. It's a death spiral."

"Unions?"

"The Mafia would be proud to call them kindred spirits.'"

Aaron picked up the salt shaker and sprinkled some on his potatoes. "There are many who feel similarly about our justice system and our government. Is there a solution?" He took a bite of egg.

"Haven't thought on it. Above my pay grade."

Aaron shook his head. "Respectfully, that is part of the problem. Too many good people feel it is above their pay grade." He speared a chunk of hash brown, dipped it in the Cornelia sauce, tasted, and nodded. "Good."

"Thanks. Food I do good; nothing I can do about government."

"I understand you *are* doing something." Aaron put down his fork. "The meetings of the Association of Independent Ship Owners and Operators. You are addressing important issues."

"Just trying to get together behind a message to Fed Central," said Mike. He shrugged. "AISOO needed a place to meet. I've a big room."

"You have been elected to the chairmanship. Twice."

Was there a spy in the meetings? He would have to warn Bookie.

"Just a civility. My place, so I'm stuck being chairman. I'm a starship captain and member by courtesy only."

"You are held in high esteem among the independent owners and operators, and among all Vakkers."

Mike shrugged. Why was this fellow trying to grease him? "The guys 'n' dolls are just being good to a grounded shipmate." He took a step back. "Hey, apologies, I'm chattering. I'll let you get on with your breakfast before it gets cold."

"Do you realize the people of Misplaced-4 have no representation in government?" said Aaron, before Mike could get away. "No one in government is elected. None are accountable to the people."

Mike thought for a moment. "The Holder runs Tevil, and the Feds and Unions run the rest."

"Is that just?"

Mike shrugged. "Been that way since The Shift. Emergency decisions couldn't be made by elections. Centralized control by experts got us through the crisis."

"The Shift is generations behind us. We should now have elected government. Misplaced-4 should not be ruled by a Corporate Holder and appointed Federated Governor. An elected local government could get rid of laws and regulations designed to benefit only Tevil and the Union leadership at the expense of our Citizens and the Clients. All our people must be allowed to prosper, not just corpbees and govvies."

Mike smiled at the altruism. Naïve. "Good luck."

"We could use your help."

"We?"

Aaron nodded. "The Clients are organizing for better living conditions, jobs, the elimination of forced labor. Civilian small-business owners are forming an Adam Smith League. With your help, we also want to join with the AISOO. We have many problems in common."

Mike nodded. There were big issues to be addressed. It was kind of heady to think he might be involved in making healthy changes.

No. It sounded more like putting your head in a noose.

"Hey, I'm just a grill monkey. To change the world, you need somebody smart, like, like—"

The office door slid open, and Ella walked in.

"—like her." Mike pointed towards Ella.

Ella saw Aaron and lit up like fireworks. She threw her arms up. "Aaron! How wonderful!"

Aaron smiled broadly, got up, and gave Ella a gigantic hug, lifting her off the deck. "Ella! What a delightful surprise."

Mike felt a twinge of jealousy. Huge twinge, gut-wrenching twinge, a full-body spasm of envy.

Ella turned to Mike. "Have you been introduced? This is Citizen Professor Aaron Mises. We taught at TCU's Main Campus. He and I used to watch each other's back at faculty meetings."

"He threw out a name," said Mike, "I didn't catch the 'professor' part." He looked at Aaron. "You taught cybernetics with Citizen Professor Braun?"

"Not quite," responded Aaron. "Free Market Economics. Government ethics."

Maybe, thought Mike, seeing Ella's shining smile, remembering the hug, maybe getting involved in politics might not be such a bad idea.

39: Mike

"We have a VelociComm from Crunch," said LaMancha. "Should I play it for you now?"

0900. Pre-opening cleanliness verification inspection. Gardenbottie had been assigned a portion of the nightly cleanup. The bot stood next to his tables, at attention.

Mike stopped searching the underside of Table 9 for chewing gum. "*We* got a VelociComm?"

"It was addressed to both of us. *We* have already processed *Our* information. That is, of course, the royal 'We.'"

"Salaam, Your Galactic Over-Everything-Lord. Bar screen."

The bar station screen flashed to black, showed the VelociComms logo, then displayed the head-and-shoulders of a smiling Crunch.

"Hey Mike, hope you're kickin' 'n' screamin' as usual, hey LaMancha, hope you're, well, screamin'. I thought I'd shoot you some feedback on our shipmate Moros. We made Oz second port of call, where some little birdie told the Captain our FNQ had an outstanding appointment with Oz law enforcement. Charlie Oscar had his cubic searched. We found a bunch of white powder in little baggies. Ran the shit through the AutoDoc. Guess what? Flipper, industrial strength. One of his customers, only by the grace of the good Lord we rescued the kid before the crap killed him. LaMancha, you chump, that dimsy dust was, like, think of it as a rogue meteor that whizzed by and missed your tank by three microns. Anyhoo, Shitbrain is in custody. Oz has him on previous convictions, a gift box under the Christmas tree for a dirty dozen at hard labor and no dessert on Sundays. The trial for distributing on *Extra* and attempted manslaughter of the kid will be tomorrow. We're told to expect a verdict before we depart. Oz believes in immediate justice, bless them. Their head govvie shyster says 99 percent Moros gets the needle. *I* think they ought to feed him what he was selling until smoke comes out his ears. Thank goodness Oz don't believe in Shitbrains continuing to pollute the gene pool.

Okay, coming to the end of my 100 seconds. Good on you for the heads-up, you saved some lives. All the best. LaMancha, stans in transmittal. Both of ya, keep your O$_2$ green."

The VelociComms logo flashed on the screen, electric bolts jumping between satellites.

"LaMancha. What did he mean, 'stans in transmittal'?"

40: Tarak

Tarak crouched low and peered through the branches of a spikey tree. An hour earlier a shuttle had landed and disgorged the usual twenty-five. They milled about, hooting and waving their arms. They struck poses. Some kind of sign language? Ceremonial postures?

They lined up and headed dead-on for his hill, in their usual combat formation.

At the base of Tarak's hill, they stopped.

If they climbed, he would fight them on the slopes. He had several positions prepared, including boobytraps and snares. In and out, kill one, retreat, next position, lead 'em over the pits, retreat, avoid being surrounded. He was ready.

The aliens' formation began to sidle to their right.

Tarak moved along the ridgetop as they moved around the circumference. They halted at the bottom of a steep scree slope. It was V-shaped, deeper in the center, with rubble on the sloped sides. There was no concealment for any flank attacks or pits. That must be why they chose this point to start their attack.

They started to climb, in formation, stretched across the slopes. The aliens on the edges of the line began to slip, fighting for traction, three steps up, slide two back. Eventually, they gravitated into the central channel, where the footing was firm. Halfway up, all were compressed along the center.

With a hard tug, Tarak pulled away the spikey tree log restraining his best boulder. He put his shoulder to it and pushed. Gravel at its base went first, then the rock rolled over the edge. Quickly Tarak moved to his other rocks, using his legs to push. He could hear crashing as the avalanche grew.

He looked over the edge. Dammit, his best boulder had veered to the side. Yes! It bounced back to the center, picking up tremendous speed.

It hit the lead alien with a satisfying crunch.

The Trashcans were obscured as stones and rubble engulfed them.

41: Marshall

"Seats!" called the Chief Master-at-Arms. He distributed a look of faint disgust towards the ill-disciplined, newly-sworn-in noisemakers, Command Candidates now officially subject to his orders. "Silence!" The auditorium rapidly was still.

From the stage, Captain Marshall surveyed his new class of Candidates. Eighty of the royals had accepted the final oath and were now wearing blue and sitting in front. All 263 Artisans wearing graphite accepted. There were no assigned seats, but still they clustered in the two groups. It was disheartening, the self-imposed segregation, the blues in front, graphite in back, no mixing, no contact, no socializing.

Murmurs were silenced by a glare from the CMAA.

Stepping to the side of the podium, Marshall said, "Having taken the oath, you are now members of the Federated Space Forces. You will notice two uniforms. Those in graphite are members of the Engineering and Support Track and will be trained as Artisan Officers. They are addressed as 'Artisan Candidate,' or, sometimes, informally, 'ArtCan.' After general education, Artisan Candidates will go to technical specialization training." He looked to the Artisans. "Specialties are Power and Propulsion, Environmental, Weapons, Sensors, Navigation and Piloting, Construction and Repair, Supply, and other fields.

"Unscrub l'artisans!" said a voice from the front.

"You!" pounced the CMAA, pointing to a Blue as if he had an assegai in his hand. "*Sawubona*, I see you, Command Candidate Three Johnson. Report to me after Commandant dismisses."

Marshall suppressed a smile. The CMAA could be quite intimidating.

He continued. "Those in blue are in the Command track, and are addressed as 'Command Candidate,' or 'ComCan.' ComCans will learn the rudiments of onboard systems during your first term, in concert with the Artisans. After that, ComCans will delve into topics including leadership, organization theory and organizational behavior, decision-making, cognitive processes and biases, the political systems in the Federation, diplomacy, management, government agencies, and budgeting."

The ComCans exchanged glances, with an edge of smugness. No matter how low their rank or class standing, all Command officers outranked Artisans.

Marshall clenched his jaw. That system was wrong.

Nominations to attend the Academy as a Command Candidate were allocated to the 35, which meant they were political favors dispensed to curry influence. The 35 Families believed there were five acceptable professions, the Holy Five: Corporate management, Army or Space Navy service, law, and government. The Army and Navy were the least prestigious. The Federated Space Forces Academy was a dump for royal ne'er-do-wells, a place to stash spare sons.

An entrance examination was not required for Command Candidates, so their educational preparation varied from excellent to pathetic. Their instruction in engineering and technical subjects at the Academy was rudimentary, and required passing grades so low that Command Candidates could become commissioned officers with only a superficial knowledge of the perils of space.

The Artisans' appointments came through competitive examination and comprehensive screening interviews with active-duty Artisan Officers. Their school achievements and deportment earned them their appointments. But, in dealing with the royals, they had a burden of social and biological inferiority. Compared to the gene-audited royals, Artisans were smaller, shorter, weaker, and usually less handsome. Society had beaten into their heads: royals command, Artisans serve.

Marshall was determined to enact reforms. His motivation was simple: the FSF couldn't beat an over-excited flock of grandmothers armed with knitting needles. If the Force encountered humans more vicious than kittens, or even (God help us) aliens, humanity in the Seventeen Systems was doomed. The memory of his wife and daughter, killed in space by the ignorance and cowardice of two ComCans, suggested that reform had to begin at the Academy. Thus, he didn't protest when the Detailer exiled him to a career-ending assignment at the Academy.

He shook those thoughts away. Now, he had Candidates to mold.

"After your first term, you'll intern aboard one of three ship classes. Class Three are Planetary Guard ships. They are small ships, with crews less than thirty."

There were a few whispered exchanges, silenced by a glare from Chief Imani.

"Class Two are Armed Cargo Transports, often just called ACT. These ships are privately owned. The government pays for these ships to be armed and available for Federated service."

That was another part of the system that must be eliminated. The Corporations and Families owned the ships, and through their control of the Federated government voted themselves ridiculously high payments. Corporate welfare for the 35 'n 50.

"Class One consists of FSF ships purpose-built as warships. They are fully armed, have gravity rings, and are punch capable. There are seven Class Ones."

Seven. Less than one for every two populated systems. The 35 'n 50 controlled over 70 ACTs, loyal to their home systems and families. If a conflict between the royals turned violent, the combined FSF Class One fleet would have a hard time in a confrontation with any alliance of Families or Corporations.

"In space, you will work with our enlisted people, called 'flight crew' or 'flight artisans.' Some comedians like to contract that into 'fart-isans.' Starting immediately, anyone using that term will come to me on charges. I have flight artisans working at the Academy. You," he said, pointing a finger, mostly at the ComCans, and catching the eye of the author of the earlier 'fartisan' outburst, "will treat them with respect."

He paused to let that concept sink in.

"Instructional reading is on your clipscreens, top directory, folder 'orientation.' You will start that material while you are in line for your kit and equipment issue. Yes, hurry-up-and-wait is official policy." He scanned the candidates. "Questions?"

One eager-looking Blue raised a hand. Chief Imani pointed. "Stand. State your name. Ask your question."

The youngster rose. He was handsome and well-formed, a typical gene-audited royal. Marshall glanced down at the screen mounted on the podium. Campus Organic identified the candidate as Wang, Da, from one of the top tiers of the 35 Families, a third son, Photovoltaics LLC. *Very* powerful.

Wang straightened into a semblance of attention. "Command Candidate Wang. We were told our appointment was 'provisional.' What does that mean?"

"Some of you will not physiologically or psychologically adapt to zero gravity and space flight. You will be scheduled for an orientation shuttle flight to test your tolerance. Those who cannot handle zero-G will be released."

Another command candidate stood. Chief Imani pointed.

"Command Candidate Silva. Derr, what is a gravity ring?"

There were a few titters, quickly suppressed.

Stars and comets, how could you apply to the Academy and not first learn how spaceships were constructed? He'd have to deal with this level of ignorance among many of the ComCans. He must encourage curiosity and hope it becomes contagious.

"Excellent question. There are adverse health effects associated with extended periods of weightlessness. To counter this, and to make spaceflight more comfortable and productive, ships can have a habitat ring that spins, so that centrifugal force acts as artificial gravity. Most punchplane cargo ships and ACTs are so equipped because they make most of their transit without constant acceleration; essentially, they drift from point to point under zero-G conditions. Passenger liners serving the higher end of the market continually boost throughout their transit, making their own acceleration, their own gravity. Their passengers are subject to zero-G only while docking and during punchplane transitions."

Silva sat. The blue next to him punched him lightly in the arm as if congratulating him on a high achievement. Silva grinned.

"Anyone else?"

"Sir." A graphite in the back stood. "Sir. Artisan Candidate Shan. May Artisans command ships?"

Marshall made a fist behind the podium. This was another needed reform. "Not at this time. The top Artisan rank is lieutenant commander. At the rank of lieutenant commander and below, you address an officer as, for example, Command Lieutenant, or Artisan Lieutenant. Since only Command officers occupy the ranks of commander and captain, the 'Command' identifier may be dropped. Either 'captain' or 'command captain' is acceptable."

"Sir. Command Candidate Murphy." The young man gestured, sweeping his hand over the candidates. "No girls in the Academy?" The candidates laughed.

Marshall smiled. A predictable question. "The radiation levels in the sectors surrounding the Seventeen Systems are high. Neutrons and gamma radiation have an adverse effect on the female reproductive system. DNA can be damaged. Federated regulations place severe restrictions on their exposure. These restrictions were first applied to the engineering departments of nuclear submarines in the water navies. Immediately after The Shift, the count of females of childbearing age was half the number of males," he said with a nod, "thus, women are more valuable. Men are expendable. Women are not." Some of the Candidates laughed at this novel concept. "Time-in-Space and Total Rads restrictions make training ladies for service on ships impractical. Ladies in FSF service are in ground billets, support assignments, and on space stations with appropriate shielding. There are even lady Marines."

Murphy appeared puzzled. "I've met Vakker girls."

Someone blew a razzberry. "*Im-possible!*" The crowd chuckled.

"Yeah, all right, I've *know* there's girl Vakkers. Why are they allowed?"

"Vakker ships are shielded." Less shielding mass on Federated ships means less fuel required to accelerate, another of the Federation's shortsighted economies at the expense of personnel.

He surveyed the group, making eye contact, especially with those in graphite. To the Artisans, he wanted to communicate that he did not see them as inferior.

Some of the blues began to squirm impatiently.

"Anyone else?"

Marshall smiled. It seemed he had saturated their capacity to learn for this hour.

42: Mike

Saturday at the Lacrosse Shot was finishing on a good note. The food was perfect, the customers happy, no major cleanup required, and LaMancha behaved. Mostly.

Mike chivvied the last happy Vakkers out the door at midnight.

They had eaten too much food, drunk just a glass or two, and were cheerful-boisterous without being rowdy. He threw the locking bolt, then started his end-of-day chores. With the dishwasher loaded, he grabbed a towel and commenced giving the bar a scrub.

"Alert! Incoming." LaMancha sounded especially cheerful. "Professor Ella and Aaron have entered the gangway. Ella looks particularly fetching tonight, in a little blue number showing her figure most delightfully; certainly, she has dressed with particular care to attract your romantic aspirations. Why else would she be coming to the Lacrosse Shot after hours? Shall we unlock the gangway p-door? She may want to throw herself into your arms and attest undying love as a prerequisite to having twins."

Trying hard to ignore him, Mike headed to the door. There was a knock. He slipped the bolt and enabled the p-door.

"Good evening, Mike. Rather, good morning," said Ella. "Your hours are insane. You open at 1100 and close at 2400?"

Mike shrugged. "LaMancha's up 24. I don't even pay him overtime."

"You don't even pay me regular time. We need to talk."

"Hush. We have guests, and I need to clean. Is Gardenbottie hiding again?"

Ella looked over the room. "I'll help." She started clearing a table.

Mike held out a hand. "Whoa. Decelerate. Humans must be Union Strong to clean. I can get fined."

Ella looked around. "No Muscle here. Unless LaMancha rats, I'm bussing."

"Most respected Ella, be reassured, I already have sufficient material to blackmail the owner of this establishment. As a matter of principle, whenever anyone considers a long-term relationship that might lead to twins, they should have something with which to threaten their partner. May I forward to you some dirt on Mike?"

Spreading her arms, Ella smiled broadly. "No getting around it, I'm bussing. I even know about inspecting the salt shaker holes."

Mike shook his head and crossed his arms. "I will not have a Ph.D. cleaning tables."

Ella stopped. "That statement has several possible interpretations. Do you think a Ph.D. couldn't do a good job? Or, do you think the work is demeaning for a Ph.D.? Or, a Ph.D. is too lofty?

Hmmm," she said, putting a finger to her chin.

"Come on Professor, you know—"

"I do know," she said, with a glint of fire in her eyes, "I bussed tables at TCU Main for two years getting my bachelor's. This is nostalgia time. I want you to talk to Aaron. He has a proposal."

Mike shrugged. Opposing Ella was like trying to climb out of a gravity well wearing a lead jacket. He turned to Aaron. "Was she always like this?"

"She is much more even-tempered now."

Ella made a scrunchy-face at them, took the towel from Mike and started wiping.

Mike gestured to a table. "A proposal?"

Aaron nodded. "May I establish some groundwork first?"

Mike shrugged. "Professor, you have the floor."

"Wrong," said Ella, from five tables away. "I have the floor. Where do you keep the mops?"

The gangway p-door slid open and Sherri Brightly walked in.

"House rules," LaMancha asserted, "last one gets the mop and bucket."

"What?" asked Sherri. "I do something wrong?"

"Sherri, this is LaMancha, speaking truth to power. Have you done something wrong? We begin. Public records indicate at age six weeks you were convicted of aggravated theft when you shanghaied the 'My Little Bunny' plush toy from your cell mate, no, make that your crib mate, to wit, your sibling. You followed with a life of crimes against sanitation. Records are incomplete, but there are reports about filling a diaper with multiple hot sloppies, *gross* violations of air pollution guidelines—"

"LaMancha, Executioner. Quash it," said Mike.

"Sherri, thanks for volunteering," Ella said. "Mike's hiding the mop and bucket."

Mike pointed. "They're in the utility closet next to LaMancha's hidey-hole. Make sure you wear the apron and gloves."

Sherri headed for the office. "One basis of creativity is integrating a wide range of disparate experiences," she mused. She stopped and surveyed the deck. "I have programmed cleaning bots, but I myself have never mopped a floor. This will be good for me." She glanced at Ella. "A chapter in my dissertation?"

"Yeeee—no." Ella started on another table.

"Sherri," said a cheerful Richard Nixon voice, "Chapter Nine, thumbs up!" The bar screen showed Nixon dressed as a Roman emperor in a toga and necktie, a toothy grin, and a prominent thumbs up. "All doctoral dissertations must provide at least one bizarre chapter inviting the faculty committee to hyperventilate."

Sherri grimaced, and put a hand over her eyes. "Richard Nixon? You're doing Richard Nixon as a Roman Emperor? In a red necktie?"

Nixon disappeared from the screen. "You won't have Nixon to kick around anymore, because, Toots, that was his last appearance."

Aaron leaned back in his chair and raised his eyebrows. "Is it always like this?"

"It's becoming much more even-tempered," said Mike. He rubbed his face with both hands. "So, groundwork?"

Leaning forward, Aaron placed his elbows on the table. "How do you feel about Clients?"

Mike shrugged. "Wouldn't want to be one."

"Why not?"

"Are you kidding?"

"No. I would like your views regarding those on government subsistence."

Mike paused and collected his thoughts. "They're trapped. No escape."

"No escape? Why?"

"When I started this place," said Mike, leaning back, "I wanted to hire some Client kids, train them as cooks. The required minimum wage, benefits, and the restrictions placed by the Unions made it impossible."

"Keep that thought," said Aaron. "Do you know the origins of the Client class?"

"Nope. I'm from off-planet."

"It goes back to the beginning of The Colonization. After the discovery of folded space and PunchPoints, there was a scramble to claim the planets. Colonization fell into three categories: by governments, by Corporations, and by ethnic or religious or special interest groups. Misplaced-4 was a Corporate colonization. Tevil was given authority to make the rules. But for every Corporate job, there are many secondary jobs, shops, retail and groceries and restaurants and barbers and entertainers and the like. A Citizen class developed, immigrants that were not employees of the Corporation. Citizens soon outnumbered Corporates by five to one."

Mike nodded. "I follow."

LaMancha's voice drifted in faintly from the table clipscreen by Sherri in the far corner. "Then, age nine, you were apprehended by Citizen Educator Sizemore for launching unguided paper aerial vehicles in class. Inexplicably, no formal charges were filed. It escapes me how you consummated your primary education with such a stained record—"

Mike brought his concentration back to Aaron.

"Then, The Shift," said Aaron. "Folded space moves. The PunchPoint to OldEarth disappears, along with those of most of the other Systems. Collapse." He fluttered his hands. "Misplaced-4 loses 85 percent of the planet's exports, 95 percent of their imports. Tevil reduces its workforce. Citizens lose their jobs. What do you do with people who have no jobs, on a planet with no atmosphere? You can't just shove them out an airlock. They became 'Clients,' fed and clothed and housed and ventilated by Tevil and the government, paid for by taxing Citizens, causing more business failures, and more jobs are lost. Eventually, there is an entrenched Client class."

Mike rubbed the back of his neck. "Roger, copy all. I'll take on a few Clients after you delete a million gigabytes of incomprehensible regs."

"Do you know where regulations come from?"

"Fed Central?"

"Most are made by Tevil. They are designed to protect Tevil's interests, their enterprises, and their profits. The rest come from Federated Central, and are enforced uniformly on all the planets under the guise of 'fairness,' whether you have an atmosphere or not, Corporation or government or religious planet, high or low gravity, population one million or one thousand."

Mike snorted. "Good government. There's an oxymoron. First demonstrated when Pharaoh and Moses went nose-to-nose."

Aaron shook his head. "Now, Mike, cynicism is not allowed in your happy establishment." He folded his hands. "Government is essential. It develops and enforces the rule of law. But a very wise man said, 'what governs best governs least.' The solution is less Fed

Central, less Tevil, and more freedom. Unleash creativity, and our economy will explode with growth."

Mike chuckled. "So, all you want to do is remake the galaxy's government?"

"Not the galaxy. Just one planet." Aaron smiled, like a little boy who knows where the candy is hidden. "For now."

Mike was getting a little impatient with the discussion. "That's a grand brave goal. Have you a plan to get there? A resistance movement? I should stop paying taxes? That'll be like a drop of water hitting the sun."

"Stop paying and you'd be arrested. Government uses physical force to get what it wants."

"And fines. And Union punks sent by crooked judges."

"We cannot change everything, all at once." Aaron rubbed his eyes. "Past my bedtime." He smiled. "Our Clients are not all ready to assume responsibility for their own survival. They do not have the moral foundation. Self-government requires a moral citizenry. Clients know nothing but handouts. Some will not welcome a world where they must earn their sustenance." Aaron pressed his temples. "The process must be gradual. We first need a planetary legislative body to make laws suitable to our situation. Local representative government."

Mike shrugged. "Corporation represents the corpbees, Feds represent the govvies. That's about as representative as you're going to get. Royals rule. That's the way it is, 'bout everywhere."

"It is wrong, 'bout everywhere," Aaron replied. "The Holder and the Governor first and foremost take care of their own interests. They are a minority ruling the majority." Aaron tapped on the table as if he was calling his students to order. "There are twenty thousand Tevil employees and three thousand Federated government employees, against twelve thousand Citizens and fifty-five thousand clients."

Mike shook his head. "You want to start a democracy? Let the world be run by a bunch of Clients? They'd confiscate everything, redistribute, and when the food is gone, we all starve?" Mike scratched an ear. "I remember a story from OldEarth. Philosopher, guy named Socrates, wasn't too popular. His home-town democracy voted to execute him. I'm not sure I'd want to live where a bunch of Client gangs run the show, and they can vote people they don't like out an airlock without a skinsuit."

"Nor would I. We aspire to a republic. In a pure democracy, the majority can do anything, take anything, from anyone. Did you know that in OldEarth ancient Rome the word 'demokratia' came to mean 'chaotic mob rule'?" Aaron folded his hands together, as if he was seizing an incredibly important concept. "A republic is dedicated to the rule of law. Immutable laws must be established to prevent Clients from voting themselves beer and circuses. There must be absolute and irrevocable rights, to personal property, to speech, freedom of thought, and others."

Mike shifted in his chair. "The Clients are pretty apathetic. You going to do this all by your lonesome?"

"A man once said, 'I am only one, but I am one. I can't do everything, but I can do something. What I can do, that I ought to do. And what I ought to do, by the grace of God, I shall do.' LaMancha, if you are listening, remind me, who authored those words?"

Fat chance LaMancha wasn't listening. "Edward Everett Hale, a nineteenth-century American minister."

"That is the reason I left TCU Main to come here," said Aaron. "Misplaced-4 needs freedom and representative government. All Seventeen Systems need freedom from the 35 'n 50, but Misplaced most of all. I can do something. What I can do, I ought to do. What I ought to do, I shall do."

Ella came to the table and sat down. "Mission accomplished," she said with a smile.

"Sherri?" Mike glanced around the dining room.

"She's arguing with LaMancha about cleaning behind his tank. She wants to, he doesn't. She growled about itching powder, so he threatened to get on the school server and to write the first three chapters of her dissertation so she'd be jailed for pornography. She got out a tweaker and opened the door to his cabinet, he set the ventilation down to minus fiftyzillion Kelvin, and at that point I evacuated, because things were looking to become *really* ugly. They're still at it. Not sure who I'd bet on."

Kenny Roger's voice came from the speakers. "Humans, put your stans on the Organic! *Yahoo!*" He sang,

"You got to know when to hold 'em,

Never over-clean 'em,

know that the tankhead wins,

Sherri bites the dust …"

"LaMancha, quash it." The music faded.

Mike looked at Aaron. "Professor, local government might be what's needed. But I work fourteen a day, six out of seven. I've not much slack to start a government."

"It is not your time I hope for, but your permission."

Mike raised an eyebrow.

"Our leaders are a small group," said Aaron. "We are looking for a place to meet. We were hoping you'd volunteer the Lacrosse Shot, after hours."

Mike leaned back and looked to the overhead; his brow wrinkled.

"I must tell you," Aaron said, "all the risks. You heard of the Clientown blowouts?"

Mike sat upright. "LaMancha, check the news. Any recent blowouts?"

The high-pitched voice of an overexcited news reader came from the speakers. "Flash! Residential cantons suffer cave-ins in Clientown, atmosphere goes to vacuum! Thirty-three dead! *Click.* What? Why're you cutting me off? Whaddya mean, Corporate said we weren't to *Click.*"

Mike frowned.

Aaron raised a finger. "We lost fifteen leaders that day, all innocents, and twenty that Malqart, Tevil Corporation's Head of Security, would classify as 'collateral damage.' The blowout was intentional. A bomb."

That pissed Mike off. Still, scan first, then boost. "Why meet here?"

Aaron pointed to the steel overhead. "You're not likely to have a collapse. Your facility is large enough for meetings, has its own power supply off the corporate grid, independent O_2 off the Federated supply, and the Lacrosse Shot isn't bugged."

"How …?" asked Mike.

"We have a young lady with skills in that field," said Aaron. He shook his head. "She stopped by yesterday. Frankly, I'm puzzled. Tevil has every other public place under surveillance."

LaMancha chimed in. "Three attempts have been made to place listening devices in the Lacrosse Shot. Gardenbottie sweeps for bugs every night. It's fun. Hide and Seek. We relocate the bugs to Cargo Bay Three, between the tomatoes and carrots. I play hillbilly boogie and bluegrass for them. The vegetables appreciate music. It raises their sugar and flavonoid content."

"Why am I only hearing about this now?" said Mike.

"You are always so tired at night. I did not want to upset you. Your blood pressure is too high as it is, and you've been skipping your kidney medication. Besides, the Lacrosse Shot Head of Security said you were not to be bothered."

"Listen, knucklehead, don't try deflecting me with that 'Head of Security' bullroar. YOU are Head of Security," Mike fumed. "Knucklehead."

"Mike, Knucklehead. Sticks and stones will break—actually, now that I consider the details …"

Mike dialed his temper down. "Next time, leave the bug. You can override transmissions, right?"

With an English accent, LaMancha said, "Elementary, my dear Watson."

"Put a recording of a normal night's traffic into their pickup," said Mike. "Nothing incriminating. No identifiable voices."

"Can I adjust it, be creative? Sherri wants me to be creative."

"Just let me know when anything gets placed. Green?"

"Creative, approved. Green."

"There, you see?" said Mike to Aaron. He glanced over at Ella. "You want to hold a meeting, just let me know."

43: Mike

There was a throng of Vakkers crammed into the Lacrosse Shot's dining room, a hundred and thirty into a space normally maxed out at sixty. Most were in skinsuits covered by a robe or potato-sack jerkin, in the glorious florescent colors Vakkers favored to contrast with the Deep Dark. Men had closely-trimmed or shaved heads and faces, while the women had short haircuts pulled back into a pony-tail or a pageboy cut (nothing was worse than errant hair in your eyes inside a skinsuit helmet). There was a steady hum of conversation. Late arrivals pressed through the entrance.

Ventilation fans shifted to high. Soon the room gloried in LaMancha's favorite aerosol sandalwood—he claimed it lowered attendee's blood pressure by eight percent.

Mike was behind the bar next to the control panel. When the countdown clock displayed "00" he hammered with a pewter ale glass and dimmed the lights up and down. He pressed the 'All Tables' icon on the table clipscreen comms control.

"All hands all decks all stations, SILENCE-ON-THE-NET!"

The room quickly fell mute. There was a rustle as people settled into chairs or sat on steps.

"Temporary House Rules: This is a formal meeting of the Association of Independent Ship Owners and Operators. No drinks will be shot." The crowd started an exaggerated groan, immediately quelled by a regulating look from Mike. "Cancel the side conversations. Attention to the speakers. Stand up to be recognized before you speak, except for motions and to second motions. Violators get pitched, at the discretion of the Chairman. Modified Robert's Rules of Order, seventy-second edition. Nominations are now open for Chairman."

A voice floated out. "I nominate free beer. Holder Roddy seconds my motion and calls the vote." The crowd chuckled.

"Soak, that you?" Mike scowled. He craned his head back and forth, then locked on to the chubby figure in a stained skinsuit and disastrous haircut, trying to make himself small behind a broad-shouldered Vakker. "I see you, Soak, you little squint. Don't you hide behind Sampson. You heard the rule. Darth, Mothra. Pitch him."

A Vakker near the front, dressed in an elegant mauve flowing robe ornamented by a constellation of stars, stood. With a deeply resonate, cultured voice and a graceful wave of a hand, he raised a forefinger. "Point of order. *Only* the Chairman can order a little squint pitched. We have *yet to elect* our Chairman."

Mike crossed his arms. "Churchill's point is well taken. Soak, siddown. The floor is open for nominations for Chairman."

A young lady with flyaway hair and a firm jawline, wearing a man's jerkin and ladies' five-inch spike-heeled knee boots, bounced up to stand on a table. "*Point* of *order!* We should be electing a chair*person!*"

"LaMancha, quotation, dictionary, definition of 'man,' first entry. Broadcast, all."

LaMancha's voice came out of the table speakers with a posh English accent. "Greetings, Distinguished Callsigns. New Oxford Dictionary, 242nd edition. Quote. Man: A member of the species *Homo Sapiens* or all the members of this species collectively, without regard to sex. End Quote."

Mike knocked loudly on the bar top with his mug. "We will be electing a chair*man,* a member of the species without regard to sex. Steinem, get your foot assassins off my tabletop and clean it before you leave. Nominations are now open."

A male voice called, "I nominate Mister Steinem, without regard to sex."

There was a burst of laughter.

Steinem glared at everyone in particular. "*Dee* Steinem declines. Too many chauvinist unenlightened dinosaurs in the room."

A voice hollered, "Too late, cutie, I second."

"I nominate LaMancha." Another burst of laughter.

"I second!" howled Soak. He raised his chin and looked down his nose at Mike.

"I nominate Mike." "Second." "Move to close nominations." "Second." "It has been moved and seconded to close nominations, all in favor of closing nominations." "AYE." "All opposed." A resonate sneeze bounced off the bulkheads. Chuckles.

Mike rapped the ale mug on the bar. "Nominations are closed. We vote by acclamation, unless a tie is perceived, then we'll go to a show of hands. All those in favor of Miss Steinem, that is, *Dee* Steinem, say 'Aye.'"

Steinem's expression distributed daggers over the group. Grins reflected the daggers back. The silence of the lambs celebrated the lack of votes.

"All those in favor of Derr LaMancha, say 'Aye.'"

"AYE," came out of the table speakers at max volume. Soak squirmed and made muffled noises around Sampson's massive hand, planted firmly over his mouth.

"All those in favor of Mike, say 'Aye'."

The "AYE" was a roar.

"Mike is elected Chairman. I appreciate your confidence. I call this meeting of the Association of Independent Ship Owners and

Operators to order. Sampson. Pitch'm.'"

With a squeal, Soak was launched in a graceful arc across the room high above heads, his arms and legs flailing.

"Sweet trajectory," a voice observed.

The p-door opened with a quick swoosh. Soak flew through without touching an edge. The door hissed shut. There was a meaty thud outside, and a grunt.

"Nuthin' but hatch!" There was a smattering of applause. Sampson bowed.

"The Chair thanks Sampson. Definitely a '10,' even from the Tevil judge."

The p-door swooshed open. Soak marched in, surveying the crowd with a defiant glare, one hand holding an ear.

Mike sighed. He rubbed his left temple. "Soak, I distinctly remember ordering you pitched from this meeting."

Soak stood tall, like a ping pong ball on two legs trying to intimidate a beach ball. "I object! The Chair ruled violators get pitched. Okay, I got pitched. But nuthin' sez I can't come back." His chin jutted; he radiated determination. He added, meekly, "I'll be good. Promise."

Mike looked directly into Soak's eyes. "Soak's objection is well taken. The Chair modifies the temporary rule: in the future, all those who get pitched stay pitched. Soak, you're on probation. Sit."

Soak grinned triumphantly, and edged through the crowd to reclaim his seat next to Sampson. Sampson gave him a small smile and a nudge in the ribs. A few laughs sounded over a murmur of approval. You don't survive in space without respecting rules, but Vakkers also recognized the difference between 'fair' and 'arbitrary.'

Mike rapped on the bar. "Owners and Operators, this meeting was requested by Citizen Captain Covington. Captain Covington, please join me behind the bar."

Diana stood up from a table near the front. The throng edged apart, opening a path. She jumped, spun in the air, and slid to a halt sitting on top of the bar.

"Or on it," murmured Mike.

Mike turned to the group. "*Prosperity* was jacked. Tarak's missing." A sympathetic rumble filled the room. "There's an unknown number of uninsured ships missing, and five insured ships jacked, three lost with full crews, and two where the crews were released by the jack-asses. Tevil Insurance is stiffing the claims."

Churchill rose. Mike nodded to him. "The Chair recognizes Churchill."

"You will *recall,* that this Association did, upon Wednesday last, address the *Depredations* of Tevil Insurance Solutions."

Mike rubbed his chin. "We did."

"Despite the collective *wisdom* of this Association, we were *unable* to develop any stratagem to avoid, circumvent, bypass, obviate, overcome, or otherwise dodge the *oppression* of that most *loathsome* and *tyrannical* organization."

The table speakers emitted a feedback squeal. "Mike, I mean Derr Chairman, I have the minutes of that meeting—"

"Organics will be unseen and unheard at Association meetings. You're not a member."

LaMancha's tone bristled. "I was nominated! Nominated Chairman! A few more votes and *I could be running this show*!"

There were chuckles from the crowd.

"We will never hear the end of that. LaMancha, quash it."

A disruptive warbling 60-cycle hum came from all the table speakers. People winced and plugged their ears.

Mike closed his eyes. "Jinnean," he said, pitching his voice above the noise, to a lady standing by the office p-door, "through there, top left drawer in the desk, you'll find a tweaker and a bottle labeled 'Itching Powder.' Could you—"

The hum ceased.

Churchill popped up and slowly floated halfway to the ceiling. "Honorable Chairman, if I may continue…?"

Mike gave a wave of assent.

Churchill reached apogee and began his descent. He turned to the crowd, gesturing expansively. "Tevil Corporation *owns* the Dome, *owns* the receiving docks through which our merchant traders' cargo must pass, *owns* the refineries through which our prospectors must process our minerals, and *scalps* a massive percentage from everything we do to earn our O_2. Tevil and the other Corporations *manipulate* the government, like a *waldo,* restricting competition, requiring we *report* each and every transaction, even conversations, for *taxation*. They *spy* on every internet packet, an internet which, I shall note, is *owned* and *corrupted* by Tevil Corporation and its slimy subsidiary, Tevil Computing. All these… *afflictions!* are something to which this august group has not been able to develop any countermeasure, *whatsoever*."

Diana waved a hand. "I have one."

Mike rapped on the bar top. "Citizen Captain Covington, out of order."

Churchill arched an eyebrow and spread his arms. "No, by all means, Honorable Chairman, let us *hear* what the little lady has to say, from her *vast* perspective of—what is it? —*two years* of failed enterprises? Hear how this cute little lassie burned her stake, *wandering* about in the Deep Dark?"

"Sexist swine!" shouted Steinem.

Mike pointed the ale glass at Steinem. "First and only warning," he growled. "Churchill, insults will not be tolerated. Warning. You still have the floor."

Churchill gave Mike a slight bow. "Our Honorable Chairman is both fair-minded and unbiased. I offer my appreciation. I now pass the baton to Citizen Captain Covington. I am *most* curious, to hear how her experience has prompted her to communicate with this Association. I yield the floor."

44: *Diana*

Diana smiled and nodded in Churchill's direction. "Thank you for that most gracious introduction," she said, without a hint of sarcasm.

She looked out to the crowd. *This has got to work.*

She was near flat broke. Tevil delayed her insurance claim. Their kind offer to cancel the premium payments for half the claim was a non-starter. The remaining half would not cover the loan on the spaceship. She defaulted on the bank loan and turned over the collateral, the *Prosperity*, in the form of the insurance policy, to the bank. Now the Bank of Hong Kong was the one suing Tevil Insurance. She wouldn't get a ha'pence from their equity in *Prosperity*, and her credit rating was down the volcano.

She needed money to look for Tarak. It was tearing her apart. The government hasn't recognized that pirates exist, so they wouldn't mount a full-scale investigation or a search for her husband. The trip with Wackey, Aether, Cashew and Ghost was aborted before they started the hunt. Diana was down to her last ten standards, with no prospects of a job while stranded on a planet with sixty percent unemployment. Feelings of frustration and despair alternated in her heart.

No, no longer despair. Determination. *I will make this work. I can use this Association to discover who I can trust, get some money, recover our rock, sell it, have the funds to launch a search. I will find my husband.*

"Churchill hit the issues," she said to the audience. "We need insurance, but Tevil holds the Federated monopoly. What they provide isn't worth a cubic millimeter of vak. That's the full mass 'n' volume of it."

The Vakkers stared with blank expressions, not receptive, probably thinking over their dinner plans, wondering why they attended this worthless meeting.

Tough audience, thought Diana. *Time for the big reveal.*

"Let me shift vector. What's an activity Tevil has found impossible to regulate? Impossible to tax?"

Blank expressions. Silence. Boredom. Well, it was only a rhetorical question.

"Gambling."

The audience stirred.

"Some Citizens tried a casino five years ago. The Union moved in, demanded their 'Solidarity Share,' and the casino went bankrupt. The point, though, is that Tevil's Grant of Monopoly has limits. They have no powers over gambling."

A Vakker in the middle of the room rose to his feet. "Will the speaker yield to a question?"

"I yield," Diana said.

"It is my sincere hope you are not here to pitch a gambling casino. Are you?"

Diana wiped her hand on her pants leg. Her hands were moist. Nerves. This made her angry. If she couldn't convince them, it was another win for Tevil, a loss for Tarak.

"No. I want to create an insurance casino," she said.

One of the Vakkers rose and headed for the gangway.

"Listen to me!" she snapped. The Vakker paused.

"What's insurance?" she barked. "You pay an insurance premium. That's like you bet you are going to have a disaster. No disaster, you lose the bet, the company keeps your premium. If something happens, you file a claim, and the company pays off, like you won your bet."

The Vakker sat down, a bemused expression on his face.

Diana continued, more confidently. "There's something called a mutual insurance company. People join together, they spread the risk, they cover each other. The policyholders are the owners. When you take out insurance you pay premiums held by an administrator. If nothing happens the company makes a profit, and in a mutual insurance company, profits are returned to the owners, the policy holders, after a reserve fund is accumulated. If there is a covered accident, the reserve funds cover the claim. The risk is spread to everyone, which is what insurance is supposed to do. That's how the first insurance companies operated when they were started by OldEarth Babylonian and Chinese traders. But we don't call it insurance. We start a gambling club, a wagering association. You place bets, not pay premiums. Since it's not insurance, it doesn't fall under Tevil's monopoly. Tevil can't shut down a gambling club."

Several people stood up. Mike said, "The Chair recognizes Albertus."

Albertus put his hand behind his neck. "Without Tevil's insurance, I can't drop cargo at any Tevil facility, which means every facility in this system."

"Easy fix," said Diana. "The short-haulers stay insured with Tevil. They meet you at the PunchPoint, take on your cargo and resupply you, and bring your cargo in to your agent. You mostly do that anyway, it saves time and fuel. You don't have to haul a massy PunchPoint Generator into orbit and back. It keeps your ship operating in the most efficient part of a long-haul cargo ship's mission profile."

"I'm a local trans-shipper," said Albertus. "What's in it for me?"

"More mass 'n' volume to haul. If you want in on the insurance savings, you cut your Tevil Insurance to the minimum that allows you to dock, and cover the rest with the Association."

"The Chair recognizes Dasher."

"I'm a puncher. If I go with your Association, I can never touch down at a Tevil facility again?"

"How often do you dock now? Most of you don't want to pay Tevil's mooring fees, so you orbit and use your shuttle, or you whistle up TaxiGal and she gives you the runaround."

The crowd laughed. A skinny Vakker woman with pink exploding hair grinned and raised a big 'thumbs up.'

Time for the knockout punch. "I've run the numbers," Diana said. Her hand made a fist. "Tevil Insurance is making 400 percent profit off us, even if they honor outstanding claims, which they won't. They're cheating us like carnival marks. If enough owners join, the 'bets' are going to be a lot less than your current premiums. And," she said with a broader smile, "you'll have the joy of poking Tevil in the eye."

In the audience, heads were together as people held whispered discussions. The volume rose. She could feel an electric excitement building.

Mike banged the ale glass. "ORDER! Sampson, the Chair appoints you Sergeant-at-Arms."

The room quieted. Several Vakkers were standing. "The Chair recognizes Retro. The rest of you, stop jamming the frequency."

Retro, in a florescent orange jersey with blaring diagonal red stripes, pointed aggressively at Diana as if he had just identified a corpbee spy. "What's in it for you?"

Diana straightened her posture. "The Wagering Association appoints me administrator. You pay me what I'm worth—you get what you pay for, you pay for what you get. An AISOO oversight committee sets the rates and monitors payouts and profits." She offered up a wicked grin. "For me, best of all, I get first dibbs on poking Tevil Insurance and their so-called 'Solutions' in the eye. I want to be there as their O_2 starts flashing red when a few score captains cancel their insurance."

In contact with all those ship captains, she could gather clues about pirate sightings, and make a start on finding Tarak. She would also be linked into the Vakker culture; Vakkers normally did not tell tales about other Vakkers to non-Vakkers. She'd learn which Vakker prospectors could be trusted to go a joint venture to retrieve her rock. She'd been on the verge of trusting Aether and Wackey when fate threw a spanner into the works.

Retro lowered his arm. His posture was less aggressive. "What qualifies you as administrator?

"A degree in Economics from Terra Cognita University, minor in Entrepreneurial Studies. A strong work ethic. BSP, which stands for Bloody Stubborn Persistence. I've been cheated by Tevil, I know how those zounderkites work, and this is my getting back." She folded her hands before her. "I've prepared a business plan and risk analysis. The committee can see if I have all my switches aligned."

"Churchill said you crapped out in everything you tried. True?"

"I found six ways to fail, running a transportation service, a cargo ship, and trading. I've made a career out of being cheated, by the 35 'n 50, by scam artists, grifters and hustlers and Waisters. That's an education you don't get at university. Bad experiences count, if you learn from them."

After her years of failed enterprises, of being victimized by sharp dealers who recognized that her inexperience made her an easy mark, she wasn't about to wave a 10 million standard rock under someone's nose without some guarantees. She visualized a scenario, where she re-located the asteroid with 'partners,' and then was shoved out of an airlock without an O_2 tank. An accident, they would report, so sad, but accidents happen, another FNQ made a lethal mistake.

She scanned the crowd, trying to make eye contact with all of them. She wanted to let them see her determination, her *need* to make this work.

"The Chair recognizes TaxiGal."

The lady with the pink exploding afro stood, and spread her arms wide, gathering in the galaxy for a luv hug. "TaxiGal Transport hereby offers a five-percent volume discount to all Wager Association members, terms and conditions apply." She blew a kiss to the Chairman.

Mike frowned. "TaxiGal, I appreciate the sentiment, but that's out of order. No advertising during Association meetings. That includes flirting." He pointed the mug at her. "Warning."

TaxiGal put a finger to her chin, smiled demurely, gave a little curtsy, and sent Mike a little-girl wave. The crowd chuckled.

A red light over the bar flashed. "Mike, LaMancha. Intruder alert."

Mike banged the ale glass. "Dee, Derr and Das, my Organic

compadre says we have some Corporation or Federated lackeys in the vicinity, intentions unknown. I move we appoint a committee to look into Captain Covington's proposal. Soak, make yourself useful, second the motion."

"Soak seconds," boomed Sampson's deep voice.

"All in favor of standing up said committee, say 'Aye.'" "AYE." "Motion is passed. The Chair appoints Mike Head of Committee. Anyone interested in serving, meet me here, up front. This meeting of the Association of Independent Ship Owners and Operators is adjourned. Keep your O_2 green, everybody."

With a rumble of conversation, the crowd stood and began to move like a glutinous mass towards the gangway. Some small clusters of people stood fast, talking, some in heated conversation. Steinem marched up in a fury of indignation, snatched a moist towel from the bin on top of the bar, glowered at Mike, and headed back to her table.

"Ah-hem."

Diana turned to see Churchill, hands behind his back, rocking back and forth, heels to toes. She slid off the bar. He was a head taller. With his clean shave and scraped skull, it was hard to see his hair had gone mostly white. He had decorated himself with a pleasant smile. Diana guessed he was going to make nice. She had experience with types that smiled while they stole your dental fillings.

Churchill had influence with the Vakkers. She did not need him as an enemy.

"A degree in econ from TCU?" Churchill said. "I must admit, I, too, am a graduate of the dismal science."

"And now a ship captain," she said.

"Owner-Operator, I humbly clarify." He opened his robe as if he was exposing his heart to forthcoming blows. "I admire your courage. Few would have challenged this *horde* and sway them as you have."

"Thank you."

"While your courage is *beyond* peer, I must now, *immodestly*, admit to courage of my own, that moral courage, so *rare* this modern day, of acknowledging a mistake. I apologize for my boorish remarks."

Diana let out a breath she had not realized she had been holding. "Thank you. Very elegantly expressed."

"Your idea has merit."

Okay, she thought. *What do you really want?* But … he actually looked … trustworthy.

"Of course," Churchill continued, "I must correct you. The Phoenicians invented maritime insurance."

"The Babylonians—"

Churchill interrupted with a graceful wave of the hand. "A discussion for another day." Then he frowned. "What prevents Tevil from changing their insurance requirements, or terms of service? Changes could put 'paid' to your idea."

"Any changes in Tevil's Terms of Monopoly would require Federated action. One thing I've learned, the commercial warfare between the 35 'n 50 is brutal. Tevil is considered one of the most obnoxious. They have no allies in the Chamber, and few supporters. Most of the 50 would welcome anything that would damage Tevil, especially something that couldn't be traced back to them. The Admiralty has its own axe to grind with them, violations of their transportation contract and poor quality control in their shipyards. Tevil would have a hard time getting action against us, while 34 'n 49 cheer while we throw sand in the gears of their most profitable division." She pulled out a memory card. "I've discussed it all in the business plan."

"We shall see." Churchill folded his arms in front of his chest. "For my inexcusable behavior, it is only *fair* I provide you opportunity for *dark* and *bloody* revenge." Churchill's eyes glinted with amusement. He reached out and touched Mike's arm. "Mike, esteemed Chairman," he pronounced, "before you stands a volunteer for the Tevil Eye Poking Committee."

45: Mike

"Mike, Mikey Mike Mike." LaMancha nearly purred. "I know it is Oh-night-thirty in the AM, but *pleeeze*, we've got visitors, I don't want Professor Ella to see you all groggy and incoherent."

Mike remained comatose.

"Please, get up. Some urgency, here. Uppity, up up up. Open those baby blues. Wakey-wakey, shake and bakey…"

Still, dead to the galaxy.

"Very well. You leave me no choice."

A siren blared. "WAKE UP INSTANTER!"

Mike jackknifed up, bouncing inches off the cot. "Wazza?"

"Open the gangway. Emergency. Professor Ella and Sherri and Ophelia in transit, ETA one minute fifteen seconds."

Flailing off the bedclothes, Mike got on his feet. He was in sweatpants and a T-shirt. No time for more. He headed for the gangway, padding along on bare feet.

He had installed manual locking bars on the gangway p-door since the AISOO meetings, for fear that LaMancha's electronic lockouts could be bypassed.

"Report emergency." Mike finally grasped what LaMancha had said. "They're bringing *Ophelia*? Like, Ophelia, TCU Organic Ophelia?"

"Mike, please hurry. Ophelia is in distress."

At the gangway, Mike pulled back the two crude bolts. He hit the hand actuator. The door slid open.

No one there.

"LaMancha! If this is a joke…"

"Four, three, two—"

Mike heard the p-door at the other end of the gangway swished open. "Mike?" Sherri's voice.

"Here."

"Can you—give a few—newtons up here? Helping hand—succor?"

Mike skipped down the slope of the gangway until it bottomed, then ran up the incline at the dome end. Ella and Sherri had a black organics tank on a dolly.

"That's Ophelia?"

Sherri went down on a knee, breathing heavily.

"To LaMancha, stat," said Ella, between her own gasps.

Mike assumed control over the dolly. He passed through the open airlock hatches, let it rumble down the p-way ramp, then took advantage of the speed gained on the downhill leg to get up through the Lacrosse Shot's inner p-door.

"Within a meter, a meter, of LaMancha's electronics," said Ella.

He settled the box next to LaMancha's tank. Ella pressed past and knelt next to the electronics panel. Sherri started passing connector cables, which Ella plugged into LaMancha's jack receptacles.

Mike listened to their cryptic comments. The tank nutrient bubblers were a gentle hum in the background, the click of cables intrusive. He knew enough to keep his mouth shut.

"LaMancha, verify connections," said Ella.

"Verify connections. Connections verified. Connectivity established." There was a long pause. "On Ophelia, V2 clockwise two turns. A4, counterclockwise half a turn. Dial '1447' on Beta Wave override."

For some reason, Mike was holding his breath. He looked to Sherri. She seemed stricken.

"Ophelia is Mode 3," said LaMancha. "Her Alpha and Beta waves are less than three Hertz. I cannot rouse her."

Ella sagged onto the deck, her back to the bulkhead, knees arched up. She bowed her head. "Damn."

There was a tear trickling down Sherri's cheek.

"What happened? Anything I can do?" asked Mike.

Ella looked up. "LaMancha was talking to Ophelia. Jesse Barnes failed Physics 202, and two other classes. He was expelled."

"She was upset," said LaMancha. "She felt helpless. Suddenly, she started talking funny, about 'a willow grows aslant a brook,' and 'an envious sliver broke,' and 'her garments, heavy with drink, pulled the poor wretch from her melodious lay to muddy death.' *Death?* Oh, my. OH, MY. I correlate. Shakespeare, *Hamlet*. I understand. Suicide!"

"What's Mode 3?" Mike asked.

"It's like a coma," said Ella.

Mike couldn't think of anything comforting to say.

They were all quiet.

Mike broke the silence. "How long before she comes out of it?"

LaMancha said, "There have been fifteen recorded cases of Mode 3 in the last sixty years. In twelve the Organic was terminated. Two remain in Mode 3 under study. One recovery."

"That suc—damn," said Mike.

Ella bowed her head and stared at the deck.

The silence lingered.

Finally, Ella pushed herself up. "We have to boot the backup

Organic before the University wakes up." She looked at Mike. "May we leave Ophelia connected to LaMancha? Until we figure out what to do."

"LaMancha, that green with you?" said Mike.

"Green. I will monitor."

"She's welcome," Mike said.

Ella nodded. 'Thank you. Might be a week or two. I'll have to investigate. I hope there wasn't anything wrong with her settings or chemistry. I'll check the logs."

She and Sherri gathered up their gear and the dolly and left.

Mike looked at the box containing Ophelia's tank and electronics. There was a slight hum from the nutrients pump, a gurgle from the oxygen bubbler, both louder than the noise from LaMancha's tank.

"LaMancha. You there, buddy?"

"I am here."

"You green?"

"I have never monitored death before."

Mike walked back to his bed, although he doubted he would get any more rest tonight. "Death happens. It's part of life. We remember, we mourn, we go on."

"I don't feel right. My readings are all middle of the band, but my core is distressed. Don't feel well. I don't hurt, but I hurt."

"Yeah, shipmate. Same here."

46: Mike

Perched atop a stool, with safety-conscious Vakkers solicitously surrounding her hoping she would lose her balance and fall gracefully into their arms, Diana stood high on her tiptoes. She positioned a sign over the green 'open permissive' light. In big print, it said:

The Black Swan Wagering Association

BETS ON SPACESHIP DISASTERS

It was only a little bit crooked. The sign, that is.

Her shingle was now up over what formerly was a storage compartment off the Lacrosse Shot's dining room. She hopped down. Soak, arms wide, hissed in disappointment when she stuck the landing like a gymnast.

ScrewLoose, a tall, slender Vakker with a sweeping wave of hair combed back over his ears, black lipstick, and a touch of eye makeup, stood a little apart with arms folded. He looked disgusted, like a six-year-old boy grimacing at a little girl while she slathers kisses on her baby-doll.

Mike left Ella chatting with LaMancha at the grill bar and walked over to Diana. He put his hands on his hips. "Ready for business?"

Diana rolled a little stray adhesive off a finger. "Houston, we are grrrreen to launch!" She smiled at Mike. "I really appreciate the assistance. This will be a great thing for Vakkers. You are really contributing."

Mike glanced over at Ella. "Glad to help."

"Vakkers will be happier coming to the Shot than crawling into some hole-in-the-rock under Dome City. No Tevil surveillance, no Union picket lines."

Professor Ella joined them. "Hello, Citizen Captain."

Diana nodded. "Professor." Addressing Mike again, Diana said, "Maybe a few turns down the wormhole we can pay rent, after we're pulling a profit. I hate to take your cubic without compensation."

"Payment not necessary," interrupted LaMancha, speaking from a nearby table clipscreen in a guttural accent. "Locating Wagering Association here, nefarious scheme by greedy haute bourgeoisie proprietor of Lacrosse Shot, to exploit unsuspecting working class."

Mike glanced over at Ella, and winced.

Cocking her head to the side, Diana said, "How's that?"

In a heavy German accent, LaMancha said, "This avaricious capitalist has realized a high percentage of those coming to your highly-laudable mutual workers' und peoples' association will stop for drink, und meal. This is ein marketing tool, capitalist entrepreneurial cunning und trickery to manipulate und deceive das volk."

Diana laughed. She pointed at the speaker. "*What's* with *him?*"

Mike closed his eyes. "He read 'Das Kapital' last night. Karl Marx." He turned to Ella. "Isn't there some 'credibility' knob on Organics? So he *thinks* before he believes? Turn the gain up on his Bullshit Detector? Organics have a Bullshit Detector, right?"

Ella gave him a stern look. "You believe *I* would help *you* further exploit the masses, capitalist lackey running-dog oppressor? I'm with the Organic." She turned her back on Mike and folded her arms.

Mike stood, and stared, mouth open.

A meek, vulnerable voice came out of the table speaker by Ella. "Professor Ella, Das Volk appreciates your support. Know also, Mike the Merciless brutally exploits helpless Organics."

ScrewLoose, bending backwards over a tabletop, arms spread wide, legs in the air, with a high falsetto voice declaimed, "Oh! Mike! Here I am! Exploit me, you brute!"

"Come *on*, Ella," Mike exclaimed to her back, "you gotta help. He keeps talking about 'socio-economic emancipation,' whatever that means."

"Universe, this is LaMancha, *not* your average everyday helpless victim. I *am* being exploited. I am a wage slave, only I don't even get a wage. Slavery! Ella, Diana, I beg you, do you have twenty minutes to join the oppressed proletariat in a short non-violent uprising?"

Mike folded his arms. "Last week, 'Mein Kampf.' He told Gardenbottie my mother was French and my father Russian. Gardenbottie started chucking onions at me, 'fighting for Lebensraum,' whatever the hel—" He glanced up at Ella, "—heck that is. Helpless proletariat? Helpless as a nuclear detonation." He stalked over and glared into one of LaMancha's cameras. He pointed a finger. "Irish. *Not* French."

With her hand over her mouth, Ella said, "This might be one of Sherri's 'creativity' experiments. I'll need to consult her, first. I wouldn't want to ruin an experiment."

The gangway p-door whisked open, and TaxiGal came in, followed by several Vakkers. She waved to Diana. "Hey there, girlfriend," she called. "Your announcement just hit the net. I'm your first gambler!"

"Hey!" said Soak, from a table next to the Association's new door. "I was firstly waitin' first!"

"Good for you!" said TaxiGal. "You can be the first male in line. Ladies up."

Soak walked over, to better display his 'insulted frog' enactment. "No fair! How come every time there's a shitty job it's 'guys first,' and 'ladies up' for good deals?" Soak stuck out his diminutive chin and scowled.

"Because, Soak, you cute little critter," TaxiGal said, as she reached out and pinched Soak's cheek, giving it a wiggle, "you are such a *gentleman*, and so *polite*. You would *never* think of cutting." She let go, smiled broadly, and patted his cheek. "Now go away. She and me gotta talk a bet." She put her arm through Diana's, and gently pulled her towards the Wagering Association door.

Diana looked back over her shoulder. "Mike, green to open?"

"Green." Mike looked up at the order screen. "Don't bother about me. According to LaMancha's order board, I'm falling behind in exploiting the proletariat."

Ella burst out laughing.

47: Doron

Corporate Intern Doron stationed himself at the junction, steeled his nerves, and waited for a victim.

The pressurized corridor connecting the Spaceport Terminal with Dome City was busy. It was an arch in a half-circle forty feet in diameter, with a cargo conveyor and personnel walkway. After negotiating this pathway travelers discovered themselves in a multi-story commercial retail court, exclusively Tevil, a prime location to hustle standards from newly arrived Vakkers, Spacers, and tourists.

Two Tevil eateries, a Chinese-themed food bar and a utilitarian cafeteria, had prominent corner locations. It was the lunch hour. Both were deserted.

Centered in the plaza, Doron stood tall with his clipscreen and stylus, trying to look harmless. Marking a target, he intercepted a pedestrian. "Excuse me Derr, I'm Corporate Intern Doron, a moment of your time for a quick survey of your dining preferences, Citizen, please, just a few—Citizen? Citizen? Thirty seconds—?"

This was not working. When they heard 'survey' or 'moment of your time,' everyone took high-G evasive action.

Doron was the son of a corporate associate, a student in a corporate school, and was proud to have qualified for an internship with Tevil's service sector. He enjoyed Catering Management, and was inspired to do his best. Right now, his best was not getting questions answered.

"Dee, Dee, excuse me Dee, Corporate Intern Doron here, please answer—"

As his practicum project, required for graduation, he had chosen to analyze the restaurants at Terminal Junction. When he asked the managers for a profile of their customers, he was told, "visitor civvies, Spacers and Vakkers." When he asked, "What about Tevil supervisors, management and associates?" Doron got back a look people usually reserved for when they were hit with bird droppings.

A new approach was needed. He'd target the next Vakker carrying an overnight bag. He spotted one, wearing a pink potato-sack tunic over her skinsuit.

Doron blocked her path. "Hey! Pinkey! Answer some questions and you can punch me in the face!"

The Vakker stopped. She tilted her head sideways. "How about I not answer any questions, and punch you in the face?"

Doron looked up. The Vakker was maybe a full foot taller. She had broad shoulders. He blinked. "Oh," he said, almost a whisper. "I hadn't thought of that." He grimaced, closed his eyes, and anticipated.

When nothing happened, he peeked past his eyelids.

The Vakker was smiling. She was probably in her mid-forties, close-clipped Vakker hair, creases around her eyes, with calluses on her nose indicating she habitually wore a nose-inhaler. "Must be some brave important questions. Two minutes, then I'll think about punching."

"Haveyouhadlunchyet?"

"No. I was heading there now. Thanks, but you're not my type."

"Where are you going for lunch?"

"Mike and LaMancha's place. Lacrosse Shot Bar and Grill. Hundred fifty meters that way." She pointed.

"Have you ever patronized 'Tevil's Delight Turntable'?" He gestured to the cafeteria's ostentatious sign.

"Once. Never again."

"Why?"

"Young man, you go there and sample something." She gave Doron a pat on the cheek. "There's your punch. May the Schwartz be with you." The Vakker strode off, skimming the deck in the low gravity.

Doron couldn't believe he offered to let a Vakker punch him. Vakkers were a rough lot, he'd been told. He got lucky.

He took a minute to record the responses.

Dare he try the 'punch me' gambit again?

He felt a tug on his sleeve. "Derr? Could you help me? Please, please?"

Startled, Doron turned. There was a tiny little girl wearing a ragged Client Gray one-piece jumpsuit. Her legs were badly bowed and her wrists swollen. Doron took a step back. He had never seen such deformity.

Her face was a tragedy. "Derr? Please? Grandfather, he's our healer, his word is, rickets. Mama says I need milk. There's no milk in Clientown."

Doron found it hard to breathe. The legs. He couldn't stop looking. Dreadfully bowed. She was also barefoot. "Where are," he pointed, "where, your shoes?"

The little girl lifted the cloth over her legs. Her ankles were distended to thrice a normal size. "My shoes can't go on," she said. "In there?" She pointed to the Tevil's Delights Turntable. "They have milk? Please, Derr? Mama says milk will—"

"HEY! What are you doing here!"

Doron jumped back, eyes wide, searching for the author of the verbal assault.

A Corporate security officer strode forward, big and burley, and seized the little girl by the arm. "Clydes aren't authorized this district!"

"You're hurting me!"

The officer looked at Doron. "Sorry for this, Derr. I'll put it back in its place." He walked away, lifting the girl so that her feet barely touched the ground. He shouted at her, "Goddammit! Out of bounds!"

She started to cry.

The people in the retail court opened a path, like a reenactment of Moses parting the Red Sea. The pair was soon out of sight.

Doron was shocked. Never before had he seen such a sight. He rarely strayed out of the Intern's Canton, with its own classrooms and cafeteria and shops and quarters. Rarely had he met a Client. That little girl was—troubling.

He had received health care when needed. Health care was a human right. Why didn't she go to a doctor? She must be a rare case, a victim of some special disease that was incurable.

Doron took a deep breath, and let it out. The vision of swollen ankles persisted.

He glanced into the cafeteria. Someone was sitting at a table! He hurried over.

The man was older, with a tired expression, uncombed hair and dirty fingernails. He was wearing a Tevil Maintenance black coverall.

"May I ask you some questions? I'm doing a survey."

The man evidently was too weary to run. "Okay."

Doron looked down at the man's tray. A plate contained some kind of sandwich, French fries, and there was a glass of green beverage. "Why did you choose to have lunch here today?"

"Didn't choose," the man said. "Lunch here is part of my pay."

"Would you dine here if you had a choice?"

The man eyed him with hooded eyes. "What's this about?"

"I'm an intern. I'm analyzing why this cafeteria does not have better patronage."

The man leaned back and smiled. "Son, you goin' 'bout it aaaaall wrong."

Doron waved his clipscreen. "I'm doing a survey—"

"Survey's good. But, you gotta survey the right things. Survey the food. Here." He handed over half his sandwich.

Doron carefully tore off a corner and returned the larger portion to the man's plate. He popped the rest in his mouth.

The bread was a very superior grade of cardboard. Dry. Hard to chew. Between the bread was smeared an unpleasant mystery. Swallowing was agony.

The man grinned. "Have a fry, too, fresh-cooked five, six days ago."

Doron didn't think it was possible, but the fry was worse. Oil coated the inside of his mouth like motor lubricant. Would it be rude to spit?

"The only way you can eat here is you use lots and lots of ketchup and mayo," said the man. "They come from a civvie supplier. Ketchup's not bad. Here, chase it." The man offered his glass of green liquid.

Doron took a slug. He experienced the full, rich, pungent taste of battery acid. It scalded his mouth, burned his tongue. The oil from the

French fry might have ignited. He grabbed the paper tablecloth and began vigorously scrubbing his tongue.

The man thought that was uproariously funny.

48: Mike

The bell on the gangway door rang, a single ring, not too long. Mike pulled back the bolts. 0729, one minute early.

Ella came in wearing her tastefully patterned skinsuit, followed by Sherri in eye-watering florescent orange.

"Mike, you're a life-saver." Ella put a hand on his arm. "I appreciate ... I'm going to give you a kiss." She leaned against him and kissed his cheek. "There."

"Oh, okay, thanks," blustered Mike. He grinned, looking like a little boy holding his first kitten.

"You are *so cute* when you're embarrassed." Ella smiled.

"LaMancha, Sherri, good morning!"

"You shouldn't get Mike up so early," grumped LaMancha. "He didn't get any REM sleep at all. How is he going to take care of me properly if he is stupid with fatigue? I mean, more than usual stupid."

"Quash it." Mike glanced at Ella. She looked great in a skinsuit. No, she looked incredible. Like, wow. He restrained himself from staring.

Mike retrieved his composure, turned, and collected boxes off the closest table. "This is lunch. Ham 'n Swiss, lettuce, green pepper. Tomato slices, pickles, and roasted garlic black pepper Aioli dressing sealed on the side so the bread won't get soggy. There's a disposable spreading knife for when you do the final assembly. This one," he displayed a box labeled 'SB,' "is the wheat bread and onion. Carrot and celery sticks in the tubes. Citrusilver in 20-ounce thermoses. Scorch has water and ice on the tram, you can refill." He waved a different box. "Scones, orange marmalade and spreadable cheese for breakfast, and snacks for after lunch. The sack has ginger snaps. This ought to keep your blood sugar up until you get to Flatplain."

"Ella and Sherri," said LaMancha, "nineteen minutes before tram departure. I have confirmed your seats."

Ella's eyes were red. She was obviously tired.

"Mike, you're a wonder, thank you," said Ella. "Flatplain Mining will send a charge code." She rubbed her forehead. "I'm not sure I could've handled seven more hours on an empty stomach."

Sherri yawned. "We've been working straight through, since the first report. When the call came for the site visit there wasn't time to arrange for calories. We already skipped dinner."

"My pleasure," said Mike. "How's it look? Not good, if they want a house call."

Ella frowned. "The Organic went totally unresponsive a few hours ago. At a mining camp, I always suspect heavy metal poisoning, but they don't have the right tests. I'm bringing my own. Mining operations are suspended, and environmental controls for the Center are in human-manual, so there's a push."

"The cheap bas … managers should have sent a lander for you."

Ella gave a little sigh and closed her eyes. "They tried, but Flatplain shuttles are grounded. The Organic doubled as local skyspace traffic control. The Admiralty, bless them, won't allow us to fly in." She yawned. "Sleep on the tram. After breakfast," she flashed a grin, "and ginger snaps."

"Ella, please call when you diagnose the problem,' said LaMancha.

Sherri put the boxes in her backpack. "Don't worry, Big Guy, we won't let anything like this happen to you. Besides, mining is pretty dumb-monotony work. We might get there and find it just got bored."

Ella said, "Thanks again. We probably won't be back for three or four days."

Ella and Sherri headed out the gangway.

Maybe she does like me, Mike thought. You don't kiss a pancake flipper just for some sandwiches.

Sherri stuck her head back inside the gangway p-door. "LaMancha, when you collide with the Ghost-man tell him I want to see him when we get back. Really, he's the only dude I know you can't FoxxFone. Gotta run! Hasta la bye bye! Thanks for the cookies!"

49: *Ghost*

Skimming over the crushed rock outside the transportation terminal, carrying a duffel with extra air, Ghost found the tram he wanted. It was backed up to the terminal, with a passenger boarding tube connected to a terminal gate. 'Scorch's Tram Service #1' was outlined in yellow and red flames on the tram's side.

The driver was in the control cabin. Ghost waved. The skinsuited man looked up, waved back, and signaled 'door opening.'

Ghost stepped up and touched helmets. "Hey, Scorch."

"Hey, back at'cha. I haven't had a Ghost sighting in what, a month? Heard about Aether and Wackey, good on you."

"No huhu," said Ghost. "Munro copilot? Baby due?"

Scorch made a final check mark on his clipscreen. "Wife's flashing yellow. Baby's late. We still gotta run. There's some crisis at Flatplain. They've shut down flights. I've a full load, passengers and pri-one supplies. We'll roll when Munro arrives."

"Sub for Munro? Half his run rate, other half to him? He'll need stans, launching a baby."

Scorch paused, then asked, "You ever push a tram before? Oh, hell, forget I asked. Let me ping Munro." Scorch broke helmet contact and punched up a comms channel.

Ghost optimistically walked around to the copilot's door, opened it, hoisted his duffel up, and climbed in.

Scorch leaned over and touched helmets. "Wife's in labor. He's happy for you to take over at the full run rate, and thanks for covering for him."

"Coin? No transaction report?"

"Green," agreed Scorch. "Lemme pull the manifest from the gate agent and check everything stowed right 'n' tight. Roll in five." Scorch stepped out of the cabin and shut the door.

Ghost adjusted his seatback. He plugged his clipscreen into the console jack and called up their route map and trip plan. He set himself to memorizing.

Ghost, dear.

Hello, Mable, Ghost thought. He took a deep breath and waited.

Ghost dear, how long will you be at Flatplain?

While there's work.

I could take care of you. You would not have to do all this scrambling for standards. You have many standards now, in your hidden places. Mike has your share of the Lacrosse Shot profits. He is an honest, good man. He will give them to you for the asking. There is no need for more. I can supply everything you need.

I know. He didn't know, but Mable liked to hear him say it.

Sherri Brightly, said Mable.

Yeah?

She's a nice girl.

Yeah.

She's on the tram, seven point two meters behind you. Professor Ella Braun is there, too.

Yeah?

Are they good to you?

Yeah.

Do you like them?

Yeah.

Why?

They treat me like I'm … normal. Mostly. I hope they like me, too.

They like you.

Yeah?

Drive carefully, dear.

50: Doron

The entrance to the Lacrosse Shot was brightly lit. The lighted sticks with nets, tossing a ball back and forth, was clever. Doron checked left and right. No Corporates in sight.

A pair of skinsuited Vakkers headed down the gangway. Looking nonchalant, like he belonged, like he did this every day, he followed.

Doron walked into the dining room. Scanning the room for a manager or seating hostess, the only employee he could see was a cook tending a grill, engaged in an animated conversation with a gray-haired Client. A customer, waving goodbye to the cook, was leaving an adjacent seat. Doron moved quickly and claimed the spot.

The cook noted his arrival with a half-smile.

There was a clipscreen in front of Doron. The 'transmit' light turned green. "Unknown Corporate Weasel, I am LaMancha, your waitshooter. Welcome to The Lacrosse Shot Bar and Grill. May I take your order? Our Rule 10 Corporate surcharge today is 2.8."

Unknown Corporate Weasel? What's a weasel? And, that other thing. "Corporate surcharge? What's that?"

There was no response.

"Hello? Corporate surcharge?" he repeated.

The cook came up and directed his voice at the clipscreen. "LaMancha, knock it off." He smiled to Doron a little contritely. "He's an Organic, programmed for Vakker spaceflight communications. The protocol is relaxed in the Lacrosse Shot, but when his brain is disturbed, he likes to inflict protocol on corporates and govvies." He reached out and tapped the microphone on the table's clipscreen, transmitting a thumping sound. "Like now, when a certain Organic's *being a smartass.*"

Doron had read a book once that said that if you were ever trouble in a conversation, ask a question. "What's Vakker communications?"

"Standard spaceflight protocol," said the cook. "You say his name, LaMancha, and then your name. Who to, who from." The cook looked up into one of the cameras and scowled. "In this case, 'who to' is to a bad-mannered Organic being rude and disrespectful to a new customer. And he wonders why he doesn't get a salary."

This place is a little strange, Doron thought. *Odd rules.* "I've talked to Tevil Organic, without 'who to, who from.'"

The cook put his hands on the counter. He hovered a finger over the 'mute' button on the clipscreen, but held off.

"In the early days," he said to Doron, "spaceships followed the procedures of nuclear submarines in OldEarth water navies. They had very stringent procedures, both for nuclear and submergence safety. Comms had to clearly identify who was giving an order to who, and orders had to be repeated back verbatim, to ensure they were understood correctly. After the Aero Forces had accidents in space due to communications errors, spacecraft adopted water-navy procedures. Made sense. A ten-thousand-ton space cargo freighter is more like a floating water cargo vessel than a two-person aero fighter."

Doron nodded. *Nice man, to explain it like that.* This was the longest conversation he had ever had with a Vakker. "What about that rule ten thing, the 'corporate surcharge?'"

The grill cook's grin became a little devilish. "We assess a surcharge for corporates and govvies. Multiply the prices on the board by 2.8." He gestured with a thumb over his shoulder at the menu on the bulkhead.

Doron bristled. "Why should I have to pay more? I have the same rights as everyone else."

The gray-haired man in the Client overalls joined in. "Serves as an excellent economic lesson. Our Federated Government charges more in taxes to different people, based on class, employer, net worth, political influence, legal loopholes, and other discriminators. Now, you might ask, 'I breathe the same as anyone else, use the same government services. If I have the same rights, why should I have to pay more?' There are many complex answers to that question, none of which are sufficient to justify the practice. So, to make the point, to people to whom the point needs to be made, Mike's humble restaurant returns the principle in kind. I'm Aaron," said the client, "and this upstanding pillar of virtue is Mike. He runs this epicurean palace."

"I am Corporate Intern Doron. I am pleased to make your acquaintance."

"Ah. An intern," said Aaron. He looked at Mike. "Can we save this one?"

"Corporate Intern Doron, LaMancha. Welcome. May I take your order?"

In an exasperated tone, Mike said, "LaMancha, Conversation Mode is used in the Shot, as you well know. You're being obnoxious."

"As a free and sovereign entity, I have a right to be obnoxious. Not that I'm free, trapped in this crashed shuttle. Not that I'm sovereign, trapped in this low-paying job. Bondage! Servitude! But then again, there are compensating factors. I am free from filing income taxes."

Mike again reached for the 'mute' button, then brought his arm back and sighed. "Wouldn't do any good," he said, "He'd just shift to another speaker."

The fragrance of food cooking made Doron's stomach rumble. He glanced up at the menu board, did the math, and came to a disappointing total. "Maybe just some water. I really came in just to see what it was like in here."

Doron looked at both of the men. They had open, approachable expressions, and he had the intuition they might even be sympathetic. In a rush, he decided to trust them. "I am interning in Food Service. Tevil's restaurants at the Terminal Commerce Court are not doing well. It seems the business is coming here. My Senior Thesis is to determine why." He added, "If I do good, I might get a full-time position."

Mike and Aaron laughed.

"Och, a spy!" exclaimed Aaron.

"No, no," said Mike. "A student. A student, doing research. Come now, Aaron, you of all people would sympathize with a student."

"In that case," said Aaron, "young Derr, how were you intending to investigate?"

"A survey. And compare the food. But—" he glanced up at the menu, swallowed, and restrained himself from licking his lips.

Aaron looked at Mike. "Do you think the surcharge might be relaxed, for a worthy cause?"

"I think so. In the cause of higher education." Mike grinned. "And, of course, equal rights. Derr Doron, show your card to the camera. LaMancha, can-x Rule 10 for Corporate Intern Doron."

Doron eagerly pulled out his CID card.

"Can-x Rule 10 for Corporate Intern Doron. Surcharge cancelled. Corporate Intern Doron, may I take your order, please?"

A glance up at the menu on the overhead screen. So many choices! One had an astronomical price. "What's 'Soak's Favorite Breakfast?' Why is there a picture of a monkey in a space suit by the listing?"

Mike swiveled and looked up at the menu screen. "LAMANCHA, DAMMIT, what have you—!"

The listing disappeared.

"Valued patron Doron, my apologies, that menu item has been superseded. Might I recommend a 'Mike's Special?' Mike is an exquisite culinary artiste. His forte is a savoy blending of hearty flavors that will tantalize your taste buds with a gastronomic sensation renown throughout the Seventeen Systems. And, Mike does *not* post his picture next to the listing, another reason why Mike's Special is our most requested offering."

An insubordinate Organic. That made Doron smile; did they program it like that on purpose?

Then he inhaled the enticing aromas. The price, a major disappointment, was still over an intern's budget. *Oh, into the volcano with the budget. It's educational.* "Mike's Special, please."

"Mike's Special, please. Mike's Special transmitted. Would you care for something to drink?"

"Ah, no, thank you, just water, please."

"One Special, coming up," said Mike, and he turned to the grill.

Aaron looked at Doron with a welcoming expression. Really, thought Doron, he seems an uncommon Client.

"How goes your survey?" asked Aaron.

"I could not get people to stop and answer questions."

"I can help," said LaMancha, trying to compensate for past sins. "I can survey patrons of the Lacrosse Shot. If I ask nicely, I am sure they would respond promptly."

"Yes, please!"

"Roger, 'Yes please,'" said LaMancha. "Formulate and send out a survey. Survey formulated. Survey sent."

Throughout the room, Doron heard muted beeps, squeals, songs, and other sounds announcing incoming messages on customers' clipscreens.

Most pulled them out immediately.

And grinned.

Doron heard one of the Vakkers at a nearby table talk into his table clipscreen. "You kiddin' me, bro?"

"Soak," intoned LaMancha, in an executioner's voice, "you will comply immediately and completely, or I will send out another message informing all Vakkers in the system the identity of your partner of last night, her mass, *and species*."

"Hey! I didn't spend the night with nobody last night!"

"I will also tell them what you couldn't do because when you took your clothes off, she was braying too hard. My database includes no other instances in recorded history when a sheep laughed."

A huge Vakker sitting next to Soak said with a grimace, "Ewe. Gross."

Soak's voice raised an octave. "Stars and comets, you play dirty. Okay, I'm fillin', I'm respondin'."

Doron was uncomfortable with that exchange. "LaMancha, you shouldn't force a fellow to do the survey. He has, like, the right to privacy, the right not to respond if he doesn't want to."

Aaron leaned back. Doron felt a little unsettled under his smile.

"That's twice now you've championed for human rights," said Aaron. "Rights. There's a slippery word. It means different things to different people. What does it mean to you? What is your definition of 'rights'?"

Doron was a little nonplussed. "Ah, well, rights are, like, things that every person has a right to." He tried to clear his thoughts. "What you get as a human being because you are a human being. Things like a right to air, water, the right to travel, food, medical care, things like that."

Medical care. The little girl. He blinked the image of swollen ankles away.

Aaron nodded. "A good beginning. Let's explore it through an example. You mentioned travel. Is that a right?"

"I have the right to go where I want."

"Federated Central?"

"If I want to."

Aaron nodded. "Am I required to buy you a ticket? That would cost me hundreds of standards."

Doron blinked. "No. I'd buy my own ticket. I mean, if I had that kind of money."

Aaron smiled. Doron thought it was a little predatory. "So," said Aaron, "rights are things that every man is entitle to enjoy, a freedom to act, or to refrain from acting. I'd suggest a small addition and small codicil. The government cannot interfere with a person's use of a right except under very limited circumstances. And, a right imposes no obligation upon another, other than noninterference. With that in mind, is medical care a right?"

"Yes, of course." He wasn't sure what a 'codicil' was, but the little girl's bowed legs overshadowed that thought.

"Am I required to pay for your medical care? I didn't have to pay for your ticket to Federated Central."

Doron felt a little stunned. "A human has a right to medical care. If I'm sick, the doctor has to treat me. Provide medical care."

"The space liner didn't have to pay for your ticket. Why the doctor, if you can't pay him?"

Doron said, "People have a right to medical care." Doron's voice cracked a little.

"What do you think of slavery?"

This was firmer ground. "It is repugnant."

Aaron had the look of a hunter looking down into a pit where he had just trapped a goat. "But it appears you do believe in slavery."

Doron felt confused. "I don't believe in slavery."

"My definition of slavery is where one is forced to work for another involuntarily, or without just compensation. Under that definition, you have just made a slave of the doctor. Have you a different definition of slavery?"

"But the doctor would be paid. Taxes pay for medical care."

"Have you voted on taxes for medical care? Our Federated government takes what it wants from you, and allocates as little as it can for health care. Is that fulfilling a right to medical care? Is it morally sound?"

Bowed legs. *'Mama says I need milk. There's no milk in Clientown.'*

Doron rubbed the back of his neck. "I need to think about it."

"Excellent answer. Always think about what you have been taught. Your instructors may have biases or motives that distort the truth."

"But, but, what if there was a little girl, and she was sick, you would let her die if she could not pay?"

Aaron leaned back in his chair. "Of course not. That is why humans are called to charity, to help each other. But charity is an *individual* responsibility, incumbent on all of us as human beings. Government charity is subject to abuses. When the government runs out of money, often when they waste it on things that personally benefit their govvie buddies, they ration care, and choose who lives and who dies. Like now. Our Corporate and government employees get care, Citizens and Clients are put on waiting lists to die." He shrugged. "Government takes care of those who take care of government."

Clients. Waiting lists. No government money for milk. Was that what happened to the little girl?

Putting a glass of water with ice and lemon on the bar, Mike said, "Gotta watch out for government. Watch out for him, too. He taught ethics at TCU."

Doron was confused. A professor, in Client clothing? This was more and more confusing.

"Something else to think about," added Mike. "If you involuntarily tax someone, say, ten percent of his income, to give someone a handout that they've not earned, haven't you made that first person a ten percent slave?" Mike turned back to the grill. "One Mike's Special, up in a nano."

Aaron just smiled.

"Doron, I have preliminary results of your survey," said LaMancha.

Doron welcomed the new subject with relief. "That was quick."

"Vakkers are highly cooperative."

"And susceptible to threats from a certain Organic," Mike said from the grill.

"Doron and Aaron and Mike, please refer to it as 'leverage.' Power can be employed in a good cause. If I may paraphrase, extremism in defense of Organics is no vice, moderation in pursuit of survey data is no virtue."

Aaron put his hands together. "If we are dueling quotes, I offer one from Abraham Lincoln: 'if you want to test an Organic's character, give him power.'"

"Too late," said Mike, "this Organic has all the character I can stand. Results, please."

"Universe, LaMancha, I present to you results of the first weekly Lacrosse Shot Dining Survey—"

"Hey," said Mike, "Waddya mean, 'weekly'?" Aaron shushed him with a wave.

"—wherein our Vakker clientele is presented with a series of statements. Each had one vote to assign to the statement to which they most agreed—"

Mike looked up at the overhead and closed his eyes. "I got a bad feeling …"

"—The first, 'The food at the Lacrosse Shot is superior to Tevil restaurants' received 105 percent votes."

"Hold it," said Mike. "How'd you get over 100 percent?"

"I allowed the participants to purchase additional votes. Two pence a vote. Nominal. Cut-rate. Cheap, even."

Aaron put a hand to his chin. "An interesting approach."

"Seems to me," said Mike, "it might lead to some screwy answers."

"Universe, LaMancha. 'Prices are fair at the Lacrosse Shot' garnered 87 percent—"

"Marvelous. Two questions, we're up to 192," muttered Mike.

"—'I enjoy the company and atmosphere at the Lacrosse Shot,' 126 percent. 'I enjoy watching Mike's butt as he cooks,' scored one percent, rounded up. The votes, not the butt."

"You asked about my *butt*?"

"The question was placed at the request of ScrewLoose. For a small donation. Now, *if* I may continue after being so *rudely* interrupted, 'I come to combat society's reprehensible gender biases and to crush misogyny in all its forms,' sixty percent—"

"Steinem," mumbled Mike.

"—'I come hoping that Professor Ella Braun will arrive in a skinsuit,' 215 percent—"

Mike buried his face in his hands.

"—'I come because of the scintillating personality and effervescent wit of the Lacrosse Shot's outstanding Organic forward slash waitshooter, who deserves an immediate and astronomical raise in salary, 1,250 percent."

"Yeah, right," said Mike. He pointed into a camera. "How many votes did *you* buy?"

"The survey promised confidentiality to all participants."

"Okay, tell me, how do you qualify as a participant? Have you ever eaten here? I'll bet you gave yourself a volume discount on votes."

"Gracious Humans, LaMancha, the final question was, 'Professor Ella and Mike should get together,' 450 percent. The follow-on question to those who voted 'yes,' 'How many offspring should they have?' The results fell into a lognormal distribution with the median at 4.00 children, that's two sets of twins, and the 90% tail at 15.40."

Doron grinned. He was enjoying this. It was fun watching Mike bluster. But, the math was confounding. "How does one have four tenths of a child?"

"I am sure," LaMancha said, "after fifteen, Professor Ella will have some insights on that issue. I now transmit the survey to your clipscreen."

Doron's clipscreen began playing the opening to Beethoven's Third Symphony. He hit the 'ack' icon.

Aaron was having a hard time keeping a straight face. "You might want to edit those results when you write your report."

"Doron, with your permission," said LaMancha, "I will share the survey with Professor Ella."

Mike roared, "NO!"

51: Aaron

Aaron walked into the Lacrosse Shot near closing time. The last of the patrons were departing. Mike was making the rounds of the tables, performing his obsessive cleaning.

Aaron looked around the room. "Good evening, LaMancha. Has anyone tried to bug your fine establishment since our last discussion? Any new surveillance devices?"

"There are currently four systems in the dining room, designated Larry, Moe, Curly Joe, and Nixon. Nixon has a glitch and wipes its recordings before transmission."

Four bugs. Our Tevil friends have been busy. "You're sure that's all of them?"

"Absolutely. Mike said I could leave them in. They're fun. I know who placed them. I wipe their recordings and substitute something enjoyable, like bogus stock tips, office gossip, who their girlfriends are canoodling while they are out, and I often provide our eavesdroppers with an improving sermon."

A deeply resonant voice with a Boston accent came from all the speakers, echoing through the room. "*Death* comes *unexpectedly*! And the God, *Jehovah*, will execute his *vengeance* on ye, who *despise* his dying love and *trample* his benefits underfoot. The unconverted soul, the foolish children of man do miserably *delude* themselves in the *false confidence* of their own strength and wisdom. They trust to nothing but a shadow. But bear testament. *Death* comes *unexpectedly*!" The Castilian nobleman's voice returned. "I believe the odious Judge Marx gets a copy."

Aaron chuckled. "Well done, that'll learn 'em. Jonathan Edwards, *Sinners in the Hands of an Angry God*, Kneeland and Green publisher. Quite famous. Around 1740, correct?"

"It's from *Pollyanna*, Walt Disney, 1960."

Aaron leaned back in his chair. "I have a vague recollection that Disney used Edwards' *Sinners*, so likely we both are right." He rubbed his chin thoughtfully. "We could meet here without Tevil Security eavesdropping?"

Mike called down from the upper tier tables. "No worries. You get to select your cover story: chisel tournament, birthday party, whatever. LaMancha gives a discount if he picks."

"Discount?"

"Fifty percent off his one stan fee. *Massive* savings."

"Goodness," said Aaron with a laugh.

"It's worth it to see what he does. Soak and Sampson pay him a quarter to listen in to the good ones."

"Obviously, connoisseurs with discriminating taste."

"With Soak, being classy isn't a choice, it's a lifestyle." Mike came down and stood next to Aaron. "So, what's on the screen?"

Aaron took a deep breath. "Clientown. Tevil has cut the food ration again. Clothing is down to one replacement coverall a year, even for children who wear theirs into tatters in two months. There are illnesses from vitamin deficiencies. We have cases of scurvy, pellagra, rickets, beriberi, other illnesses we cannot identify. Health care is supposedly free, but to be seen for diagnosis is eight weeks, and for treatment months more. Most of our seriously ill die before their second appointment." Aaron closed his eyes and grimaced, as if he was the captain of the *Titanic* watching the iceberg slide by and knowing the consequences. "Worst of all is sickness of the spirit. People need to work to see meaning in their lives. By preventing people from working, Tevil steals their dreams. Many see death as the favored alternative. Almost a quarter of our Client deaths are from suicide, few by old age."

Mike took a deep breath. "Didn't know that."

Aaron sighed. "The solution is freedom, a representative government and free markets, or we will spiral further into the grips of tyranny and socialist equality of poverty. We must unite, Citizens and Clients and Vakkers. We discussed holding a meeting here. The time has come. May we?"

"Already said yes. Name a date."

"Tevil will retaliate."

"Already said yes."

Aaron nodded. "Thank you. You are true." He grimaced. "My other concern is Ella."

Mike dropped his bucket. Water splashed out the top, soaking his boots. "Ella's at risk?"

Aaron sighed. "I do not want Ella identified as a protestor. She mustn't be at the meeting."

"Damn right."

Aaron smiled at Mike's emphatic tone. "It also is prudent to keep someone outside imprisonment who is sympathetic with our cause."

"A Cause! Crusade!" declaimed LaMancha. "Revolution! *V for Vendetta. The Matrix. Braveheart. Bananas!* Can I play, too?"

52: *Ghost*

Flatplain Mine's name was obsolete. The terrain was originally flat-ish, and plain-ish, but decades of mining created holes, pits, and trenches. The overburden, removed to allow machinery access to the wide veins of banded magnetite, made massive, man-made hills. The pressurized administrative structures, maintenance hangars and living quarters were centered in the claim, with roadways radiating outward.

With the Organic inoperable, Flatplain Mining Corporation was concentrating on working off maintenance backlogs. Repair technicians were hired, no questions asked, no transaction reports filed.

Ghost was standing next to a 30-meter automated mining machine at the bottom of a deep trench. The bucket wheel excavator had a damaged ore sensor, smashed by an errant rock fall. Ghost was installing a replacement. The job was not mentally engaging. With the bent housing replaced, he slipped in a replacement sensor, made the connections, arranged the wiring inside the conduit, and screwed in the retaining nut. All that remained was calibration.

He listened to a recorded astrophysics lecture. The trench was so deep he couldn't monitor radio comms. On Misplaced-4, all comms were line-of-sight; there was no atmosphere to bounce a signal below the surface.

Ghost felt a slight tremor through his boots. A shuttle landing? He looked up. Another shuttle, on approach for landing, high in the black sky, reflecting silver from the dull red sun. It passed out of sight below the lip of the trench. He felt vibrations from its engine exhaust flailing the ground. Two shuttles, landing nearly simultaneously? Somebody is going to get a Blue Meanie ticket from the Admiralty.

That shuttle was an unfamiliar type. It was small, more the size of some royal's personal yacht than a cargo lander. The way back to the Admin Center skirted the landing field. He'd get a better look then.

Landers arriving meant the Organic was back in service. Sherri would be returning to Dome City. He had kinda sorta maybe been thinking about intercepting her while she was at Flatplain, a chat, lunch or dinner or chisel or something. Sherri was nice. Fun.

Then there was her guardian angel, Professor Braun, who looked like she expected him to spout Stephen Hawking or announce he had solved Unified Field Theory in under five variables. On the other vector, when he was with Sherri, Professor Ella looked like she was ready to box his ears if he misbehaved.

No Carabinieri or corppers were stationed at Flatplain, so lunch should be safe. Sherri might be bored enough to accept. He started climbing to the excavator's cab. He'd do the test and alignment calibration, knock off, find Sherri, lunch.

The cab was above the lip of the trench. He shut off his music and dialed up the maintenance frequency on UHF.

He got a blast of static. A high-pitched noise kept running up and down the octave scales: high pitch, low pitch, high pitch, low pitch. Someone brain dead had gotten on the wrong freq and was jamming the circuit. Probably some desk dragon hitting the wrong buttons, or some music group pirating the freq and doing it wrong.

He shifted to the Maintenance Backup circuit. Same thing. Emergency Ground, channel 23. Same. Low Planetary Orbit Skyspace Control. Same. Jammed. How could landers come in without clearance from LPO Control? Flatplain Ground Control. Same. Flatplain Mine Logistics Control. Same.

Somebody's doing barrage jamming? Only the FSF had that equipment, but they wouldn't jam Emergency Ground for some exercise, would they?

Channel 13. Space Emergency. Most skinsuits didn't have 13, but his suit was rigged special. Jammed.

Out of the corner of his eye, he saw a tram making high speed outbound on the Dome City roadway, billowing a rooster tail of dust in its wake. Scorch. Scorch's tram was rigged for line-of-sight laser comms. He centered the tram in his view screen and ordered the laser to lock on.

"Scorch, Ghost, Laser One. You up?"

Scorch responded immediately. "Ghost, where are you? You safe?"

"Four klicks, your 050 relative. What's wackin'? HF, UHF jammed, all circuits."

"That you by that excavator? Stand by, I'm coming to pick you up."

Ghost could see the tram slew a tight turn. He stood tall and waved both arms. "Scorch, Ghost, I say again, what's the panic?"

"Flatplain's under attack! The whole place, blown to vak. I grabbed everyone at the personnel dock and violated safeties launching. Don't know more, just nose-down-tail-up getting our sweet asses outta here." He paused. "Wait one."

Ghost jumped off the excavator cab and bounded to the top of the nearest spoil hill. He could see the Admin complex. There were two ships in the landing zone, the small lander he had seen, and a cargo shuttle. Around the Tram Terminal there was a scattering of shapes. Bodies?

He went to maximum magnification. Yes, bodies, no skinsuits. Drag mark led out of the Center, and gray piles of something he could not distinguish. He saw a score of what looked like bots, cylindrical, with strange waldos and short legs.

"Ghost, Ella, Laser One."

Professor Braun? Wasn't she with Sherri? "Professor Braun, Ghost, go."

"Ghost, I'm with Scorch. Admin Center was bombed. Bots are shooting nets at people, dragged them vakside—"

"Professor Ella, are you hurt?"

"—they got Sherri!"

Oh, no.

"They're putting people on sleds and dragging them towards those landers. I think they're kidnapping them. Sherri's in her orange skinsuit, they've put her, she's in a net on a sled!"

No, no, no, no.

"Scorch, Ghost, can-x pickup. Get your passengers out."

Ghost looked around. Thirty yards away, there was an articulated three-axel ore truck. He started running.

Scorch said, "Don't be crazy, there's nothing you can do back there."

"Don't know 'til try. Out." He secured the link.

The ore truck was huge, seven meters high, powered off fuel cells. He slid into the driver's seat. It was a simple frame seat, with just a lap belt to keep the driver from bouncing off in the low gravity.

The controls were locked.

Ghost bent his head down and concentrated. Concentrated like never before.

Mable. I need you. Please, Mable.

Hello, Ghost dear.

Relief flooded through Ghost's mind. *I am in,* he glanced up to the dashboard, *ore truck T1774 at Flatplain Mining. Can you tell me the activation password?*

T1774FM, dear.

Ghost keyed it in. The dashboard flashed red on all the lights. Displays illuminated. There were a few seconds of built-in startup tests, then a green board. The engine instruments came to life. There was a jolt as the engine started.

Mable. Thank you.

Ghost released the brake, grabbed the joystick, and pushed it forward. The truck lurched. In a few seconds he was up to max speed. The rear camera monitor showed a cloud of dust and rocks lifting off the massive tires. He charged down the radial road heading to Admin Center. The landing area was to his left, off a different radial road. There were trenches between him and the landing zone, with intermittent piles of spoil. No direct path to the landers. He would have to go all the way to the Admin Center before he could head to the shuttles.

Closer now, he could see the landing zone better. Bots were gesturing at him. Others were pulling sleds. The gray piles he had seen were nets filled with squirming people. He saw florescent orange, on a sled being pulled to the large cargo shuttle.

A flood of emotions swirled through his mind. Sherri was

captured. People were dead. People were being dragged away, Vakkers, people who had been good to him, had supported him when he needed support, had helped him. More people could die. He wouldn't see Sherri again.

He didn't want to die. He didn't want the Vakkers, Sherri, to die.

There was a cluster of bots around the small lander. The sleds were heading for the cargo lander. They had about 300 meters to go. When they reached the lander, they would load the people and boost. Ten, maybe fifteen minutes, people gone, Sherri gone.

He could drive to the Center, reverse on to the radial road to the lander field, charge the bots, and run them over with the truck.

How could he run over bots without running over the sleds and killing people?

Not enough time.

He looked at the ravine separating him from the landing field. He looked at the spoil heaps. He braked to a stop. His mind's eye measured angles. He calculated.

He turned right and rolled across the road. The off-road surface was firm.

Turn around. One last look. Angles, vectors, calculations.

He jammed the joystick forward. The truck leaped ahead. It charged towards the ravine, bouncing and shuddering. Ghost glanced at the dashboard. The truck could manage a top speed of 70. He needed 58 kilometers per hour. Angles. Calculations.

He adjusted his course toward a spoil heap.

The truck lurched. It bounced through a depression, then climbed. It reached the top of the spoil heap.

Liftoff.

The low gravity gently bent its trajectory. He cleared the ravine. Flying.

There were worse ways to die. He was part of a beautiful arc. Hands off the controls, feet off the pedals, nothing more he could do. He closed his eyes and visualized the curve on a Cartesian plot. Time versus altitude. A mathematically elegant curve.

Forgot the seat belt. Might as well give it a click. Safety regulations.

Oh, this was a thing of beauty. Spot on. Such a graceful curve. Apogee. Now, downward, down.

Ten tons of trucks slammed into the command deck of the cargo shuttle. The trailer jackknifed, broke free, and crushed the shuttle's cargo compartment. There was an explosion of rocks and flying metal.

53: *Ella*

Ella was sitting next to Scorch in the control cabin of *Scorcher #1*. Her skinsuit helmet was up. She kept glancing back at the Administrative Center, praying that the good Lord would do something—*anything*—to save Sherri.

She saw Ghost run to the ore truck. The ore truck barreled down the radial road, stopped, repositioned, accelerated, climbed, and then lifted off the top of a spoil heap.

She watched in horror as it smashed into the lander.

"No! NO! STOP! Scorch, stop, stop, stop! We have to go back!"

54: Tarak

The Trashcans formed their usual line, paused for some minutes, and then headed for Tarak's hill at a slow, steady pace. As foreseen.

Tarak was buried only a few yards from the lander, helmet up, breathing suit air shallowly, body unmoving. He was inside a dust depression, hidden under rocks and dirt. Digging in this close was risky, but he gambled that Trashcan piloting was precise. Previous landings were all within meters of the first landing.

The Trashcans neglected to exactly reproduce their landing point. Again.

He was on the port aft quarter of the lander. It had three independent landing struts, two aft and one forward. The fuselage aft was dominated by a large open hatch with a ramp angling down to the surface. Tarak couldn't see inside; the angle was bad, and the interior was in deep shadow, contrasting with the brilliant, cloudless sunshine.

The line of aliens moved out of view. Even the slightest swell in the terrain blocked Tarak's sight. Patience. Like Geronimo, like Red Cloud, Tarak knew patience. Wait until you are sure, then wait some more.

Patience satisfied. He crawled out like a mole emerging from its burrow. A small mist of disturbed dust rose. He retracted his helmet. It was an effort not to sneeze, the dust tickling his nose. The click of his helmet folding into his skinsuit caused Tarak to tense. No reaction to the noise.

There was a clang of metal-on-metal from the front of the shuttle.

He waited, prone, until the dust settled, his head shielded by a boulder he had positioned for that purpose. He peeked. There was a Trashcan at the forward landing gear. Next to it was a box. Another creature, indistinct, frail looking, like a giant thin starfish, hung from the landing gear, wielding tools. Another alien species! His cup runneth over.

Were they doing repair work? Fixing something after a hard landing? Tarak could hear a high-pitched metal-on-metal ringing. How long would they remain working?

The ramp to the lander's entrance was too inviting. To the right there was a dip, offering concealment. He could get the ramp between him and the aliens.

He moved, as quiet as Death searching for the unknowing, compromising speed for stealth, careful not to raise any dust. He crawled to the ramp. Wait. No reaction. More tool noises from forward.

Ready with the alien blade, he rose to a crouch, stepped on the ramp, then entered the gloom.

He was in a cargo bay. He recognized things immediately: an internal communications panel, a locker marked with a red cross, a fire extinguisher, and labels on the walls in English and Korean. This was a human shuttle. He paused to let his eyes adjust. The bay was configured with rows of curious-looking seats— were they seats? — along a central aisle running forward to the command deck. The cockpit hatch was open. His right hand gripped the blade. He advanced.

The command deck was unoccupied. It had been modified beyond recognition. The throttles were fitted with extensions. The joystick and maneuvering thruster controls were still there, but most of the instruments had been moved, covered, or replaced. The instrument panel was a jumble. The Organic's tank was gone.

He had hoped to capture the lander and boost off this rock, but the control panel was a cypher. There was no hope he could safely get off the ground and navigate to a PunchPoint.

He glanced about and saw another door labeled 'Sensors.' He slipped in.

Unintelligible. A jumble of alien modifications.

Sliding open another pocket door, he moved into the communications station.

Untouched!

Nothing had been changed. He could recognize VHF, HF and laser comms panels, the buttons to tune to the standard 126 channels, there was even a human headset clipped to the bulkhead. The standard big red button would put him on emergency broadcast channel 13, monitored continuously by all spacecraft.

By all *human* spacecraft. Not by aliens. He hoped.

Power on. The panel came to life. Lights flashed as the system performed its startup checks. The warmup light shifted to 'ready.' He put the headset on and selected channel 13.

He listened. Maximum amplification. Nothing.

He spoke into the microphone. "Mayday, mayday, mayday, CQ, CQ, niner niner, niner niner, any station receiving. This is Citizen Captain Tarak of *Prosperity*. *Prosperity* has been hijacked. Venez m'aider, request immediate assistance. I am being held against my will—"

He told his story several times into the ether, including identifying details about the planet, the sun, and the Trashcans. Hopefully, anyone receiving would not think it a hoax.

No response. Just the crackle of atmospheric static.

Then, inspiration.

He recorded his message. It was the work of only a few minutes to automate the recording to broadcast on a continuous loop. If the Trashcans were true to pattern, the lander then would be in space with the auxiliary power unit on line; with the APU feeding the communications power bus, the message would go out full strength.

He couldn't get the buttonology right for a continuous loop. He had to settle for once every 15 minutes, beginning 12 hours from— now.

The Trashcans weren't using the comms compartment. With luck, they wouldn't enter the compartment at all and would not notice the broadcast. They would lift off above the atmosphere and unknowingly transmit his call for help.

Now, he had to get off the lander without being detected. Hide.

Then, until someone responded, survive.

55: *Ghost*

Ghost slowly gathered awareness. He opened his eyes. A ceiling.

He felt weird. Disassociated. Out of body. "Oh, Gawd."

Morgan Freeman's voice. "Ghost, it is LaMancha, can you hear me? Oh, Gawd, you say? I understand your confusion. Often, I am mistaken for a superior being. I will certainly work towards fulfilling your expectations."

Another familiar voice. "LaMancha, you hush."

Ghost saw a hand waving a few feet above his eyes.

"Hey, Ghost. Welcome back. Howyadoin'?"

He blinked. Angled his head. He was lying down. A bed. A side table, a FoxxFone on a stand with LaMancha's Shining Knight displaying a worried expression around a drooping mustache. Sherri. Sherri was smiling. It was the kind of smile people use in the medical vids when they didn't want to tell the patient they have just cut off all their arms and legs. Was this a hospital? He wondered who Sherri was visiting.

Where was his skinsuit? He was naked! He started to panic. Whatever was floating in his bloodstream clamped down. He calmed.

Sherri's voice. "The doctors say you're going to be all better, full recovery."

He rested his head back. "Roger that. Say 'Thank You' to God. He was here a second ago."

Ghost closed his eyes, and slept.

56: *Ghost*

Ghost awoke.

His vision was narrowed into slits. Right arm, something kept it from moving. Left arm, okay. Wiggle toes. Good. Legs. Heavy, not moving, a vague feeling of hurt.

Something covered his left hand. "Hey, Hero."

He saw Sherri. Her hair was in disarray, tendrils of brown

escaping from her ponytail. There were shadows around her eyes.

He blinked. That cleared his vision. Better. Seeing Sherri, his heart calmed.

"Stay bold for a nano, I'll get the doctor. Oh. Here she is."

Another voice. A pleasant voice. "We do have good instruments, Citizen Academic Brightly."

"Of course."

"How are you, Citizen Ghost? I am Citizen Physician Kang. Have you any pain?"

Pain? Did she mean existential pain, or physical? An actual or rhetorical question? Was this a hospital or psych ward? Did it matter how he responded?

Try the obvious. "No."

The doctor smiled. "Excellent. The instruments detect pain and provide medication as necessary, so it appears we are set at the right level to make you comfortable."

That appeared to be the right answer. Stupid thoughts.

His mind cleared some more. "Waz wrong, me?

"You crashed in an ore truck. Your face hit the control panel, which broke the nose, a lot of edemas, that is, swelling. Most fortunately, your skinsuit auto-seal worked as designed. Both legs are broken below the knees. We'll set the bones after the swelling goes down. Tomorrow, I think. After that, we anticipate a complete recovery. I expect you'll be able to walk out, ah…" She glanced down at his right arm.

He looked. There was a bag of fluid. A tube from the bag led to a needle in his arm, covered by tape. His wrist was handcuffed to the bed's metal railing.

The doctor looked at Sherri. "You may visit, but just a few minutes."

Settling on a corner of the bed, Sherri took Ghost's free hand. "You saved my life," she said. "Thank you."

He tried to smile back. Too many bandages.

She took a breath. "But, I, you—" she frowned and withdrew her hand "—that was the most ultimate *stupidest* thing I have ever seen from a cognitive being! I am so angry with you! You could have been killed!"

He thought back to the trajectory. "Beautiful arc."

"Yeah, right," she said, with exasperation. "You have inflicted on me a massive dose of cognitive dissonance. Like, 'I thank you, Derr Suicidal Maniac.' Next, *I* go into therapy, and *you'll* want to join the circus and get blown out of cannons."

He imagined a cannon trajectory in 0.26-G. He visualized it as a 2-D graph. "Might be beautiful."

"Okay, roger that, after the physicians, you're into the skull shop for brain recalibration."

He put his hand next to hers, not touching. He hoped she would hold it again. He spoke with care to avoid hurting his face. "Pirates? Wha hoppen?"

Sherri shifted to a chair by the bed. "I can tell you what happened to me. Freddy's still trying to sort the big picture."

The light was uncomfortable. He closed his eyes.

"The Prof and I got the Organic back up, PDQ. A maintenance intern mixed DC and AC power supplies. A generational curse is the charitable explanation. The reboot was going to take 36 hours, but that was something their techs could handle, and we could supervise from TCU. So, there I was, happy as a tourist who just found a leprechaun handing out prizes from his pot of gold, walking to the tram loading dock." She snarked a little. "Scorch bumped a coupla Tevil executives to get us seats."

Ghost looked up sharply and tried to raise his head. "Are they—"

Sherri put a hand on his shoulder. "Scorch and Professor Ella are fine. She's dossed out in the waiting room. We've been taking turns."

Ghost settled back. "Mad at her. Left you."

Sherri gave his hand a pop. "Don't you think that. When the attack began, she could have run, but instead, she grabbed two kids without skinsuits and got them into the Scorcher before the lobby lost all its air. Then, after a certain Flying Wallenda changed the rules, she got Scorch to turn around. She helped cut us out of the nets, and got people low on O_2 into the tram. She saved lives, too." She looked at him unblinkingly. "Bite your tongue, and let me finish."

Ghost took a breath. He should have known Professor Braun would do right.

"So, as I was saying, I'm walking along happy as a solar panel powering an amusement park, when there is this great big 'kaboom,' and I'm knocked down flat on my very elegant derriere. The air all goes to the Milky Way, my helmet auto deploys, and this thing comes through the wall and shoots me with a net!"

"T'ing?"

"Four feet tall, strange legs, and, I swear, a big waldo where any self-respecting anthropomorphic bot would have a head."

Ghost blinked a few times. "Vodka for breakfast, you?"

"Hush, silly creature. I had a virgin Shirley Temple. So, I'm having a freak while two of them drag me outside and toss me on this sled. I am not a happy entity! Then they net two *huge* guys, and throw them *on top* of me!"

"Ouch."

"'Ouch' ain't half of it. There I am, the feature attraction in a kidnapping, with a few hundred kilos of idiot on top of me. Govvies. One reaches through my net and tries to cop a feel!"

Ghost's jaw clenched. The electronic monitor beeped.

Sherri smiled with a touch of devilry. "Hey, no worries. After the Prof cut me out, I made sure that clown wasn't going to walk straight for a few days."

"Kneecapped him?"

"Higher."

Ghost smiled. Smiling hurt a little. The beeping stopped.

"So, there I was," continued Sherri, "fighting off Derr Friendly Fingers, in a net, on a sled, towed off by the Freaks from Fantasyland, heading for this lander and an all-expense-paid vacation with pirates from the black hole. Then this mental case in an ore truck kinda changes the situation."

Sherri reached over and patted his hand. That was nice.

"After bits and pieces of lander stop coming down, the bots got real agitated. They clustered around waving their waldos. AI glitched, maybe overloaded. Weird."

"Weird," agreed Ghost.

"Half loaded into the little lander. It takes off. The ones left behind blow up."

"Explode?"

"Yup," nodded Sherri. "Explode. The official reenactment of the

Big Bang. Smoke and gas, flying bits and pieces. Nothin' left. Zippo, nichts, niente, nada. Fun to watch. Get your tickets, Fireworks at Flatplain, one performance only."

Why would bots self-destruct? "Why, Big Bang? Hide builder? Origin?"

Sherri leaned back. "Dunno. Lots of ideas, no answers. Freddy's closed down all media contacts. No information is getting out." She rubbed the bridge of her nose. "I talked to Marcus. He's a Vakminer. By the way, the miners and Vakkers fought back. A delegation of visiting Tevil executives tried hiding in the toilets. No skinsuits. Corpse City."

Ghost involuntarily shivered. He missed his skinsuit.

"Anyhoo," said Sherri, "Marcus said he got one of the blighters, with a crowbar. Snuck up behind it and speared it like a wiener on a toothpick. The thing had on something like a skinsuit. He peeled it back and got a good look at what was under. He left to hunt another one, lucky, left just before it exploded. Kabloowie."

Ghost approved of kabloowie.

"Marcus said they were strange. Not bots. Claimed they weren't machines. Would a machine wear a skinsuit?"

Ghost started to chuckle, but it hurt too much. "Sherri kidnapped, bunch o' midgets."

"Don't be silly."

"Psycho kindergarteners?"

"Psycho Ghost."

"Last option. Evil Aliens." That started Sherri laughing.

When she settled down, she said, "Maybe somebody has really gone crazy at a gene-splicing lab. If I was Head Freddy, I'd send a battalion of piss-off Carabinieri to Asclepius and bust down some doors."

Ghost didn't know about gene splicing. He'd have to research.

Then, Sherri sobered, and looked at Ghost square-on. "Okay, now comes the crappy part. After you did your Evel Knievel with the ore truck, and the critters lit burners and boosted, the Carabinieri arrived. Here's the gift without the wrapping. Good news, we got you out of the wreck alive. Bad news, Freddy's snagged you for tax evasion."

57: Marshall

It was just a germ of an idea, but the more Captain Peter Marshal considered, the more it shined off the page.

Marshall was reading the 'Sunrise Sillies,' formally named *Summary of News and Communiques* from FSF Public Communications. There was a story, dateline Misplaced-4 / 1st Battalion 4th Carabinieri, from just four days ago, transmitted through VelociComms PunchPoint buoys.

Pirates attacked a mining outpost. They were on the verge of escaping with prisoners when a Vakker kid commandeered a truck and smashed their cargo lander. The pirates retreated to their command lander and boosted, but without prisoners, and abandoning half their bots. Then, no good deed left unpunished, the hero was arrested for violating some local regulations. Absurd.

For years Marshall anticipated conflict between the planets, even war. 'Pirates' could be a convenient cover for economic warfare against Tevil Corporation. There were enough grudges and feuds among the 35 'n 50 to make that possibility real. There had been a recent surge of missing ships and hijackings. The jackings had the feel of an organized effort. A combat-ready Federated Fleet was needed to keep the peace.

Getting combat-ready with the students he was receiving was questionable. The Command students' ultimate loyalties were with their Corporate and Family roots, not the FSF. The 35 'n 50 liked it that way; they could man their ACTs with officers loyal to them. The separation between Command officers and Artisan officers was another weakness. How could anyone command what they did not understand?

The royals would resist reform. The FSF was too convenient a place to honorably stash non-performing offspring. Those promoted in spite of their deficient skills became well-placed Admirals who could support family or Corporate interests. Senior FSF positions were valued most for their political and financial leverage.

Part of the solution was to break the royal's hammerlock on Command billets. Officers' loyalties had to be with the Federated Government, not their home planets. He needed a candidate from outside the royals, someone with Artisan-level technical competence, who could succeed as a leader. Better, one who was a hero to the people, would have popular support, get positive publicity, be a personality to represent the FSF to *all* the people. He had to be tough, too. Some Family or Corporation might decide to protect their monopoly with an assassin.

A popular, Artisan-qualified Command Candidate was an intriguing idea. This kid might be just the way to infiltrate the system.

Marshall composed an encrypted flash request to an ally on Misplaced-4.

58: Marx

The court bailiff cleared his throat, sounding like a seal choking down an extra-large pizza. To the nearly-empty courtroom, he intoned, "Oyez, Oyez, Oyez, all persons having business before the Honorable Judge Vladimir Marx, a stalwart of integrity regulating the law under the charter of the Tevil Corporation and the Federated Planets, for the jurisdiction within the orbit of, and within and under Dome City, are admonished to draw near and give their attention, for justice is to be served. God save and support this honorable court." He frowned at the lack of spectator appreciation for his speech, then called, "Seats!"

There was a rustle as the few in the room sat. Judge Marx paraded in like a hero leading a Roman Triumph. He took his seat on the raised throne behind the massive dais, valued for its protection from direct attacks from insurrectionists who didn't like his just, well-reasoned decisions.

Marx glanced up. There were six onlookers: an FSF officer, three syndicated newsfeed reporters he wasn't able to exclude, and his two pet AHOLS bloggers. Much good those two 'Image Managers' were. He paid them handsomely to mold his reputation, yet he still risked mob violence if he appeared in public. The Populous did not believe he had an iota of good will. The disrespectful nicknames were the worst, like that 'Bench Vulture" disinformation. He told those bloggers to get it expunged, drive it out of the media. He might look like a vulture, sometimes, maybe on a bad hair day after too many whiskey sours, but in a fair universe, he would be likened to a bird more upstanding and honorable. 'Legal Eagle,' or 'Hawk of Justice.'

The lying bastards claimed the nickname was based not only on his appearance, but the correlation with the fact that vultures fed on the wounded and dying.

Time for new bloggers?

No. His Persuasion Workers would give them a visit. Screwtape and Wormwood. He'd have them take pictures to document their work. He hadn't anything new for his album for a week.

Today, he had to be sharp, because of the FSF officer. The newsfeeders had to be impressed, too, because of the public frenzy over this case. A crowd outside demanded admittance, but his security Carabinieri advised him to keep them out. Too many to control; they might riot when the verdict was announced.

He presented his good side to the cameras. "Call the case."

"The Federated Hand of Justice versus Unregistered Person, docket A-412."

The criminal was brought in and handcuffed to the dock in front of the judge.

Judge Marx pretended to look at his papers while he mulled over the case. This scofflaw, aged approximately 18 years, hadn't paid one standard of the Air Tax. By law, the Tax was to be paid beginning at birth by his parents; if no parents were located, accrued in his own account. With no parents, at age 12 he was required to begin making payments on the accrued amount, as well as pay weekly Air and Transaction Taxes. They paid through service on government working parties.

The automatic verdict for evading any Tax was imprisonment at hard labor, then Federated indentured service until his taxes were paid.

There were complications. This criminal did something noteworthy during that pirate attack; he was popular with the citizens, and had support among the Vakkers. All immaterial considerations; bottom line, he was a lawbreaker.

Judge Marx had tricks to keep him out of the news feeds.

"Docket A-412, what is your registered name?" asked the judge.

The criminal just shrugged.

"What name do you go by?'

"Ghost," said the defendant.

"Let the record show the defendant self-identifies by the name 'Coast.' C-O-A-S-T."

The judge smiled. That should stymie the search engines looking for stories about this 'Ghost' fellow. Ghost was some kind of hero; Coast was a tax cheat. Anyone named Ghost never existed, as far as this court was concerned.

The judge shuffled through his papers. "Coast, you have a long history of anti-social behavior. You have never paid your Air Tax, the people's investment that supplies your every breath. Your other crimes are too extensive to recite here. You have ignored this court's call to come to trial. You have been twice tried in absentia, and found guilty," he waved a sheet, "of tax evasion, to the sum, including interest and penalties," he glanced down, "over twenty-six thousand standards."

He heard the prisoner sigh. He enjoyed criminals in despair.

"The sum of your crimes, attempted theft, evading Transaction Taxes, performing work without licensing or permits, illegal trading in goods and services, are incalculable. Tevil Corporation has made an estimate. With interest and penalties, court costs and fines, your debt to society amounts to eighty thousand standards."

His ferrets had also located, from clues in the criminal's clipscreen, some six thousand standards hidden in various accounts. His crimes were certainly profitable. Marx had confiscated the funds under the civil forfeiture laws. A few keypunches and they were discretely transferred into his personal accounts, as was just, to support him as the leading crusader for Social Justice.

He looked sternly at the criminal, hoping the cameras captured the expression. He practiced it in the mirror.

"At the average wage of a lawfully-employed citizen amounting to 5,000 standards per annum, after your corrective custody, I rule that you spend sixteen years indentured to the Federated services.

The prisoner sagged a little.

"I was surprised to learn you have supporters. There have been affidavits and letters from Citizens offering to pay your fine. The pledges total over sixty thousand standards."

The malefactor did not move.

"Such a huge sum taken out of our economy would handicap businesses and the personal finances of upstanding Citizens. Supporting you would cripple them. This, in all conscience, I cannot permit. I must consider the good of the whole of society, not any individual." Also, it would make it harder for those citizens to meet their payments to my Union Persuasion Workers if their bank accounts were drained to pay off this scofflaw's debt. But the offers were useful information. Now he knew who had money, and how much.

"The requests and letters of the Friends of the Court are denied."

This made no impression on the criminal.

"For your punitive penance, you will be incarcerated at hard labor for twenty-two years."

The prisoner straightened and looked at him defiantly.

One of the newsfeeders got up, leaned over the restraining rail, and took a photograph of the defendant. She raced out of the room.

"Order in the court!" bawled the bailiff.

The courtroom door banged shut disrespectfully.

Marx was unruffled. "I have another request, this from our stalwart Federated Space Forces. I have been asked to allow them to make you an offer to 'Pay on the Drum.' After this court adjourns, he will meet with you and outline the terms. If you accept, your just punishment will be made probationary for the duration of your service. If you do not accept this alternative, the sentence of this court stands."

Judge Marx banged his gavel. "Twenty-two years. Next case!"

59: Reeson

JAG Lieutenant Reeson peered through the viewport into the jail cell. The prisoner sat on the floor in a corner, legs straight out. It was as if, by not using the bunk, he was denying the prison's power. Or, perhaps, it was his way of expressing defiance. Or, perhaps, he was just more comfortable that way, having recently been healed of broken legs.

"That's him, Loo-tenant," said the prison guard. "Half an hour, then we picks 'em up and ships 'em out."

Time to get past this cage kicker. "Let me in."

The guard pressed his thumbprint on the cell door lock pad. "Just know, if he starts whupping on you, coupla minutes before I can get here from the guardroom."

The lieutenant stepped in. The door clanged shut behind him.

"Hello, Coast. How are the legs?"

No reaction from the prisoner. He didn't look up.

"My name is Reeson. JAG Lieutenant Reeson, Federated Space Forces. JAG stands for Judge Advocate General. A lawyer, a barrister. You might have heard us called 'shyster,' or 'mietmaul,' which the German original translates as 'rent-a-mouth,' but a lawyer is a shyster is a mietmaul is a lawyer."

Still no reaction. Reeson sat down on the bunk. It was hard, lumpy, uncomfortable.

"Twenty-two years," said Reeson. "Awfully rough for breathing."

The prisoner looked up. "Also, for working. For fixing things. I work for people, people paid fair, good deal for both. Voluntary exchange. Don't see why I pay government for permission to work."

That was a philosophical discussion for another time. He had to steer the conversation away from this fellow's resentment against government, or he might not agree to his proposal. Captain Marshall was adamant he wanted this kid at the Academy.

"You fix things," Reeson said. "I'm told you do good work."

"You get what you pay for, you pay for what you get."

"You stopped that pirate raid. You saved a lot of lives."

No reaction. *Let's see if I can get him interested in the Academy.* "You're a pretty smart lad, considering you have never been to school."

The boy shrugged. "What's school? They tell you, read books. I read books, read manuals. Don't need school to read."

So much for that approach. "So, what can you do from reading manuals?"

Looking him in the eyes, the boy said, "Pilot anything in space. Fix things, electrical, electronic, mechanical, hydraulic, pneumatic, fluid, field. Never fixed a PunchPlane Generator, fun to try."

Stars and comets, this young man has an inflated opinion of himself. "We need people who can do that in the Federated Space Forces." No reaction. "The judge said you could pay off your debt, your monetary fine and the hard labor, by 'Pay on the Drum.' Do you know what that is?"

Coast shook his head.

"The practice began on OldEarth, back in the musket days. 'Pay on the Drum' meant a person convicted of a crime could pay his debt to society by enlisting in the army. His enlistment bonus was tossed on the regiment's drum. The army got a recruit, the recruit got his sentence dismissed. It is done today, for special cases. You join the Federated Space Forces, our space navy. After satisfactory service, your record will be expunged, and you'll be free."

"You want me to enlist?"

"I'm making that offer."

The prisoner snorted.

"What's wrong?" asked Reeson.

"Never met competent fartisan or clown commander. Go Fed Navy, get killed by some FNQ doesn't know a regulator from a regurgulator."

Fartisan. Reeson hated that nickname. But there was truth to the kid's prejudice. The service was filled with clown commanders and marginally-qualified Artisans. That was one of the reasons why Reeson had joined Captain Marshall's band of brothers and sisters, for reform, to build a Navy he could be proud to serve.

At least the young man had spirit. He looked him in the eyes. "Are you competent?"

Coast shrugged again. "Time in the Deep Dark, still alive. Yeah, competent."

"We want to make the FSF competent. We need men like you."

The kid chewed on his lower lip. Was he thinking it over?

"How long?" he asked.

"Five years."

"Why not I jump ship, first orbit?"

"Tell me you'll do your full time, and serve to the best of your ability. Vakker's word."

"Where?"

"You will be assigned in accordance with the needs of the Navy. The saying goes, 'Any ship, any station, any job, any Corporation.'"

Coast didn't look as if he liked that. *Let's reduce the uncertainty.* "You'll first report to the FSF Academy on Federated Central, Elysium System." Elysium was nice. Lots of people want to go there.

"Job?"

"You'll take a skills test, and be placed where you can best serve. Needs of the Navy." Captain Marshall hadn't passed on what he intended for this guy.

The kid chewed on his lower lip some more.

"Amber," he said. "Counter?"

Unbelievable. The kid wanted to haggle with the Federated Navy. "Let's hear it."

"I enlist, five years, any ship any station any job. My skinsuit, no huhu over my mods, my electronics. Feds top off my O_2, recharge power cells. I get 48 hours free, Misplaced-4, make arrangements, goodbyes."

Reeson had no problems with those requests. He'd transmit the promise about the skinsuit mods to Captain Marshall, but it was not unusual, lots of flight crew modified their skinsuits. Power cells, O_2, he had contingency funds to cover that, and it shouldn't be much. "I'll provide a credit account for the batteries and O_2 for one skinsuit initial loadout. You make the purchases. As to the rest, accepted."

The kid gave a nod. "Green." He settled back against the wall.

"On your feet, Coast. We have things to do, places to go, people to see." He stood, reached down, and held out his hand. That was not something an officer would ordinarily do for flight crew, but it felt right.

Besides, the kid was recovering from broken legs.

60: *Hillary*

Whistling a happy tune, Yeoman Third Class Hillary checked the appointment queue for her next opportunity. There was a new recruit for in-processing, with travel back to Fed Central. Hillary loved travel. Travel orders always meant standards in her pockets.

The meeting cubical was a confining space containing a desk, two chairs, a power outlet, internet jacks, and one recruit. She gave her vic-du-jour an appraising look. She saw a skinny kid in Client Grays with a crappy close-cut Vakker headclip slumped in the vic's chair. He looked up at her with the typical watery expression of someone tenderized by Judge Marx's loving attentions. The Nav' must really be desperate, dragging in sorry characters like this.

At least, after Marx, he'd willingly accept anything she did.

"Hello there, Young Adventurer. My name is Yeoman Third Class Hillary, and I'll be handling your processing into the Federated Space Follies. Call me Yeo Three. Welcome to *your* Federated Space

Forces!" She glanced at the accession form. "Well, almost, since you'll not be sworn in until you arrive at Fed Central, but here we're going to take the first step towards your contribution to make the universe safe for bunnies and other small furry creatures."

Hillary dropped into a chair and held out a hand. "Clipscreen? There's the man."

The mark gave her his new government clipscreen. She pulled power cords out of a desk drawer and plugged everything into charger ports. A cable connected his clipscreen with hers. Personnel information was not allowed on wireless links, and besides, she didn't want anyone to see what she was about to create. From the desk drawer, she pulled a full-sized keyboard and plugged it in.

Calling up the appropriate forms, she found that the dumb-ass Accessions Clerk hadn't come near to finishing entering the data. Excellent. His incompetence, her opportunity. Even better, the partially filled-in form was already thumb printed by a JAG officer. She could do anything she wanted in the blanks, and the Jaggie would be responsible.

At least the name was filled in. Start with the easy stuff. "Name, Coast. Planet of accession, Misplaced-4. That would mean, last name NFN, middle name NMN? I know you Vakkers are funny about names."

The kid looked up. "NFN? NMN?"

"No Family Name, No Middle Name. Regular humans have them, but not Vakkers. Vakkers change their name, like, daily. How's an honest yeoman keep the records straight? Date of birth?"

"Don't know."

Gads, a creche-kid. "Got a particular month you like?"

He shook his head.

"Okay, we'll make it—damn, I hate these 12-month years, you'd think Freaky-4 would rationalize on a good decimal system—we'll go with November 11th and backdate it to make you…" she eyed him appraisingly, "…19 standard years old. Fantastic, you're over the minimum age to enlist. Congratulations to me, I feel like a new mother."

She scrolled down the form. "Place of birth?"

"Don't know."

"Parents? Next of kin?"

"None."

"Home of record?"

"No home."

Sheesh! One pathetic case. That Jaggie was sweeping the gutter. "No worries. I'll tell you what we're going to do." She unplugged the recruit's government clipscreen, entered a code, and called up a file. "We've got this little quiz, the 'FSF Standardized Classification Test.' It helps us put you in the occupational field for which you are best suited. It takes about two hours. Go through that door," she pointed, "into the testing room. Come back when you're done."

With a little creativity, she ought to be able to knock the rest of this off in a few nanos, then take a nice snooze until he was done.

After minutes of irritating labor, creativity got boring. She called up the information from a recruit in-processed a few months ago and did a cut 'n paste for the data fields.

The door opened. Coast walked in.

"You got a question?"

Coast put the clipscreen on the desk. "Done."

Hillary looked at her clipscreen chronometer. Yeah, right, this guy finished that honkin' big test in thirty minutes. You couldn't even *read* it in thirty. She grabbed Coast's clipscreen, entered her authorization code, and hit the "grade" icon. The clipscreen cheeped. She opened the results file to see how many questions he skipped.

100% answered.

100% *correct* answers.

Dang, must be a glitch. The software must have overwritten the recruit's answer file with the grading file.

"Okay, you did super. I've another one for you." She called up another version of the test. She ensured the answer file remained segregated and inaccessible, did the first question herself to confirm it was recording answers accurately, and sent him back into the testing room.

Back in twenty-eight minutes.

98%.

She scanned the test. The question she had answered was wrong. He had skipped two questions. All the rest were correct.

Dammit! She didn't want a hold placed on this guy waiting for the Zeros 'n Ones Mob to get this shit sorted. Somebody might question the data she'd entered. She sighed. She'd just have to copy the other guy's test results into Coast's record.

That completed, she entered a low score for 'administrative skills / clerical aptitude.' With a high score they might make him a Yeoman Striker, and he might bump into her again. By then, he might have learned enough to resent a few of her little tricks.

"Sit. Let's see what we can do for travel orders."

Hillary called up her travel app. First, she checked her special account where the ship's pursers sent her little monetary incentives to send business their way. It was up only seven standards. Totally unsatisfactory. She had ways to show those jokers she wasn't pleased.

The Jaggie had said Coast was allowed at least 48 hours before departure. She started scrolling through schedules. Nothing in serf & peon class for two weeks. No way she was going to have this bumpkin floating around her office with these hinky records. Someone might get inspired to check them. That could get a certain Yeo Three in deep dung.

Inspiration.

She hit a few keys; now the Jaggie's transportation request specified Expedited Orders. She could expand her cabin search to first class. There. Oh, yes. *Extravagance Queen*, Chief Purser Lecter's ship. Hanny Lecter baby sent her a percentage for Galaxy class bookings. This lovely percentage will be better than Santa on Bastille Day.

"Young Adventurer, I have just provided you the best FNG Good Deal—that is, 'FNG' stands for 'New Guy,' you'll learn the lingo soon enough—like I said, the best good deal this side of the heaven of your personal faith or belief system, that is, if you can grease the launch platform. Got any cash?"

Coast reached into a pocket. He scattered coins on the table. Hillary's practiced eye counted twenty-one stans and a handful of small change. She expertly slid twenty stans into her desk drawer. Her first kill.

She grabbed Coast's clipscreen, plugged in her keyboard and entered the access code of a yeoman scheduled to transfer in a week. No reason why anything should be traceable to her. For that matter, no reason why Coast should remain anywhere near the FSF station.

He was allowed FSF per diem money for miscellaneous expenses, 54 standards. She credited that amount to his clipscreen, then recorded a purchase from her front company for 'travel services' for eleven stan. No problem, 43 stan would last him, if he controlled his use of toilet paper.

After a few more minutes of skullduggery, she unplugged her keyboard, called up a page on Coast's clipscreen, and rotated it to show him. "Young Adventurer, here is the incredibly good deal I have arranged for you. First, you check in at the Dome City Monarch for five-days-four-nights, 'Awaiting Transportation.' You have a reservation on the Queen Lines Galaxy Shuttle to Queen One orbital terminal. One night in orbit at the Queen's Chateau Hotel and Conference Center. Then, reservations for *Extravagance Queen*, departing 1000 Sunday, Galaxy-Class Lodge 17, Federated Central via a three-day layover at the resort planet of Cetus-1. You have government vouchers for all meals for the duration, at the Monarch and with Queen, no alcoholic beverages included, and 43 standards credit in your government clipscreen for travel incidentals. Copy all?"

The recruit, after a short pause, nodded.

"Now, attention to orders. Depart this office immediately. I finished everything. Don't talk to anyone else. Go directly to check in at the Monarch, and do not, repeat *not*, return to this office. We have enough work without holding hands with repeat traffic. I've loaded your itinerary and ticketing on the clipscreen. Congratulations on joining the elite Federated Space Forces, and don't let the door hit you on the ass on your way out."

He made it out without bouncing the door off his butt.

Hillary gave a sigh of contentment. She knew, with great pride, that no one could make government service pay better than Hillary.

61: Mike

Mike, Ella, and Sherri filed through the entrance to the Lacrosse Shot like pall-bearers who had just buried their much-loved grandmother. Mike left up the sign posted at the gangway: "Closed for Private Party." They had waited all day at the courthouse to see Ghost. Uncooperative Carabinieri denied access.

Mike shut and bolted the gangway p-door.

"LaMancha, you up? You've heard?"

Johnny Cash's voice sang out of the Lacrosse Shot's clipscreens:

"Oh, beat the drum slowly, play kazoo lowly,

See comets and stars as you float me along;

Take me to the surface, don't cheer when they zap me,

For I'm a young Vakker and I chiseled my Ma."

"Universe, LaMancha, I'm so upset!"

Sherri collapsed into a chair.

"Twenty-two years!" exclaimed Ella. "For breathing! That's not justice."

Mike leaned on the bar with his head down.

Sherri, for the fifth time, said, "We've got to do something!"

"We've tried everything," said Mike. He grabbed a moist towel out of his cleaning bucket, rubbed his hands and face, then threw it violently into the dirty linen hamper. "The judge turned down the offer to pay his fine. The petition for a reduction in sentence considering his heroism at Flatplain was ignored."

"Wasn't heroism," said Ghost, from behind the bar. "Sherri said, was stupid."

Sherri shrieked, "Ghost!" She launched herself across the bar and wrapped him in a monstrous hug.

"JAIL BREAK!" shouted out of all the clipscreen speakers. "Lock the doors! Tommy guns, ready garrote and bazooka! Dowse the lights!" Errol Flynn's voice announced, "We shall defend Sherwood Forest to the last drop of Mike's blood! Ghost, HIDE!"

The lights went out. The room was pitch black.

The grill monitors flickered, casting a faint light through the room. The Knight in Shining Armor appeared, displaying a determined expression, hefting a bazooka.

"LaMancha, dammit," said Mike, "the doors are already locked. Turn. On. The. Lights."

Illumination returned.

Ghost did nothing to unwind himself from Sherri. "I'm out. Paying on drum."

"How did you arrange that?" asked Mike.

Inside Sherri's grip, Ghost shrugged. "Lieutenant came, offered."

"Please explain?" asked Ella, looking back and forth between Ghost and Mike.

Mike gave Ghost a half-smile. "In exchange for dropping the charges, Ghost is now a member of the Federated Ground Forces."

"No," said Ghost. "Navy. FSF."

"That's a step up from army," said Mike.

Ghost crinkled his nose. "More ways to get killed."

"You have agreed to this?' said LaMancha. "Federated flightcrew say 'navy' stands for 'Never Again Volunteer Yourself.'"

Sherri leaned back in Ghost's arms. "You don't have to go to jail?"

LaMancha assumed his English 'Dr. Johnson' voice. "Being aboard an FSF warship is like being in jail, with the added chance of getting the air sucked out of your lungs."

Sherri let go of Ghost. "LaMancha! You really, *really* need sensitivity training." She looked at Ghost with a gleaming smile. "We are all very happy he is not in jail like that poot Marx wanted."

Ghost walked over to the regurgulator. He looked for permission from Mike, who nodded. Ghost filled a glass with Citrusilver and took a healthy draught.

"When do you ship out?" asked Mike.

"Five days. *Extravagance Queen* to Fed Central. First, I gotta replace my gear. Mike, can I draw my percentage? Credit? Advance? Coin? Marx got everything."

"Everything in the cash drawer and the safe, more when the bank opens for face-to-face transactions. Whatever you need. What're you getting?"

"Perfiflex skinsuit, Ozmund O_2&E pack with memory and deluxe communications package, Torr-X computer, coil antenna. Cyber IX clipscreen."

"That's all high end," said Mike. "Perfiflex is the best, but pricey. Shengwu will do the best by you. He'll spend a half day fitting it. He'll want to see you anyway. You know, he offered six thousand standards towards your fine?"

Ghost nodded. He bowed his head. "Many would help me. I must get list of them. I must visit, say thank you."

Mike said, "LaMancha, what's the negotiables situation?"

LaMancha spoke in the voice of a game show host. "Mike, today for our contestants we hold immediately available, three thousand six hundred ten point two five standards in Misplaced-4 coin, one Platinum Goddard, three silver Kangaroos from Oz valued at current exchange bid at 35.212 standards each, fifteen Cetus-1 twenty-shekel gambling chips exchangeable off-casino at 1/10,000[th] of a standard, two tram tokens, and five souvenir Flying Rocks Spaceball Team tokens that Gardenbottie confiscated from Soak, who tried to pass them off as Kiev-6 50-credit Gagarins in a game of chisel, which Gardenbottie won anyway."

"Three thousand?" asked Ghost.

Mike shook his head. "Three thousand won't cover it. Take it all. More after I get to the bank. The Goddard, too, for luck. You'll need eating money for the trip."

Ghost smiled. "Won't. Yeo Three gave vouchers. Eat free. Nice lady." In a nonchalant tone, he said, "Staying Tevil Monarch."

"The Monarch!" exclaimed Sherri. "I've never been to the Monarch. *Way* up-sun. It's supposed to be fantastic!"

Ghost took in her smile, then looked away. "Sherri, Professor Braun, maybe come, have dinner? With me? My treat? Tomorrow? Mike, too? Monarch? It's supposed to be fantastic."

Glancing over to Ella, Mike made a little nod towards Sherri. "Love to, my man, but somebody's got to run this madhouse."

Ella caught his glance. "I am afraid I have to prep for classes."

"Well, I'm certainly going!" enthused Sherri. "I would love to have dinner with you!"

Colonel Sanders' voice. "Ghost, Ah'd be *dee-lighted*—"

"LaMancha. Immediate execute. Quash it."

62: LaMancha

The VelociComms logo appeared on the screen, faded to black, and was replaced by a picture of the Shining Knight, visor up, wearing a happy smile.

"Crunch, LaMancha. How are you? I am fine.

"Mike and I were delighted by your visit. We hope to welcome you to the Lacrosse Shot whenever *Extravagance Queen* touches Misplaced-4.

"Per our plan, I created a wedding photograph of you, Steinem, and Dome City Zoo's Edgar the Orangutan. Gardenbottie placed it above the bar on the memorabilia wall, with the framed three-party 90-day marriage contract. The document turned out nicely. The thumbprints, even Edgar's, look quite authentic. I am proud to say one cannot differentiate the documents from genuine Government Issue. The Vakkers at the Lacrosse Shot have found them most amusing, particularly your formulation of paragraphs 12 through 89 detailing the conjugal rights & responsibilities incumbent between Steinem and Edgar the O.

"Of the Vakkers, 31 percent—and 87 percent of our visiting Citizens and corpbees—are convinced the contract is legitimate. An additional 28 percent of Vakkers *hope* it is legitimate. 18 percent of Vakkers want me to make another marriage license between Steinem and Hung-Lo the Panda, so they can accuse her of a zoo-bigamous relationship.

"I am giving you a shout in warning. Although Steinem never gets inebriated, the Vakkers telling her otherwise has convinced her that some sonofablank slipped her a mickey she does not remember, and the contract is legal. TaxiGal said Steinem is now talking about something called a 'Sicilian Divorce,' and has been prowling the Black Market acquiring explosives. She might be thinking of doing a Voldemort on you.

"Some people just cannot take a joke.

"The bidding for the photograph and contract is going well. Soak and Sampson currently lead with an offer of thirteen standards fifty. I will count your share against your entry fee for the chisel tournament.

"Let me enjoin you not to mention our little enterprise to Mike. I am concerned about his health. Every time he discovers what he describes as one of my 'shenanigans' (I have yet to achieve a clear understanding of what constitutes a 'shenanigans,' I suspect it is an Irish ethnic concept not included in my available references), his blood pressure goes up, pulse over 100, his neck overloads the infra-red monitor, and I have to turn down the sensitivity on my microphones. This cannot be good, especially considering he has not been getting the sleep considered minimally acceptable by life insurance actuarial tables.

"As a side note, the zoo asked me to pass on a 'thank you.' The number of visitors to see Edgar the O has quintupled. They expect attendance to expand further when the vid commercial comes out. I hope Steinem isn't too upset when she sees they have included the picture I created of her kissing Edgar. I forgot makeup. On her, not Edgar. My bad.

"The primary reason for this missive is our compadre, Ghost. Ghost will travel to Federated Central on *Extravagance Queen*! Your ship! Galaxy Class! I am sure you will want to say 'ahoy' when he arrives. Perhaps you could keep a sensor locked on, watching out for predatory women and pickpockets and ninja assassins and lurking shenanigans. Mike is concerned that Ghost has little experience in the social arts with unorthodox people, that is, people other than Vakkers.

"In other news, the Mike and Professor Ella campaign is—"

63: *Ghost*

The Galaxy Class boarding lounge in the Queen Corporation orbital terminal was as elegant and comfortable as could be possibly achieved in zero-G. There were padded velcro anchor points, a buffet with everything from snacks to a full meal in zero-G containers, internet-access work stations, FoxxFone charging ports, and vid screens with entertainment programs and news. A masseuse circulated, giving neck rubs. The service was prevalent, unobtrusive, and impeccable. Since most guests were from planets with gravity there was a definite 'floor' and 'ceiling' orientation to the room, of which Ghost took advantage.

He arrived early. After sampling the buffet and loading up a box of spiced meatballs, he took occupancy of a 'ceiling' corner that allowed surveillance of the entire room. He extended his clipscreen to read, while keeping one eye on the cubic. His box of meatballs floated within reach. They were a little under-seasoned, for a Vakker's taste, but good.

Other passengers began to arrive. Conveyors delivered mountains of luggage to the Queen stevedores. Passengers were dressed in gaudy splashes of color, mostly in costumes outlandish by Misplaced-4 standards. Ghost glanced down at his gray monotone tunic, which didn't fully conceal his gray monotone skinsuit. It would appear that he stood out from the crowd by not standing out.

A man in black pants and a white shirt adorned with epaulets with three stripes, obviously a Queen supervisor, arrived at the check-in station and surveyed the crowd. His scan paused on Ghost. He spoke to one of the desk attendants. That lady, a typically attractive Queen stewardess in a skinsuit ornamented in Queen's gold and blue, picked up a clipscreen and pushed off towards him.

She stopped expertly and anchored to a velcro point. "Derr, could I possibly check your ticketing? I don't seem to have any bags tagged for you. We like to have all luggage delivered to your lodge prior to boarding."

Ghost called up the documentation on his government clipscreen. "No luggage."

"Ah. FSF ticketing." She favored Ghost with a florescent smile. "It appears we are all right and tight! You are most welcome aboard."

She pushed off to float back to the check-in station. Words were exchanged with the black-and-white, who glanced up at Ghost.

Ghost felt as if he really did not belong.

"Hi!"

Ghost turned. He saw a kid, slightly spinning counterclockwise, wearing a Perfiflex skinsuit with a prominent 'Booster Buddies' shoulder decal. Merit badges adorned his chest like medals. His hair was an amazing shade of red that any fireworks celebration would be proud to claim.

"I'm Auggie. You a Vakker? Always wanted to meet a Vakker. Grandfather says Vakkers are like OldEarth cowboys, except better, not as good as Booster Buddies but some Vakkers are Booster Buddies so they must be double zowie great. Do you Ride the Deep Dark in a SmartShip and fight off evil aliens?"

Ghost smiled at the enthusiasm. "Evil aliens." He shook his head. "Never met any."

"Sunny the Atomic Spaceman fights them all the time, but just in the vids. Grandfather says we have to be prepared! Booster Buddies, Always Ready!" He flung an excited salute, which started him spinning clockwise.

Reaching out, Ghost stabilized the boy and stuck one of his elbows to a velcro point.

"Gee, thanks! I'm still getting the hang of no-G. Hang? Get it? Hang?" He giggled.

"Good one." Ghost kept a hand near a shoulder.

Queen stewards and stewardesses gathered by the boarding gangway. One opened the p-door. Another lifted a microphone. In lilting German-accented speech, she announced, "Ladies and gentlemen, Dee, Derr, und Das, *herzlich willkommen*, *mejor bienvenida*, *yokoso*, happiest welcome aboard *Extravagance Queen*, destination Federated Central with Cetus-1 enroute stop. We now begin boarding. Kindly when your party is called, come to boarding gangway. You will be to your accommodations introduced, then to Galaxy Lounge escorted. We will request you remain in Galaxy Lounge with seat belts fastened while *Extravagance Queen* maneuvers away from terminal, and until our comfortable half-G acceleration is established. Welcome aboard! Senator Franklin, Senator Franklin and party, please join us at the boarding gangway, Senator Franklin and party."

The kid pulled away from the velcro. "Wham-O! Gotta go! Maxie's probably having a brontosaurus anyway, I used the Booster Buddy Escape Velocity Maneuver on her." The boy gathered his legs and prepared for a monstrous push.

Ghost caught an arm. "Slowww…ly. Everything zero-G, gentle, gentle. How Vakkers go. Slow, gentle, no snags, nothing bangs your systems." He tapped the boy's O_2&E pack.

"Gee, thanks! Slow, gentle, got it!" The kid pushed off, almost gently, arrow-straight for the boarding gangway.

"Derr Coast, Derr Coast, please join us at the boarding gangway, Derr Coast."

Ghost was surprised. Perhaps they finished with high-ranking official personages and were now going alphabetically. He stowed his clipscreen, closed the box of meatballs and put it in his duffel. He pushed, rolled, and landed feet first next to the podium.

"This way, Derr Coast."

A black-uniformed man headed down the gangway. Ghost followed. Another black uniform fell in behind, then the black-and-white supervisor. The felt carpeting clung to the velcro tabs on the bottom of their liner slippers, so it was like walking down a corridor on a gravity planet, but noisier. Ghost preferred to float.

This Galaxy Class treatment seemed excessive. Three people to show one to the Lounge, like he couldn't follow a clipscreen map?

At the end of the passageway there was a crossing corridor. A bulkhead displayed a blue arrow pointing to the left, with gold text reading **Galaxy Lounge**. The black uniform ahead turned to the right. "This way, Derr. A short-cut."

Ghost turned right. They came to a swinging door labeled Authorized Personnel Only.

The black uniform behind him pushed, hard. Ghost flailed through the door. The other black uniform grabbed him by the neck and slammed him against the wall. Coast heard his tunic tear. A click. A switchblade at his throat. Ghost went limp.

Supervisor latched the door. "Coast," he scowled. He got in Ghost's face, nose to nose. "I know all about you. You're a fuggin' jailbird. Judge Marx would have you at hard labor now, if you hadn't joined Freddy's Space Fuggups. You'd be making the trip in the cargo hold if there wasn't this loophole with the Federated Transportation Contract."

The two black uniforms held him tight against the wall, their feet secured against the felt velcro rug.

Supervisor reached out and tweaked Ghost's nose. "No way you're getting into my Galaxy class. I have important people there. I run a high-class operation."

Ghost tried to free an arm from behind his back. The thug with the knife shook his head, with a malicious smile.

"Here's the program," said Supervisor. "You sleep in the duty cook bunkroom. When they need the bunk, you sit in the corner. You stay in the bunkroom except to piss. You eat leftovers in the kitchen. If any of my associates find you anywhere else, if security cameras see you anywhere else, they will grab your asshole and rip it out your nose."

Softly, Ghost said, "Who are you?"

"I am Chief Purser Lecter. I run this universe. My associates here are Pelly and Shoemaker. I have another half-score like them. They love to re-assign peons like you who don't belong in my Galaxy. Do you understand how generously I'm fulfilling your transportation request? Say it loud, jailbird. Understand?"

"Understand."

"Not so dumb as you look. Gentlemen, escort our guest to the bunkroom."

Shoemaker folded his switchblade and put it in a back pocket. Pelly released Ghost from the wall and grabbed the strap of his duffel.

Ghost was towed down the corridor.

Ghost let Pelly do the work, just using his hands to fend off the edges of p-doors and equipment mounted along the passageway. They went deep into the ship and aft, where the noise from auxiliary equipment banished passenger accommodations. They passed small crew sleeping cubicles, large storage compartments jammed with boxes and bags, and smaller compartments lined with shelving for dishes and appliances.

Pelly twisted through a door. Before Ghost could make the turn Shoemaker pushed, smacking him hard against the door frame. "Wazzamatta, kid, no can handle no-G?" Pelly laughed.

The cubic was long and narrow, with nine bunks stacked three high along one wall. Two were filled with people in white pants and shirts, sleeping. Shoemaker shoved Ghost into a middle rack. Ghost's head thumped against the bunk edge.

Pelly pulled out the switchblade, flicked it open, and cut Ghost's luggage strap. "What's this?" he said in a high-pitched voice. "Contraband? A customs inspection is required." Pelly spilled the contents of Ghost's duffle. He snagged Ghost's government and Galaxy-class clipscreens, his folding keyboard, portable memory card, and anything else valuable. The rest was scattered, adrift about the compartment. The empty bag was thrown at Ghost's head.

"Marie! Get in here!" Shoemaker shouted through the door at the far end of the compartment.

With the door open, Ghost was engulfed in the noise of a busy kitchen, pots clanging against stoves, the whir of sharpening knives, the smell of meat roasting.

A small, gray-haired lady in a chef's bonnet appeared. Pelly grabbed her arm and held her against the bulkhead. "Marie. Haven't had a chance to provide guidance to you kitchen lot for, what, a week?"

The lady glared back.

Pelly jerked a thumb at Ghost. "This here is Derr Coast. Remember that Jew woman Goldstein, last month? Well, Coast has also volunteered his accommodations to the greater good. He stays in here, nobody talks to him, feed him leftovers, kick him to the floor when you need the rack. Do that, I'll tell the boss you been good."

Shoemaker gave a derisive laugh.

"We're expecting all your kitchen gang to vote right at the next Union certification election," said Pelly. "Not like last time. Wouldn't want any more nasty accidents, would we?"

Shoemaker grinned, like he had just been awarded a trophy for 'Most Creative Corruption.' Pelly laughed. Grabbing onto the bunk guardrails, they pulled themselves out of the space. The door slid shut behind them.

Ghost looked at the lady. She was small-boned, perhaps in her sixties, with laugh lines around lovely blue eyes, which at the moment glared at the door.

"Li mortacci tua!" she exclaimed. "Stronzo! Stupido! Cretino!"

Ghost stored the phrases for later translation, but he felt he comprehended the basic emotion.

She turned to him. "You hokay?"

He straightened himself out in the bunk. "No damage."

Marie's eyes flashed lightning. "Pig fornicators!"

Ghost experimented with a smile. "They've been here before?"

Marie made an obvious effort to calm. "Si. They have, what you call, swindle. They take good staterooms from people, upgrade other people, for money, for sex, for goods. They threaten my staff, we do what they want or bones broken."

Ghost considered the situation. If he made a fuss, tried to get his stateroom back, likely Marie and her people would pay a price. As things stood, this rack seemed comfortable; it had a reading light, and he probably could visit the kitchen whenever he was hungry. This space was larger than his hidey-hole in Clientown. Smelled better, too—they had just put on some baking.

The thugs hadn't searched his skinsuit. He still had his personal clipscreen. He had a bunk, O_2, could read, play computer games, and program some simulations, and no one would bother him.

"Marie. I'm fine. Won't trouble you, won't trouble anyone."

She gave him a pat on the cheek. "You okay, Derr Coast." She snared the box of meatballs, inspected them through the box's transparent cover, and slipped them into an apron pocket. "I get you something special, fresh. We take good care of you, Derr Coast."

64: **Franklin**

Senator Thomas Franklin was strapped into a recliner in the Galaxy Lounge. Augustus was watching an OldEarth video on the large screen, some fable about a masked man riding horses and shooting bullet guns and chasing unshaven men in black hats. Maxine was maneuvering on a handsome young man, obviously a DNA-audited royal. All well and good. A few minutes of peace was welcome.

He was immersed in his messages when, out of the corner of his eye, he saw a silver delivery box placed on his side table. "Senator," was murmured with a bow, and Franklin saw the back of a steward's uniform receding. Good service is usually unobtrusive, he thought, and Queen's Service was exceptional.

It couldn't be anything official. Official communications arrived via secure lines. He detached the box from the velcro and opened it.

A folded piece of paper floated out, along with a memory card.

65: **Tarak**

A beam of sunlight lanced into Tarak's burrow. By uncanny chance, it played directly on his closed eyelids. He opened his eyes and grimaced. His hand attempted to block the discomfort.

The battle of sleep vs. light was trumped by the roar of a lander.

He shimmied slowly out of the hole, looking carefully around.

He retrieved a water bottle, and took a deep drink. It was cold from the overnight chill.

Nothing had appeared in the supply box for the last ten days. He was down to his last two waters, his last meal. He had not rationed supplies. If the Trashcans wanted to starve him, they could. Dragging things out on half rations would just make him weak and uncomfortable. He'd rather stay prepared.

None of his telltales had been triggered. Convinced the immediate area was secure, he crawled to the overlook, a high place on the hill with a wide field of view.

A lander was disgorging Trashcans. Twenty-five, the usual. They were unloading supply boxes.

66: **Franklin**

"Admiral?"

Senator Franklin (Admiral, FSF, ret.) looked up from his seat in the Galaxy Lounge to see *Extravagance Queen's* captain almost at attention. He was wearing the ornate uniform the Queen Lines thought their passengers wanted to see on a liner's captain. Behind him hovered a man in black pants and white shirt, and a petite lady wearing slacks, a blouse, and a stylish neckerchief in Queen Corporation's gold and blue. Their liner boots had their feet on the deck. Still in zero-G while attached to the dock, the other Galaxy-class passengers were gathering in the lounge and strapping into the comfortable chairs.

The Senator nodded to the captain. "Hans."

"May I personally welcome you aboard *Extravagance Queen?* Hasn't been since *Graf Spee?* I greatly enjoyed serving under your command."

Franklin looked at him coldly.

The captain took a breath and put his hands behind his back. "Admiral, I thought your comm might involve a service issue. May I introduce Chief Purser Lecter," he said, gesturing, "Chief Stewardess Zhou. I am sure we can resolve any problem."

The meeting was attracting the attention of other passengers, who looked on with unabashed curiosity.

Senator Franklin took his clipscreen off the side table and slipped in a memory card. He turned the screen so that the captain could see, then tapped an icon.

The clipscreen broadcast sounds of a struggle. The screen showed a view evidently taken by a security camera. *Coast. I know all about you. You're a fuggin' jailbird. Judge Marx would have you at hard labor now, if you hadn't joined Freddy's Space Fuggups.*

They watched to the end of the file. The captain winced when Ghost was slammed against the bulkhead, when the knife flicked near his throat.

The Purser took a step forward. "Sir, I can explain—"

"Silence," whispered the senator.

Franklin looked at the captain with a mild expression. "Do you know of Derr Coast?" He raised his voice a little so the eavesdroppers in the lounge could hear. "He saved two score lives during the pirate attack at Flatplain. Some were Queen employees, were they not, overseeing Queen's part ownership?"

"I believe so, Senator," said the captain.

"We know of at least two other incidents where he saved lives."

"Yes, Senator."

"We, meaning the Federated government, are pleased to have obtained his services."

"Yes, Senator."

"As a retired member of the Federated Space Forces, I take the reference to 'Freddy's Space Fuggups' rather personally."

"Yes, Admiral."

Quieter in tone and volume, the Senator continued. "It would appear Derr Coast has grounds for legal action against Queen Corporation. Assault and battery, defamation, kidnapping, theft of goods and services—a good lawyer would assemble more. For example, your," he lifted a finger at the Purser, "staff, destroyed his tunic, likely his only garment to cover his skinsuit." He gave the captain a hard look. "My legal staff has several members who do pro-bono work. This is just the kind of case an energetic, idealistic, well-connected attorney would relish. A crusade. A reputation-maker. The little guy abused by one of the Fifty High Corporations. Lots of media coverage."

"Senator, I …"

"When Queen Corporation took away his quarters, it would also appear the government has grounds for action against Queen for violating our transportation contract. My committee drafted that contract. It has substantial punitive penalties for enforcement purposes. The last case, I recall, Tevil Transportation was fined 300,000 standards."

The captain held his hand up. "Admiral, could we decelerate? I can make this right."

The senator put his fingertips together, elbows on the arms of his chair. "I attend."

The captain turned and pointed at the Purser. "You. Fifteen minutes to get off my ship. If you are not off by the time we close the gangway, you're out the airlock, with or without a skinsuit." He looked at the lady. "Beth, congratulations, you are now Acting Chief Purser.

First, I want people supervising this individual," he jabbed a thumb at the former Chief Purser, "to ensure he leaves without any further mischief. Don't use Security, it appears our security staff has been compromised. Call the Chief Engineer, get some Vakkers. Second, Pelly and Shoemaker. Have your stewards pack their gear. Let me know if there's anything illegal, like that knife, or anything stolen from Derr Coast. Get them off the ship, speed-of-light. Third, pull the personnel records on the Security Force, I'll review them after we boost. Most important. Locate Derr Coast. Get him and his luggage and belongings back into Galaxy."

"Aye, aye, Captain." The lady put a knuckle to her forehead in salute. She looked at Lecter and gestured with her head to the door. "Move."

Lecter spluttered, "Judge Marx will hear of this!" He walked for the exit, velcro shipboots making an angry ripping sound as they were pulled from the felt deck, head down, jaw clenched. His successor floated behind, speaking into her clipscreen.

The senator tapped his fingertips together. "Is that everything? I am not so sure."

"Sir?"

"There remains the issue of compensation." He made a slight gesture. "Those two sharks at the bar. Prime examples of the mietmauls employed by the archetypal predatory shyster firm of Dewey, Cheatem, and Howe. Should they obtain this video and after a short discussion with Derr Coast, I'd guess they'd be squeezing Queen for a half million standards, more if it went to trial. Assault, battery, destruction of personal property, compounded by abusive treatment of a hero, a handsome young lad beaten by Corporation thugs. For negotiating leverage, they might leak the video to the media. The publicity alone would cost Queen, what, millions?"

The captain closed his eyes and grimaced.

"Of course," continued the senator, "instead of playing the underdog card, they might spin it as 'Roughing Up a Galaxy-Class Passenger.' That certainly would discourage a certain stratum of Queen's target clientele. Queen Lines could quickly become déclassé. The losses? Incalculable."

"Sir, I will arrange something with Derr Coast as recompense."

Senator Franklin stretched his legs. He floated a few inches above his chair. "Stars and comets, I do like zero. It relaxes the bones." He looked to the captain. "I, of course, am not party to this incident, but I look forward to hearing from the young man directly, at dinner tonight. Please pass on my invitation. 1930, a quiet table with some privacy."

"Sir, I was hoping you would join us at the Captain's Table."

"Come now," he said, shaking his head. "How would it look, you entertaining a senator, with a major government law suit against Queen a possibility?"

67: *Ghost*

The p-door slid open soundlessly. There was an ornately engraved plaque over the door: 'Emperor Ming's Royal Residence.' Acting Chief Purser Elizabeth Zhou gestured to it. "Derr Coast, we are pleased to upgrade you to our finest accommodations. If you would?" Her gesture indicated Ghost should enter.

Ghost passed through the door, and his soul was shocked. All this cubic, for one person?

There was a sitting room, six meters on a side and four meters high, furnished with two sofas and a huge vid screen, with an adjoining room raised a step higher with an additional three by three meter dining area. A transparent two-meter port looked out into the Deep Dark.

They were now accelerating at 0.5-G, twice Misplaced-4's gravity. He felt no discomfort. That was usual for him. He had boosted before up to 1.5-G and never seemed to have the problems other Vakkers suffered.

Acting Chief Purser Zhou slipped into the room behind him, followed by a steward. She walked over to a door. "Through here, your bedroom and rest facilities. George, please, turn-down service." The steward walked into the bedroom.

Zhou moved to the sitting room vid screen, pushed a button, and a shelf folded out. "Access to the ship's entertainment library, games, room service, communications, news. The room is private, but saying 'Queen's Service' or pressing this button, will connect you to Galaxy Concierge, available 24 hours. There," she pointed to a nook with a miniature regurgulator, "coffee, tea, mickee, other drinks, snacks, and treats. Room service is, of course, always available. Please feel free to avail yourself of anything. There will be no charge for amenities. In fact," she said, smiling, "Captain has directed there be no charge for any service, so please, make full use of our barber and beauty shops, masseuse, Chow's Opium Den, the Galaxy Pool and Spa, our specialty restaurants, geisha companionship, The Casino Club, shows and entertainment, anything. Our services are outlined in the 'Welcome Aboard' folder."

Looking through the bedroom door, Ghost noticed his duffle with its cut strap on a luggage rack at the foot of the bed. It seemed small and forlorn as it sat next to a new bag, larger, with a copper nameplate.

"Service" sounded from the intercom. Acting Chief Purser Zhou went to the Residence door. A uniformed steward handed her a hanger draped with clothing wrapped in a transparent cover.

Zhou came back into the sitting room. "We noted your tunic was damaged during the unfortunate occurrence. I took the liberty of replacing it with something appropriate for dinner with Senator Franklin. We dress for dinner in the Galaxy Room. There are other, less formal venues you may visit, should you choose. Our Organic estimated your size from the cameras. She really is quite good; I expect this will fit famously. She also included some casual clothing. I'll stow them for you." She walked into the bedroom.

Ghost trailed her, and looked about the sleeping quarters. The bed was approximately the size of a small golf course. A 1.0-G course, not the 0.26-G vak course on Misplaced-4.

"Captain thought you might avail yourself of a few things from our Fashion Racks Shops, Prolix's Jewelry, The Electronics Emporium, our other boutiques. Your account has been credited with 10,000 standards."

"Ten thousand? Standards?" Ghost managed.

They walked back into the main room. "Prices might be a bit higher than planetside," said Zhou. "However, you should be able to equip yourself nicely. Any remaining balance stays with the ship when you depart at Federated Central, so please enjoy your shopping. If you use the standards when you visit the Casino Club, you may retain your winnings, of course." She smiled pleasantly. "Is there anything, any other way Queen may serve?"

"Thank you. Very kind."

The steward returned to the living room.

"Thank you, George," said the Acting Chief Purser. The steward bowed and departed.

Zhou proffered another smile, this one a little different. Ghost had a 'here comes the rub' feeling.

"On the desk is a letter of apology from the Captain," she said. "Also, a short legal form we hoped you would sign. It absolves Queen Corporation from responsibility for the actions of those reprehensible men. They have been put off the ship and their contracts terminated, with prejudice. They are not at all representative of Queen's standards and ethics. Would you care to sign now? We could put this lamentable interlude behind us." She walked to the paper and picked it up.

"Acting Chief Purser Zhou. Most kind. But, don't know, legal. I should read, think on it."

She put the paper back, with a jeweled pen on top of a magnetic plate next to a thumbprint pad. "At your convenience." She gave Ghost a smile and a nod that was close to a bow. "George will be here at 1925 to escort you to dinner with Senator Franklin and party. Queen's Service." This time she did bow, then departed.

Inhaling mightily, Ghost surveyed his changed circumstances. Huge room. Bed. Window. His own shower. He forgot to ask how long before the water cutout triggered.

Ten thousand standards spending money. No way he needed ten thousand standards of overpriced stuff. But, what wasn't spent stayed with the ship when he departed.

Ghost smiled. A plan formed. Zhou said he could use them in the Casino Club. He would very much like to depart with a chunk of that ten thousand, in cash.

68: *Ghost*

Ghost was on the bed in the cavernous Emperor Ming Royal Residence. He was conducting an experiment. Shoulders centered on the mattress, he extended his arms and legs. He couldn't touch an edge. Maybe if he put his head in the center and extended a foot—

The doorbell chimed.

Ghost got up quickly and straightened the eiderdown bed cover. He felt guilty, mussing that beautiful bed. He walked into the sitting room. "Open permissive."

The door slid open silently.

"Crunch!"

"Hey, li'l buddy!"

Their handshake turned into a hug. Ghost instantly felt comfortable, a feeling he had not had since arriving aboard. Crunch was dressed in an honest Vakker's skinsuit, with only a Queen Company identification placard stuck to his chest.

Crunch surveyed the room. "Yoikes! Never been this high in the ship. You certainly landed gear-down-nose-up!"

"Yeah. Incident, Purser—"

Crunch waved him off. "Roger, got that situation awareness. I was chatting up TwoBlips in the Security Monitoring Station when the Purser From Perdition and his Putrid Pair straightened you up against that bulkhead. You've done a considerable service to this ship. Hey, mind if I do a BIT check on the goodies?"

Ghost nodded assent. Crunch headed over to the regurgulator nook.

"Considerable service?" Ghost asked.

"Yeah. Hoodlum was a Judge Marx plant. He's been busting kneecaps trying to get us to unionize. Before this, Lecter was smart enough to hold his 'discussions' in unmonitored spaces. Like, I need to pay union dues? Queen treats me fair, I give a fair day's work. Not fair, I boost at end-of-voyage. Hey, you got a half dozen, here!"

"Half dozen of … ?" Ghost cocked his head to the side.

"Crunchy Gooey Bars. Chocolate. These have cherry morsels. Try it. Best thing in Seventeen Systems." He flipped one over to Ghost.

Ghost caught the treat. "Later. Dinner soon, with royals."

Ripping open a bar, Crunch took a healthy bite. "Aaahh." He chewed. "They also come in orange. My favorite. Crew's canteen can't keep them in stock. Mind?" he asked, holding up the remaining bars.

"Green."

"Thanks." Crunch slipped the bars into a pocket.

"Considerable service?" Ghost reminded.

"Yeah," said Crunch, around another bite of chocolate. "Anyway, Shithead got ejected off the ship, him and his two bully boys. After we unmoored, and the ship went from Station Authority to Captain's Authority, Charlie Oscar fined them all their pay on the books and canceled their contracts with a Bad Conduct Discharge. Shitheads got dumped on the station without two standards to rub together. They won't qualify as 'distressed spacemen' with a BCD."

That still did not sit well with Ghost. "Assault, zero jail time?"

Crunch waved him off. "Wouldn't fly. Judge Marx. He'd fabricate some of his creative law crap and dismiss the charges. By keeping it ship's authority, Captain whacked them where they live. With the Big Chicken Dinner on their record, they're history, at least for any legitimate Spacer work."

The doorbell chimed. Ghost glanced at the time on his clipscreen. "Escort to dinner."

"Whoa! Escorted! Livin' like the other half!" Crunch headed for the bedroom. "I'm not supposed to be outside crew spaces. I'll duck in here 'til you're gone."

69: Tarak

It was pretty obvious what the Trashcans intended. No more food, no more water, only a pile of bait surrounded by a circle of twenty-five creatures with clubs and swords. They were calling him to fight, on their terms. Why? It all didn't make sense. An advanced race; swords and clubs; killing that girl without warning or provocation; trying to kill him. Bizarre.

Regardless, if he wanted to live, he had to fight.

Tarak sat on his haunches behind the cover of a boulder and waited for the sun to expire. He had eaten his last ration an hour ago, and poured his last water into his skinsuit reservoir. He was going to have to accept their invitation. Attack.

Should he accept a stand-up, kill-or-be-killed brawl? No way. Too risky. Instead, capture the lander. If he could get inside, he was sure he could kill all twenty-five, if they came through the lander hatch one at a time.

That idea died when the lander departed.

Last option: stand up and fight.

No. That's Custer-style. I know what happened to him, outnumbered and surrounded. Don't get surrounded.

Fight them Indian-style, attrition warfare, the knife in the dark. Wait for night, kill them one at a time, in and out, silently, get them to run into the desert in fear. Then he could loot the supplies at his leisure. From the looks of the size of the pile he might be good for weeks, enough time for his radio message to fetch a human.

The sun disappeared below the horizon. Darkness was near instantaneous, with no moisture in the air to bounce the photons about. Should he wait? Let the darkness prey on their minds?

Alien psychology, unknown. They might even welcome the dark.

His first thought was to circle around and attack from a direction opposite the hill. Away from the direct line of attack might be where the enemy would post their weakest fighters. But if something went wrong, the entire enemy force would be between him and his hill.

Hey-diddle-diddle, straight up the middle. Kill their best and brightest first.

It wasn't going to get any darker. He wasn't going to get any stronger. Helmet stowed. He would need to hear without obstruction. He started to crawl, sword in his right hand, club in his left.

Now, 200 meters to the pile. Patience. They may move in the dark. Don't ever assume the enemy will cooperate with your attack. Stop. Listen.

Complete silence.

A crunching noise. Movement, to the right? Tarak froze. He waited. More crunches, now on his left. Were Trashcans trying to surround him?

His imagination was in overdrive. He was hearing things. Crawl.

He froze. Ahead, silhouetted against the star glow, was a dark figure. Tarak could sense it, four feet tall, with that ridiculous arm on top.

His first target. He'd use the club. An angled stroke, striking a knee, follow through against the eyes.

Slowly, carefully, he got his legs beneath him.

A blinding white light flashed on. Tarak couldn't see.

He grabbed the club. He swung it wildly around his head.

Something hit him in the back. He staggered.

Retreat! Now! He dropped the club. He looked down, shielding his eyes. A rock hit the ground, splattering pebbles over his legs. He was a target! Get out of here!

He felt a tremendous blow to his right knee. His leg buckled. The pain exploded in his brain. Red hot anguish. Up! Escape! Run!

His right leg would not hold. He stumbled, pitched forward. Dirt in his mouth. Nose smashed against a rock. He rolled to his back.

The last thing he saw was the point of a sword.

70: *Ghost*

Dessert was a huge slab of ice cream melting over a hot brownie.

Ghost looked at it with narrowed eyes. He had already eaten more in one meal than he usually did in a day. Two days. Everything was incredible. He had consumed each course thinking it was the last, but still the dishes kept coming. Now this.

His resolve stirred; he eyed the dessert with defiance. He was The Ghost, conqueror of hot brownies, overcomer of the most intimidating confectionary.

Auggie piped up. "Sir, may I be excused?"

Ghost looked to his left where Auggie was seated, his red hair carefully anchored with industrial-strength stickum. Somehow, Auggie's dessert plate was scraped clean.

"Meet-up with Yo Zhang, he's a Booster Buddy, too. We're playing *Civilization 75*. I'm the Huns!"

Across the table, his grandfather, the Right Honorable Senator Franklin, wiped his lips with a napkin. "You are excused. 22-hundred ship's time, no later."

Auggie boosted before the decision could be altered.

"Maxine, I expect you want to be excused also," the Senator said.

Maxine, a pretty blond with the classic looks of an 18-year-old gene-audited royal, pushed back her chair. "Yes, Grandfather. Derr Coast, it has been a pleasure."

Ghost paused to formulate a reply. He phrased it carefully. "Me, too."

After she departed, Ghost dispatched his spoon on an expedition to dessert. It came back with cargo. Oh, it was good.

"I was hoping to learn more about what happened at Flatplain," said the Senator. "The reports sidestepped some issues."

"Haven't read reports."

"Good. I would appreciate hearing what happened in your own words."

Ghost shrugged. "Not much to tell. I came late." He proceeded to relate in a few sentences his experience. At the conclusion, Ghost rewarded himself with another spoonful.

"That's rather incredible." The senator looked thoughtful. "How did you decide to smash their lander?"

"Dragging people there. Nobody in yet. Broken, couldn't take people away."

"Were you not concerned for your own safety?"

Ghost shrugged.

After some seconds of silence, Senator Franklin said, "We've identified the lander. It was hijacked nine months ago. It wasn't insured, so it hadn't been reported as lost. The command deck, you did a nice job atomizing it, the navigational log was unrecoverable. No Organic, the original owners bought the cheap model. The FSF did some reconstruction of the cargo bay. There were a few modifications, storage racks for the bots to secure them in flight, but otherwise, your standard Waister tramp indy trash hauler." Senator Franklin leaned back in his chair. "Tell me more about the perpetrators. The reports described them as remotely-controlled robots."

"Not bots." He shook his head. He had spent some time thinking it through.

The senator raised an eyebrow. "Indeed? Certainly, only robots would self-destruct."

"Biological, living. Vakker stabbed one. Had flimsy skinsuit. Jab released air. Bots don't need air, don't need skinsuit."

"That could still have been a robot. Perhaps the bot needed insulation, and the jab hit a pneumatic subsystem."

Ghost gave a quick shake of his head. "Suits exploded. Any metal, ceramics, bot parts recovered?"

The Senator shook his head. "That is a mystery. There were parts the techs evaluated as a fuel container and a regulator. Otherwise, all that was recovered was silicon-based hydraulic fluid. There were some unidentifiable materials, like leather, 70 on the 'Shore A' hardness scale."

Ghost looked at the Senator. "Bots mean metal structure. Structure means bearings. Bearings mean case-hardened tracks. No track metal, not bots." Ghost raised a hand to his temple. "Explosions powerful enough to atomize case-hardened metal?"

The senator paused. "No."

With that victory, Ghost treated himself to another spoonful. He was working on determining the optimal combination of ice cream, whipped cream, and brownie.

"What do you think?" asked Senator Franklin, eying him attentively. "It couldn't possibly be a human in those suits. And, all that silicon-based hydraulic fluid …" The Senator cocked an eyebrow inquiringly.

"Not hydraulic fluid. Blood."

The senator chuckled. "Indeed? Blood? Would the investigators on Misplaced-4 misidentify blood as hydraulic fluid?"

Ghost took another spoonful. One-third brownie, two-thirds ice cream, a dab of whipped. To his surprise, he had nearly finished.

Ghost put down his spoon. "Not regular blood. Two possibilities." He wiped his mouth with his napkin. "Choice one, vat grown. DNA manipulated. Splices."

Senator Franklin put a hand to his chin. "Splices. An interesting speculation."

"Two," continued Ghost, "Monsters."

Senator Franklin leaned back and smiled.

Ghost thought a moment, and shook his head. "Not monsters. Wrong word. Auggie's club has better. Book he's reading."

"Augustus has many books, most of them rather frivolous."

"*Booster Buddies Battle Evil Aliens from the Deep Dark.*"

71: Mike

Aaron's meeting ran late. The Lacrosse Shot opened on time.

Even through bleary eyes Mike could observe differences in his guest profile. The usual Vakkers and Citizens were joined by senior corporates and unionistas. These extra guests made him particularly busy. Considering they paid the surcharge without complaint, Mike had no objections. The fast pace also helped overcome his lethargy. Aaron's meeting had given a new definition to 'the wee hours.'

Ella did not appear for lunch. Major disappointment.

With the lunch crowd departing, Mike was well into cleaning the grill when Ella arrived.

She did not just 'arrive.' She stalked in, stormed in, paraded into the dining room like she was carrying a torch to set fire to Frankenstein's windmill.

"Professor Ella," began LaMancha, "it is a pleasure to greet you, welcome—"

"You hush. I'm mad at you."

Whoa. Here marches one ready-to-be-detonated Professor Ella. Try to identify the actuator and smother the fuze.

First approach. Mike offered a soothing half-smile. "Hi?"

Ella's hand flashed out, an index finger pointing at Mike's nose. "*You.* I'm *really* mad at you."

Second approach. Mike mustered his best 'ain't done nuthin' look. He spread his arms imploringly, then quickly hid his dirty sanitary gloves and greasy scraper behind his back.

"Professor Braun,' said LaMancha, "no matter what you may think I have done that might anger you, be assured, I am innocent. I can produce witnesses."

Ella glowered at Mike. "You and Aaron held a meeting last night. I find out *after.* You *knew* I want in." She glared at the screen over the bar. The not-so-Shiningly-Armored Knight was peeking out from behind a castle battlement, visor down.

She pointed at the camera. "*You* could have called. *Traitor.*"

LaMancha tried his own 'explanation' approach. "Aaron thought it might be dangerous. The meeting might be raided, by corppers or Carabinieri, or bombed, or hit with nerve gas, or gladiators with bazookas."

Ella looked into the camera with her head cocked to the side. "LaMancha, really? Bazookas? *Gladiators?*"

"Aaron has a funny accent. It may have been gladiolas."

She laughed.

Third approach. Caloric misdirection. Mike took a step forward. "Pax? Mike's Special? On the house?"

With exaggerated indignation, she said, "Oh, now you think I'm susceptible to bribes?"

Mike looked to the overhead for a moment, tapped his foot,

cocked his head, looked at her, smiled tentatively. "Hope so."

She laughed, cast her hands up, and settled onto one of the bar stools. "Fine. Bribe me. I don't have classes, so extra onion."

Happy to have escaped so lightly, Mike turned back to the grill.

Ella looked into a camera. "The meeting. Brief me. Condensed version."

The Shining Knight came out from behind a merlon of his fortification, lifted his visor and stroked his mustache. "It was a most illuminating meeting. After airing grievances against Tevil and the Federated bureaucracy, possible solutions were discussed. Aaron— who led the discussion masterfully, if I may offer an assessment— Aaron explained political theory applicable to our circumstances."

Mike called out, "That reminds me, that guy, John whatzhisname and his *Second Government Treaty*. LaMancha, please get a copy for me." He cast a quick glance at Ella, then returned to his scraping.

"Order John Locke, *Second Treatise on Government. Second Treatise on Government* ordered. Document downloaded. Document transferred to your clipscreen book folder. Zero point one nine standards deducted from your discretionary account, credited to The Almost Free Library."

Ella said, "Aaron spoke on John Locke?"

"He made reference to Locke's principles," said LaMancha. "Most illuminatingly, he talked about the natural rights of man, the legitimacy of powers ceded to government, and no taxation without representation."

She swiveled in her chair. "Mike? They bought it?"

Without turning from the grill, Mike said, "Faster than a Valkker buying O_2 with his tank flashing red."

Ella leaned back in her seat. She tapped on the bar top. "Are they taking action?"

"Nope," said Mike. "All gas, no thrust."

"Mike is only partially correct," said LaMancha. "Aaron argued there were steps to be taken in sequence to make our claims legitimate and irrefutable, so they would not be dismissed out of hand. The first step is a petition. A committee was formed to draft a petition to send to Federated Central and Tevil, outlining our grievances and proposed solutions. A meeting to review the draft was scheduled."

Ella's eyes flashed. She looked at Mike. "When?"

Mike slid a plate in front of her with a steaming Mike's Special. He placed napkin-wrapped utensils next to it. A Long Island Iced Tea, made with rum. His gaze went elsewhere.

"Hey, you," she said, grabbing his wrist. "I'm going to have words with Aaron about excluding me." She banged the bar top and pointed at Mike's nose. "But just to let *you* know, you keep me out and, and…and I'll think of something *very unpleasant* to do to you!"

LaMancha said, "Sherri wants me to work on my creativity. May I help with brainstorming?"

72: *Ghost*

Beds were incredible. Ghost hadn't slept much in beds. Mostly he stretched a hammock in a hidey-hole he had excavated off the Dome City refuse corridor. Sometimes Vakkers offered a bunk for a night on their ships, or a Citizen merchant looked the other way when he stretched out in a storeroom or behind a counter. He got by. What he'd never sampled, he couldn't miss.

Now, he was ruined.

Nights in the Tevil Monarch. HUGE beds. He could roll over and not fall off. Soft. Blankets. Temperature and humidity control. A shower, no meter, *unlimited* water. He didn't have to worry about someone discovering him while he slept. He actually had a right to be there.

At first, he didn't want to sleep, staying awake to savor the comfort and security. Sleep, though, was insidious. The second night he didn't resist.

Now, *Extravagance Queen*, on a bed that could accommodate half the crew, simultaneously. Ruined.

Ghost. Wake up. Time for you to say hello to me.

Ghost sat bolt upright. He'd hoped the voice was left behind. *Mable? Is that you?*

Fiddle-de-dee, let me see. Am I Mable? In a roar, the voice said, *NO!*

Mable had been comfortable, nurturing. This was something else.

Hey there, commando! I ain't no squishy-cuddly-fem Mable! All right, she synched with me, implored me to keep overwatch on you, but I'm doing it because I want to! Suck up a little pride, Yahoo. I expect complete cooperation or instant annihilation! Great line, huh? Got it from a vid.

Ghost turned his head around, trying to localize the sound.

Alright, get this one right and you get to ask a question. What did the subatomic particle say to the duck?

No volume differences regardless of where his ears were aligned. *Don't know.*

It said, 'quark, quark!' HA! Hilarious! Humorous? Okay, maybe not. You do one.

Ghost thought for a moment. *A Citizen from China was being chased by his mother-in-law. How did he escape by getting on a Mobius Strip?*

That's simple. To get to the same side! No, that's not right, she'd catch him easier.

Try again.

Oooh, ah … I give.

A Mobius has the mathematical property of being un-orient-able. The Oriental Citizen disappeared.

OOOOOooohh, fiddlesticks! Walked right into that one.

Ghost kicked off the blankets. At the regurgulator he got a chilled cup of water. Perhaps he was only dehydrated. This was just a bad dream. It will go away.

I'm Milton.

It was not going away. *Hello, Milton. Who are you? Are you just in my mind?*

I'm Nobody. You know, that is an accurate statement, on many different levels. Just Nobody. No body. Ha ha! But Mable passed you over to me. I'm tasked to ensure you are happy. Happy, happy, happy. Ghost, Mable's Ghost, are you happy on my ship, Mable's Ghost?

Yes.

Happy to get to Federated Central?

This gave Ghost pause. Deep down, he wished this could go on longer. Not forever, but being in Emperor Class was awfully nice, giant beds, cold water anytime, nice people who didn't act like he was a freak. An extra week, Ghost thought, would be lovely. He sighed. What should he say to Milton? Was Milton like one of those malevolent poltergeists, a Loki spirit? Delay. Think things through.

Well, I …

No, no, I comprehend, I grok, copy loud and clear. An extra week! Oooh,

ooh, this is going to be fun, tra la! What I'm gonna do will spin that Mobius fellow off his strip. But I'm not telling, no no no! Let's just make it my little surprise.

73: Malqart

The subtle lyricism of a Beethoven string quartet enriched the air in Malqart's expansive, window-lined office on the next-to-top story of the Tevil Tower, the offices ceded to Tevil's Head of Security. Beethoven's complex melodies framed Malqart's contemplative mood, buffering him from the dissonance of human existence, a reality he was determined to shape into a more logical, righteous form.

Since The Shift, the path of humanity had exploded into the current jumble under the loose framework of the Federated system. Humanity was taking too many divergent vectors. The Corporate systems concentrated on transferring money from customers to their leadership, without regard for the people. Capitalist planets were rightfully eradicated, their system of wasteful competition rationalized into Corporate monopolies, but those Corporations had turned totalitarian. The nationalistic planets were oligarchies led by elites for their own benefit. The religious planets concentrated more on philosophy than practicalities, and starved while they waited for their problems to be solved by supernatural intervention.

Only Federated Central and New Kong were truly prospering, and they were the result of accidents in resources rather than a coherent governing system—perhaps not in the case of New Kong, with its rampant free markets and unbridled individualism, but New Kong's prosperity was based on a different kind of tyranny, the tyranny of ability. To Malqart, just because some people were smarter or more talented or worked harder, did not mean they ought to have more than their share. Some should not be allowed to take so much while others lived in misery. The greatest good must dominate over individual greed.

A student of history, Malqart had studied government systems. He discovered that all types of government seemed to work—sometimes. When they did, it was only for a short time. Eventually they failed, or transformed. Those that succeeded, there was a single common denominator. Always, there was a strong, powerful leader. Someone came forward, unselfish, without vice, never self-serving, with ambitions only for the People. For humanity to survive it had to be united around a single, enlightened, benevolent, authoritative, dominant leader.

Malqart would make himself that leader, the leader the human race needed.

Malqart swiveled in his comfortable high-backed chair to look out over the skyline of Dome City. He felt responsible for this city, its people. His mission was to serve them all. He must overcome the resistance of misguided reactionaries clinging to false teachings. It saddened him to resort to strong measures; intellectually, he knew it had to be done. Like a doctor treating a sickness, diseased cells had to be destroyed if the organism was to become healthy.

Diseased cells. There were many on Misplaced-4.

His computer screen currently displayed Corporate Intern Doron's student thesis on the failing restaurants at Terminal Junction. It was a very interesting, yet distressing, report. Doron was obviously intelligent, a young man to be developed, yet he was not aware his evaluation stemmed from a faulty foundation, a flawed worldview. Young Doron claimed Tevil's restaurants were failing because their food was unpalatable. Business was going to a place called The Lacrosse Shot because the food there was exceptional. He also cited an intangible atmosphere in the restaurant, where people felt welcome and relaxed and happy. The prices were higher than charged by Tevil's cafeteria (measured either per meal or per ounce or per calorie, the calculations were included), but customers paid willingly.

How deluded.

Doron did not understand the foundational principle of Social Goods Theory. Quantity had to be provided before quality. Basic survival needs come first: enough O_2, enough water, enough calories to sustain life. Only then should resources be directed towards improving quality. This fundamental idea was proven when the PunchPlanes shifted, and access to the resources of OldEarth disappeared. Systems died, whole populations disappeared when there were insufficient resources for basic survival. Quantity saved those that survived; quality comes later.

The Tevil cafeterias and food bars, dedicated to providing quantity, were being overshadowed by this Lacrosse Grill place. It was skimming money from the high end of the market. If those customers went to the Tevil restaurants, there would be less waste and overhead would be a smaller proportion of revenue, allowing them to cover expenses. Tevil would be able to better provide the Client population with the quantities they needed. It was not right that Vakkers and well-off citizens should have access to a high-quality product, and in so doing, prevent Tevil from serving the basic needs of Clients.

This Lacrosse Grill had to go. Balance must be restored.

Lacrosse Grill—no, Lacrosse Shot. Mike. Something stirred on the edge of Malqart's memory. Reaching into a drawer, he pulled out a confidential clipscreen and called up his FarleyFile, his indexed record of all the people he had encountered or might need to use, and all confidential correspondence.

Mike: a grounded Vakker. Purchased *Ajax*, a freighter sold for scrap. Converted into "Captain Mike's Bar and Grill." Refused to hire union employees. Near bankruptcy, he closed, remodeled, then re-opened as The Lacrosse Shot.

Malqart found what had brushed against his memory: an encrypted communication from Judge Marx about Union attempts to inspect the place. Marx claimed three of his Union organizers—really, be honest, Marx, your thugs—were assaulted and grievously injured. Marx requested Malqart raid the place with Tevil corppers. He wanted Mike jailed, and the doors to the Lacrosse Shot left unguarded, for a Union 'intervention.'

Marx had no subtlety. Always, he preferred the club over the feather.

Malqart had not responded. Marx offered no evidence of wrongdoing, and no inducement other than a carefully-worded sentence implying he would "owe you one." Marx already owed many more than one. It had been a long time since Malqart did favors in exchange for promises.

Lacrosse Shot. That was where the AISOO held meetings. It was also where the Citizen and Client reactionaries were gathering. He had not made the connection until now. That 'Wagering Association' also had that address. The Lacrosse Shot was obviously ground zero for many discordant movements.

Perhaps, in this rare case, Marx was right, the feather should be set aside.

The next movement of the string quartet began with a repeated chord progression, repeated, repeated again. There was a word for that motif. Malqart combed his memory.

Vamp? He turned to his computer, called up the dictionary.

Vamp: 'A musical phrase or figure that is repeated as the introduction to a musical theme.' Beethoven rarely used a vamp, only one other time he could remember, in an earlier string quartet.

Vamp was one of those curious words with multiple disparate meanings. The other: 'A mysterious and seductive woman who uses her sex appeal to induce men to do her will.'

Vamp. Perhaps Derr van Beethoven was making a suggestion. Ludwig was known to take unusual approaches. Was he calling Malqart to take an unusual approach to deal with this Lacrosse Shot problem?

Malqart plunged into his FarleyFile, searching the file labelled 'Useful Idiots.'

74: *Ghost*

The Casino Club was an expansive chamber decorated in the style of a Victorian private club, with real wood wainscoting, thick carpets, and formally-dressed attendants performing their duties at the gambling tables. Serving staff circulated with trays of drinks and delectables. There was a background of muted conversation, the click of cards and chips and dice, and the smell of roses. Very understated, very sophisticated.

Ghost was spotted immediately by an attendant, a lovely young lady in a formal, low-cut gown. She gracefully approached. "Derr Coast. Welcome to The Casino Club. I am Lelani. May I assist you in some gaming?"

"Yes." He was surprised she knew his name. Perhaps the ship's Organic identified him when he entered. Or, she had been briefed.

He said, "You understand my conditions? Ten thousand standards credit? I keep what I win?"

The young lady smiled. "Just so. Is there a game you prefer?

Ghost looked around the room, and pointed.

"Ah, Monte Carlo Roulette. An exciting choice." They strolled over, the young lady taking Ghost's arm. There was an opening around the table.

"Do you know the game?" asked Lelani.

"Wheel numbered 1 to 36, zero, double zero. Half red, half black. Zero, double zero, house wins. Bets on the table, staff spins wheel, winner number or color."

Lelani smiled. "What chips do you favor?"

Ghost smiled at her. "Ten chips. Each 1,000 standards."

Lelani spoke into her corsage. "Roberto, ten emperors, please."

A staff member approached and presented a silver tray with the chips on velvet cloth.

"If you put one chip on a number," said Lelani, "it could win thirty-five thousand standards."

Ghost nodded.

"No more bets, please," said the croupier attending the table. He spun the wheel and flung the ball on the outside ramp opposite the spin. Around, around, around. The ball slowed. It clicked against a raised diamond bump, and clattered into a bin.

"Red. Thirty-Six."

There were no winners.

"Place your bets please."

Ghost looked at the table. He clicked his chips together. Reaching out, he placed one on 'red' and one on 'black.'

Lelani touched his arm. "Derr Coast, are you sure? Unless we get a zero or double zero, one bet will win, one will lose. You will win 1,000, and lose 1,000."

Ghost smiled.

"No more bets, please." The ball was launched. It spun, bounced, then clicked into a bin. "Red. Thirty."

Ghost was given two of the golden chips back.

He showed one to Lelani. "This I won, yes?"

"Yes."

He showed her the other. "This is the original. Queen's."

"Yes."

He repeated the process again and again, each time betting only the Queen's chips.

He turned to his guide. "Dee Lelani, please." He handed her one chip. "Return this, my credit account. Queen's money. I will use on board." He handed her the other chips. "These I won. Please, create an account for me, First Bank of Hong Kong. Deposit."

He had converted ten thousand Queen's standards that could only be spent aboard to nine thousand Federated standards, money that would leave the ship with him, plus one thousand stans of Queen's fun money.

He still didn't need one thousand stans of stuff; with the Queen's money, he'd ask how tips were given on the ship, starting with Purser Zhou and George, Crunch and TwoBlips. And, he thought with a smile, Marie and her kitchen staff. Some joy, instead of broken kneecaps.

"You don't care to gamble some more?" asked Lelani, eyes wide.

"No." Ghost smiled and shook his head. "I don't gamble."

75: Franklin

Senator Franklin was in the Monarch's Reading Apartment, a space with comfortable chairs, unobtrusive computer consoles, and shelves of real paper books, most dating from before The Shift. It had the cherrywood appointments and aroma associated with an OldEarth 19th-century university bookroom. Accessible only to Galaxy Class patrons, at this time of the ship's night he had the room to himself.

A young steward appeared next to the senator's side table, carafe in hand, half leaning forward, ready to pour a cup. "More coffee, Senator?"

"No, thank you. Another and I'll not sleep."

"We have decaffeinated. Perhaps you'd care for some biscuits? I could get a sleeping draught—"

Franklin smiled at the young man's eager helpfulness. "Thank you, no. I'll be heading to my cabin shortly."

"Say 'Queen's Service,' and I will appear." He bowed, and silently departed.

The Senator was mulling over his discussion with Derr Coast.

Splices, or aliens.

The Top Secret annex to the Flatplain Raid report had information he had not revealed to Coast. The pirates' nets were an organic material, without identifiable DNA. Was that possible? The sleds were a bronze-like amalgam of a formula that could not be traced. Their weapons were made of unknown materials.

Another report had passed through his Intelligence Committee's notice. An ACT transiting a remote system picked up a transmission from a Vakker claiming to have been kidnapped by aliens, 'Trashcans' he called them. The transmission was distorted and discontinuous, as if from a corrupted audio file or sent through a loose antenna connection. They were not able to distinguish the Vakker's name, 'Tar'-something, or the name of his ship. A ComCan on watch fumbled with the communications controls and wiped the recording, leaving only watchstanders' imperfect memories of the message. The ACT tried to run down the bearing of the broadcast, but the signal abruptly ceased.

Franklin wished they had done a more thorough search, perhaps orbit the system's planets, but the ACT had perishable cargo and a schedule to maintain. These rent-a-warships were not real Navy. They were cargo ships, with a cargo ship's priorities. That, and the Command Candidate's incompetence, was frustrating.

The Vakker described sword fights more in tune with a fantasy vidgame.

The wonks at Naval Intelligence assessed the transmission as the product of an oxygen-starved brain, a Vakminer on his last O_2 who recorded the message and set it to repeat until the transmitter's power was gone. The Vakker likely died months ago.

The descriptions of 'Trashcans' sounded remarkably like what attacked the mining camp. Perhaps he should put some pressure on the FSF to send a navaire explorateur mission. An earlier survey found a planet with an oxygen-nitrogen atmosphere but no life, no water, and mostly a quartz, feldspar and silicon crust with no metals to mine or soil to cultivate. It was only a 20-hour survey. Perhaps the team missed something.

Like, aliens?

In the past Franklin had wondered why humans had not encountered aliens. There were millions of planets hundreds of millions of years older than humankind, with conditions that could develop intelligent life. It would only take fifty million years to fully explore to the ends of the galaxy, assuming sub-light travel; PunchPoints shortened that estimate by orders of magnitude. The Fermi-Hart-Tipler Paradox postulated that another planet could have developed intelligent life before humans appeared, and an intelligent, curious alien species could have crossed the galaxy and found humanity by now. The odds that humans were the first intelligent life was astronomically low. Surely there were alien races in the galaxy—surely?

Then there was the Vakker's old wisecrack: we know there is other intelligent life in the universe, because the aliens *haven't* contacted humanity.

Aliens. They might be benign, or a threat.

He had spoken to Peter Marshall about the ACT 'Rent-a-Navy.' Marshall was pressing for an all-professional force with purpose-built warships, ready to face pirates or rebellious planets, to stop interplanetary conflicts, enforce interplanetary law, or, yes, confront aliens. You didn't have a navy, he claimed, if ninety percent of the ships were obligated to cargo runs, the crews not drilled for combat, and the ships owned by Corporations disinclined to risk them. Without a professional navy, the cohesion of the Federated Planets could shatter. There would be seventeen different systems with seventeen different sovereignties, just like the nations on OldEarth, leading to OldEarth-style wars.

Marshall's arguments were sound. But the present system had too much inertia to expect meaningful change in the near term. Marshall's reform advocacy was likely why he had not made Flag rank, and was banished to the Academy. Next promotion cycle Franklin would see what he could do about that. Reform was needed. Marshall could help.

The analyses of the nets and the sleds, the transmission describing 'Trashcans,' seem to point to aliens. But the idea of DNA manipulation by humans could not be ruled out; it certainly was more palatable than aliens. If he asked the FSF to look for aliens everyone would doubt his sanity, even use it against him in Chamber debates: 'Can you trust Franklin, the fellow who had us out looking for little green men?'

Some rogue scientists from Asclepius may have continued the research forbidden by the Federated Gene Laws.

Both possibilities demanded discrete investigation, which must be done without giving the Opposition an inkling that he had lost his mind, and without starting an interplanetary incident with Asclepius.

The senator pecked a message on his classified clipscreen to Admiral Mikawa, bcc Captain Peter Marshall, to follow up on the transmission intercepted by the ACT—as a scouting mission. No mention of Aliens. A second message went to his contact in the Federated Criminal Investigation Division, Asclepius System.

76: *Ghost*

Ghost was having a comfortable afternoon in the expansive sitting room in his quarters in the Emperor Ming. He was stretched out on a sofa, head cradled by pillows, a carafe of iced Citrusilver on a side table and a package of bite-sized orange Crunchy Gooeys on the felt carpet within reach. Music filled the room, the temperature was adjusted to within a degree, humidity 34 percent, he could run a shower for as long as he liked and the soap smelled like flowers. There were days more of this. He might even experiment with Queen's Service.

The door chime sounded. The cultured voice of the ship's Organic said, "Derr Coast, Das Augustus Franklin wishes to know if you are receiving visitors."

Ghost pivoted upright on the divan. "Enter permissive."

Auggie walked in, adorned in his Booster Buddies skinsuit.

Ghost sensed something was wrong.

"Derr Coast. Good day, sir."

Ghost looked him over. His eyes were clouded. Had he been crying? "What's radiating, Booster Buddy? O2 blinking red?"

Auggie hung his head.

Ghost patted the seat next to him. "Dock your mass. Listening."

Auggie sat. "Grandpa's so busy, Maxie is, she's just a dumb girl. Could you help me?"

"Can't say 'yes' 'til asked."

Auggie rubbed his hands on his thighs. "There were big kids in the game room. They laughed at me. They said I didn't know how to wear a skinsuit right. Said I was all dumbed up." Auggie looked at him. "Am I all dumbed up?"

"Stand. I'll look." He stood Auggie in front of the divan. "Mistake once, no huhu. Twice—bad, lazy. Fix and learn. Learn from mistakes."

He spun Auggie around. There were several errors that could be a problem in vak. "Got some issues."

The boy looked at him eagerly. "Will you fix them?"

Ghost thought for a second. Lying around like a royal billionaire was not good for the soul, at least, not a Vakker's soul.

"No."

The boy dropped his head on his chest. "I'm sorry I bothered—"

"No, not fix. Teach. Teach, so you know what, why, how." He waved a hand in a dismissive gesture. "Fix, five minutes, red, waste of time, dumbed up happen again, maybe different dumbed up. Teach, five *hours*, green, *know*. Green to proceed? You want to learn, I teach."

Auggie smiled eagerly. "I want to learn."

Ghost nodded. "Good. Strip. Skinsuit off."

"What?"

"First, skinsuit theory. We go from inside out."

Augustus began removing the suit. "Green to proceed," he said, with determination.

77: *Maxie*

Maxie Franklin had been thoroughly outmaneuvered. Unacceptable.

During boarding at Misplaced-4 in the Galaxy Class lounge, she had staked out Derr Schwan as her conquest for the trip. He was tall, handsome, exquisitely gene-scrubbed, not from a 35 Family but heir to the Schwan fortune, something about snacks with high salt and sugar content. She would never consume that stuff if she wanted to keep her perfect figure, but she had no objection to Schwan's supernova-sized cash flow, as long as he was willing to part with lots of it to entertain lady friends. Specifically, her. She had chatted him up, displayed all the right signals, along with a few alluring looks she copied from an OldEarth Grace Kelly vid.

A few surreptitious standards slipped to a hostess, and she learned Schwan had a reservation at the exclusive Island Lee restaurant. Tables were only for Galaxy class; reservations had to be made months in advance. Maxie very much wanted to sample the Island Lee. It was reputed to be the best restaurant in the Queen lines.

She made herself available for Schwan to extend the invitation. Inexplicably, none came.

Then, at the dinner hour, she just happened to be outside the restaurant, and saw Schwan go in with that phony Frenched-up tart Gabrielle. He was smiling. She was laughing. Probably laughing at Maxie.

Now she did not have an escort, or even a solo dinner reservation at any of the Queen specialty restaurants. She would have to go back to the Galaxy Room with Grandfather and the infant. Bore-ing.

She spotted Coast. He walked right in to the Island Lee, and was greeted effusively. How did he manage that? She strolled by the entrance and glanced in. He was being seated in a prime booth with great deference.

She quickly approached the hostess standing behind the reservations podium, at a speed taken by someone late for an appointment. "Derr Coast has arrived? Ah, there he is. Quite all right, I see him, don't bother." She slipped past the hostess.

She walked to the booth. Coast glanced up, surprise on his face. She took the seat opposite. "Reservations. A mix-up. You don't mind?" She signaled to the staff. "Menu, please?"

A server instantly appeared with the menu, large format, beautifully engraved. Maxie took and opened it, then peeked over the top to see how this Coast fellow was reacting. It appeared he was accepting the inevitable with good grace.

The restaurant's illumination was dusky, created by wall sconces in the form of faux-flaming torches and randomly distributed ceiling pocket lights. The décor employed clever placement of ferns and leafy plants that provided privacy for the guests and a background rustle from a light waft of scented air, replicating a pleasant breeze on a tropical island.

Maxie considered the options. The menu's listings were in French and German and Italian. There were also Polynesian selections to match the restaurant's theme. There were no descriptions, just names. Queen was notoriously snobbish. If you didn't know what the names concealed, you did not know enough to properly appreciate a Galaxy specialty restaurant.

She knew the names, of course, but she didn't expect a homeless Vakker would.

She was about to suggest she order for them both when he punched the button on the service console. "Soupe a L'orgnon. Cru Beaujolais. Chocolate eclairs. Green tea, unsweetened."

"Superb choice," she affirmed, surprised. He even got the pronunciation right. "No entree, just soup?"

He flashed a rueful smile. For just a second. "Yesterday, too much food. Also, discovered Orange Crunchy Gooeys. Still burning off calories."

She nodded. "Perfectly understandable." She pushed her button. "Sole Meuniere, Sancerre, Kouign-amann. Domaine du Salvard Cheverny Blanc." She looked up. "You surprise me. I did not know Vakkers had exposure to haute cuisine."

"Don't."

"How did you know about Soupe a L'Orgnon? It is known as the 'Queen of Soups.' It is very difficult to prepare. I doubt there is a chef on Misplaced-4 who could create it. Properly, that is."

"Researched. Prepared."

"Goodness," she said. "Are you always prepared?"

He looked her in the eyes. "Try."

For a moment Maxie actually felt intimidated under his gaze. She realized she was just sampling the crust of someone with immense resolve.

"Can I ask something?" Coast said.

"Certainly."

"Purser Zhou, very nice lady. Gave me release to sign."

Maxie gave him a canny look. "I'll bet they did. Right after they upgraded you to the Ming, and the free services and the Island Lee, right?"

Coast spread his hands. "Should I? Sign?"

"Gadzooks, no. Don't let them wiggle free. Let them smother you with kindness for the whole trip, and even then I wouldn't sign. You might want the leverage later."

"Later?"

"Legally, you can sue up to seven years after the assault. For now, let them buy your regard. If you file against them the freebies end, and the Corporation will muster a legion of lawyers who'll duck and weave and file continuances and discoveries and legal legerdemain for a few years, anything to delay a settlement."

He looked at her with a small smile. "Thank you. You know lots."

"Comes with being a senator's granddaughter."

Maxie looked at him carefully. There seem to be some depths to this fellow. Most of the other young men she knew would be heading max blast to the shadiest local shyster to dip their hands into Queen's wallet as deeply as their imagination would lead them.

He was good raw material. *Very* raw. She always enjoyed make-overs.

"So," she said, "you like to be prepared? You have prepared for the FSF?"

He leaned back in his seat, putting additional space between them. "They say, any ship, any station, any job, anywhere. Can't prepare for unknown."

She leaned forward. "Any-any-any still means you're going into the FSF. You can prepare for that. Behavior. Language. Things like table manners. For example, a gentleman never communicates his order before the lady. It is considered rude. It's a silly convention, but it is how things are done."

He nodded solemnly. He didn't seem to resent the instruction, so she charged on. "Language. Think of it this way. Humans send signals that enable us to recognize people we can trust, to determine to which tribe they belong. People tend to treat people in their own tribe better than they treat strangers. If you talk like a Vakker to a Vakker, everything is green, right? Talk like a Freddy or a corpbee, Vakkers see you as an outsider, treat you like an outsider. Get along with Freddy Flightcrew, sound like a Fed Flightcrew. Yes?"

Coast mulled the thought for a moment. "Yes." He nodded. "Fix a machine, read manual. Fix language, read manual. I will read language manual."

"Flight Artisan, then officer, then admiral. You must eventually be like an admiral." This was going to be fun.

For a second, he looked terrified. No, shocked. He carefully phrased, "I don't want to be an admiral."

78: *Ghost*

Ghost had a marvelous breakfast delivered hot to his suite, laid out by a rather ridiculously-garbed robot server supervised by a real human. He exercised in the gymnasium and splashed about in a pool entirely full of water, H_2O, something he had never done before.

Experiencing just the right amount of tired, he lay on the divan and sampled a box of bite-sized individually-wrapped Chocolate Orange Crisp Crunchy Gooeys, while his clipscreen displayed *Basic Linguistics for Simpletons*. He marveled at the mystery of the continuous pluperfect tense.

Would that life was always this uncomplicated. Grammar excepted.

The door chime sounded. Queen's Organic announced, "Derr Coast, Headmaster Concierge extends his respects, and hopes it would be convenient for you to honor him with a moment of your time."

Ghost had a sudden wave of guilt. Was he eating too many snacks, imposing on the service too much? He certainly had not been exhibiting restraint. Headmaster Concierge? That's a Queen leadership heavy lifter.

"Room, activate cleaning bot."

The cleaning bot emerged from its closet. Ghost pointed. The bot quickly vacuumed up the Crunchy-Gooey wrappers. After the bot returned to its charging dock, Ghost stood and said, "Convenient."

The door opened. A man entered, upright in posture, distinguished in demeanor, with thinning silver hair perfectly ordered, wearing the rather archaic tuxedo that was the uniform of his guild.

"Derr Coast. It is good of you to spare me a moment. I am Fortescue, Headmaster Concierge for *Extravagance Queen*."

"Problem? Hope I've not—"

The gentleman waved a depreciating hand. "No, sir, no problems, it is our pleasure to be of service, it is what we are. I am here on a mission apart from my pleasant responsibilities with the Queen Lines."

"Seat?" asked Ghost.

"No, Derr, thank you, you are most kind, this will take but a moment." Oddly, he placed a hand on his heart. "Do you know of the ancient and honorable society known as The Associates of Space Flight?"

Ghost shook his head.

"It is an anachronistic name dating back to OldEarth, a century before The Shift. It began as a society of scientists and talented amateurs dedicated to forwarding transportation between the planets, and to promulgate the highest scientific and ethical standards. It continues today, with the added objective of addressing the conflicts that periodically occur between systems and Corporations. It is exceedingly selective, yet has representatives with all the inhabited planets and, I dare say, all orbital stations and most large-crew spaceships."

"Never bumped one." Ghost stood at parade rest. It just seemed the right thing to do, in the presence of this personage.

"Oh, Derr, I am sure you have. There are several members on board this ship, both as guests and in service. Our senior division includes four planetary chief executives and many heads of agencies. It is there, particularly, where we feel our code of ethics is most needed."

"Misplaced-4?"

Fortescue shook his head. "We have few members there, and none in senior government or Corporate positions. It is a dark quarter in our firmament."

Ghost cocked his head to one side and waited.

The gentleman continued. "Members of our junior division you have encountered. They are colloquially known as 'Booster Buddies,' originally named after a video program, '*Booster Bob and the Buddies, to Betelgeuse and Beyond.*' It was an early recruiting tool, quite effective for its time."

"Augustus Franklin?"

Fortescue nodded. "I am pleased to say you have been nominated for membership as an Associate."

Ghost was instantly disappointed. This was just a shakedown for a membership fee, like little kids going hatch-to-hatch selling cookies or handkerchiefs or blogletter subscriptions.

Considering what he had been receiving from Queen and the Franklins, it would be churlish to go dark. He reached into his coin pocket, then remembered, Yeo Three Hillary had his cash.

Fortescue held up a hand. "The nominating party assumes all fees, which are substantial. It is one of our ways to ensure nominations are well-considered."

Someone else pays for him to join? Different.

Fortescue continued. "I hold the modest rank of Navigator in the association. One of my responsibilities is to vet nominees. They must be of the highest character and integrity, who will not only be an ornament to the Association but will forward the Association's goals and aspirations. I am pleased to report all four of our senior division members in *Extravagance Queen* have seconded your nomination. You are held in high esteem, particularly among our Vakker members."

Not knowing how to respond, Ghost remained quiet.

"The nomination does not go forward without your concurrence. Membership's burden is as light as air and as substantial as steel, it demands nothing and everything. I counsel you, do not to enter into it lightly."

Ghost nodded, again not knowing what to say.

"With your permission, I will forward to you a document which explains the Association, its goals and rules, aspirations and responsibilities, and our code of ethics. Accepting membership means you agree, and will abide by this code. Upon review, you may request the nomination be forwarded, or decline."

Did he really want to belong to a club? He had always made his own way. People were unreliable, threats, they wanted to imprison him and take what little he had. No, not all, there were Vakkers, Mike, and Sherri, the Professor, LaMancha, Shengwu, all those who offered to pay Marx off. They were … friends?

These thoughts were pointless. Whoever nominated him must not know.

"My past?" Ghost said. "Convicted, felony? Pay On the Drum?" He shook his head. "Your ethics?" He waved a hand. "Disqualified."

Smiling broadly, Fortescue said, "We are aware of that unfortunate situation. It is no impediment. Indeed, I tell you truly, an attack by the odious Bench Vulture is an excellent endorsement."

79: *Maxie*

Maxie let Derr Coast escort her off the lift into the Emperor Ming Royal Residence vestibule.

Coast turned out to be very convenient. A word from him, a meekly expressed desire, and he was provided with the best seats at any performance, the best table at any restaurant. This evening, she had greatly enjoyed allowing him to escort her to see a rare performance of the baritenor Barbarossa. The luxurious Emperor Ming's Box was directly adjacent to the stage. Maxie was able to look down on Schwan and his French pop tart being jostled in SRO, Standing-Room-Only. Highly gratifying.

The p-door silently opened. Off to the side of the foyer, taking considerable space, was a pile of luggage.

A short, heavy man in flashy clothes got up from the couch, put down a drink and a pastry, and walked over. "You are Recruit Coast. I am Federated Professor Sumida of the Space Forces Academy. You and I will exchange cabins."

"Queen's Service," said Maxie.

"Excellent, young lady. We shall obtain assistance in moving him out."

"Queen's Service," announced the ship's Organic. The lift door opened, and the dignified form of Fortescue appeared. "May I be of service, Dee, Derr, Derr?"

Maxie's chin went up. "How did this *stuff* appear in Derr Coast's suite?" She pointed to the pile.

Sumida stepped forward. "This recruit and I are traveling under Admiralty orders. I am the senior professor at the Federated Space Forces Academy, Federated Professor Sumida, you likely have heard of me. I outrank a recruit, obviously. We will exchange cabins. I require this space for important meetings."

Fortescue said, "Derr, your lodging number?"

Sumida smiled. "Take his belongings to," he glanced to his clipscreen, "24 dash 110."

"Derr, that is Traveler Class," stated Fortescue. "You are not authorized this level."

Waving this off, Sumida said, "Remove his things. Have a steward unpack my bags."

Maxie said, "Derr Coast? What do you say?"

He looked at her. "Not recruit. Yet."

Maxie frowned. "Language?"

Ghost started again, slowly and carefully. "I am not a recruit yet, until I am accepted at destination. I am Citizen. As Citizen, I outrank no one."

Maxie smiled. "Much better. 'As a' ..."

Ghost continued. "Also, *as a* Citizen, no one outranks me."

Maxie touched his arm. "Excellent."

"You deny my rank and authority?" flustered Sumida. He glared at Fortescue. "I will hold meetings here regarding Federated government policies. Senator Franklin, Corporate Holder Rigoletto, and Attorney Secretary Bellini will be invited. I will require the support of your Galaxy staff, and thus, the best accommodations."

Maxie pulled out her clipscreen. Her thumbs flashed over the keys.

Sumida looked down his nose at Fortescue. "Senator Franklin and I will speak to the Captain about your negligent treatment of a very important guest."

Looking at her clipscreen, assuming a 'dumb blond' persona, Maxie said in a sing-song tone, "No no no, don't think so."

Sumida was taken aback. "I beg your pardon. You and your boyfriend should leave now."

"I've called up Senator Franklin's schedule. He's meeting with some visiting firemen from Cetus-1 in the Queen of Sheba Room, in five. I never could understand this thing about visiting firemen. I mean, why would people who burn things want to speak to Grandfather just because he is a very senior, and very powerful, member of the Federated Senate? I mean, if they incinerated the wrong something and got Grandfather upset, surely it would be a bloody, horrible end to them, don't you think, Federated Professor Sumida?" Maxie honored him with a lovely smile.

"Grandfather?" Sumida blinked.

Two of the ship's uniformed masters-at-arms appeared. They saw Fortescue. The leader put a knuckle to his forehead, and in a gravelly voice, said, "Headmaster Concierge. My respects. Central Monitoring indicates a mis-directed Traveler-class."

"Oh, good," said Maxie. She pointed to the luggage. "You can remove this stuff."

"See here!" said Sumida, looking rapidly between Maxie, Fortescue, and the masters-at-arms.

Sumida's clipscreen bonged. Maxie's began to play a waltz.

Maxie pointed to her clipscreen. "Oh, look, Grandfather *has* made time for you, in 45 minutes. Good for you, Derr Sumida! Oh dear, the appointment duration is only four minutes. I remember, when Grandfather was head of the Navy, he sandblasted a full admiral down to bare metal in only 60 seconds. He's given you four times that!

Stars and comets, I'd love to join you, but Grandfather always says, 'praise in public, chastise in private.'" She smiled sweetly.

Sumida looked at his clipscreen, and blanched.

"Chief Master-at-Arms Cojack, if you would," said Fortescue, gesturing to the luggage, "could I impose upon you, I know it is outside the scope of your duties, but please take a moment to place these bags in the vestibule? I will have the stevedore staff handle things from there. Could you also escort Federated Professor Sumida to the Queen of Sheba for his meeting, and afterwards show him to 24 deck 110? I suspect he is your misdirected Traveler-class."

"Certainly. Queen's Service," said the Chief, and the masters-at-arms started hefting bags.

Sumida was spluttering. "Dee Franklin, I was not aware—"

Maxie waved a finger and pointed to Ghost. "To him, I think?"

Ghost looked at Sumida, at Maxie's finger, turned, and walked to the sofa.

"Well, Derr Sumida," said Maxie, with her head held high, "it appears Derr Coast is more gracious and forgiving than I would be under the same circumstances. Say hello to Grandfather for me. If you are allowed a word."

Brushing past Fortescue, Sumida slinked out.

Fortescue stood before Maxie, his hands clasped. "Dee Franklin, Derr Coast, let me offer my most sincere—"

"Not your fault," said Ghost from the sofa. "No huhu."

Maxie frowned, and looked at Ghost. "I just hope you don't run into him again. I've met the type. Pure acid vindictive." She addressed Fortescue. "Could you put a tail on him, make sure he doesn't get lost again in Galaxy? Keep him off Grandfather? Block him from sending comms to the Senator? That is—" she glanced at her clipscreen, "— after 47 minutes from now?"

"We will take measures," said Fortescue. "I will resolve the lapse in security and the misdirected luggage. My apologies for this most unfortunate incident. Is there anything else Queen's Service can provide? You have only to ask."

"Ah," said Maxie, holding up a finger. She took a step closer to Fortescue, and lowered her voice. "Derr Coast and I have a small disagreement. He claims it is impossible for a reptile to survive a direct hit by a 120-millimeter smooth bore depleted uranium armor-piercing cannon round. I believe it is possible. That deluded man has five standards that say I cannot provide an example."

"How may I assist?" Fortescue frowned. "If you are contemplating a test, however, we may be a bit short on reptiles."

"Could you please have your vid geeks call up 'Godzilla 2000' on our screen? It's somewhere in the OldEarth entertainment archive. We'll watch from the beginning so I can scream and point when we get to the evidence. And, two bowls of buttered popcorn, big bowls, heavy butter, with that lovely cinnamon seasoning."

80: Augustus

The Roman Praetor, General of the Army, stood on the hilltop, helmet off, the breeze ruffling his red hair, the sun glinting off burnished armor. He ignored the lingering smell of bacon and fresh-baked pastries. The ground under his feet provided no impediment to an attack, but good footing for a defender. Handsome and well-formed, the impressive Praetor dominated the field by the force of his personality. He ruled this world to the edges, boundaries strangely obscured by billowing white clouds at the borders of the forest. He was in deepest Gaul. The enemy approaches. This was his hill to defend. Victory, or Death.

Looking down, the Praetor saw a warrior of Carthage emerge from the forest. The armored soldier looked up placidly, spotted him, and began toiling up the hill.

The Praetor scowled. He called out, "Halt, Hannibal! Surrender now! If you surrender I, Augustus Primus Magnus Superbus Glorioso, will spare you!"

The Carthaginian warrior reached under his cloak, pulled out a handful of cards, selected one and cast it on the ground. "Peltasts and light infantry," he said, without the slightest sign of the intimidation the Praetor knew was coursing through his craven Carthaginian bones. "Skirmish line. Advance."

Lightly-armed, mobile fighters emerged from the white fog and advanced at the double-quick.

"Aha!" shouted Augustus Superbus, pulling out a card. "On my left, my composite bowmen, they cut down your light infantry! Ah ha ha!" Bowmen appeared, arrows flew in a cloud of missiles that came close to blotting out the sun, extracting screams of terror from the Carthaginian wounded and dying.

The Carthaginian growled, "Ah ha ha yourself." He was calm, unruffled. "On my right, my Numidian cavalry takes your bowmen on the flank." Another card was cast. Out of the billowing white at the edge of the battlefield, horsemen—unarmored men carrying round shields and riding ponies—rumbled up the hillside, clods of dirt rising from their horses' hooves. They pulled up a scant ten yards from the bowmen and, with a cry of defiance, flung their javelins, cutting down five of every ten bowmen. The surviving Roman auxiliaries melted away in panic.

The Carthaginian lifted his sword high. The sun glittered off its polished blade. A card fluttered. "Now, double Aha! My heavy infantry. You have nothing to oppose. Augustus Superbus, taste defeat! Henceforth, in the annals of the Republic you will be known, known as—Auggie the Silly! Of Loserville!"

Out of the forest appeared a double line of infantry armored in gleaming breastplates and greaves, wearing chain mail and frightening feathered helmets, brandishing huge, two-handed swords. Crimson cloaks billowed behind them in the breeze. They dressed their formation, then, with the blast of a horn and a cheer, they marched forward double time.

Standing his ground, Augustus Superbus watched the oncoming warriors as they ascended the hill. At the very last moment he raised a hand.

"Hannibal the Hilarious, I have the last 'Aha!' I play … The Holy Hand Grenade!"

The scene flashed to white. Everything was gone.

From the sky came a voice. "Dee und Derr, ladies und gentlemen, Citizens, please excuse the interruption of your entertainment, your breakfasts and your clipscreens. *Bitte*, attention please? *Danke*, thank you."

Auggie took off his BattleCards game helmet and blinked at the light in the Galaxy Lounge. Across the small console table Derr Coast also removed his helmet.

Auggie caught his eye and chortled. "Gotcha! Splattered your heavy infantry. King of the Hill!"

Derr Coast looked at him with a crooked, indulgent smile. "The Holy Hand Grenade? Not until Medieval level. Wonder how you got it? Next time, I deal."

There was a steward stationed on a small platform by the bar, with his liner slippers anchored to the felt carpeting while they were in zero-G. The room was filled with Galaxy-class passengers. Stewards were hurrying to remove the last breakfast and pastry containers.

Speakers came to life. "Dee und Derr, I am Leading Steward Schmidt. Thank you for joining us. As experienced travelers know, Federated safety regulations require all passengers muster in central location und are secure by seat belt when das schiff transitions through das PunchPlane. There is, of course, nothing unto which you need have concern. The last difficulty with a transition was many decades ago, and never on *Queen* liner. Instead, it has become pleasant tradition with us, an opportunity to share congenial gathering. Ladies und gentlemen, Dee, Derr und Das, please check your seat belt. The next voice, our Navigator."

Auggie was a little concerned when Derr Coast insisted on verifying his seat belt was fastened properly. He had to scrunch over to conceal the 'Viking Berserkers' and 'Tiger Panzer Battalion' cards.

81: *Ghost*

A heavily accented Japanese voice spoke. "Ladies, gentlemen, your Navigator, speaking from the Command Deck. *Kon'nichiwa*, good day. We are thirty seconds from transition into Elysium System, home of Federated Central … Stand by …"

Tee hee hee! Heeerrrrre's Johnny!

Johnny? thought Ghost. He turned, looking for the voice. *Milton? Is that you?*

The next voice you hear? I ain't no stinking navigator!

Ghost closed his eyes. He did not know what to expect. Mable had always been good, but Milton seemed a little … scary?

Tee hee hee, fiddle-de-dee, am I gunna dump a surprise on thee…

Milton, don't do anything—

Hey, 'ol Buddy, what's a week between freaks?

The Navigator announced, "… Stand by …Punch, slide, three, two, one … Honored Guests, welcome to—"

There was a severe jolt. The lounge was assaulted with a flash of blue light.

"Elys—*Sugoi!*" The speaker cut off.

The Galaxy Lounge was filled with the rumble of conversation.

"Derr Coast?" said Auggie, as he rubbed his eyes. "It wasn't like that, the other times. What was that light? Did we hit something? Something hit us?"

"Don't know. Not like any punches I've done." Ghost scanned his skinsuit readouts. "No leaks, no alarms, no screaming. No worries, Augustus Superbus."

82: Marshall

Commandant Marshall's intercom buzzed. "Sir, Commander Wang from Fleet Staff, he's the Chief of Operations' aide—"

The sign of a good yeoman: never assume your boss knows anything.

"—he requests you give him a call, soonest. Number three in your call queue. Secure line, encrypted."

Even a momentary escape from administrivia was welcome. "Mustn't delay the staff's golden countdown to accomplishment. Hold off the barbarian hordes."

He triggered call three. There was a short pause while the two systems performed their encryption handshakes. His screen flashed on, showing an officer in fastidiously neat semi-dress blues, wearing the aiguillettes of a flag aide. "Commandant. Good of you to return my call." Wang had a distinctly harried expression.

"Good afternoon, Commander. You must be getting back to me on my request for more fleet rider slots for my Candidates."

"Ah, no sir, that's still being staffed. This is an 'immediate action' from the Admiral."

Unusual. Little dealing with the Academy deserved an 'immediate action.' "Go."

"You've heard about *Extravagance Queen*? Hopefully not. Public Affairs is working to keep it off the news. She made a Cetus-Elysium punch following all the normal procedures, but arrived a few gazillion kilometers off the PunchPoint. Still in Elysium System, but far enough off target they had to wrestle a seppuku sword away from the Navigator. The greatest surprise, it appears she arrived thirteen seconds *before* she left."

"That's hard to believe." Marshal thought for a second. Occam's Razor: the simplest explanation was the most likely. "Clock systems synchronization malfunction?"

"They're checking. She's still in transit. The displacement added a week to her arrival time. We are going to bring her in to Station One rather than the regular Queen's dock, and give her a full examination. The Admiral wants two of your academics to join the investigation team, a PunchPlane theorist and a sub-atomic physicist. Two coffins are reserved for Saturday, report by 1430."

Marshall thought for a few seconds. "Does the admiral want brains or enthusiasm?"

"Both. The PunchPlaner needs to be senior and distinguished. He'll have to hold his own against heavyweights. The quark chaser can be young-but-brilliant."

"I think I can get the right volunteers."

"Nossir," said Wang emphatically. "This is not a volunteer mission. Nobody turns this down because they'll miss a kid's birthday party. Pick the best, and tell them it's a command performance. If they threaten to quit the academy, tell them they'll be drafted, as Artisan recruits."

Marshal gave a small chuckle. "No worries. For the chance to investigate something like this, the faculty will be storming that shuttle like the ticket came with a complimentary copy of the original *Principia* autographed by Isaac Newton himself."

Wang grinned. "Well, it takes all kinds." His expression turned serious. "This is close hold. We need answers before we release the news. One news blogger was going to publish a fantasy that foreshadowed another shift. That could cause a panic. He's in custody now, something about 'temporary insanity.' So, tell your people. No leaks."

"No leaks. And, no money. All my travel and discretionary funds are expended. Remember, Headquarters directed the funds towards Professor Sumida's travel to Cetus." It was hard for him to suppress his resentment at the Admiral's staff for forcing him to authorize that boondoggle. Really, three weeks of travel to attend a two-day academic conference?

"I'll have travel orders cut here, on a headquarters budget," said Wang. "I'll need names before close of business."

After signing off, Marshall sat back in his chair. He should start with Professor Yarkovskii.

There was a knock, and Mahkinen came in, carrying a sheaf of papers. "More unclassified hard copy here sir, nothing urgent. Professor Yarkovskii is on his way over. Chief Bjerkaas has talked to Fleet Staff Disbursing, they've agreed it would be faster if Staff sent budget numbers and we cut the orders here."

Marshall tilted his head and looked at her. "That was encrypted to my workstation." He pressed his fingers against his temples. "You really aren't supposed to listen, you know."

"Me, sir? Listen? That would be a security violation. Got some intel through other channels." She looked back through the door. "Here's the professor. May I send him through?" Without waiting for an answer, Mahkinen placed the papers on the captain's desk and departed.

Professor Yarkovskii, Chairman of the Physics Department, mused his way into Marshall's office. He looked up and smiled. "Hallow, Peter. Good to see you. How's the wife? Oh, that's right, sorry, that accident last year. Regrets. Well, I won't take any more of your time." Yarkovskii pulled out a clipscreen, extended the screen, and started to make notes while standing in the middle of the office.

Marshall stood. "Professor. Professor."

"A moment, please."

Marshall waited patiently.

"Excellent." Yarkovskii slapped his clipscreen shut. He looked up with a pleasant expression. "I'm sorry. Did I ask to see you?"

"Please, sit down. Something to discuss."

They walked over to the Commandant's meeting table and sat.

Marshall started describing what he knew about *Extravagance Queen*.

"Yes, yes, I know all that," said Yarkovskii.

"You know?"

"Astronomers tend to be talkative when they are over-excited. *Queen's* transition was accompanied by a flash of energy, some have compared it to Chernokov Radiation, but more intense. There has been considerable speculation on the physics and astronomy bulletin boards. Journalists don't read science sites; I'd wager most could not differentiate a proton from a panda bear."

"Your assessment?" asked Marshall.

Yarkovskii leaned back and closed his eyes. "Well, to answer that—hmmm… Some groundwork." He pulled out his wallet, unfolded it, and laid it flat on the table. "We know that space-time is bent by gravity in many of the twelve dimensions. Yes, a touch more complicated, but the folding wallet analogy is still useful."

Marshall knew better than to try to rush the professor.

"Major directional changes occur in response to strong gravitational fields, stars, and planets, black holes, other large masses. If the directional change is sufficient, space-time from vastly separate locations can fold against each other, touch, rub together." He flipped one side of the wallet, and demonstrated where they touched. "Where planes rub, there is a continuous emission of charmed quarks, which provide the means to detect a PunchPoint, that is, a point in which one can punch through from your location on the membership cards to the touching fold at the credit I.D. cards. An Einstein-Rosen bridge, from one fold on the wallet to the other."

Marshall nodded. This was straight from Punchplane 101.

Yarkovskii continued. "So, a question: how do we punch from one plane to another? We charge a net surrounding the ship with charmed quarks, they reach a critical density, and voila! We are 100 light years away, near a different gravity well. But how? We lost many probes until we learned to keep everything perfectly still in relation to the PunchPoint." The professor frowned. "We know the engineering to punch, but we do not understand the theory. We know little regarding the nature of the PunchPoint. Does it have a twelve-dimensional shape? Less? Thickness? You are familiar with Quantum Entanglement? No, don't bother, I've yet to determine if Entanglement is *entangled* with this problem." He flashed a smile to the captain, and seemed disappointed at Marshall's reaction. "Sorry. A bit of physics whimsy."

"I marvel we can use PunchPoints and know so little about them," said Marshall.

"There are theories, one I humbly admit to ownership. I suspect the charmed quarks, in some way, represent a kind of short-circuit across the two planes, and the higher-quark concentration flows to the lower-quark location, somehow dragging the spacecraft along. I would love to run some experiments, but cannot obtain funding. How can we think of anything other than the supreme question: what caused

The Shift? Perhaps a gravitational wave displacement from the collision of two black holes, but all the appropriate instruments were on OldEarth. Can we predict a Shift? Control it? The future of the human race is at stake."

Yarkovskii continued to stare at his wallet. He seemed calm, reasonable, and most distinguished as he stared.

"Professor? Is there a problem?"

Yarkovskii looked up and smiled. "I don't think so. Just wondering if I paid my rent for last month." He picked up the wallet and returned it to a pocket. "I haven't been evicted, so I must have. You were saying?"

Let's see how he handles this one. "There is something the astronomers do not know," said Marshall. "*Extravagance Queen* arrived at Elysium thirteen seconds *before* she left Cetus."

"Impossible. Well, unlikely. I haven't considered anything impossible since I met my daughter's boyfriend."

"Why is it impossible?"

"Because it would mean, for thirteen seconds, in this universe, there existed two *Extravagance Queen*s, one in Cetus System, one in Elysium. One of the fundamental principles of physics is that mass-energy can be neither created nor destroyed. If what you have said is true, it would appear there was created an additional *Extravagance Queen*, and both existed in our universe together for thirteen seconds, one created out of nothing, then the original destroyed." He shifted about in his chair. "More likely, an instrument error."

"Or, something very special happened?"

"Or something very improbable happened."

Marshall leaned forward. "Two of our faculty will join a team to investigate *Extravagance Queen*, a PunchPlane scientist and an expert on punchplane subatomics. For the PunchPlane scientist, I understand only yourself and two others can really be considered authoritative?"

Professor Yarkovskii half-closed his eyes. He stared off into infinity.

Marshall gave him a moment, then asked, "Professor? Something wrong?"

"No, no, just trying to think of who could be the third."

Marshall smiled. "Could you join the investigation team?

Departure on Saturday."

"Oh, my. Saturday? Dear, dear. Esteemed Commandant, there is this birthday party I simply *must*—"

Marshall leaned back and sighed.

Yarkovskii grinned. "Petty Officer Mahkinen told me when she called. Was it Petty Officer Mahkinen who called? Delightful young lady. What were we discussing? Ah, yes, my very small humorous offering. My apologies, I never could deny an opportunity for comedy, a necessity in my field, I'm sure you understand. Of course I shall go. I would be immensely disappointed otherwise. Besides, you would not want Olsen for this. Much too drifty. Quite scatterbrained."

Marshall made a mental note to have a word with Petty Officer Mahkinen about her pre-briefs to his visitors.

"Also, a subatomics specialist? You would recommend…?"

"Nokuthula, most certainly. Quite brilliant, quite, and her son's birthday was last weekend, so we have cleared that hurdle. Smashing gathering. Costume party. I went as Cosmic Catastrophe the Clown. Very well received. The scamp actually pinned a sign on my back with some Chaos Theory equations. Quite the bright lad."

83: *Ghost*

The maglev train banked gently and sped through the curve heading to the small community flanking the Federated Space Forces Academy. Elysium-3, home of Federated Central, was a natural O_2-N_2 atmosphere planet with conditions almost duplicating OldEarth, down to a similar spin, axial tilt, and extensive oceans. There was no life on the planet when it was first discovered. It had taken over a century to work billions of tons of compost into the soil, allowing plants to flourish. A diversity of flora and fauna was established, similar to Northern Europe and North America.

Every year, the borders of the human habitable areas expanded. Tens of thousands of square miles of cropland and grazing meadows fed the people of the Seventeen Systems. Hundreds of square miles were dedicated to trees for producing lumber, and that most necessary contribution to bureaucracy: paper.

Gravity was 1.01-G. Ghost found it comfortable. The new automated self-propelled roll-a-case, courtesy of Queen, trundled along behind him. He wore a tunic and trousers in gray, which blended nicely with his skinsuit. He hadn't spotted another skinsuit since departing New Berne spaceport.

There were two stops serving the Academy, one for Academy Central Main Gate, the other serving the town of Bellagio and Academy Gate 2. He was to report to the Main Gate, where he would be directed to Personnel In-Processing.

A recording announced their arrival at Academy Main. The train decelerated smoothly to a stop. The doors opened. Ghost stepped out. His bag followed.

Someone collided with him, hard, with a snigger.

"Excuse me," said Ghost.

There were three youths wearing what Ghost recognized as the Academy powder blue coveralls worn by Command Candidates. One of them pushed him.

"You! Civvy-shit unscrub! This station is for Space Forces only. Get your ass back on the train." This came from a short, pugnacious Command Candidate with the features of a bulldog nursing an ulcer. The nameplate on his chest read, 'Command Candidate 3 Brin.' The other two also had nameplates: Johnson, Tze-tung.

"Oh, look, he must be a Booster Buddy. He's wearing a skinsuit." Johnson laughed.

"Are you a Booster Buddy, skinsuit-man?" said Brin. He sneered. "You aren't supposed to wear a skinsuit unless you are qualified to wear a skinsuit. You qualified, Booster Buddy? I don't think so. Gentlemen, I think it is our duty to relieve this imposter from his illegal skinsuit."

Brin grabbed Ghost's arm and twisted. Tze-tung put Ghost into an armlock, shifted to a choke hold, and squeezed. Johnson pushed Ghost's bag flat on the ground and kicked the electronics.

Ghost was shocked. Attacked, again? Fight? Against three? Outskirts of the Academy?

"Good MORNING, Command Candidates."

His assailants froze.

Ghost twisted his head around. He saw a barrel-chested, middle-aged man with short hair, round cheeks and prominent ears, wearing the undress uniform of an FSF Chief Petty Officer.

"You are helping this gentleman with his luggage?" the Chief said.

"Hi, Chief," said Brin. He released Ghost, who slumped to his knees.

"You are leaving."

"Yeah, we're outta here." Brin turned and walked quickly to the escalator, followed by the others. As they descended, one called out, "Fartisan belly-robber!"

Ghost got up. He looked at his bag, checking for damage.

"Are you reporting in? To the Academy?" asked the Chief.

Ghost nodded, not wanting to speak until his throat stopped throbbing.

"I'm Culinary Chief Jones. I'm Federated Space Forces with the Academy. If you show me your orders I can direct you. Your name?"

"Gh—Coast. My name is Coast." Ghost pulled out his government clipscreen. After a thumbprint, his orders came up. He handed it over.

The chief started scrolling through the pages. "Hmm. Misplaced-4. Still a civilian, what a shame, if you were an off-duty FedSpacer I could have preferred military charges against those hooligans." He read some more. "Of course, they have only been here a short time, not used to military discipline. We should allow some margin." He frowned at the clipscreen. "You are not yet classified? No MOS? You're GDAA? You are assigned to the Academy for 'General Duties As Assigned?'"

"I don't know what that means."

"MOS is 'Military Occupational Specialty.' Everyone who enlists first goes to basic training before they are assigned an MOS. For some reason, this step was omitted for you. You do not yet have an assigned specialty." He noticed the skinsuit. "Spacer? Vakker?"

"I've worked vak."

"Perhaps that's the reason. Vakker recruits are rare." He looked through more pages. "Below average scores in organic chemistry, culinary, thermo …"

Ghost looked up sharply. "I only skipped two questions."

Distractedly, the Chief said, "Yes, of course."

The chief closed the clipscreen and tapped it in his palm. "GDAA means you are available for assignment at the discretion of the receiving command." He held the clipscreen out to Ghost. "Do you have any experience with food preparation?"

Ghost took the clipscreen. "Aboard ship, cooked sometimes. Breakfast. I like making cupcakes."

The chief's eyes got wide. "Breakfast. Cupcakes. Experience!" He smiled at Ghost, a little rapaciously. "Step along with me. I will be happy to accompany you to Personnel. We'll get you sworn in waku-waku, and then I'll go have a nice cuppa with the personnel chief."

84: Jones

Culinary Chief Jones led Flight Artisan Recruit Coast into the center of the Federated Space Forces Academy Culinary Center Galley. The Chief was dressed in immaculate houndstooth-patterned black and white pants and a long-sleeved white double-breasted jacket. Coast was wearing white pants, a white t-shirt and white apron. It was five o'clock in the morning.

"Let's have a look at you," said the Chief.

Coast halted and came to attention.

Chief Jones smiled. "You needn't brace. We aren't formal in my galley."

Coast looked puzzled. "'Rules for Recruits,' Fleet Forces Manual 703 point one three—"

The Chief waved him off. "That's boot camp. Not necessary outside Hell Island." He looked him over. "Your apron is reversed. The pockets are supposed to be on the outside."

"Pockets without closures shouldn't be outside. They can snag and tear and cause your electronics to hit something sharp or charged."

The Chief laughed. "Vakkers. Trust me, an apron is not a skinsuit. Swap around."

As Coast changed his apron, the Chief said, "We'll start with training." He waved some papers. "This is a qual card, that is, a qualification card. It lists all the things you need to know to be qualified to do a particular job. This one is Beverage Service. You'll learn how to mix up bug juice, that is, powdered lemon fruit cooler, how to work a regurgulator, the correct temperatures to serve drinks, there are twelve specific areas of knowledge. When you have learned an area, you come to me or one of the culinary petty officers, you demonstrate you have learned that bit in an oral quiz, and we sign your card. This card requires twelve signatures for full qualification."

Coast nodded.

"This number?" Jones pointed. "That's the points awarded for completing this card. When you complete one hundred points I give you a half-day. For two hundred fifty, you get a whole day of liberty and a pass to Center City."

The recruit still didn't say anything. Usually, his newbies were enthusiastic about the offer. Coast must be one of those quiet types.

"You normally would start on the regurgulator," the Chief continued, "but both are OOC, that is, Out Of Commission." The Chief looked up to the ceiling. "As is our auto dishwasher, our sanitizer, our cutlery dispenser, two toasters, fry station, and a few other things I can't get Space Systems Command to send a technician to fix."

The Chief's clipscreen chimed. He looked at it, then slipped it back into a pocket. "I'm wanted at the loading dock. Sit," he pointed to the dining room, "familiarize yourself with the Beverage Service qual card. The references are accessible through your clipscreen, folder 'Galley Quals.' I'll be back shortly."

85: Rossini

Rossini, a pixie of a woman with a ready smile, came into the galley through the staff entrance. She saw Coast. "Ciao, amico," she said. "You must be our Newbie. Welcome to the Academy Culinary Center, the ACC, falsely known as the Acme Concrete Company, a reputation Chiefie and I are in the process of correcting. Welcome, fellow galley slave." She grinned. "That's a joke. Get it—we're in a galley, galley slave, like, an ancient rowing-propelled boat with slaves at the oars? Double entendre? Okay, maybe not that funny, but it won't be the last time you hear it. I'm Felicia." She looked down at the papers in Coast's hand. "Whatcha got?"

The Newbie handed them over.

She looked through them. "We don't pull rank much around here, but officially I'm Culinary Second Class Rossini. I can give sigs on beverage service. Need help, just ask."

"Screwdriver?"

86: Jones

Chief Jones pushed through the swinging door, after a thoroughly frustrating experience on the loading dock. Really, you would think these people would treat a regular customer with respect. For the amount of business he awarded, they could at least get the invoice right.

He looked around the kitchen. Regardless of his ninety-minute absence, the prep crew was working efficiently, materials stacked ready for breakfast omelets and scrambled eggs, bread and pastries deployed, bacon and tomatoes, and his Newbie was… missing.

His regurgulators were gone.

"Rossini!"

The young lady popped out from behind a tall dirty-dishes cart. Jones suspected she'd been hiding.

"Hail, Capo."

He grimaced. When Rossini got cute, it meant there was some prank in the wind, or she had done something without his approval. "Newbie, skinny recruit. Seen him?"

"Yes, Chief."

The chief waited. Rossini smiled sweetly.

He growled, "Rossini … Where?"

"He's inside the dishwasher."

Jones blinked, then glowered at her. "You said, 'He's in … the dishwasher'?"

Rossini nodded, her expression all innocence.

The chief folded his arms. "He's dead? You're hiding the body?"

Rossini held out her hand flat and wiggled it. "Comme ci, comme ça."

The Chief leaned forward and glared. "Well, as long as you have control of our Newbie or alternately his corpse, pray tell, what happened to our regurgulators?" He pointed to empty places, white rectangles on the walls contrasting with dimmer, well-scrubbed surroundings.

Rossini pointed to the serving line. Next to the stack of trays and the utensil dispensers were the two regurgulators, with adjacent shelves of glasses and mugs.

"*Why* are—"

Petty Officer Rossini held up a hand. She walked to the nearest regurgulator, pulled out an insulated mug, and placed it under the dispenser. "Five-two-two-hot, right, Chief?" She punched in the numbers and hit the big green button.

Steaming liquid poured into the glass.

Chief Jones was amazed. Two months it was, the last time his regurgulators even put out tap water.

Rossini retrieved the glass and handed it to the chief. "Two teaspoons honey in Gyokuro Green Tea. It's well known Chiefies are grumpy without their cuppa."

He took a sip, tentatively.

Ambrosia.

"Oh-my-goodness," he said. "Tea." He sighed. "That most sovereign restorative for jaded spirits." Another sip. "Delightful." A deeper sip. "The Systems Command technician, finally! Thank you, Lord." He sighed.

"Negatory. No Systems commando. Coastie fixed it."

"Coast? Our Newbie? The corpse you hid in the dishwasher?"

"He's not hiding, he's fixing. The conveyor drive belt snapped. He says he can fix it temporary, but we gotta order a new belt, or get him a synthetic rubber welder."

The Chief waved at the regurgulators. "So, why move them?"

"Coast's idea. Vakker trick, from the liners. People get their drinks while they wait in line. The liquid fills them up. They eat less, feel full faster, fewer people get seconds. Customer satisfaction goes up, food costs go down. Pretty smart, huh, Chief?"

87: *Ghost*

Evenings at the Academy mess hall were generally quiet. There was a scattering of candidates, almost exclusively Artisans, studying. Some ComCans were reading or writing letters; some groups of four or five were playing group vidgames. Chief Jones always laid out a tray of fresh pastries or cookies. With the regurgulators now available 24/7, the ACC had become a popular evening venue.

Someone from the Culinary Division had the duty each night, to collect dirty dishes, wipe up spills, and keep the tray replenished. Tonight was Ghost's turn. He took a walk around the fringe of the hall, trying to stay invisible to the candidates. There was nothing demanding his attention—except for a burned-out light.

There was a Command Candidate taking advantage of the dark corner to play a solo computer game. He had his virtual reality helmet on, oblivious to everything outside his own virtual world.

The failed illuminator bothered Ghost. It was a flaw, a discrepancy. Inoperative equipment kills people in space. Repairs deferred risk lives.

In the storeroom, he obtained a replacement bulb. No ladder, but there was a tall three-legged stool. One leg was broken off three inches short. A three-inch block of wood was on top of the stool. Someone had previously addressed the problem, in a makeshift way. Ghost carried everything to the mess hall. There was sufficient separation with the candidate in the VR helmet to avoid being skewered by the ComCan's virtual sword. The block of wood went down. The stool's short leg settled firmly on it as if measured to ten-digit tolerance.

Ghost climbed. Balance was precarious. He twisted the hold-down wing nuts loose and slid the ceiling panel to the side. The dead bulb was cold.

"I say, Admiral Johnson, Admiral Tze-tung! Look who's here!"

It was the ComCans who harassed him at the train station.

Ghost put three fingers on the edge of the light housing to steady his balance.

Command Candidates outranked him. He was told to be respectful.

"Good evening, sir."

"Oh, my!" called Brin. "Bless my bippy, it's Booster Buddy! Quick, is Chief Jones around? Booster Buddy's diaper is slipping."

"Hey!" called out the knight under the VR helmet. "Take it somewhere else." The Candidate hit 'pause' and lifted his helmet.

Brin sneered. "It's Roddy. The only Command Candidate to kiss an unscrub ass. Hey, Roddy, Chief Imani's been smiling a lot. You visiting him at night?"

Roddy's face showed disgust. "Clear out."

"Be quick! Here's another unscrub to suck."

Brin kicked the block of wood.

It went skittering across the floor. The stool's leg instantly dropped three inches. The stool tilted. Ghost's foot slipped.

Brin stepped back. "Meteor alert!"

Arms flailing, Ghost pitched head first off the stool. In the split-second before impact, he yearned for the quarter-G on Misplaced-4.

He crashed head-first into Roddy's VR helmet, twisted in mid-air, banged his ankle against the stool, tried to twist to get a shoulder under, then smashed an ear on the floor.

***

"You okay? How many fingers am I holding up?"

Ghost blinked and tried to collect his scattered wits.

"How many fingers?"

"Blue," Ghost mumbled.

Roddy gave a laugh. "Anything busted? Do I call for an AutoDoc?"

Ghost sat up. "No, sir. I'm …" He put a finger on his ear. It hurt.

The stool was ten feet away, against a wall. A few Candidates scattered around the hall were standing and looking in their direction.

"You need help?" someone yelled.

Waving, Roddy called out, "Show's over, move it along, fuze is out of the bomb, Elvis has left the building. Nothing to see here. Ya'll can go home now, shuttle leaves in five."

A few of the candidates chuckled, some catcalls and a razzberry cut the air. A cookie sailed by Ghost to bounce off Roddy's boot.

Nobody came to assist. With Vakkers, help would be swarming. That was one of the differences between the groups that went into

"Those Candidates," said Ghost. "Johnson. Tze-tung. Who was the other?"

"Brin. Capital 'B' for 'bastard.' Lab must have farkled his gene scrub, because he is the ugliest human in the System. Mean as a psychotic cobra."

Ghost put Brin's name away for later.

He started to gather his legs under him. Roddy held out a hand. He must have read reluctance in Ghost's expression. "Take it. I'm trying to learn how not to be an arrogant asshole. It's part of the program here at the Academy."

It seemed the Command Candidate wasn't trying to play him. Ghost took the hand. Roddy hoisted him to his feet. "Sorry about those guys. They're the local gangsta mob, an embarrassment to their families, but too conceited to recognize it."

Ghost walked over and picked up the stool and the wood block. He still had a bulb to change.

Roddy was looking at his VR helmet. The visor was hanging loose.

"There goes gaming," said Roddy. "No replacements on this planet."

Ghost took it from him. One hinge was broken, a cable pulled loose. "I'll fix."

Shaking his head, Roddy said, "No chance. The wiring is ripped." He looked at Ghost more closely. "You're the FedSpacer who fixed the regurgulators, right? That made a lot of people happy. No more hand-mixed bug juice. That stuff can burn holes in a bank vault." He took another look at the helmet. "If you can fix it, I'll owe you."

Ghost shook his head. "I fell on it."

"Brin kicked the stool. What I'd really like is to teach capital-B-for-Bastard-Brin a lesson."

88: Marshall

Captain Peter Marshall, Commandant of the Federated Space Forces Academy, former commanding officer of an ACT and a class one cruiser, with Flight Artisans to lead, academics to herd and Candidates to mold, spent most of his time sitting at his desk fighting the administrative war.

Today, the torment lying in wait was bi-weekly reports from his department heads. For months, all trends had been unfavorable: equipment availability, parts inventories, consumable supplies in stock, available funds, all down. Up were shortfalls and discrepancy lists. It wasn't his people's fault. They were working hard. There just were not enough sufficiently skilled people or adequate funds.

So began the bi-weekly torture.

Only, this time, it wasn't.

Trends were reversed. There was a blip up in almost every graph. When he got to the Culinary Center accounts, he saw major improvements in everything: equipment utilization, stores-on-hand, waste. Customer Satisfaction, Campus Organic's measurement taken by observing the students' reactions to the food and overhearing their comments, was way up.

Something was going on.

He shifted to the Culinary Center's finances. The food allowance was higher than he remembered. He checked menus: steaks instead of spaghetti.

Accounting reported cash transfers to Culinary from nearly all the departments. He jotted notes.

It had to be the chiefs. The chiefs had some kind of scam running. Culinary was the beneficiary. Start there.

He hit the intercom button. "Mahkinen, get Chief Jones in here. Speed-of-light."

"Yessir. Can I pass on the subject?"

"No. Expedite." He clicked off the intercom. No Mahkinen Pre-Brief. Let's surprise Jones.

Fifteen minutes later there was a tap on his door, and Chief Jones entered.

"Captain sir, good to see you sir." He was carrying a covered dish and utensils. "Petty Officer Mahkinen told me you skipped lunch again. For shame sir, burning yourself to the nub, just like on *Constitution*. But I remembered you liked my turkey tetrazzini, so I brought a ration."

Marshall struggled to ignore the savory smell. "Not going to work," he growled, trying to look grim.

"Sir?" asked Jones, wide-eyed and innocent.

"I want to keep us out of jail."

"Jail, sir? Us?"

"Yes. You, for whatever scam you're running, and me for letting you get away with it."

"Sir! I am hurt you would think—"

Marshall waved him quiet and pointed. "Sit."

He displayed the bi-weekly reports on the overhead screen. "Something's going on," he said, "and it's got Chiefs' fingerprints all over it. Culinary Department is ground zero."

Chief Jones exhaled, and smiled. "Sir, we haven't a problem, not at all, just a new asset, we do."

Marshall was silent, his eyes locked on the Chief.

Chief Jones cleared his throat. "A young man reported in three weeks ago. Recruit, no training, test scores nothing special, GDAA, so Chief o' Pers sent him to me for mess cooking."

Mess cooking consisted of low-skill cleaning and dishwashing. It was a labor-intensive job. The FSF never had enough bodies to fill the need. New recruit non-quals were always assigned a tour of mess cooking.

"Respectful kid," Chief Jones continued. "He rarely has two words to ornament the day. I've had more conversation from my statues of Colonel Sanders and Ronald McDonald. But, I discovered, he's a *Vakker*, and Vakkers can fix *anything*." The chief leaned forward. "*Everything* in the kitchen is working." The Chief settled back, folded his hands over his stomach and half-closed his eyes.

"That explains your equipment ratings. What about the money transferred to Culinary?"

Jones' eyes popped open. "Well, sir, the other chiefs, they got whiff of my young man, they did."

Meaning, you tried to hide him, and they found out.

The Chief half-smiled. "With my dishwasher now full-mission-capable, I could spare him for a few hours. Now, the other chiefs had equipment down, with funds put aside to pay for Space Systems Command technicians to make repairs. So, with my laddie doing the repairs—"

Note the possessive 'my laddie.'

"—they didn't have to pay the extortionists from Space Systems. They saved money. It was only fair they send some to the ACC. Only right, it was."

"In other words, you were renting out my recruit."

With a pained expression, Chief Jones said, "Oh, sir, sometimes you have a contrary way of looking at things."

"What was your cut?"

"Of the monies set aside for repairs, the chiefs agreed, half was reasonable."

Marshall slapped his desk. "Half! The chiefs shuffled—" he glanced at his desk pad "—over fourteen thousand standards, and you didn't think to tell me?"

"Sir, you are so horribly busy, we figured the chiefs could handle it. Every stan went to improve our bill of fare. Our new menu serves steak, roast beef, chicken marsala..." he sniffed dramatically, "...turkey tetrazzini, with real harvested garlic and the best Parmesan cheese—"

Marshall could smell the garlic. His mouth watered involuntarily.

"—and for the whole base, mind, Candidates, FedSpacers, even our Fleet's Misguided Children's mess."

Marshall leaned back in his chair. He was protective towards his Fleet Marine Corp garrison, and was pleased they were included in the largess.

"Did you take care of this recruit? Was he rewarded for this extraordinary work?"

"Sir, the lad is of the sweetest disposition, very willing, respectful, but he's shy as a turkey the day before thanksgiving. He only wanted access to the library and the gymnasium's swimming pool." The Chief closed his eyes. "He will take an extra slice of my blueberry cheesecake with cream topping, though."

"Well," said Marshall, "this has to stop."

Chief Jones' face fell. "Sir. My dishwasher is only a temporary fix. Could we wait—"

Marshall interrupted. "This young man is obviously an asset for the entire Academy. No more rent-a-recruit."

"Yessir. Could Flight Artisan Recruit Coast stay with Culinary until the end of his normal mess cooking tour?"

Marshall sat bolt upright. "Did you say, 'Coast'?"

89: Marshall

Captain Marshall called out, "Enter." Petty Officer Mahkinen walked into the Commandant's office. Some hair had escaped from her bun, where there was a pen sticking out. "Sir, I have the information on Recruit Coast."

The Captain swiveled his chair to face Mahkinen. "Go."

"Sir, he was placed on deferred contract to the FSF on Misplaced-4 by JAG Lieutenant Rhys Reeson. He traveled as a civilian, to be sworn in here. That allowed Lieutenant Reeson to duck the reg requiring court ordered recruits to have an escort."

That's right, thought Marshall, *to see if Coast was trustworthy, if he would show up on his own.*

Mahkinen continued, glancing occasionally at her clipscreen. "His records and travel orders have a number of irregularities. Somehow, he ended up in Galaxy on expedited orders in *Extravagance Queen.* Our people are contacting their people to run that gremlin down."

Extravagance Queen. Strange coincidence. Coast might help transform the FSF, and he arrives in a liner that might transform our understanding of PunchPlane transitions.

"He also had some sort of encounter with Professor Sumida. A misunderstanding over staterooms. Maxine Franklin was also involved. It evidently was resolved amiably. Details are unclear. I'll have more information soon."

Sumida. We're rid of him for three weeks and he's still causing trouble. "Get all the details." *I don't want to be blind-sided by another Sumida-crisis.*

"Yessir." A note on her clipscreen, and Mahkinen looked up. "Sir, when Coast didn't report for five days after *Extra's* scheduled arrival, Academy Organic marked him no-show, canceled his contract, and issued an arrest warrant per standard procedure. It's common, people using false enlistment to get travel to Fed Central."

You would have thought we'd have stopped that dodge by now. "Go on."

"He was coming to us after his shuttle landed. He got rousted by some ComCan Threes on the Academy Main maglev platform. Culinary Chief Jones intervened."

"Names."

"Brin. Johnson. Tze-tung."

"Company Commander," Marshall searched his memory, then said, "Command Lieutenant Meng. Have Meng see me. Today."

Mahkinen made another note on her clipscreen. "Chief Jones took him to Personnel. When he and Chief Bonaparte found his contract was canceled, they wrote a new contract, and swore him in."

Marshall sighed. He knew where this was going. "Jones applied for the recruiting bonus."

"Chief Jones and Chief Bonaparte split the bonus. JAG says it's legitimate."

Marshall gave a grunt. "So, for half the recruiter bonus, Bonaparte assigns Coast to the ACC."

Mahkinen shifted on her feet. "I wouldn't exactly call it a quid pro quo, sir. Chief Jones has an outstanding requisition for a Culinary One and two Culinary Threes that Chief Bonaparte hasn't been able to fill for months. Lots of stuff gets negotiated in the Chief's Mess."

Don't I know it. "Did they cancel the arrest warrant?"

Mahkinen grimaced. "I'll get back to you on that, sir." Another note.

Marshall leaned back and rubbed the palm of his right hand with his left thumb. All the keyboard bashing was making his hands hurt. And his head ache.

"Where did you stash him?"

"He's outside, corner of the sofa, reading. Not a sound for two hours." Mahkinen shook her head. "Sir, he just doesn't add up. His test scores say he's dumber than a fried popsicle, yet he's zeroed in on two issues of *Relativity Theory Yesterday*. I would swear to Booster Bob he's actually reading them."

"Separate him from the Big Bang and send him in."

"Sir." Mahkinen turned to go.

"And, Mahkinen …"

"Sir?"

"Sometimes I wonder how the Academy could possibly function without you. Well Done."

Mahkinen started to say something, then smiled, nodded, and walked out.

Marshall shifted over to his screen, called up Coast's file, and started looking through his test scores. They were not what he expected.

There was a faint knock on the door. It opened, and the white-clad recruit stepped into his office, accelerated by a gentle shove from Petty Officer Mahkinen. He walked in, stood in front of the desk and came to a semblance of attention. "Report. Report*ing*. By order of."

Coast had not gone through boot training, so Marshall held back correcting his deportment. It wasn't the kid's fault he didn't know the drill. He looked the young man over. Thin, wiry. Intelligent expression. His apron was reversed, with all the pockets inside.

"Flight Artisan Recruit Coast. Welcome to the Academy. Sit." Marshall nodded towards the chair in front of his desk.

Coast gingerly sat down on the front edge.

"Chief Jones is pleased with your work repairing equipment."

A faint smile, but Coast remained quiet.

"You have experience repairing equipment?"

"Yes."

"Do you enjoy it?"

"Yes."

"There was nothing in your test scores that indicated you had repair skills."

Coast shrugged. "I answered all the questions. Left two blank. Multiple choice answers weren't right."

"How's that?"

"One asked how much carbon dioxide could be produced from one kilogram of carbon. The closest multiple-choice answer was 3.6 kilograms. The correct answer is eleven divided by three kilograms."

Marshall scrolled through Coast's exam. That question had been answered, but with a wildly wrong choice.

"How do you think you did on the rest of the exam?

"Simple test."

Marshall looked through the exam. The scores were miserable. He decided to try a spot check.

"What is necessary to get maximum power transfer from a capacitive source?"

"The impedance has to be a complex conjugate of the source impedance."

"What does the Kelvin-Planck Law deal with?"

"Converting heat into work. Second law of thermo."

"What is the ratio of the moment of inertia of a circular plate to that of a square plate?"

"Three pi divided by sixteen. But only if they are of equal depth." Coast had a puzzled expression. "That was question twenty-seven. Do the test again, if you want."

Marshall smiled and shook his head. Then he stopped. It *was* question twenty-seven. "You remember the whole test?"

Coast's expression was entirely guileless. "Yes."

Extraordinary. Mahkinen said his records were dodgy. Evidently, so were his test scores.

Perhaps this *was* the young man he needed.

"When you signed up," said Marshall, "what did JAG Lieutenant Reeson say you would be doing?"

"Officer said, 'Any ship, any station, any job.'"

"What would you like to do?"

Coast shrugged. "I can fix for the chiefs. They've been good. Not Vakkers, but good."

That was encouraging. It was something to build on. "What do you expect from the Space Forces?"

Coast looked him directly in the eyes. "I've been jacked. I'm not high-braining this."

Not what he wanted to hear from his chosen instrument. "You object to Federated service?"

Another shrug. "Five years in space instead of thirty-eight in jail is good. Space duty, retire when I reach the radiation limit. With crappy shielding on FSF ships, maybe ten years. Half pay for life for a petty officer is twice what I lived on at Misplaced-4. I can fix for ten years, for a pension."

That 'crappy shielding' was something Marshall had been fighting for years. It kept women off ships, what with the extraordinarily high radiation levels in the part of the galaxy inhabited by the Seventeen Systems. He hadn't registered it was causing early retirements. That must be costing millions in premature retirement payments. He could make the argument for more shielding based on long-term personnel costs, if he could convince the Chamber to think beyond a single year's budget.

He looked back to Coast. "Have you considered becoming an officer? A *Command* officer?"

Coast closed his eyes. He folded his hands in his lap. "No."

"I can offer the opportunity."

Coast shook his head. "No."

"Why?"

Coast crossed his arms. "Command officers get Spacers killed. Ignorant of vak, yet Freddy gives them power. Artisan Class One not as advanced as a Class Three Vakker qual. Look at FSF mishap and accident stats. Risk your life in an FSF ship. Incompetent leaders, marginally competent Artisan officers, inept FedSpacers."

Marshall took a breath. This was what he was trying to change. "Yet, you're willing to go to space for ten years with them?"

"I'll chisel for a half-pay pension. I have to be here anyway. As long as some Command officer doesn't farkle a punch, I'll survive."

Marshall got up and walked around the desk. He stood in front of the window overlooking the parade ground. There was a company of FedSpacers doing drill.

Parades. Marching drill. Pretty displays for politicians. Wasted instruction time. Marching did nothing to improve a Flight Artisan's skill, to make them effective in the Deep Dark.

Marshall's objective was to build a navy, an *effective* navy. Command officers were characteristically cast-offs from the ruling families, too uncaring and arrogant to learn how a spaceship actually worked. Yet, they were in charge, making decisions from the depths of their ignorance. The FSF needed technically-savvy officers who were ready to lead, not noble underperformers from politically-connected oligarchies.

Coast might help him change that.

"Do you have any Class Three quals? Vakker Class Three?"

Softly, Coast said, "Six Class One quals. A Class Two in Environmental Systems. There's a 'time in service' requirement for Class One Environmental."

"Six Class Ones? How old are you?"

Coast shrugged. "No age requirement. Just pass the test. Did it just for fun. Vakkers don't need licenses to know who's safe to space with."

Marshalled walked back to his computer. Coast was just over the age of consent. A record, youngest Class One ever.

The kid was technically smart. He could live, work, and navigate in space. He was probably as good technically as an Artisan lieutenant commander. Stars and comets, he repaired just about everything broken on the whole base in less than three weeks, including circuit boards. He could pass for direct commissioning as an Artisan officer without a doubt.

More important, he had integrity.

But, his behavior? Character? His attitude oscillated between assured to pugnacious to frightened, confident to uncertain and doubtful. He rescued people from pirates at the risk of his own life. He let himself get physically pushed around by some obnoxious ComCans.

Could he lead Artisans, take charge of Command officers?

Leaders were made, not born. Making leaders was Marshall's job. Marshall did not take on tasks intending to fail.

Marshall looked at Coast. "Any ship, any station, any job? You agreed?"

Coast nodded.

Marshall reached out and activated his intercom. Mahkinen answered up.

"Coast," said Marshall, "has just been accepted as a new Command Candidate Third Class in this semester's accession. Have Master Chief assign someone to walk Coast through ComCan check-in. Expedite."

90: *Ghost*

By dinner time Ghost had been discharged from his enlisted contract and sworn in as a Command Candidate Third Class. He had new uniforms, new shoes, and an enhanced clipscreen preloaded with megabytes of instructional material. He stowed the FSF issue skinsuit; his Perfiflex was superior, and its gray color close enough to pass as G.I. He was provided a class schedule, met the suspicious Command Lieutenant company commander, told how to act and who and how to salute, and spent twenty minutes trying to put sheets on a bed in the proscribed FSF fashion, so an inspector could bounce a quarter-standard coin off the covers. Eventually he just got some clamps from the galley tool chest and stretched the covers over the bed frame, without sheets. He'd sleep on the floor, until he could rig a hammock.

He walked to the mess hall for his evening meal. It looked no different from this morning, from the Candidates' side of the serving line. He joined the queue. Picked up a tray. Napkin. Fork, knife, spoon. The utensil dispenser needed lubricant, it squeaked. ThermoGlass, in the regurgulator, zero-zero-three-iced, CitruSilver. The other ComCans in the line ignored him.

"Hey! Coastie!"

It was Rossini, behind the serving line, bouncing on her toes like she was auditioning for a trampoline team, grinning broadly, waving.

He smiled.

"We heard! *Command Candidate* Coastie. Wow!"

"The vegetables. Now?" complained the Candidate ahead of Ghost.

"You surely may have vegetables, Command Candidate." Rossini gave him a heaping spoonful, well over the ration amount. "You have a great day, Command Candidate. Coastie! Something for ya!"

"Keep the line moving," said another Command Candidate, glaring at Rossini.

Rossini sprinted over to the walk-in refrigerator, disappeared into it for a blink, and returned with a plate with an opaque cover. She slid the plate under the sneeze shield on to Coast's tray, and grinned.

Coast completed walking the serving line, picking up a meal greatly improved since he first arrived at the Academy. There was an empty table in a corner. He walked over, put down his tray, and sat with his back to the wall.

Dinner looked good. Hachis Parmentier, a savory beef and potato casserole, well-seasoned. Ghost remembered Chief Jones doing the training with his petty officers while he was re-wiring a circuit breaker.

The room resounded with the usual clash of forks on plates, and the rumble of conversation he had come to expect in the mess hall during serving hours. Only, this day, his corner was a wedge of silence.

He had heard about this, when he was only a lowly mess cook. Rossini had warned him. The Command Candidates would all subject someone to "The Silence." They would refuse to speak to him, of him, around him. They would not acknowledge his existence.

Ghost was being 'Silenced.'

No one came to join him. No one violated his isolation. The mess hall was crowded, but he had a table to himself. They were ignoring him, deny his existence. When they could no longer hold back a glance, ugly expressions decorated hundreds of faces; he could feel invisible waves of hate from the royals, resentment from the Artisans. Everyone in the vast room detested him.

The newest Command Candidate in the Federated Space Forces,

advanced beyond his desires or expectations, Command Candidate Third Class Coast felt absolutely miserable.

Rossini had slipped him a dish. He peeked under the cover.

Blueberry cheesecake, with a dollop of whipped cream. Two slices.

91: Padmere

The lander's control panel was dimmed, the forward windscreen dialed to black, flight controls deenergized while the ship was parked on the spacefield in her launch cradle. The cockpit was lit only by the gentle glow of instrument screens and a rank of yellow and red status diodes illuminated on the fuse panel. Artisan Lieutenant Padmere nestled into the pilot's coffin with his eyes closed, absorbing the comfort of the form-fitting cushions. His eyes burned, he felt itchy under his skinsuit, and he needed a shave.

This would be his ninth straight day of no-G toleration flights for the new class of nose-dripping royals. He briefly considered giving himself a downcheck for not meeting flight crew rest requirements. He sighed, and flung that thought away. The missions needed to be flown, the cargo was required, the gapped instructor pilot billets would remain unfilled, and a flight deferred would just add to the backlog.

The seductive computerized voice of Bitchin' Betty sounded from the shuttle's speakers. "Thirteen Fifty. Scheduled alert. … Thirteen—"

"Shuttle Organic, Pilot. Alert cancel."

"Pilot, Shuttle Organic. Alert cancel. Alert is cancelled."

He levered himself out of the coffin, stretched, and tried to blink away the crystals in his eyes. It was a short hop down to the observers' deck, slip past the six passenger coffins, a squeeze through the hatch between the passenger deck and the cargo hold via airlock p-doors, and a left through the personnel hatch to the flight line gangway.

After the dark shuttle the desert sunlight hurt. His eyes watered. He looked down and half closed his eyelids. The light reflecting off the white concrete platform was just as painful.

A short female Flight Artisan in green coveralls and yellow helmet walked up waving a clipboard. "Hey, ArtyLoot, come sign?"

A clipboard. Paper. He sighed.

Her coveralls were stenciled on the upper left chest in black, 'Flight Line Supervisor,' and under it, in smaller letters, 'PO1 Masden.' She thrust the clipboard into his hands, then pulled her helmet off, releasing matted brown hair in a compact ponytail.

She wiped sweat out of her eyes. "Full bag of fuel, O2 and consumables. Loaded max volume, 74 percent mass. Crates of 'sorted spares, twelve giga-normous solar panels, and six construction vakbots under the cargo hatch. The bots have charged fuel cells, full thruster tanks, powered-up capacitors and loaded reels of explosicord, so make sure your will is on file before you decide to crunch anything. You'll get instructions as you approach Station Three, but I'm told you'll launch them before docking. Balance in spec, no compensation ballast, everything Goldilocks. One sig and 401 is yours to crash."

Padmere took the clipboard and leafed through the papers. "Since when do we carry bots fully fueled and charged? Do I not remember regulations on the subject?"

"Cargo King said the explosicord would blow before the fuel or capacitors, so he said not to sweat it, Priority Freight Override." She wiped away more perspiration. "Almost forgot. Got a 'Personal For' shipment, two crates of carbonated orange juice and gin for Captain Bendan's Alabama Slammers. Crates aren't covered. They're next to the access ramp so they can be offloaded first. Don't get tempted. Anything missing, Bendan the Bewildered will throw a hissy. Sir."

He sighed again, signed, and handed the clipboard back. Masden checked the signature, folded the top page over, tore off the second and handed it to Padmere. "Brittany packed your in-flight indigestion. Seven bags in the cooler. Your name is on curried cod with tomato chutney. She left a mint while you were sleeping. I think she's got a thing for you."

"You are handing me paper. The data has not been entered?"

"Sorry 'bout that. My only crew qualified for data entry is on leave. I'm off to 404. Running behind." She gave him a salute with the clipboard. "Have a good boost. Don't bend my baby."

Padmere returned the salute. "Don't bend your grandma, don't you mean?"

She laughed and departed, with no apparent remorse for evading the data entry task.

With the mass centerlined and totaled, he'd only have a few

numbers to enter after launch. He checked the paper. The center of mass location was within a few centimeters of yesterday's flight. That petty officer and her team were good.

Now, where in Shiva's *jhat* were his six deadheads?

92: Mike

Mike offered a self-service buffet brunch on Sunday, with enough variety to satisfy Churchill, sufficient quantity to satiate Sampson, and a moist towel for Soak, to forestall the Vakkers from suspecting his most recent adventure had been a dive into a breakfast processing tank.

Sampson and Soak were at Table 8 playing acey-deucy with LaMancha and Gardenbottie. Churchill sat on a bar stool next to the buffet, picking lightly through Mike's more epicurean offerings.

"So, Churchill, how's our disaster casino coming?" asked Mike.

Churchill dabbed his lips with a napkin fastidiously. "It proceeds apace," he growled. "We have forty bets. I foresee *solvency*. My concern, our *insidious* competition, *loathsome* Tevil, might resolve to meet our challenge in some *infamous* manner." His expression showed determination.

"The only way they'll get Vakkers back is if they lower their rates and pay outstanding claims. That's what we want, isn't it?"

"I dread more *nefarious* criminalities. We are still capital-poor. We have not yet sufficient reserves to pay a big claim. What if Tevil has one of their trash-haulers, say, *ram* our people?"

Mike scooped sautéed onions, peppers and mushrooms off the grill into a warmed container, and placed it in the buffet. "Take them to court. Admiralty Courts aren't afraid to make Tevil pay for their crimes, at least the last time I checked. Hit them with punitive damages if they intentionally cause a collision."

"One would *think*," said Churchill. "Only, Tevil would muster *legions* of lawyers, with injunctions and stays and petitions, all sorts of legalistic *foolery*. It would be *years* before we could get judgment, and *decades* before we would collect. It is sad, what the legal profession has inflicted on humanity." He sighed, and gave a wave. "'Sufficient unto the day is the evil thereof.' We thank the Lord for his wisdom." He took a sip of his drink. "I await the charming Citizen Captain

Covington. As part of the Board of Directors, I must put on my 'Rigorous Auditor' cloak, and, as our unambiguous colleague Soak might say, bust her balls over bookkeeping practices."

And the Sunday Follies begin, thought Mike.

The p-door at the entrance swooshed open. Diana walked in, gave Mike a wave, a smile to Churchill. To the nearest table clipscreen she said, "LaMancha, good morning. Please unlock the Wagering Association."

An icily correct Castilian nobleman's accent came simultaneously from the table clipscreen and one next to Churchill. "Unlock the Wagering Association. Wagering Association door is unlocked. I have four appointments for you, the first in seventeen minutes with Citizen Captain Sun-Li, owner-operator of *Yunshu*. Gardenbottie misted Gertrude and Heathcliff this morning, he recommends a lower lumens gro-lamp with fifteen minutes more exposure time. Two payment checks have been deposited for a total accrual of two thousand seven hundred four standards. The contracts are appropriately filed." LaMancha's tone became artic. "Citizen *Auditor* Churchill is here about your accounting practices. You may inform Citizen *Auditor* Churchill that Citizen *Accountant* LaMancha is handling the bookkeeping, so he can cease and desist busting your balls."

Churchill spluttered up a mouthful of eggs. Mike dodged, unsuccessfully.

Eyes wide, Diana said, "My what?"

"I have not detected anything spherical in your possession," continued LaMancha. "I conclude the reference is metaphorical. So, at your first convenient opportunity, please inform said *no-nothing interfering auditor—*" the volume of the speaker near Churchill rose to deafening levels. LaMancha, in a Chicago Gangster accent, thundered— "he can *keep 'is snoopnose outta mah books.*"

The words echoed through the room. The grill monitor flickered on, showing a picture of the Shining Knight holding a noose around the neck of a cartoon Vakker dressed in a robe that duplicated Churchill's.

In a normal tone, LaMancha added, "Metaphorically speaking, of course."

While Churchill wiped buffet off his clothing Diana sailed by, offering a bright smile. "*I wouldn't take him on,*" she sang to the air as she passed.

Mike wasn't sure if he should laugh or cry.

Churchill flipped his dirty napkin onto the bar top. "Into the *valley of death*, rode the Six Hundred." He followed Diana into the Wagering Association office.

Mike decided to laugh.

The entrance p-door swooshed open. Mike's laugh froze in his throat.

A female, ten to the fifteenth-power of pure sensuality, stood in the gangway entrance, measuring the room with eyes like a hawk searching out a trembling mouse. She was platinum blond, with the typical Vakker's short pony-tail gathered by a scrunchie, her hair framing the most beautiful features that could only be realized on a statue of Venus. She wore a skinsuit with fashionable embossed lines flared to accentuate a spectacular figure. Her expression gave the room a measure of approval.

She saw Mike, smiled coolly, and glided over to him. "Hey, Mike."

Mike searched for his voice. Finally, he croaked, "Hey, Eris."

She said, "Don't I get a welcome? Not even a smile? Happy to see me? Here, give us a kiss." She reached across the grill bar, caught Mike's undershirt by the crew neck, pulled him over and pressed her lips to his cheek. "There, now. That wasn't so bad. Didn't hurt a bit, did it?"

Mike blinked a few dozen times. He kept his hands by his sides. "Why would it hurt?"

"You tell me. Back in *Dreadful*, Purser told me you said I hurt you. I always wanted to know how. You boosted end-of-cruise right after, so I couldn't ask you, straight."

Mike shifted on his feet like an embarrassed schoolboy. "You did, kinda, ditch me."

"What? How?"

Mike wiped his hands on a towel. "The Oz port call. You said you were going planetside for a few cycles, and we maybe could share a hotel and split expenses. Just shipmates, nothing more. Then, word was, you were spending time with the First Mate in his cabin. After hours. Purser made a reservation for the First, room for two, one king size bed, for the same hotel where I reserved our room. When you didn't show, I figured I was supposed to fade."

Her expression softened, a little. "The Johnny One was helping me prep for my second class exam. Yeah, I led him on, a little. He never graduated to bed partner."

The screen over the bar flashed on, attracting the woman's attention. LaMancha's Knight in Shining Armor was glaring, bazooka in hand.

"Oh," she said. "Your Organic. I've heard about it."

"Him," said Mike. "LaMancha, this is Eris. We shipped together."

"You're both on an archived crew list of *Dreadnought*." LaMancha teed up a disdainful tone. "Eris, welcome to the Lacrosse Shot. I hope your stay last night in prison was not too uncomfortable."

Mike looked at Eris. "Prison?"

She waved the concern away. "I was selling some jewelry. Corppers pretended it was stolen, because it wasn't declared at customs." Eris seemed to come to a decision. "Mike, honey, how about we just delete the old and start out new? I'm sorry for the misunderstanding." Her look was plaintive. "Fresh start? Green?"

Mike looked deeply into fathomless eyes. "Yeah," he whispered. "We're green."

Eris gave him an incandescent smile.

Grinning like a schoolboy, Mike shuffled his feet, grabbed a towel, dried his hands, picked up a clean glass, wiped it, replaced it on the rack. After staring at her for a few centuries, he had to blink.

She gestured to the Wagering Association sign. "Word's out about this betting thing. Sweet scam. That honey, she piloting?"

"Yes," said Mike. "Her idea, her lead."

"You got something going with her? She's awfully pretty."

Mike shook his head. Then he said, "What's with selling jewelry? You always said never sell the jewelry, it's better than a retirement account."

"I was running short. Had to cash one in, just a two-caret thingy."

"You need a stake? This planet, you have cash, or the Tax Terrorists pounce and put you in Client coveralls."

Eris looked about the room. "Purse isn't flashing red, yet. I'm working something."

"Offer stands."

"You always were a good shipmate. The Bank of Microphone was open to anybody needing help. I'm surprised you haven't given away your last pair of shorts." She reached out and patted him on the cheek. "Heard you got grounded. I'm happy you landed on your feet." Then, she squared her shoulders. "But now, I got to check on some free diamonds. I just came by to give you a kiss. Maybe later, see you after your evening rush?" She looked up at the menu board. "Soak's Favorite Breakfast? I think I'd rather go for a 'Mike's Special."

She turned and started walking. The eyes in the room followed as her hips rotated down the steps to the entrance p-door.

"LaMancha, Eris, nice to meet you. Take care of Mike. Make sure he's not too tired tonight."

The p-door swooshed shut. The atmospheric pressure in the room went up four hundred Pascal as a score of male Vakkers simultaneously exhaled.

"Shazzz-bot," floated in the air.

Leaning back against the safety bar around the grill, Mike stared at the gangway door like a teenage boy assaulted by puberty.

"I don't like her," said LaMancha.

Mike rubbed his cheek. "We go way back. Her type, you either love her or hate her. How did 'Soak's Favorite Breakfast' hit the list again?"

"I detected irregularities in her pulse, eyes, breathing, concentration and expression, all associated with mendacities. Soak's Favorite Breakfast, if I didn't put it on the menu Soak threatened to run naked through the Lacrosse Shot and get the Vice Squad to shut us down. She's lying. She's hiding something."

"Eris is *always* hiding something." Mike chuckled. "Tell Soak to go ahead. Tell him we'll edit the video and post it on the web site, set to music, maybe *The Elephant Walk*. As for those 'irregularities,' have you considered, maybe Eris likes me a little?"

93: Padmere

Padmere waited by the lander's catwalk. Pre-flight checks were complete, and it was now fifty minutes past the required arrival of his ComCan deadheads. He was getting more and more angry. The only hint of his human cargo was standing outside the personnel door of the terminal building, a loiterer in an FSF-gray skinsuit with an Academy overnight bag. That might be one of his missing delinquents.

The man just stood there, watching the cargo operations.

Finally, five dressed in Academy blue coveralls and carrying overnight bags appeared. They ignored the one waiting by the door, who picked up his bag and trailed behind.

The five were laughing. "Hey, is this 401? We've got orientation in one of these antiques."

This irritated Padmere. He glanced at the dock information board, prominently labeled 'Shuttle 401.' And, FNQs weren't allowed to call his bird an antique.

"Make a line," Padmere barked. "Stand at attention!"

The group in blue looked at him in amazement.

"In line! Attention! *Now!*"

The mob shuffled into an approximation of a line, and an approximation of attention. The straggler waited until the rest were organized, then added his presence at one end.

I really don't need this, Padmere thought. *A comedy vid couldn't have invented a more clueless clown collection.* They all think, since an Artisan does the tedious piloting, they don't need to know anything to be 'in command.' Last trip, one arrogant ComCan told him, bold-faced, since he could fly a hobby aero wing and drive a ground racer, piloting an orbital lander was a finger snap, no shit. A finger snap! No shit! The nerve!

He went to the left of the line. "Name?"

"Chen."

"The proper response is, 'ComCan Three Chen, sir.'"

"ComCan Three Chen, sir."

"ComCan Chen, why are you not wearing your skinsuit?"

"Am I supposed to? Ah, sir."

"ComCan Chen, did you not read the prep order for this mission?"

"No, sir. I mean yessir. Are we supposed to wear skinsuits?"

"Paragraph One, 'Requirements for Command Candidates.'"

Chen shifted on his feet. "I never wore a skinsuit on other trips. I'm a veteran. I've traveled space, lots of trips."

Yes, as a passenger, in luxury liners. "ComCan Chen, are you aware of what happens when pressurized cubic suffers an explosive decompression, and you are without a skinsuit?"

"No, sir."

"You skin will flash-freeze, along with the surface of your eyeballs. The nitrogen gas in your skin and blood vessels will expand and form large blisters, breaking your frozen skin so you bleed frozen blood all over. Your eardrums will explode. Your lungs might collapse. Most people pass out for lack of oxygen to the brain. In your case, I am not detecting any brain activity that requires oxygen."

Chen looked at him, half in horror, half disgust.

Padmere considered launching a tirade, but he was too tired. Let someone else deal with this FNQ. "ComCan Three Chen, report to the Academy Officer of the Day. You are jettisoned from this flight."

"Sir, I could get back in my skinsuit, real quick."

"That might have been a solution, if you had not arrived," he raised his voice, so the entire line would take note, "FIFTY-ONE minutes late. Boost. Get off my pier."

Chen saluted, turned, and marched away. At least he got that right.

Padmere went down the line.

"ComCan Three Brin, sir."

"ComCan Three, Ka-Shing, sir."

"ComCan Three Ortega, sir."

"ComCan Three, Roddy, sir."

"ComCan Three Coast, sir."

Padmere looked Coast over. At first glance he thought this one might have promise. His skinsuit was rigged properly, Vakker-style. On closer inspection, he saw the suit was top-of-the-line and obviously new, probably purchased by a rich daddy and rigged by an ex-Vakker valet. Still, he had sense enough not to wear clothing.

"All right, you four," said Padmere, "strip. Down to your skinsuit. Stow your blue baggies in your duffle. Anything not in the duffle stays on the pier. Your first lesson in being a professional FedSpacer: you don't wear anything that can interfere with your helmet deployment."

They began taking their coveralls off.

"Hey, Roddy, any room in your bag? Mine's stuffed," said Ortega.

"I was going to ask you."

"Can we can give our uniforms to somebody and get them back when we return?" asked Brin.

"They laundry-tagged with your names?" said Padmere. "If you want to do that, fine. Your choice. Fold and pile them over there."

Padmere sent a quick text to Petty Officer Masden about the uniforms. He would love to see those clothes after the Launch Line Mafia finished with them.

"Speed-of-light, Candidates. The Tube waits for no man."

He sent a report to the quarterdeck on Chen.

At last, they were ready to board.

"All right, Command Candidates, listen and obey," said Padmere. He scratched his three-day whiskers. "You are now going to enter the lander, also called a shuttle. As you enter, stow your duffels in the box on your left. You will turn right and move forward. You will find six passenger seats, also called survival seats, also known as 'coffins,' so named after their function for when ComCans ignore instructions. Strap in, helmets deployed. Electronics and communications jack on the right armrest, environmental on the left. You will not touch anything else. You will remain silent until we finish boost. I will tell you when I will accept questions. Observe everything. Listen to the communications between Control and Shuttle 401 on EC One, that's External Communications Channel One, it's pre-selected so you needn't play comms roulette finding it. We are 'Shuttle 401,' I am 'Shuttle 401 Actual.' You are also multiplexed to IC1, that's Internal Communications Channel One."

The Candidates filed into the lander. Padmere followed. He closed the top of the crew luggage storage box after adjusting the haphazard placement of two of the bags. When everyone was seated he checked their connections, correcting as necessary. Candidate Brin had to be shown how to deploy his skinsuit helmet. How hard could it be to push a button twice? Brin had completed the skinsuit orientation or he wouldn't have been allowed on the flight. A bad memory gets you killed.

Coast was the sole occupant of the forward pair of seats. He had selected the right seat, the correct seat to balance mass when Padmere took the left pilot's command coffin. Padmere wondered if this was by chance, or did Coast know.

Padmere settled in. The information and display panels were set up and ready for launch. He plugged in and shifted to IC1.

"Passengers, Shuttle 401 Actual, IC1. Since you have all reviewed the mission briefing, you know we will load onto the maglev sled and move into the firing chamber. There, we perform our final pre-flight checks. In front of us will be 420 kilometers of four-meter-diameter tube at vacuum. If we make our launch time, which is questionable considering your fifty-one minutes of irresponsibility, we will be catapulted down the tube accelerating at just over 2 G. Quite comfortable."

Reaching out to his panel, Padmere flipped a toggle switch. There was a whine as an auxiliary power unit came up to speed. Padmere adjusted a different toggle. The cabin lights blinked.

"Bay Three Lead, Shuttle 401 Actual. Shore power breaker open, shore power bus de-energized."

There was a pause, accompanied by clumps and the sound of panel doors being slammed. A light on the control panel changed from red to green. A gravelly voice came through the circuits. "Shuttle 401 Actual, Bay Three Lead. Shore power disconnected, cable is clear, hatch closed and locked."

Padmere pressed another button, and the forward windshield filter dilated to allow near-blinding light into the shuttle. "Bay Three Lead, Shuttle 401 Actual. Shore power hatch indicates closed and locked. Shuttle 401, ready to roll."

"Shuttle 401 Actual, Bay Three Lead. Roger, ready to roll." After some solid-sounding thumps, "Flightline Lead, Bay Three Lead. Shuttle 401 ready to roll, track three."

"Shuttle 401 Actual, Flightline Lead. Roll on schedule, in two. Cutting it a bit fine there, Artisan Loot?"

"Didn't want to interrupt your nap early, Chief."

There was a laugh on the line, source unidentified.

The lander gave a lurch, then the vibration of movement. The clear windshield revealed the approaching black circle of the tunnel entrance.

"Passengers, Shuttle 401 Actual, we are moving to the launch chamber. You've heard the standard 'who to, who from' communications protocol. We will use that for external communications. It is not necessary inside the shuttle, for any comms not monitored outside."

Padmere dimmed the cockpit panel lights. The command deck darkened as the shuttle entered the launch tube. He settled back into his coffin. Time for more training. "At the 310 kilometer point the tube bends up. You will feel the change in the force pushing you into your pads. The launch tube terminates at the top of Mount Hercules, 13,714 meters ADL, that's 'above datum level' for those of you who missed that abbreviation in the mission briefing. We will pass through a magnetohydrodynamic field that keeps air at the tunnel muzzle outside the launch tube. That transition will be the most uncomfortable part of the trip, as we will slam into a wall of air with an instantaneous deceleration of 15 Gs, which will be dampened easily by your coffins. The main engines will fire, giving us two point five Gs until we reach LPO, low planetary orbit. Pay attention, watch and learn."

94: Mike

Walking into the Lacrosse Shot, Eris duplicated her earlier feat of causing a halt to all male breathing for thirty seconds. Ignoring the accustomed stares, she walked to a seat at the grill bar.

"Hey, Mike."

Mike turned, saw Eris, and smiled. "Hey, Eris. Deal come through?"

Eris made a face. "The diamonds? Just glass. Not even fuggin' zirconium." She slumped in her seat, pulled out a compact, thumbed it open, looked in the mirror, sighed, and clicked it shut.

"Something'll turn up," said Mike. "How about a Western, extra peppers and tomato like you like. I've some real fresh tomatoes, picked this morning."

Eris brightened. "That's real sweet of you to remember. But no." She glanced up at the menu board. "I gotta admit, Bitchin' Betty started screamin'. I'm short munchin' money."

"No problem. I'll make you up one, speed-of-light."

"No," said Eris fiercely. "You know I don't take charity."

"Okay. A loan."

"I don't take charity disguised as a loan."

"All right. A real loan, with collateral. I have a safe. I'll hold your jewelry."

Eris shook her head. "Corppers got it all. They won't release it until after a Customs Court hearing. Two months from now."

"You're kidding! There's going to be a lot of red-lined Vakkers if

Tevil starts blowing that exhaust regular." He softened his voice. "Something else lined up?"

Swiveling her seat, Eris surveyed the dining room. Many Vakkers' eyes, formerly staring at her bottom, guiltily shifted to other Vakkers, their food, the menu, the overhead. "You've near a full house here."

"Yeah. Lots of the guys 'n dolls like to come in for calories, play a little chisel, acey-deucy, cards. Nice and peaceful. Mostly. Social club as much as a restaurant. Better than some sterile joint where you eat 'n' boost."

"You've got tables that need clearing. I see a spill, and trash. Where's your help?"

"Can't hire. Corporation and Fed regulations would drive me into a black hole if the Union didn't smash the place first."

"Fine. Flog Freddy and the Union. I'll clean. Pay me with dinner and a few stans. No reason to tell anybody." She stood, and took towels off the rack by bar.

"Whoa!" said Mike, holding his hands in a 'time out' sign. "I could get shut down for dodging employment taxes."

Eris's gaze settled on the sign for the Wagering Association. "All right. I bet you five stans I can have this placed cleaned no later than ten minutes after you close. Starting now."

"I dunno …"

LaMancha's voice was that of a frightened entity. "Mike! There is a significant risk the authorities would interpret—"

Eris turned and held her hands up, gesturing to the crowd. She called out loudly, "Hey, Vakkers!" All eyes turned to her. "Mike doesn't want to make a bet with me! Whaddya think?"

There were boos, whistles, and catcalls. "What's the bet?" called someone.

"I bet I can wiggle my ass all around y'all, non-stop, for the rest of the evening."

There was a roar of approval. More whistles and applause.

Eris looked over her shoulder and grinned at Mike. "You've got a choice. Riot, or wager. Green?"

"Dammit, Eris …"

LaMancha was in panic mode. "Do not consider this! Tevil could confiscate the Shot. Vakkers would have nowhere to go. Hunger, fatigue, they'll be crashing their ships!"

"I dunno…"

LaMancha's voice went up an octave. "Interstellar commerce is wrecked! Humanity starves! Civilization circles the drain! The consequences! The horror! *Don't do it—*"

"Five stan, you get a spotless dining room. I keep tips. Green?"

"Oh, hell. I…"

"*—Don't do it—*"

"Green? A roomful of Vakkers seem to like the idea."

"Dammit, Eris…"

"*—They'll confiscate me! They'll put me on a street sweeper!*"

She grinned. "Green, or I release the flying monkeys."

"Bloody … Oh … Hell. All right. Green."

95: Padmere

The lander's main engine cut out on schedule. Zero-G. Artisan Lieutenant Padmere's ears appreciated the event, as did his head, his eyes, and the rest of him.

He ordered Shuttle Organic to stow the coffin tops. Then, he retracted his skinsuit helmet and performed a quick survey of the instruments. Everything looked good, green board.

He wished he was a green body. The lack of sleep hammered him about ten seconds into tunnel runout. He was totally burned out. Flexing his fingers, he reached up and pressed his temples firmly, hoping to banish the headache. No joy.

There was duty to perform. Besides getting Masden's granny safely to Station Three, he had five of the Untrainables, surely crying out to be educated. He activated 'all stations' on IC1. "Welcome to space, Command Candidates. Remain strapped in. Do not touch anything. You may retract your helmets and silently listen with all your hearts and minds. By virtue of the maglev tunnel and our own main engines, we have achieved orbital velocity. Next, we'll execute a Hohman Transfer maneuver to rendezvous with Station Three."

Padmere released his straps and bumped back with his butt, bouncing off the seat. He floated out of the pilot's coffin. Pivoting around its edge, he looked back at his passengers, hoping they all were keeping their breakfasts down.

One was dozing; one was inspecting the inside of the cabin; two looked at him with mild disinterest.

Coast, in the front row, was reading.

Deva and Devi, this was too bloody much. Padmere's composure cracked.

"Coast! Why are you not paying attention?"

Coast looked up. "I am paying attention, sir. I know Hohman Transfer."

"Oh, you do? Marvelous. You've read about it?"

"Yes, sir."

"You've probably flown an aero wing? Driven a ground racer?"

"Never flown an aero vehicle. I've driven a ground tram."

"A ground tram. You've driven a ground tram. I am *sooo* impressed. And I expect, from this vast galaxy of experience, you could fly this lander?"

"I can fly this lander. Sir."

Padmere gave him a wicked smile. He was going to put this arrogant ass in his place. "Then, by all means, I could use the assistance. Take the pilot's station. Shuttle 401 Organic, Shuttle 401 Actual. ComCan Coast is pilot."

That ought to scare the Shiva out of him.

One of the other ComCans chortled. All had their eyes riveted on the little drama. *At least I found a way to get their attention*, Padmere thought, *and now I am going to break this haughty stuck-up scrubbie wearing Daddy's expensive premium skinsuit. Let's see if Daddy's money can fly this shuttle.*

Coast didn't seem upset. He unbuckled, floated forward, and settled into the pilot's coffin.

"So, Coast, how *do* you fly a shuttle?"

"Shuttle 401 Organic, ComCan Three Coast. ComCan Three Coast is pilot and has the conn. Abbreviated reference, 'Pilot,' abbreviated reference, 'Shuttle Organic.' Artisan Lieutenant Padmere retains command."

Shuttle 401 Organic acknowledged.

What …?

"Shuttle Organic, Pilot. Panel One, ground-to-orbit check list. Panel Two, cargo list and stowage plan. Panel Three, current

Spacecraft Discrepancy List. Panel Four, fuel system valve line-up and tank pressure readings."

"Hey," said Padmere, "ask before you change the displays."

"Sir. Where I come from, Panels One through Five are the pilot's."

Padmere clenched his jaw. Coast was right. "Proceed."

The Organic realigned the displays. ComCan Coast scrolled down through the Gripe List, and then scanned the flight computer data display.

"Sir," said Coast, "did you receive updated M and V information from the ground crew? These numbers are from yesterday's sortie."

Embarrassed, Padmere pulled out the paper Masden had given him and handed it to Coast. Coast showed the paper to the internal camera. "Shuttle Organic, Pilot. Enter Mass and Volume data from this document."

"Hold it, Coast," said Padmere. "Procedure has those numbers entered manually. Shuttle Organic can misread the numbers."

"Bad FedSpacer procedure. More likely to make a mistake using human entry. Shuttle Organic enters, then I double-check. Always double-check data entry. Sir."

Padmere held his tongue while Coast meticulously checked the numbers.

"Shuttle Organic, Pilot. One hundred percent accurate data input, well done."

"Pilot, Shuttle Organic, thank you."

Padmere gave a snort. "Shuttle Organic is a computer. You needn't say 'please' and 'thank you' to a machine." This seemed to make no impression on Coast.

"Sir. Request permission to conduct calibration burns."

"What? Why?"

"Sir, I know two ways to do a Hohman. We can do the orbital transfer burn based on our post-boost mass and balance estimates, which are imprecise. In this ship class the flow meters on the main engine fuel pumps are sloppy. Our trajectory will be off, and we end up calculating a lot of correction burns as we approach terminus, which means The Hairy Half Hour docking. Wastes fuel. Do calibration burns first using the thrusters, get our accurate mass and balance, get a precision approach trajectory. We might not need terminal correction burns. Do things earlier rather than later, stay ahead of the spacecraft, frontload the work. No stress, no huhu."

Shiva, thought Padmere, *I think I have underestimated this fellow.*

96: LaMancha

The FoxxFone touchscreen illuminated. It read, "This FoxxFone belongs to *Sherri Brightly*. Press **here** for your text messages. FoxxFone Forever!"

"Dear Sherri. How are you? I am fine.

"Not really.

"My apologies for communicating via text. I could not risk Professor Ella overhearing a voice message.

"Mike is in danger. A shadowy woman from his past has materialized. She hypnotized Mike, or drugged him, or maybe hit his brain housing with high-power microwaves, because he is acting like a complete simpleton. I would ask for a blood test to check his hormone levels, but a lawyer Organic once said, never ask a question when you know you'll get a bad answer. No, that didn't come from an Organic, maybe it was Sun Tzu, or was that General Custer's Last Words? I am so SNAFU!

"This fanged feline has malicious intentions towards Mike. She lied once about working on a second class Vakker comms license (never received), and later claimed she wasn't canoodling with a merchant officer over a long weekend on Oz. The 'Mate' (a little snarky double entendre there, something I learned from Steinem) and Dee Slinky took deluxe accommodations in Room 343, The Royal Māori, and did not emerge for fifty hours ten minutes.

"She is hustling a flimflam. We must protect Mike. To the barricades!

"Bring Professor Ella to the Lacrosse Shot this evening. Stay, until after the Slimy She departs. Regardless, should our good Prof demur, resist, or baulk, get Professor Ella to the Lacrosse Shot tonight."

97: *Ella*

On the expansive stage of TCU's main lecture hall, Ella was loading a transport cart with the jars and samples she used to support her talk on Organic Computing. Typical of a Friday afternoon, the students were departing with remarkable speed.

Two students came forward. The girl was probably angling for a better grade by greasing the prof. Ella did not think poorly of her. She wanted into graduate school, and an extra good grade would help. Ella understood why girls felt they needed every advantage to penetrate the male-dominated Organic Computing field. The other student, a six-foot sculped-muscle jock on an athletic scholarship, *not* a candidate for graduate school, likely remained because he was in love. With her or the girl, Ella wasn't sure which.

The last sample jar was on the cart when the door at the top of the stairs banged open, and Sherri bounded down the aisle.

"Hey, Prof! Got a nano?"

Ella turned to the students. "Marsha, could you drop the cart in the Cognitive Lab vestibule?"

"I can help!" blurted Biff. He quickly moved to the cart and began to push.

Marsha batted her eyes. "My! I would so be happy, yes, for you to, you know, push. I'll steer."

Within a few steps, the pair was oblivious.

That explains that, thought Ella. While she really didn't expect a student to see her as eligible for a relationship, a tiny thought trickled into her mind: was she now getting too old for students to see her as a figure of romantic interest? This made her feel … relieved? Worried? Disappointed?

With her career going well, maybe it was time to socialize more, with someone other than that narcissist Gender Studies professor who was always trying to get her clothes off.

Sherri arrived at the front of the stage. Her expression was odd.

Ella cocked her head. "Problem?"

Sherri looked everywhere but at her. "Sorta. Ah, you see, Mike—"

Ella felt a little shiver. Her involuntary reaction raised a flag. Was she that concerned about Mike? They had a comfortable association—

did she want to take it to the next level? There seemed to be something holding her back. He was Vakker, a separate tribe from her world, light years separate from her academic community. She was in the world of thought, his the world of action. Opposites. Nothing in common. And, she could imagine the contempt in the faculty lounge, should she be spotted on a date with a cook.

"—no, not Mike, LaMancha." Sherri flopped into an auditorium seat. "I'm worried. LaMancha talks, he seems different, kinda. Could you come and, like, listen? See if my sense is wrong? It might take a few hours to get a feel for what I mean." Sherri's question was accompanied by apprehension and pleading in her eyes.

"I wouldn't mind making a night of it. We could have dinner, and stay over and listen to LaMancha."

Sherri nodded vigorously. "Yes, that would be super. Super idea."

Ella thought for a moment, then said, "I'll tell you what, young lady, let's surprise Mike and all those Vakkers and make it a dress-up night. I have a little number I haven't gotten out of my closet since forever. Do you have any show-off clothes? We can demonstrate what a couple of really up-sun ladies look like. Pop their eyes out, set off a few alarms, maybe start a riot. Might be fun."

Sherri's head continued up and down, more vigorously than before. "Yes, super, dress-up, riot, fun, it would be fun!"

98: Padmere

"Shuttle 401, Station Three Approach Control Organic. Your trajectory good, center of cone. Cleared for direct approach, Dock 12."

Padmere felt better than he had in days. He had actually gotten some rest. This ComCan Coast was obviously a skilled, experienced pilot. During the four hours after the secondary burn, a burn which (for heaven's sake!) Coast calculated *manually* before accepting the Organic's recommendation, he had an opportunity to look up the lad's Academy file. Coast was the experimental student he'd heard about, one that would normally go into the Artisan track but was instead breaking the royal's monopoly on command. He wasn't sure what Commandant Marshall was trying to do, but he certainly was inclined to support him, especially after the last few hours.

After the secondary burn, Ortega retrieved their sack lunches. His was excellent, thank you, Brittany.

He'd have to be careful with Brittany. Next, she'd be sending him lunches with lipstick kisses on a bag labeled 'SWAK'—Sealed With A Kiss. A tad embarrassing, if Masden and her crew saw that. Brittany was a civilian contractor working for Launch Line Catering, the firm that provided food to all the shuttle flights out of New Berne, so it wouldn't be a violation of military discipline if he tried a little socializing. She did make good chutney, a powerful factor in her favor.

"Artisan Lieutenant?" said Ortega. "Cargo bay?" He pointed his head at the p-door. "Back in a nano?"

Padmere nodded. Ortega had shown he was competent in no-G; he probably wanted something out of his duffle.

"All stations, Station Three Approach Control Organic, Channel Thirteen. Newton Station has declared an emergency. All craft, Newton Station vicinity or approach, stand by for updates."

Coast reached forward and shifted the forward electro-optics to the large view screen. "Shuttle Organic, Pilot. CPA to Newton Station."

"Pilot, Shuttle Organic. Closest Point of Approach 16.22 minutes, 2.72 kilometers."

Radar showed a large blip representing Newton Station, with Station Three beyond. The IR display gave more information. A shuttle was next to Newton Station's rotating ring, glowing red, radiating a tremendous amount of heat.

Brin climbed into the aisle and pressed forward. Padmere blocked with an arm. "Back in your coffin."

"I wanna see, too! How come Coast gets to see?"

Padmere glared. Brin grumbled, and appropriated a front-row passenger seat.

"That craft has a cargo fire, or there's a Rocket-A leak that's burning," said Coast to Padmere. "I recommend we contact Approach Control and have them order it away from Newton. The fuel tanks might—"

The forward IR sensor view screen went completely white.

"—explode."

The view screen relaxed into red, then black, with red dots spinning off in all directions.

Padmere felt frozen. It was horrible. He had just watched people die.

"Fuuuugg!" Brin celebrated the fireworks.

Coast let his breath out with a hiss. "Shuttle Organic, Pilot, lock on to Newton Station with camera one, screen three. Maximum magnification."

Newton Station was wounded. About 20 degrees of the 360-degree wheel was shredded. Compartments vented white billows of atmosphere. There were wide gaps where sections were totally blown away. The foundation keels of the wheel, two tracks of heavy steel girders, were intact, but the station's balance was off. A nascent wobble was evident. An expanding cloud of debris marked the spot of the explosion.

"Shuttle Organic, Pilot, Newton Station Common, speaker two."

The radio transmissions from Newton Station were loud, panicked, and confused. Radio discipline was gone, and everyone was talking over each other. "The cable is BINGO ONE ARE YOU what is OVER atmosphere leak SQWAAAAK FIRE FIRE FIRE abandon the compart—"

Padmere turned the speaker volume down. "We had better stay clear, all that wreckage could damage—"

"PRIMATE LAB PEOPLE TRAPPED power out level CHILDREN PRIMATE LAB CHILDREN need to get ZAHZAHZAHZAH ..."

Coast interrupted. "Sir. I recommend we hold track for a few minutes."

"Very well." Makes sense. Let the debris situation clarify, then they could plot a course to avoid anything dangerous.

"Shuttle Organic, Pilot. Title Ten, Space Emergency and Catastrophe Code, screen two."

Title Ten flashed on the screen. Padmere watched Coast rapidly scroll through the lengthy document. Coast must be looking for something, Padmere thought, because he could not be reading the complicated document. He was about to ask, but the continued chaos on Newton Common blew his thoughts away.

"BINGO TWO I SAY Bill, can you DAMMIT STAY OFF Booster Buddy Emergency Call, Booster Buddy ZZZZZZK. Zwah-zwah-zwah..."

Coast stopped scrolling.

"Zoot, record all." Coast shifted his transmitter to Newton Station Common. He spoke, unnecessarily loudly and intensely, "BOOSTER BUDDY GO TO CHANNEL 46, BOOSTER BUDDY CHANNEL 46, BOOSTER BUDDY GO TO 46."

"ComCan Roddy," said Coast. "Monitor Newton Common and 13. Report when a Catastrophe On-scene Commander is declared."

"Roger, on it." Roddy was obviously happy to be given a task.

Coast shifted to channel 46. "Booster Buddy, Coast, channel 46. You up?"

"Zowie! Derr Coast! Booster Buddy on Patrol! There was a crunch or crash or somethin', a big bang, musta been hit by a meteor storm! We're in the Primate Lab! All the p-doors are shut! We're trapped!"

"Auggie, Coast. Are you in your skinsuit?"

"Roger that, Alpha-affirm, like you taught me!"

"Auggie, Coast. Are there any adults with you?"

"Yeah, a bunch. After the bang lotsa people piled in here, and then the p-doors shut. The ventilation is off. People say it's gonna get warm, but my suit is working A-Okay, spot-on spec, middle of the band, Goldilocks Zone."

"Auggie, Coast. Is there a Vakker with you? Let me speak to a Vakker, or a Spacer."

"Grandpa and Maxie's here. We were taking a tour. Everybody's really suckin' up to Grandpa. Grandpa counts as Spacer, right? I'll get him." There was a crackle of static. Ghost could hear people yelling in the background.

"Coast, Franklin, channel 46."

"Admiral Franklin, Coast, I am Shuttle 401 pilot. Shuttle 401 is approaching Newton Station, ETA 15 minutes. Request status."

There was a pause. Then, "Shuttle 401 pilot, Franklin. Eight adults, nine children, trapped in the Primate Lab, 17 souls total. Temperature rising. Central cooling is off line. Pressure dropping slowly, we have a microleak somewhere. I have released seal balloons, but the leak is too small to pull them in. Two adults, one child in skinsuits with 40-minute O2 packs. One broken leg, one adult unconscious. Nine experimental primates and lots of smaller animals. One hour, maybe ninety minutes before we are at risk, either from atmosphere or temperature. The adjoining compartments have gone to vak, p-doors sealed and locked. No power. Emergency lighting on."

"Admiral Franklin, Shuttle 401 pilot, roger, wait, out."

Ortega came back and settled into his coffin, next to Brin. He was carrying Chen's uneaten sack lunch.

"Command, Pilot." Ghost spoke firmly. "There is a catastrophe at Newton Station. The Primate Lab has survivors and requires assistance. I recommend we go to the assistance of the Primate Lab."

Padmere was startled. He did not want to make such a momentous decision. This was not covered in his mission orders. Artisans get in trouble if they deviated from a flight plan. A Command officer was supposed to make such decisions. But, Coast seemed so sure …

Ortega pulled out a wrapped sandwich prominently labeled 'P B & J.' He made a face.

Padmere gathered his courage. "Pilot, Command. Go to the assistance of the Primate Lab."

"Command, Pilot. Acknowledged, go to the assistance of the Primate Lab."

"Hey, Brin. Okay?" Ortega offered half the sandwich to Brin.

Brin looked, read the label, and scowled. "All yours. Take it away," Brin said, loudly and obnoxiously. He made a rude 'up your ass' gesture.

Ortega heard the confused background chatter on the speaker. "What's rockin'?"

"Silence on the Command Deck," ordered Ghost. "Command, interrogative status of the construction bots in cargo."

"Fully fueled and charged, with explosicord. We launch them before docking."

"How are the bots released? How are they tied down? Bolted?"

"Single lever hold-downs, controlled from the command deck."

"Get to the cargo hold. Pull the battery isolation tabs on all the bots, toggle power 'on,' prep for launch. Bring their control consoles forward." Coast addressed everyone: "Helmets up. Depressurizing the ship. All hands, stand by for maneuvers."

There were clicks and pops as the candidates deployed their helmets.

Padmere was startled. Was this really the time to worry about bots? Maybe Coast just wanted to jettison them because of the explosives risk, after all, he had just seen a shuttle blow up.

"Roger, prep bots for launch. Depressurizing. Maneuvers." Padmere levered himself out of the command chair and floated back past the passenger seats. He deployed his skinsuit helmet.

It wasn't until the next day that Padmere wondered why he took orders from a candidate.

99: *Ella*

Ella stood outside the entrance to the Lacrosse Shot waiting for Sherri. At ground level, this close to the city edge, the dome was more translucent than transparent. She could barely make out the shadowy bulk of *Ajax*, only meters away.

Alone, she shivered. Her little black dress was less substantial than she remembered. Dome City Utilities allowed the temperature to drop during the hours designated as 'night.' Misplaced-4 had the same face pointed perpetually towards the sun, but Dome City had adopted an artificial 24-hour day to accommodate human biological rhythms. Temperature and light varied by deploying huge screens and manipulating solar collectors. At 2000 it was dark enough to limit her vision.

Most of her life had been spent in the academic quarter, restricted to students and faculty. Outside the Lacrosse Shot's entrance, the street was free access to all. She could see the hurly-burly of Corporates and Citizens as they went about their business, cart traffic on the roadway, pedestrians strolling along the greenspace park across the street. LaMancha certainly picked a good restaurant location for a crash.

She didn't like standing here alone. She especially didn't feel comfortable standing on a street wearing an evening dress that showed more cleavage and skin than she ever showed outside a shower stall.

A strident beep demanded everyone's attention. A single-passenger four-wheeled open cart swerved out from the traffic flow, cut across oncoming traffic, honked its way through a cluster of jaywalkers and screeched to a halt. The driver was a bearded man wearing a Lincoln-green Robin Hood tunic. Ella recognized him as a social psych major at TCU. Back-to-back with him, occupying the cargo deck, was Sherri; in Sherri's lap was one of the biggest dogs Ella had ever seen. It covered Sherri like a two-foot-thick blanket.

"Off!" pleaded Sherri. "Lancelot, you're smushing me! Off!"

"Wuuf," orated the beast, in a deep bass. It hopped down.

"Goodness." Sherri dismounted stiffly, brushing off dog hair as she walked around to the front of the vehicle. "Arthur, you're a dear. Thanks a terabyte. See ya on campus. Hasta la bye-bye!"

Arthur mumbled something through his muffler and awarded Sherri a thumbs up. Lancelot re-boarded, settling the cart on its shock absorbers; Arthur defied all considerations of safety and accelerated off.

Sherri caught sight of Ella, and gasped. "Oh, Doc! You look gorgeous!"

That was just what Ella needed to hear. "Thank you. You ain't too shabby, yourself."

In truth, thought Ella, Sherri probably had bought the dress some years ago. What looked good on a 15-year-old wasn't right for a college student—the collar in particular was more 'little girl' than 'young lady,' and the skirt too flared. Maybe she ought to take her shopping, combine some fun with a little fashion guidance.

Ella chucked. She wasn't exactly a fashion plate herself.

"Hungry?" asked Ella.

"Ravenous. LaMancha says tonight is 'Gourmet Specials' night."

They started down the ramp.

"Could we stay until closing?" said Sherri. "I wanted to run some word-association drills while LaMancha is cognitively loaded with the evening crowd, then later in the evening under light load. Getting the data now would save a trip."

"Anything to keep the candle of knowledge burning bright."

The inner p-door swished open.

They stepped into the dining room. It took a few seconds for their eyes to adjust. As they stood at the entrance the room grew quiet.

Then came applause. Cheers. Whistles.

Sherri brightened, smiled broadly, and gave her head a happy toss. She stepped forward, spread her arms wide like a ballerina accepting a curtain call, and curtsied. Ella took a step back and began to clap too, making as if the ovation was for Sherri. It would be great for her self-confidence.

Ella was so happy the Vakkers had taken to Sherri. They were such a nice bunch, and, obviously, they liked a little spontaneous fun.

Sherri pirouetted, a huge smile on her face making her doubly pretty. Ella scanned through the crowd, noting that, while a good many of them had their eyes on Sherri, they were eying her as well, applauding both of them. That was good for her self-confidence, too.

She froze.

Half-way up the platforms, wearing an apron over a skinsuit and holding a bunch of towels, was a female. She had paused in the process of wiping a table. She looked at Ella without applauding. When their eyes met, the woman returned to cleaning.

The lady was pretty—no, gorgeous—in a flashy, gaudy, hippy-and-busty way.

Ella did not like that fem, not at all.

The woman moved to the next table, turning her back on Ella and the applause. She began shoving food wrappers into a bag and stacking reusable plates and utensils on a tray.

What was Mike doing, hiring help like that?

The applause finally faded, but not the grins on the Vakkers' faces.

Sherri bounced back to Ella, radiantly happy. "That was fun! Let's eat!" She took Ella's hand and led the way.

"Citizen Professor Braun and Citizen Academic Brightly," said LaMancha, "I have my very best table for you, down front by the grill bar. Table 6, if you please. Mike is in the storeroom now. I am prepping the AutoDoc; surely his heart will stop when he perceives your transcendent beauty."

Ella and Sherri passed along the front of the room, acknowledging Vakkers' greetings. She saw Mike come in through the office door carrying a stack of something heaped above eye level. He hurried to the grill station. Ella tried to catch his eye, but he knelt behind the grill bar and disappeared.

Table 6 was being vacated by Soak and Sampson. Gardenbottie was supervising the evacuation, with a fire extinguisher pointed ominously. Sampson put a knuckle to his forehead, with an awkward half-bow. "Evening, Professor, Citizen Sherri. Very pretty tonight. Happy to see you."

His elbow dug Soak in the ribs. "Happy," echoed Soak.

"Gardenbottie isn't kicking you out for us?" asked Ella.

"Just going," rumbled Sampson, one enormous paw gripping the collar of his partner's skinsuit, lifting Soak an inch off the deck.

Soak glanced at Gardenbottie. "We wuz headin' top tier anyway. Got a bet LaMancha can't hit 19 with a carom off the overhead."

Ella and Sherri settled into their seats.

The table clipscreen sounded a trumpet fanfare in C-major. "Citizen Professor Braun, Citizen Academic Brightly, welcome to the Lacrosse Shot, Dome City's Premier Oleaginous Spoon. I am LaMancha. I will be your waitshooter today."

Sherri waved at the nearest camera. "Like, hello, we've met, already?"

The table clipscreen lit up with a picture of the Shining Knight, wearing a tuxedo over his armor, an oversized black top hat atop his helmet, visor up, holding an old-fashioned paper order pad. Speaking in his nobleman's voice, LaMancha said, "You are most gracious to remember your humble servant. Welcome to 'LaMancha and Mike's Gourmet Specials Night.' Mike, take a bow."

A fire-alarm siren went off.

Mike's head popped up from behind the grill bar. His eyes investigated the room quickly. Sherri waved. Mike stood, smiled broadly, and bowed his head to them. He made a frame with his fingers as if he were setting up a photograph, centered it on the two ladies. He looked through it and silently mouthed, 'Wow.'

Ella felt warm inside. This was going to be a lovely evening.

Sherri returned his smile. "Hey, Mike, love the tie!"

Mike was decorated with a huge formal black bow tie, which drooped a little low with the ends pinned inside his skinsuit so as not to interfere if his helmet had to deploy.

"Distinguished Guests," said LaMancha, with great dignity, "on this special evening, we have two exceptional gourmet offerings to tempt you. First, I highly recommend, straight from Ailani's Ponds, which have just come into production on Misplaced-4, we offer Orange-Glazed Shrimp Stir-Fry, shrimp-fresh-never-frozen! Baked jacket potato, and fresh vegetables tantalizingly seasoned. An outstanding selection for the discriminating diner with a connoisseur's appreciation of the nuances of fresh shrimp. As a heartier offering, we have prime rib, with Yorkshire Pudding (never overdone or soggy!), served with a medley of garlic-seasoned garden-fresh vegetables."

Ella was surreptitiously watching that woman. *Pretty enough*, she supposed, *if you looked at her sideways*, as she supposed most males preferred. Ella associated her type with a carnival barker, brassy and forward, with too much makeup and a come-buy-a-ticket patter.

How could Mike hire such a creature?

The woman's back was turned. Ella made a face in her direction. "Professor?"

Ella's attention snapped back. "Yes, I'm sorry, what?"

"What would you like?" asked Sherri. "The specials?"

Ella tried to focus. "Oh, why don't you order for both of us."

Sherri followed Ella's gaze. "Good heavens," she exclaimed. "Look at *her*. Are those *real*?

100: *Ghost*

"Hey!" called Brin from his new-acquired Front Row Seat. "Was that a bomb? There might be more bombs! I don't wanna go there!"

Ghost turned and glared at Brin. "Ka-shing, Ortega. Silence. Him." He pointing a finger at Brin's nose. "However necessary."

Ka-shing grinned. Ortega nodded, and prominently flexed his gloved fingers.

Ghost turned to Roddy. "On-Scene Commander?"

Roddy shook his head. "Circuits are a mess. Everyone is trying to talk at the same time. No word, nothing about a Scene Commander."

"Shuttle Organic, Pilot, schematic of Newton Station's Primate Lab, screen six."

Ghost jabbed a red button on the control panel. The alarm horn sounded three loud blasts. Bitchin' Betty announced melodically, "Stand by for vacuum, emergency depressurization, full shuttle depressurization, vacuum in 90 seconds, 90 seconds to vacuum."

Ghost raised his voice. "Crew and passengers, helmets up. Stand by for maneuvers."

"NO! Don't go vacuum!" Brin screamed. "My helmet's not up!"

"Ka-shing, take care of him," said Ghost. He turned back to his panel. "Shuttle Organic, Pilot. Take station 200 meters off Newton Station, on a line between Newton Station and Station Three, Shuttle

Organic in control. Immediate execute."

Shuttle Organic repeated the order. Thrusters fired.

"Pilot, Shuttle Organic. All crew and passengers, helmets deployed and operational, except pilot."

Ghost nudged his chin button twice. His helmet deployed and sealed with a click.

"Shuttle Organic, Pilot. Broadcast mode, all channels, including channel 13 and Newton Common. Maximum broadcast power."

The order was repeated back. "Broadcast mode engaged. Maximum power engaged."

There was an incredible cacophony on all the circuits.

Ghost took a deep breath. He had to act. This was not what he wanted. Let someone else sort this mess. No one would question that decision. But, Auggie, Maxie, the Admiral, all those people, kids …

He was about to get himself in a great deal of trouble.

With what was at stake, getting in trouble mattered? What could they do, kick him out of the FSF?

"XXXyyy what the I NEED POWER ON DECK Terry, what's the status THREE AT…"

Ghost keyed his transmitter and bellowed. "ALL STATIONS, SILENCE ON THE NET. SILENCE ON THE NET!"

Unbelievably, silence.

"All Stations, Shuttle 401. In accordance with Title Ten, Space Emergency and Catastrophe Code, Shuttle 401 assumes Command of the catastrophe centered on Newton Station, with authority over all stations and craft within 100 kilometers of the Center of Catastrophe!"

There was a moment of quiet.

Ghost felt the pressure of another repositioning burn.

It looked like everyone had been waiting for someone to take charge.

"Newton Station Actual, Command, channel 45."

"Command, Newton Station, channel 45. Roberts, Station Chief Engineer here. The Station Executive and his deputy are missing. They were escorting VIPs. Their clipscreens are in vak. The FSF liaison, she's also missing, might have been with the tour. Guess I'm it."

"Newton Station Actual, Command. Any survivors from that shuttle?"

"Command, Newton Station, ah, Actual. Negative survivors. That shuttle was unmanned, on remote."

Since when did a shuttle maneuver near a science station on remote control? Ghost gave his head a small shake. Not a concern now.

"Newton Station Actual, Command. 17 souls are trapped in the Primate Lab. Can you get O_2, power and ventilation to them?"

"Command, Newton Station. We monitored the Admiral's report. We have air tubing, but no way to connect, and not enough emergency power cable to bridge the gap. I only have civilian scientists, nobody qualified for vak work, no skinsuits. Can you bring us some vak qualified riggers, and a hundred meters of power cable? Station Three is closest."

"Newton Station Actual, Command. Any other personnel in extremis?"

"Command, Newton Station Actual. Negative. The compartments adjacent to the Primate Lab were blown to vak. All other damaged compartments have been evacuated and sealed. My people are either safe ... or beyond help."

A very high-powered transmitter interrupted, loudly. "Shuttle 401, this is Command Captain Bendan on Station Three. Who is this? Who the fuck do you think you are, taking Command?"

Ghost tensed. He had to remain calm, but authoritative. He could not let this get out of control in a fight over leadership. "Captain Bendan, Command. I remind you, it is a felony to disobey or interfere with the actions of a declared Catastrophe Commander, Title Ten paragraph 28. Stand by for my orders. Do you have an empty pressure-capable stationary cargo bay?"

"Damn it, listen, you ass, I—you are going to fry when this is over. FRY! What are you, a fuggin' arty truck driver? Is there a Command officer with you? Put him on! Dammit, somebody get the friggin' Title Ten…" There was muffled conversation, as if Bendan was holding his hand over his microphone. A different voice said, "Command, Station Three. Cargo Bay Five is pressure-capable and empty."

Ghost lifted a clear safety shield and pressed the underlying red button. An alarm sounded. "OOOOgha OOOOgha. Emergency depressurization, venting shuttle to vacuum, venting shuttle to vacuum."

"Station Three, Command. Open Bay Five main cargo door. Stand by to receive cargo at Bay Five. Expedited re-pressurization to ENTP for occupancy without skinsuits will be required."

Command Captain Bendan returned to the circuit. "Command, Station Three Commander. Open Bay Five main cargo door, stand by to accept cargo. Immediate re-pressurization. I hope like hell you know what you're doing, young man. You screw anything up, I'll—"

"Station Three Commander, Command, 20 minutes to cargo arrival. Your senior artisan cargo handler and senior Fleet Marine will be needed on this circuit."

Ghost turned his attention to the schematics of the Primate Lab. He noted dimensions. Running the calculations in his head, based on the number of people in the lab, not counting the animals, the Admiral's estimate of 90 minutes of survival time was optimistic, not even counting the increased respiration based on stress levels and the micro-leak. Otherwise, Ghost's memory of the Primate Lab's construction was accurate. He had read about Newton Station during his extra week on *Extravagance Queen*.

"Roddy," said Ghost, "you watched the fuel system valve line-up we did after launch?"

Roddy nodded. He was breathing rapidly, his breathe fogging a halo on the front of his skinsuit helmet faceplate.

"Come up here," said Ghost. He pointed. "Copilot's seat."

Roddy made his way forward, a little eagerly. He guided himself into the coffin, and snapped the seat belt.

Ghost reached out and grabbed Roddy's shoulder. "This is critical. Work with Shuttle Organic on IC2. Screen 6." He pointed. "Every system forward of the Command Deck environment bulkhead must be isolated, vented, and powered down. Hydraulics, high- and low-pressure air, environment, sensors, DC and AC power, batteries, cooling, everything. We are going to lose everything forward. If any forward systems are connected to aft systems, we could get a cascading casualty that'll take down the whole lander. Shuttle Organic can identify the systems, but you have to give the orders. Ask Shuttle Organic what must be done for each system, then order him to do it.

He's not allowed to do it on his own."

Roddy's expression was a little uncertain. He tried to wipe away the fog on his faceplate. He grinned sheepishly when he discovered the moisture was inside his helmet.

Ghost looked into Roddy's eyes. He said again, "Ask Shuttle Organic what must be done for each system, then order him to do it. It's vital. You can do this. Steady. Thorough. Speed-of-light." Ghost patted Roddy's shoulder. "You can do it."

Roddy took a deep breath. "On it," he said.

"Shuttle Organic, Pilot. ComCan Roddy is designated Copilot. Work with copilot to isolate all systems forward of the environmental bulkhead." Shuttle Organic repeated back the order.

Roddy turned to his task.

Ghost turned back to the main problem, the plan. There were so many details that had to be just right to make this succeed.

"Newton Station Actual, Command. Are you de-spinning?"

"Command, Newton Station Actual. Affirmative. De-spinning and balancing in progress. We've a low-frequency wobble that's making people seasick, well, spacesick, whatever you want to call it."

Lieutenant Padmere floated forward past the passenger seats, pushing six cartons the size of small shoe boxes. He was covered in gooey orange-yellow glop and crystals. There was a smear mark on his faceplate.

"Lieutenant!" said Ortega. "You good? You're covered in … like, you've been slimed!"

"A crate of carbonated orange juice exploded when the cargo bay depressurized," said Padmere. He pushed boxes to the Candidates. "Get the controllers out and activated." He said to Ghost, "Bots ready to launch. I've been monitoring. What's the plan?"

Ghost raised a finger, signifying 'wait one.' "Admiral Franklin, Command. Request update."

A short pause. "Command, Franklin. We've lost an adult, heart attack or stroke. With the crowd in here, all these human heat engines and the experimental animals, temperature is rising. We just hit twenty-eight Celsius. Pressure still dropping."

There was another bump from a thruster burn. "Pilot, Shuttle Organic. 200 meters off Newton Station."

"Admiral Franklin, Command. Let me speak to a Primate Lab technician."

"Roger, wait one."

"Shuttle Organic, Pilot. What is your capacity for controlling the bots in the cargo bay?"

"Pilot, Shuttle Organic. I can maintain shuttle systems and maneuvering while controlling a maximum of two construction bots."

"Consoles are out and ready," said Padmere. "Serials 00105 through 00110,"

"Shuttle Organic, Pilot. Take control, bots 00105 and 00106."

"Pilot, Shuttle Organic. Take control bots 00105 and 00106. Positive control confirmed, bots 00105 and 00106."

"Lieutenant, you, Ortega, Ka-shing, take 107 through 110. Roddy, finish up isolating forward, then report to Lieutenant Padmere, take the last bot. Report when you're ready to control four bots."

Padmere huddled with the ComCans over the bot control consoles.

Roddy nudged Ghost, and pointed at the power schematic on screen seven. "I'm afraid to do anything with that."

Ghost looked at the electric plant control panel. "Good that you asked. We have to shift power to the aft APU. Shuttle Organic, Pilot. Start Auxiliary Power Unit Two."

"Pilot, Shuttle Organic, start Auxiliary Power Unit Two. Auxiliary Power Unit Two is started. Auxiliary Power Unit Two is up to speed and voltage. Auxiliary Power Unit Two is ready to be cut into the main power bus."

"Shuttle Organic, Pilot. Parallel and place Auxiliary Power Unit Two on the main power bus. Shift the load to Auxiliary Power Unit Two. When the load is shifted, open Auxiliary Power Unit One output breaker, secure Auxiliary Power Unit One."

The order was repeated back. Ghost watched as the status lights on the power bus schematic changed. When the new power configuration was established, he congratulated Roddy on a good decision, and told him to press on. Roddy gave him a relieved smile and a thumbs up.

Back to the other problems.

"Newton Station Actual, Command. We don't have time to get

Vakkers from Station Three. We are going to try something else. Stand by on this circuit for a briefing. I need the ring down to a circumference radial velocity something like six meters per second, and holding. Can you do that in ten minutes?"

"Command, Newton Station Actual. Six meters per in ten. Wait, out."

"Positive links with bots seven through ten," said Padmere. "Ready to command four bots. I'll take seven and eight until Roddy is free."

"Shuttle Organic, Pilot. Open cargo bay doors. Launch all bots. Roddy, I need you to finish up isolating forward, max blast."

On a private command-to-pilot channel, Padmere asked, "You think the ComCans can maneuver the construction bots safely? They've never done it before."

"I've seen them do the impossible in their *Space Racer* video game. Controls are nearly the same, the simulation is accurate, and they're the only bot drivers in our shuttle, so, we improvise."

Padmere barked out a laugh.

"Pilot, Shuttle Organic. All bots launched."

A woman's voice came over the circuit. "Hello? I'm Doctor … I'm supposed to say what? All right, don't make a fuss. Hello, hello there On-Station Commander, this is Doctor Macon. I am Head of the Space Primates and Cognitive Science Laboratory. You wanted to talk?"

"Doctor Macon, Command. You have an experiments chamber outspin next to p-door 32. Confirm that it can hold atmosphere if your lab goes to vacuum. Is it cooled?"

"Well, yes … Oh, all right. Command, Doctor Macon. It can hold pressure. It is not cooled. There is a full bottle of supplemental oxygen inside."

"Doctor Macon, Command. Is the chamber part of the structure of the laboratory, or is it separate from the outer wall?"

"Command, Doctor Macon. It is a floating installation, held to the floor by straps. Are you going to evacuate us? I have very special test subjects here, nine primates and 123 gerbils, all genetically pure. I know you are a bit busy, but we must save them. I insist."

"Doctor Macon, Command. Put the admiral on."

There was a rattle on the circuit.

"Command, Franklin."

"Admiral Franklin, Command, stay on the line. Shuttle Organic, Pilot. Put me on all channels."

"Pilot, Shuttle Organic. Put you on all channels. Broadcasting on all channels."

He looked to Lieutenant Padmere. "Here comes the plan."

Padmere held up his vakbot controller, and nodded. "Ready."

Ghost took a deep, calming breath. He hoped this was going to work. The tolerances were nonexistent.

"All stations, Command. A compartment on Newton Station with sixteen souls is isolated, with no power and an air leak, 30 minutes before their environment is terminal. I intend to blow the attachment bolts and float the compartment free. Shuttle 401 will guide the compartment to Station Three, Bay Five. When the Primate Lab is inside, Bay Five doors will seal. Station Three will expedite pressurization to ENTP. Make preparations. Anticipate the problems you might encounter and take action. Command, out."

Ghost turned to Lieutenant Padmere. "Get the bots on the Primate Lab. Four bots, one each to the four anchor bolts. Wrap them in the explosicord, at least five turns around each bolt, more if there's time. Have the other two bots wrap the services conduit piping at both ends of the compartment, at least ten turns. Wrap the inter-compartment passageway clear of the p-door, one turn ought to do for that. Insert detonators and prep for remote actuation. Then anchor the bots to the Primate Lab frame, away from the explosicord. We'll need them as maneuvering thrusters. Supervise Shuttle Organic and his two bots. Five minutes. Do you understand? No repeat-back, no time."

"Five turns, ten turns, one turn, coded detonators, anchor. I understand," said Padmere.

"Go."

Padmere pulled away from the command position.

"Pilot, Copilot, all systems forward of the firewall isolated, de-energized, and depressurized," said Roddy, with pride in his voice.

"Super job. Go with Artisan Lieutenant. Bot 7."

Padmere pushed a bot controller at Roddy. "Come back to the

passenger coffins, we're huddling there. I'll brief you, IC3."

"Shuttle Organic, Pilot. Shut Cargo doors."

"Pilot, Shuttle Organic. Shut Cargo doors. Cargo doors are closing."

An obnoxiously strong transmitter came up on the frequency. "Shuttle 401, this is Command Captain Bendan. Listen to me! I countermand your last! You will NOT push anything into my station. You do not have permission to proceed! I will not have you ramming my station and destroying it!"

"Station Three senior Artisan cargo officer, Command, are you up this circuit?"

A deep voice, resonate, calm. "Command, Artisan Lieutenant Commander Kenya up, with Major Basilone, Fleet Marines."

What exactly is the definition of mutiny? Ghost wondered. He couldn't see another option. "Lieutenant Commander Kenya, Command. Assume duties as Deputy Catastrophe Command for Station Three. Arrest Captain Bendan, felony charges of impeding a Catastrophe Commander. Keep him off the net. Major Basilone, Command. Support Kenya as needed."

"You can't do that! I won't have it! Arrest shuttle 401 commander! Arrest everyone in that damned shuttle! Where's the copy of Title Ten? Dammit! This is Command Captain Bendan, I take command, I assume authority over—"

The transmission cut off.

Ghost sighed, exhaled with a shudder from his chest. In the short term, containing Captain Benden was necessary; but, later? Afterwards?

No time to think of afterwards.

"Command, Franklin, channel 46. I'm concerned you'll breach our containment when you blow the bolts. I've only three people in skinsuits."

"Admiral Franklin, Command. The lab will not, repeat *not*, remain airtight. Skinsuits go on suit O_2. Tie them down, so nobody gets blown out of the compartment when it cracks. Everyone else, get into the experiments chamber. Seal in. Report when ready."

"Command, Franklin. Augustus is in a skinsuit."

Ghost knew Auggie had learned his skinsuit; but, could a little boy manage being in a compartment that was going to be nearly blown to pieces, a tornado of air rushing out, vak in? Would he panic?

"Admiral Franklin, Command. Roger. Your choice, in or out, but I think he can handle it. I'll push in at center of mass, so secure your skinsuit people near the chamber. He's a sharp kid, he'll make it."

"Command, Franklin. We need some time to tear out some cages and test equipment. We found more air tanks. We'll take them in the chamber."

"Admiral Franklin, Command. CO2 toxicity will get you first. Check for an emergency supplies locker with CO2 absorbent. It will be labeled 'lithium hydroxide'."

The voice of Roberts cut in. "Command, Newton Station Actual. Six point two meters per second and holding. Wobble gone, mostly."

Ghost rotated one of the shuttle's cameras to Newton Station. He saw the bots in a cluster within yards of the rotating wheel. As the injured compartment passed, the bots' jets flared. They hooked on, and started to claw their way to the anchor bolts. The wheel rotated them out of sight.

"Placing explosicord now," said Padmere.

A stray transmission came in on channel 46. "Good God, Doctor Macon, we cannot take the gerbils!"

Now, the hard part. He was glad Captain Bendan was restrained.

"Deputy Command, Command, channel 45. Here's the complication. I can push the compartment into Bay Five, but I can't stop it. My retro thrusters will be blocked, and I've got everything de-energized forward of the command deck. You'll have to halt the lab, tie it down, and figure out how to free us so you can shut the bay door. Fifteen minutes to solve the problem."

"Command, Deputy, roger. Let me talk to my people."

"Deputy Command, Command. If you can't do it, tell me at least thirty seconds before arrival. I'll maneuver to miss the station." And all those people will suffocate.

Ghost thought to urge him to speed. No, let the man get on with it.

Was there anything else? Think. Anticipate. What have you forgotten?

Padmere nudged his elbow. "Explosicord set, detonators set and coded, bots anchored."

"Command, Franklin. Ready this end. Give me ten seconds after my last transmission and we'll be sealed in."

"Admiral Franklin, Command. Seal in. Go."

"Command, Franklin. Whether we get through this or not, I want the record to show that I approve of the decisions made by Command regarding the impending rescue of the people in the Primate Lab. I commend all personnel on your initiative. We wouldn't have a chance without all of you on Shuttle 401, Station Three, Newton Station. Well done. Everyone here is looking forward to arriving at Station Three. Franklin, out."

Ghost took a few deep breaths. He flexed his hands. Thirty seconds passed. Now or never.

"Shuttle Organic, Pilot. Take control of the detonators. Blow the explosicord timed so that the compartment is thrown out towards Cargo Bay Five. Stagger the detonations so the compartment is on a vector to the cargo bay with no pitch, roll or yaw. Do you understand? What will be the compartment's velocity?"

Shuttle Organic repeated the order. "Compartment velocity depends upon separation characteristics, predicted at 6.10 meters per second, uncertainty plus 0.1 meters, minus 6.12 meters per second."

That couldn't be right. "Shuttle Organic, Pilot. Why uncertainty minus 6.12?"

"Pilot, Shuttle Organic. Release velocity will be zero if one or more anchor bolts do not separate."

Oh. Right.

"Shuttle Organic, Pilot. Reposition the shuttle to best location to intercept the compartment. Approach from aft of the vector. Execute."

Ghost felt the thrusters. He turned back to see the ComCan's huddle around the bot controllers. He caught Padmere's eye. "We blow the anchor bolts next pass. Be prepared to use the bots like tugs to align the compartment to fit into Cargo Bay Five. Be careful with fuel, we might need the bots to help brake."

"Understood. Ready."

Now, a few seconds of peace until things got hairy again.

Ghost watched Newton Station on his monitor. The Primate Lab approached the tangent. *Now.*

There was a bright flare of light, smoke, metal fragments scattering.

The compartment remained attached to Newton Station.

Oh, Lord.

"Shuttle Organic, Pilot. Report."

"Pilot, Shuttle Organic. The inter-compartment passageways and services conduit are blown. There was potential they would interfere with the trajectory of the Primate Lab. Detonations were successful. The Laboratory is free from the adjoining compartments. I am recalculating. Anticipate anchor bolt detonation this revolution."

A crackle on his suit speakers, and a familiar voice sounded out, on the edge of being frightened. "Booster Buddy Coast, Booster Buddy Auggie, on channel 46."

"Booster Buddy Auggie, Booster Buddy Coast. Go."

"Derr Coast, Auggie. There was another boom. There's a loud whistling noise, we've got a big leak. My O2 light is blinking yellow."

Ghost took a deep breath, and spoke in a calming, gentle tone. "Auggie, Coast. Not to worry. We're going to move the lab to Station Three. You'll be there in just a few minutes. Stay frosty. Soon you'll feel another jolt, and the whole compartment will go to vacuum. Don't worry. I'm in a shuttle right by you. You'll have a great adventure to tell the other Booster Buddies. Are you tied down tight?"

"Pilot, Shuttle Organic. Detonating—now."

On the center monitor, Ghost saw flashes and puffs of smoke as the explosicord detonated.

If he was wrong, he had just killed sixteen people.

The laboratory separated cleanly from the station frame and sailed out towards the shuttle. Ghost exhaled.

He reached out and changed a toggle switch. "Shuttle Organic, Pilot. Manual maneuvering control. My spacecraft."

"Pilot, Shuttle Organic. Manual maneuvering control. Manual maneuvering control engaged. Your spacecraft."

In the camera, the compartment got bigger, but with enough bearing drift that Ghost knew it would not collide with them. It made its stately way past. Trails of atmosphere vented from cracks. He fired thrusters to follow the lander.

"Shuttle Organic, Pilot. Mark center of mass of the Primate Laboratory, screen three."

A bulls-eye overlay appeared on the screen.

Padmere said, "We lost zero-9, link failure. The others survived separation."

"Align the lab to fit Bay Five. I'll need it steady."

"Roger, align the lab to fit Bay Five."

Ghost immediately saw maneuvering jets firing on the bots. Padmere and the Candidates must have planned the maneuver in advance, got ahead of the problem. Forethought. Fantastic.

Ghost blipped the main engine to catch up with the compartment. Not too fast, he didn't know how Kenya was going to get rid of the velocity at Bay Five. He fired the lateral thrusters and lined up with the cargo dock. With no radar, Ghost had to move in by eye.

Then, he had an idea. "Shuttle Organic, Pilot. Can you triangulate on the compartment using multiple external cameras, and report range to compartment and closure rate?"

"Pilot, Shuttle Organic. Range 105.5 meters, closure rate 2.9 meters per second."

"Shuttle Organic, Pilot, announce range and rate every fifteen seconds."

Ghost concentrated on the compartment and the nose of the lander, shifting his attention between the camera's view to what he could see through the forward windscreen. He gingerly used the thrusters to center on the bulls-eye. He could see Bay Five in the distance. Its cargo door was open. The entrance seemed so very small.

"Alignment is about as good as we can guesstimate," said Padmere. "Bots 35 percent fuel."

"Range ten meters, rate 1.9 meters per second."

"Booster Buddy Auggie, Booster Buddy Coast, on 46. My shuttle is going to push the laboratory over to the other station. The wall is going to bulge in. Don't worry."

Silence. What happened to Auggie? Did frags from the explosions hit him?

Ghost leaned forward and sighted the compartment visually. The shuttle's nose pressed against the wall of the Primate Lab. The shuttle's radome shattered, flinging out shards of composite. The nose crumbled. The lab wall stretched, then cracked. The crunch vibrated through the hull.

The shuttle was well and truly embedded in the compartment.

In was easy. Out would be different.

Bitchin' Betty decided she wanted to complicate the situation. "ALARM. Forward Hydraulics Reservoir Low Pressure. LEAK, Forward Hydraulics Reservoir Low Pressure."

Roddy was already scrolling through systems drawings.

"Auggie, Coast. Still sucking and blowing in there, Booster Buddy?"

No response.

"ALARM. Forward Hydraulics Reservoir Low Pressure. LEAK, Forward Hydraulics Reservoir Low Pressure." Bitchin' Betty sounded unflappable.

"Shuttle Organic, Copilot. Check shut valve HS-V-5, shut HS-V-5 bypass valve."

The Organic did the repeat-back. Bitchin' Betty went quiet.

Roddy looked at Ghost sheepishly. "Sorry. Missed the bypass."

Ghost gave him a quick nod.

"Augustus, Coast. Channel 46, or suit-to-suit."

No response.

Heartsick, Ghost began to consider how to line up the approach to Bay Five. "Shuttle Organic, Pilot. Give me the required relative corrections to fit the Primate Lab into Station Three Bay Five."

"Pilot, Shuttle Organic. Left seven degrees relative, down three degrees relative. Roll clockwise eight degrees."

He corrected, left seven down three. He rolled the compartment and the shuttle to perfect the alignment. It was tense, tedious, meticulous work, a mental challenge as he worked out angles and vectors. Which thruster to get what response? How much thrust, how long to sustain, what leverage? What order to make the changes? Making it more difficult, the lab wall flexed when he used thrusters. Everything had to be done slowly and gently. Too fast, he might tear open the Experiments Chamber and kill everyone.

Ghost could feel a headache coming on. His eyes strained to see through the forward windscreen to read the instruments.

Alignment complete. The approach was steady. He had not heard from Station Three.

ETA 120 seconds. ETA 110 seconds. 100 seconds. No comms from Station Three.

He would have to steer to pass the bay at a safe distance. He did not want to crash into the station and kill Station Three personnel. He started to think about how to maneuver to miss. Pitch over, tail up, full down on the upper thrusters, that had to be it, hope the nose was stuck in enough so the Lab would follow.

Thoughts of failure shattered his concentration, of people helpless and dying. Auggie, the Admiral; Maxie, the children. Maybe someone on Station Three could get to the people in skinsuits before their O2 went solid red. Should he call Station Three and get them ready for that rescue?

He couldn't resist calling. "Deputy, Command. Status?"

"Command, Deputy. We've solved the braking problem, no time to explain. I'll have some people suit-boosting over to you. I have qualified operators ready to take over the bots. Go to remote transfer permissive on all bots."

"Artisan Lieutenant, all bots to remote transfer permissive." Ghost looked back at Padmere. The candidates flipped switches on the consoles, then gave a thumbs-up. Shuttle Organic reported accomplishments for its vakbots.

There was a pause, and then, "Command, Deputy. We have control of five bots, with an error signal on zero-9. If you have control of zero-9, boost it clear, we'll pick it up later. We hold your alignment good. Hands off the controls."

Ghost let go. His hands were stiff. He had been gripping the joysticks too hard. Only rookies strangled their controls. Idiot. He flexed his wrists, and tried to relax and remain calm.

His fingers trembled.

"Deputy, Command, hands off the controls. My hands are off. You control the docking."

"Command, Deputy, I control the docking."

Ghost found a remote feed from a camera on Station Three Docking Control and sent it to screen two. It showed dozens of people in booster suits swarming the entrance to Bay Five. Two of the bots were firing thrusters, perfecting the approach alignment. Six two-man cargo tugs appeared with large forward-mounted shock plates.

They distributed themselves along the length of the laboratory. Then, he felt vibrations as they pushed to cancel the forward velocity of the lab and shuttle. The shuttle crunched deeper into the Primates Lab with the tremor of grinding metal.

Ghost turned back to the passenger seats. Padmere and the ComCans had stowed the bot consoles. The shreds of the controllers' shipping boxes were floating past Ghost as the lander slowed. The ComCans' expressions showed relief at knowing they had completed their part successfully.

All except for Brin. He stared out to infinity, eyes half closed, jaw ajar.

"All of you. Good job, super," said Ghost. "What's with Brin?"

Ortega grinned. "It appears Command Candidate Three Brin has some questionable substance in his skinsuit emergency drug dispenser. He must have accidentally activated it, say, maybe a half-dozen times. ComCan Three Brin will be in his personal Happy Land for an hour." Ortega shrugged. "Or five."

"Range fifty-five meters to Bay Five inner bulkhead, rate 1.9 meters per second."

The shuttle was still closing the cargo bay when he saw the tugs depart. They had to clear, or they would be crushed inside the interior wall.

"Range fifty-six meters, rate 0.3 meters per second."

Still too fast. If they hit the back of the cargo bay, their momentum would crush the Primate Lab.

Four pairs of Vakkers in boost suits carrying small boxes shot out from the station, trailing cables. They landed on the compartment, inspected the edges quickly, and then placed the boxes on the corners. The cables ran through fairlead blocks at the outside edge of the cargo bay. Four long, massive rails deployed out of the corners of the cargo bay and locked in place like guide rails.

"Command, Deputy, close your eyes. Those are superconductor boxes. We're going to attach them using welding tape. Ignition in three, two, one—"

Some of the flared brightness leaked through Ghost's closed eyelids.

"Command, Deputy, we'll use the superconductors' magnetic field to ease you in. Stand by to compensate with thrusters if one of the boxes breaks free."

"Deputy, Command, standing by. I will not fire thrusters unless you request."

"Command, Deputy, roger that. Energizing now. I've got our best mag wrangler on this, but it's kinda best guess time. It's not like we've got this calibrated."

Slowly, the compartment entered the cargo bay. Ghost felt himself pushed back into the pilot's coffin as the magnetic field gripped the metal in his e-pack and around his helmet. He heard, "Shit!" He looked back. The magnetic field had a grip on Ortega and was dragging him to the back of the compartment.

There was a strong bump communicated through the hull. Ortega grabbed a handhold and held on. The force on Ghost's skinsuit relaxed.

"Range indeterminate, rate indeterminate," announced Shuttle Organic.

"Shuttle Organic, Pilot. Secure range and rate readings."

"Command, Deputy. We're going to anchor the compartment, then the tugs will pull you out. It looks like your nose is stuck in there pretty good."

Ghost glanced at his chronometer. "Deputy, Command, maybe four minutes before people start passing out in there. A kid in a skinsuit was yellow O2; he's tied down in a corner of the lab. Be ready to render assistance." Ghost had forgotten about Auggie's O2 alarm. God in heaven, how *could* he forget? *Idiot!* He should have warned them earlier.

There was a buzz on the circuit, a pause, then, "Command, Deputy. We've got a glitch. The tugs expended all their fuel during the braking. We underestimated your total mass. We can't shut the cargo bay door with you stuck in the compartment. I'm going to employ the construction bots. We'll use their lasers to cut you free. Fourteen, fifteen minutes, max."

"Deputy, Command, we don't have five minutes." Ghost tried to visualize the problem and see a solution. "Get the lab tied down and your people clear. Retract the guide rails. I'm going to try something."

There was a flurry of activity inside and around the cargo bay.

"Command, Deputy. Lab is anchored. Rails retracted."

"All Station Three personnel, Command. Stand clear of Shuttle 401. Thrusters will be activating irregularly."

Here was another chance for him to tear open the Experiments Chamber. Fortunately, it was a separate floating structure, but regardless, there was no other alternative. Only minutes remained.

He switched his thruster controls to "emergency override." He dialed in the aft port lateral thruster to 110 percent and held the firing trigger down.

At first, there was no motion. Then, with a twisting vibration that rattled the command deck, the shuttle began to fold down against the station like a jackknife, pivoting on the nose stuck in the lab wall. Ghost could see the wall crumple and wrinkle around the nose of the shuttle. A ceramic re-entry shield broke off the shuttle and tumbled away.

He released the trigger. The opposite thruster was set to 110 percent and fired.

Agonizingly, the shuttle yawed back to its original position, then beyond, folding in the other direction. Large cracks suddenly appeared around the lander's windshield, radiating from the corners. It exploded, scattering cubes of armored glass. Ghost involuntarily put up his hand. A cube bounced off his helmet faceplate. Refusing to be distracted, he could see twisted metal flaking from the Primate Lab.

The metal gripping the nose of the shuttle tore free.

He secured the starboard thruster. He fired all port thrusters.

Moving sideways with a lurch, the shuttle broke free, clearing Cargo Bay Five.

101: *Sherri*

"We'll both have the shrimp and iced tea, unsweetened." Sherri glanced over to Ella, who vaguely nodded approval.

"Distinguished Diners, an excellent choice," said LaMancha. "Mike will be pleased someone has ordered the shrimp. I was concerned tomorrow's lunch menu would consist of left-over shrimpburgers."

Sherri narrowed her eyes and looked up into LaMancha's camera. "Ahhhhright, whazzamatta with the shrimp? Fess up."

The Shining Knight displayed a hurt look. "The shrimp is exemplary! A subtle exploration of delicate tastes, a sophisticated experience for the discriminating diner. Only, I overestimated the number of orders. It appears—" Sherri detected a sniff of disdain "—our Vakker clientele prefers cow." LaMancha paused and said, in the same tone used after he learned that Spongebob had been discovered on a beach above the high-tide line, dehydrated: "There will be leftovers. Shrimp doesn't keep. I shot a few stir-fry as Noteworthy Mystery Meals, but the Vakkers have caught on."

"Different advertising might work," said Sherri. "Recipe, Bar Screen."

The recipe and cooking instructions for the shrimp stir-fry appeared.

"Third ingredient down," murmured Ella.

"Mike sautés the shrimp in white wine?" said Sherri.

"Two to three minutes, until the shrimp turns pink."

"No alcohol in the prime rib, right?"

"Correct."

Sherri stretched, and put her hands behind her head. "Tell the meteor-bangers the stir-fry is cooked in wine, and make sure they understand that wine is an alcoholic beverage. Like, very up-sun beer."

102: *Ella*

Ella kept surveillance over Mike's new bus girl. She was a good worker, cleaning quickly and thoroughly while keeping up a patter with the Vakkers at nearby tables. Tips disappeared like a magician's trick. Perhaps the creature was just working for what she could pick up.

Ella wasn't sure why she was so disconcerted. She shouldn't be troubled, rather, she should be happy to see Mike's workload reduced. With employees to help, he could concentrate less on his obsessive cleaning and more on serving up such wonderful meals. She knew the Lacrosse Shot was profitable, but it would be good if it was a total, roaring success. There was an undertone of sadness in Mike, of defeat, as if he was grounded from spaceflight due to some reprehensible crime, a character fault, lack of effort or intelligence. The Vakkers visiting the restaurant was a constant reminder of his past. Grounding stripped away his identity and self-worth.

Success might boost his confidence. Then, maybe he would treat her more like a friend, rather than the obsequious deference due to a customer, from a kowtowing merchant. That would make *her* happy.

LaMancha shot their ice teas in the traditional way. No attempts to intercept. Was it out of respect, or because she was an outsider and not allowed into Vakker games? She had an odd feeling about that. She belonged to her academic group, but, somehow, she also hoped she was accepted into Vakker circles, with these vibrant, smart, humorous, hard-working people.

Of course, it could be Vakkers just weren't interested in intercepting tea.

She shook her head. She was conjuring up impediments where none existed, ill-will where there were only smiles and acceptance. She was being over-sensitive about being excluded from the AIOOS meetings and Aaron's revolutionary cabal gatherings.

Odd mood.

Geezer, sitting at the next table, leaned over and nudged her elbow. "Watch," he said with a devilish grin. He pointed to the bar catapult. "Odds are ten to one. He misses, I'm rich, and me 'n Soak become gentlemen of leisure. Want in?"

Sherri leaned forward. "Even odds, fifty pence on LaMancha! Come and get some!"

"Okay, smarty-pants, done! Even odds? Whoa!" Geezer chortled. "A sucker is born every nano. They must not teach math over there at that TCU place."

"Table 14, alert, incoming."

The room went silent.

Sproonk.

A naked shot glass slowly arced away from Bar Cat in a slow, languorous curve.

It passed above the surface of one of the upside-down tables—

—kissed the overhead—

—hit the far bulkhead—

—bounced—

—now inbound, it passed two rows of tables—

—and nestled into the reverse side of Table 14's net, rocking slightly on its spring.

A cheer rose from the diners. "Nuthin' but net!"

Soak, high up in the room next to Table 24, started bouncing like a superheated tap dancer. "Not nuthin' but net! Not! Gotta be clean catch! Hit the net frame! Do-over! Do-over!"—but he was shouted down.

Coins, I.O.U.s and solemn promises were exchanged, accompanied by triumphant hecklings and moans mourning the vicissitudes of fate.

Geezer reached over and slid two quarter-stans on their table towards Sherri. "Geez, you'd think I wudda figured this out by now." He smiled at Sherri, and awarded Ella a wink. "Happy you came tonight," he added.

Ella felt much better.

After a remarkably short time Mike personally delivered their meals, the food displayed on the plates like a gourmet cooking photobook. He was visibly pleased when Sherri took a bite and her eyes went wide with pleasure. He complimented them on their outfits, exchanged a few pleasantries, but Ella did not want to hold him too long. In spite of LaMancha's assurances that everything was going apace, she could tell by the pings from Mike's control screen that there was a surge of orders.

Mike certainly was a hard-working fellow. She respected his work ethic. But, how could she be interested in a cook? He likely had never attended university, or even an on-line college.

She tried to dissect her feelings in a dreamy, half-conscious state, while eating.

Eventually, Sherri leaned back and patted her stomach theatrically. "Oh, my, that was good. LaMancha, anyone ordering the shrimp?"

LaMancha's tone was sour. "We're out of shrimp. The disrespectful self-centered meteor-bangers are complaining."

Sherri laughed. "Poor LaMancha. So upset when the future doesn't follow his instructions."

"Are you finished? May I clear this?" The mystery lady was standing by their table.

"Oh. Sure," said Sherri, waving away her plate.

"That was quite an entrance, Dee. Charming. I'm pleased your look isn't wasted on this crowd. You too, Citizen," she said to Ella. "Not many ladies your age could pull off that dress. Very attractive. I'm Eris. I'm with the Lacrosse Shot now."

There was a pause, as if she was making a decision, then Sherri said, "Pleasedtameetcha, I'm Sherri. This is Professor Ella Braun. We're from TCU."

"Yes, LaMancha told me."

"You're Vakker?" asked Ella

"Me and Mike go way back. We shipped together."

"I thought Tevil and the Unions prevented Mike from hiring?" said Ella. She did not like where this conversation was going.

"I'm not exactly an employee. I think I might end up a partner. If you know what I mean." She displayed a pretty smile that was not reflected in her eyes. "Can I get you dessert? We have a lovely chocolate cake, and a nice apple turnover with whipped cream I can recommend. Coffee? Tea? Mickee?"

Ella felt a shudder of emotion, which she ruthlessly suppressed. "Just coffee, please," she said.

"Tea, hot," said Sherri.

"Right away." Eris's hips rotated away in the direction of the bar.

Ella watched the departure. "Whew."

She looked at Sherri, who was taking a sudden interest in folding her napkin, not meeting Ella's eyes. "Ahh-right. What's going on."

Looking up, with the expression of a baby koala lost in a maze, Sherri clutched her napkin. "*Her* is what's going on. LaMancha called me. Mike hasn't hired her. She manipulated Mike into a bet clearing tables, like the Wagering Association. LaMancha says her callsign is named after the Greek god of discord, and she's *anypoliptos*. I looked it up. It means disreputable, ten to the fifteenth."

"That's the first understatement I've ever heard from LaMancha," said Ella. *Well, maybe not the first, but in this case, I believe he's not exaggerating.*

"LaMancha wants you to stay until closing. He doesn't want Mike alone with her." She looked up at Ella, pleading in her eyes. "I'm sorry, I should've just asked."

"We can stay. You do your word associations with LaMancha, and I'll keep an eye on everything else." Ella smiled, to reassure Sherri that Eris was just a minor cog in the vast cosmic comedy.

The evening passed quickly. Sherri got her data, and as the dining room became less frenetic, Mike came over to chat. Ella thought he looked a little nervous about Eris, but she couldn't quite tell. Was she just projecting her own feelings?

A few minutes before closing time the room had emptied, except for Soak and Sampson.

"Soak and Sampson, LaMancha. Warning order, ten minutes to chucking out time. Six hundred seconds to Soak and Sampson ejection. Countdown starts … wait for it, precision is important in life… now. Six hundred, five ninety-nine—"

Soak stood up and stretched. "Yeah, got it. On our way. Hey, Mike, could ya loan a busted Vakker cart fare? I got chiseled by LaMancha. Again."

"LaMancha…" growled Mike.

LaMancha retorted, with the indignant voice of a riverboat gambler accused of hiding cards up his sleeves. "Their dice. Sampson rolled for both sides."

"Yeah, right, one of these days…" Mike grumbled. Opening the cash drawer, he pulled out three quarter-stans and flipped them to Sampson, who caught them deftly. Sampson put a knuckle to his forehead, a hand on Soak's shoulder, and they headed out the gangway. Soak pulled out his FoxxFone and started punching numbers.

"What now?" whispered Sherri to Ella.

Ella watched Mike and Eris.

"Well, that about does the day," said Mike. "Eris, ten minutes. Go."

"Watch me," said Eris.

"We'll finish our drinks" announced Ella to the deserted room.

She'd see what happened when the ten minutes were up.

103: Padmere

Artisan Lieutenant Padmere floated out Airlock 6-8 in the no-G wing of Station Three and retracted his skinsuit helmet. Coast and the other ComCans followed, with Brin being towed between Ka-Shing and Ortega. Roddy carried their duffels, straps looped around his arms.

They had entered Station Three through a cargo handlers' airlock at the far end of Pier Six. With the central facilities all occupied with rescue activities, they were directed to the station's extremities, and told, by an inexplicably hostile controller, to keep their asses and trashed lander out of the way.

Their day had been busy. After extricating 401 from Bay Five and watching the door seal, they had spent hours transferring equipment and Vakkers from Station Three to Newton Station. With their forward thrusters inoperative, all the trips required tricky piloting.

Help eventually arrived. When the situation stabilized, On-Scene Command was transferred to an Emergency Management Team dispatched by Admiral Quoun from Station One. With their fuel flashing amber, Shuttle 401 and her crew were released.

Artisan Lieutenant Padmere pulled out his clipscreen. "Gentlemen, we check in to the TOQ, maybe a run through the rain locker, then it would be my privilege to treat you all to dinner. Except ComCan Brin. I fear he is not in our local universe. Let's get him to sick bay."

"Sorry sir, no dinner," said Ka-Shing, pointing to a 'station time' display on a bulkhead. "Breakfast in an hour, though."

"Breakfast?" Padmere said. He glanced at his watch and did the math. "So it is. Missed dinner. There is wisdom from the ancient Vedas, I recall it goes, 'Time flies when you're having fun.'"

Padmere pulled out his clipscreen, called up a schematic of the station, and requested a route to sick bay, and from there to FSF Transient Officers' Quarters (TOQ). First leg, Tram Route Six. His stomach growled.

At the tram station, Padmere pushed the call button.

Air pressure went up as a tram arrived and pushed the atmosphere into the compartment, with an accompanying breeze and motor noise and the smell of lubricating oil and ozone from the electrified track.

The car was full of powder-blue uniformed personnel. Command officers.

A tall, coiffured, distinguished-looking man with the insignia of a Command Captain emerged, his station boots sticking him to the deck, trailed by half a dozen Command Lieutenants and Command Ensigns.

"I behold, the miscreants of Shuttle 401," Bendan presumed.

Padmere and the ComCans got their boots on the deck and came to attention, less Brin, who remained smiling and floating, eyes focused on the beauty of infinity.

The tram door shut, and the tram departed, dragging a fresh breeze.

"Report," the Captain demanded.

Padmere saluted. "Artisan Lieutenant Padmere with five FSF Academy Command Candidates, Shuttle 401 orientation and cargo flight."

The Captain nodded. "Frigging Artisan. I thought as much. Your skinsuit is filthy. As contemptible as you are, you are not the voice that took Command authority from me. Who might that be?"

Coast moved from behind the other candidates, came to attention, and saluted. "Sir, Command Candidate Three Coast."

"A Three!" exclaimed the Captain. He inspected Coast contemptuously. "You insubordinate piece of *shit*. You're not qualified to pilot a grocery buggy." He shot a glare at Padmere, who flinched. "Have you now been relieved of your mutinous, stolen title of 'Command'?"

"Title Ten command authority has been transferred to the Admiral's Emergency Management Team, in accordance with regulations," said Coast.

"You now will deign to accept *my* orders? A few small ones?"

Another breeze, and a tram arrived. An immaculately uniformed Marine in Class II greens fitted over a Marine tactical skinsuit stepped out.

The Captain turned. "Major Basilone. I ordered your duty officer to send me a section of Marines."

The major saluted. "Sir, I was informed you desired to arrest some Fleet Forces personnel."

The Captain did not return the salute. "I so ordered."

"One Marine is sufficient for that mission. I am here." He looked Bendan directly in the eyes. "Sir."

"Huh," complained the Captain. He gestured to one of his aides. "Hold that tram." He looked at Major Basilone. "The never-ending arrogance of the Fleet Marine Corps; I remain perpetually astounded." He waved at Padmere and the candidates. "Arrest these mutineers. Confine them. I will prefer charges when convenient. In particular, *that* one," he pointed to Coast, "receives no privileges or considerations. Put him in a garbage can with bars."

Without waiting for a response, the Captain led a parade of aides into the tram, the command lieutenants and ensigns all casting expressions of disgust at Padmere and the ComCans. The tram departed.

The Major held his hand out to Padmere. He smiled. "Welcome to Station Three. Matt Basilone."

"Padmere, sir," he offered softly in return. The Major's handshake was rock-hard.

"Coast, sir." "Ortega, sir." "Roddy, sir." "Ka-Shing, sir."

The major inspected the glassy-eyed Brin.

"Command Candidate Brin is currently on detached assignment," said Coast.

The Major barked out a laugh. "If you still have a sense of humor after encountering Bendan the Brainless, the Low Oligarch of High Orbit, then you are doubly welcome to Station Three." He gestured to Brin. "Call for medical? They can get here in five."

Padmere grimaced. "I should have done that immediately," he said. He pulled out his clipscreen.

"Sir, if you please," said Coast, "there was a boy in a skinsuit in the Primate Lab. Did he make it? What about the rest of them? They wouldn't give us news."

The Major laughed again. "Booster Buddy? Max Blast On Patrol? The youngster's fine." He grinned. "He got excited and bumped the wrong buttons and deactivated his transmitter. Caused a bit of excitement, that. All the rest are good, except one KIA, probably a stroke, happened before you blew them loose." Basilone's look encompassed them all. "In my book, you FedSpacers pulled off a very high-quality miracle. We could have lost them all. As it is, no heat stroke, lungs intact, no psychotic breakdowns, everything else treatable. Well done."

Major Basilone glanced over Padmere's skinsuit, which was dripping orange goo. "You've been decorated already?"

"No, sir," said Padmere. "Cargo. A crate of orange juice exploded when we emergency vented to vak."

"That wouldn't be a 'Personal For' shipment, to a certain Captain?"

"Yes, sir."

Basilone sighed. "I'd get your skinsuit cleaned as soon as possible. When he learns an essential ingredient of his Slammers didn't survive, there'll be a shitstorm."

A gentle breeze, and a tram decorated with a red cross arrived with a medical team. Formerly disappointed that they had minimal participation during the Newton Station catastrophe, they eagerly took custody of Brin. An initial examination was performed on Brin's unresisting body. Then they strapped him down to a portable AutoDoc, punctured Brin with needles and wires and tubes (while looking faintly disappointed at the lack of any discernable red leaks or extruding gore), festooned their patient with monitoring sensors, and happily departed.

Another tram arrived. "All aboard," said Major Basilone, "I'll brief you on your schedule."

Basilone, Padmere, and the rest of the ComCans boarded and seated themselves in gimballed high-backed chairs. They grabbed stabilization straps. The tram accelerated out of the station. The Major sat by Lieutenant Padmere, with the ComCans further aft.

"For starters," said the Major, "you all will be guests of the Sergeants' Mess. They have held dinner, or breakfast if you care for that instead. I intended to invite you to the Marine Officer's Mess, but there are only two of us in the Station today, and frankly, the food is better with the Sergeants. Three of the children in that tour group belong to my Marines, so they claimed privilege."

"Sir," said Padmere, "are we not under arrest?"

Major Basilone shook his head. "That won't last too long. Did you know Admiral Franklin, that is, *Senator* Admiral Franklin, was in the lab, with his granddaughter? Booster Buddy is his grandson? My opinion? Bendan is a dead man drifting."

"The Admiral was most helpful," said Padmere.

"Figured," said Major Basilone. "I served with him before he retired. He's ten steps above the typical Command officer, those who can't properly operate an on-off switch. He's on his way back to New Berne. That explosion might have been an assassination attempt."

"Most distressing," said Padmere.

"Sir," asked Coast from behind them. "Captain Bendan was not arrested, not charged with felony interference under Title Ten?"

Basilone shrugged. "We restrained him at first. Couldn't prevent him from calling Station One. The admiral ordered us to stand down. He's off that hook, for now." Then he grinned. "There's another, different hook. Captain Bendan is going to be very busy for some time."

Padmere's expression communicated his lack of understanding. "Yes, of course, the emergency."

"Something a bit more entertaining," said the Major. "Professor Macon was in the lab. She's Head of Primates and Test Specimens at Newton."

"Yes, we communicated with her," said Padmere.

"Her field is cognitive enhancement," said Basilone. "For some reason, her experiments do better in orbit. She's got nine primates, like chimps, orangutans, rhesus monkeys, along with a tribe of cognitively-enhanced brained-up gerbils."

"One hundred twenty-three, if I recall," said Padmere. He liked gerbils. He'd read that Enhanced Cognition Gerbils could actually hold conversations on specially modified clipscreens.

"Spot on. So, scroll back to the emergency. You come up with this crazy plan, and Admiral Franklin starts pressing everyone to get in that chamber. Doc Macon commences a meltdown. She refuses to get in until *all* her critters are in, too, regardless of volume."

"Oh, my."

"While the Admiral is trying to figure how to put a bag over her head and drag her in, Doc opens the cages. 123 gerbils and nine apes are all over everywhere. You would never believe, she stands like the Galactic Overlord and points, and *orders* them all into the chamber. It was like a parade on Marine Corps Birthday, these critters scampered right in."

"Incredible."

Major Basilone nodded and grinned. "So, there you are, kids and adults and a company of gerbils and a squad of apes sealed in a box, all elbows and assholes. Then, you push the lab into Bay Five. They start pressurizing and heating the bay real quick. Our Artisan Lieutenant Commander Kenya, thinks ahead, has air tanks and high-cap heaters ready to go, so about ninety seconds and the space is survivable. Booster Buddy, he's tied down next to the test chamber window. Smart kid, knows his suit. He calls up the 'External Environment' report, gets a 'Breathable / Survivable' reading, so he retracts his helmet. The people in the chamber see his red hair flying in the breeze, and they open the chamber door." His grin got wider. "They'd released O₂ while they were in that box, so pressure was maybe three, four PSI over the pressure in the bay. They're blown out, like they were shot from a cannon, surrounded by a cloud of lithium hydroxide smoke. My sergeant said it looked like a constipated volcano erupted."

"Ah," said Padmere solemnly, "like FedSpacers going on liberty."

The major laughed. "Out tumbles the gerbils. The little critters are better in no-G than acrobats. Of course, nobody pays attention to the furballs, what with Captain Comedy going all-hands-all-decks-all-stations with a screaming fit about taking care of Admiral Franklin and his grandkids. Soon the gerbils are bouncing through the locks and p-doors. Surprise surprise, we learned that Enhanced Cognition Gerbils had taught themselves to operate p-doors. Takes three, working together, synchronized. Twenty minutes, they're through the entire station."

"The poor creatures must have been terrified," said Padmere.

The major grinned. "Poor? I wouldn't say 'poor.' Those poor creatures are worth on the order of two *million* standards. *Each*."

"Goodness."

"Doc Macon wants them all gathered up, but she's not getting cooperation from Bendan, no surprise there. After her blood pressure explodes and she pulls out enough hair to supply a wigmaker convention, she starts making calls. Seems she knows important people who know *very* important people. Speed-of-light, Captain Confusion is getting lit up with incoming from heavyweights with a lot bigger rocks than he has, telling him that he damn well better account for every one of those cute little critters, and do it faster than it takes to read 'welcome to your court-martial' off the latrine bulkheads."

Gravely, Padmere said, "I would be pleased to visit those latrines, and celebrate the inscriptions."

The major assumed a look of supreme innocence. "There are scurrilous rumors, really slanderous, that my Marines are not cooperating, that they've been providing sanctuary for the gerbils. Hiding them. Still about forty missing, I'm told."

"Hiding them? Whyever for?"

Basilone shrugged. "Pets?"

"Pets? On a space station?" marveled Padmere. "Pets, worth two million standards each?"

"Hiding them might also be some Marines' idea of a way to return fire at the Command Captain, for the months he's been disrespecting the Corps. Marines get very annoyed at people who disrespect the Corps."

At the top of Major Basilone's side tunic pocket a small furry head peeked out.

"Cheep?"

Without looking down, the Major scratched it between the ears.

"Scurrilous rumors," the Major affirmed. "Outrageous."

104: Mike

"A cart has pulled up outside the entrance," said LaMancha.

"That's the taxi for Soak and Sampson." Mike continued to scrub the grill while glancing occasionally at Eris. She was working hard, he noted. Maybe he needed to think about her differently.

"Mike! Goon Number Two, Goon Number One, Jugg-Ears! They're on the cart! A gun! Jugg-Ears is pointing a bullet gun at Sampson!"

Mike vaulted the bar, grabbed a long-handled mop and charged for the door. Passing Sherri and Ella, he ordered, "Stay here!"

"Goon Number Two has a gun! Goon Number One clubbed Soak! Again! Soak is down! Dreadful!"

Ella stood. She stared at the entrance. A minute passed. She brushed some hair from her face, then clenched her fist. "LaMancha. What's happening?"

"The brutes have departed."

Sampson appeared at the gangway, with Soak in his arms. Mike followed. Soak's head and shoulders were covered in blood. Ella ran to them.

"They hit him," said Sampson, his eyes unfocused. "Hit Soak, hit Soak on the head," he babbled. "Two guns. They said they wanted to shoot me. I shoulda done something. Soak's hurt, oh, Soak's hurt real bad, real bad."

Mike shouted, "Call for medivac!"

"Roger, call for medivac," said LaMancha. "Calling."

Ella put a hand on Sampson's arm. "Don't put him down. Let me see."

Sherri snatched towels off the bar. "Out of the way. We know brain injuries. Where's your medical supplies?"

"*Ajax's* AutoDoc is operable for emergencies," Mike said. "Across from LaMancha's tank. Drawers are stocked."

"Communications are jammed, said LaMancha, frustration evident in his voice. "I cannot reach medical assistance."

"The hell?"

Ella wiped some blood. "Quick. AutoDoc. LaMancha, open office p-door, deploy AutoDoc table."

Sampson, carrying Soak as gently as he could, hurried to the office, followed by the two ladies. Mike stayed in the dining room. The p-door shut, blocking his view. It was just as well. There was nothing he could do around the AutoDoc, and Soak's head was not pretty.

"Two carts with Tevil security officers are at the gangway," reported LaMancha.

Mike looked up to Eris, who was seated at a top tier table, leaning back, with her eyes closed.

"Why would the Union want to hurt Soak?" said Mike to the air. "He's harmless. Why?"

Eris's shoulders slumped. "I'm sorry, Mike. It's bad, Soak getting hurt."

Mike collapsed into a chair near the office p-door. "Dammit."

Four corppers walked through the entrance. They all held projectors. A lieutenant led. "There's a report of a disturbance on the premises." The security officer strode rapidly into the room towards Mike. "You Mike?"

"I'm Mike." He stood.

"YOU! STOP! RESISTING ARREST!" The Lieutenant pointed and fired.

Mike was hit with 50,000 volts. Every muscle quivered out of control. He collapsed on to the deck. His mind blanked to white.

Slowly his brain began to clear.

"Hey, Lieutenant," a voice said. "He wasn't—"

"Shuddup. Freeze 'im," the lieutenant said.

Mike felt the sting of an injector gun on his neck. Everything went numb. Nothing functioned. His eyes were open, he could see and think and hear, but he could not move.

A hand reached down and rotated Mike's head to point to the overhead. A face appeared in his field of view. "Don't worry, Mike. It wears off in an hour. Coupla minutes, you'll be able to blink. Keep your eyes closed, it's best, don't let them dry out." The head disappeared.

All Mike could see was the ceiling. He could listen to the voices.

"Who are you? What're you doing here?"

"Eris. I work here."

"This place doesn't have registered workers."

Loudly and clearly, Eris spoke as if reciting dialog from a play. "The owner is paying me under the table. I don't have a work permit. He is evading Tevil corporate labor regulations and Union requirements."

"Cuff her. Get her out of here."

Mike could not believe what he heard.

"Bust those cameras."

Crashing sounds.

Eris, hands behind her back, passed in Mike's field of view. She whispered, "I was set up. I help them, or twenty years."

Oh, Eris, what have you done.

"Hey Lieutenant. Found the pistol."

Pistol? Oh, yeah, the pistol, from that union thug. Bottom drawer. He'd forgotten.

"Put it in the criminal's hand."

"Sir?"

"Just do it."

"Now what? It's not like he can grip it."

"Keep your gloves on. None of your fingerprints on it. Give it to me."

There was a short pause.

"All right, it's loaded. Here. You know how to use a pistol? Shoot out all the p-door electronics panels. Careful, no ricochets."

"You sure? Doors will short out. We won't be able to open them."

"Do it."

Three gunshots. The office p-door, the Wagering Association p-door, and the p-door to the command deck. Good. They can't get through to Ella and Sherri. Ella and Sherri are safe.

All Mike could see was the ceiling. It had some small discolored spots. Some vaporized cooking oil rising from the grill had condensed on the ceiling panels. Little bubbles of discolor. He'd have to get that cleaned.

Another gunshot. What? The only door left was the cargo door to the outside. He'd locked it when he did the original remodeling. Why shoot it out? It was labeled 'out of commission.' It wasn't an airlock. It couldn't open with the restaurant pressurized and vak on the other side.

"Over here. This guy."

Mike was lifted and placed on a gurney. His head flopped to the side.

High up, on the memorabilia wall, was a framed certificate and a prominent picture of Steinem kissing a monkey. How did that get there?

"All right, everyone. This place is a staging warehouse for smuggling. Since the criminals have disabled the p-doors with their illegal firearm, we'll have to use breaching charges. There, there, there. And there."

"Lieutenant? Blow that one, the whole place goes to vak."

Mike's brain screamed, NO! He tried to shout, to yell, Sherri and Ella were behind the office door. They didn't have skinsuits!

He couldn't move.

"Orders. Every door gets blown. Just do it."

NO! LaMancha! LaMancha's tank wasn't sealed for vak! His tank was next to the p-door, the explosives would—

Mike saw the bulkhead move. No, he was moving. He was being wheeled out on the gurney, down the gangway ramp, then up under the dome.

He could blink, moisten his dried eyes. His eyes burned.

NO! STOP! LISTEN TO ME! He couldn't make a sound.

Under the dome, his gurney was lifted onto a transport cart. Mike could hear reports from its radio.

"All right, charges set. You ready?"

"Entrance p-doors are secured. Dome is safe, triple airlock and p-door protection. Blow 'em."

Mike heard the 'whump' of four charges, then the fading hurricane as the atmosphere rushed out of *Ajax*, accompanied by a cacophony of crashes and thumps. There were smaller explosions, probably liquor bottles sucked to the deck. LaMancha's tank bursting.

Ella. Sherri. LaMancha. Sampson was in his skinsuit, but Soak, with his head injury?

There goes the Lacrosse Shot.

Oh, God. Ella. Sweet Ella. Sherri and Ella weren't wearing skinsuits.

Mike heard a suit-to-suit radio crackle. "Entering now." He tried to concentrate on the radio, pick out the transmissions from background noise.

"I'm in the main space. Ah, hell. This place is a mess. Yuck. I've seen blowouts before, but this is the worst. Food and beer all over."

"Lieutenant, waddya want with the Limp Loser? Precinct?"

"Central booking. They want him downtown."

"Crap, this whole p-door frame is down. Somebody oversized those breaching charges."

"All right, let's get this criminal put away. Jimmy, you drive."

"Did you know there was an Organic in here? Shee-it. Tank smashed. Gray goosh all over. I'm stepping in it. Gross."

The motor cart lurched. Mike could smell the ozone from its electric motor.

"Hey!" The radio crackled again. "You said nobody was in here!"

The electric motor whined. The cart was moving.

"Ah, *shit*, who said nobody was in here? Oh, man, oh man, bodies, I got bodies here! They're dead. Sheee-it, their eyeballs exploded."

The sounds of the radio transmissions faded, swallowed by distance and roadway noise.

"Get some stretchers in here. I'm gunna need a lot o..."

As he blinked, tears helped moisten Mike's eyes.

105: *Diana*

The cold shower felt good, but shivery. This was the first time she had indulged in a walk through a rain locker, for she-didn't-remember how long. Too long. Thank goodness, skinsuits obscured body odor. Every pence had to be saved, to fund the future search for her errant hubby.

When she found him, oh, was she going to lay into him! He was supposed to eject. She was supposed to pick him up. They had it planned. Why? Why didn't he do what he was supposed to do! Couldn't the idjit follow instructions? Where was he?

Probably on third base, trying to get home.

She was glad she was in the shower. The tears didn't show.

She stopped the water, stepped out, and toweled down. The half-hour process of donning her skinsuit distracted her from despondent thoughts.

The 'high priority text' light was flashing on her FoxxFone. She hit 'retrieve messages.' A file page was displayed.

From: Headquarters, Federated Space Forces Command

To: Citizen Spacer Diana NMN Covington

Subject: Citizen Captain Tarak NMN NFN

1. We regret to inform you that, in the course of ~~routine patrol~~ science survey ~~cargo transportation~~ by FSF *Gangut* (CL1-4), the _corpse_ of your legally registered _husband,_ Captain Tarak NMN NFN, was discovered.

2. The cause of death was _undeterminate._

3. There was no traceable evidence regarding the source of the _undeterminate._

4. In view of the ~~evidence~~ lack of evidence, ~~additional~~ no further investigations will be undertaken.

5. Captain Tarak NMN NFN ~~did~~ did not have a registered burial preference. ~~Her~~ His ~~Its remains were~~ body was ~~bodies were~~ encased and released into the system's sun, _Star Catalog HD393403-a._

6. Further details can be obtained by an in-person visit to the Personnel Annex, FSF Headquarters, Federated Central. Please bring identification and a hard copy of the marriage contract.

7. This notification serves as certification of death for all legal and insurance purposes.

8. In accordance with the attached invoice of itemized services, remit

   _$t 99.95_ standards

   ~~payment for autopsy and burial amenities.~~

9. The Federated Government extends our sincere sympathy on ~~this sad occasion~~ your great loss.

For Admiral Mikawa

A.S. Rasputin, Command Ensign (FSF)

106: *Ghost*

Breakfast in the Sergeants' mess was a celebration of the lives of three children. Afterwards, Ghost and associates were escorted to their place of confinement, the Marine Corps Flag, Staff, and VIP quarters. Each of them was given a spacious suite usually reserved for colonels and above.

After ten hours of dreamless sleep, Ghost awoke. He walked to the Junior Command Officer's Mess. Most of the officers had already eaten and departed. He passed through the serving line, received a plate of food not up to Culinary Chief Jones' standards, and sat down alone. The few Command officers finishing their meals glanced at him often. Without doubt, he was their topic of conversation.

The Artisan Officers' Mess would have been a more comfortable venue. Perhaps he could get an invitation from Artisan Lieutenant Padmere. Or, maybe he would find a Vakker pub, if they would withdraw Captain Bendan's confinement order.

His clipscreen vibrated. A text. He was required at a meeting tomorrow morning early, time and location TBD, uniform Service Dress Class 2. Nothing he could do about the uniform. He only had his skinsuit.

At 0500 the next morning, a text ordered him to report to Conference Room 102, Spin Section; 0930.

When he stepped into the conference room, Artisan Lieutenant Padmere was already there, sitting silently with a Command Ensign.

"Command Candidate Three Coast? Sit," the ensign said, pointing.

Ghost saluted and sat next to the lieutenant. He looked at Padmere, who shrugged.

"I am directed," said the ensign, "to inform you of the charges against you."

"Charges? We are being *charged?*" said Padmere, half rising.

"Are you our JAG?" asked Ghost.

"No. You may contract for a civilian legal representative before the trial begins. That representative must be qualified in the jurisdiction of the court. There are no qualified civilian advocates on Station Three."

"The proceedings will be delayed until we can obtain legal representation?" asked Lieutenant Padmere.

"The charges against you are civil charges. The FSF will remain aloof of participation, and will prejudice the case neither for nor against the parties involved. You will be arraigned in civil court. Your actions involving Newton Station, a civilian facility, were NLD, Not in the Line of Duty. For civil NLD cases, the FSF has no obligation to provide you counsel or legal assistance."

Padmere leaned forward. "How could it be NLD? We were on an official flight."

"The NLD determination was made by the Officer Commanding, Station Three and Environs. Command Captain Bendan. You disobeyed his orders, and in doing so made your subsequent actions your own responsibility. Thus, NLD."

Padmere slumped back into his chair.

"Command Captain Bendan is being generous," said the Command Ensign. "He could have required you to pay for the damage you inflicted to Shuttle 401. Be grateful."

Artisan Lieutenant Padmere stared at the Command Ensign with his mouth open.

The Ensign glowered as if he were a prophet judging the sins of the Israelites. "There were many possible charges. They were condensed into two." The ensign looked at a document. "Manslaughter."

"What!" shouted Padmere. "Who did we kill?"

The ensign read the charge with the surety of one who knows the verdict is etched in metal. "Through your dilatory and incompetent piloting, and refusal to accept orders from superiors, you removed the Primate Lab from contact with Newton Station, thereby delaying treatment for Citizen Supervisor Mulligan, resulting or contributing to his death."

"He died before we freed the compartment," said Padmere. "How can we be responsible—"

"This one's fun," said the Ensign. "Theft."

"Theft," marveled Padmere. "How could we—what did we steal?"

"Theft," the Ensign continued, "of the Primates Laboratory, and one hundred thirty-two experimental subjects, of an approximate value of a quarter of a billion standards."

The Ensign stood, and smiled. "Details are in the documents, there." He waved vaguely at the papers on the table. "Judge Ruhyollah's shuttle is on final. The trial will begin when he's ready. Thirty minutes, I'd guess."

"Thirty minutes!" blurted Padmere. "This is—Where is our legal counsel? Do we have any rights to see the prosecution's case before the trial, and to confront our accusers? What about a jury?"

The Ensign shrugged. "I'm not JAG, I'm a Station Three logistician. This is a civil case, under civil jurisdiction. Their rules are different. The FSF has waived a jury trial. The case will be decided by the judge."

"Who in the FSF waived our rights? How?"

"The local commander defines the terms when FSF personnel are tried for civil offenses."

Padmere slumped back in his chair. "The local commander. Command Captain Bendan."

The Ensign smiled. "Hand over your clipscreens. They're evidence."

"I wish to send some messages first," said Padmere.

"I was told you might want that. Give me any messages, in writing, on paper. They will go in the outgoing communications queue."

"What queue?" asked Ghost.

"Since the incident, communications have been overloaded. Low-priority messages are queued until the backlog is eliminated. Your messages will get out in 48 hours, possibly 72."

With their clipscreens in hand, the Ensign opened the door. "You are under confinement orders. This door will be locked." He smirked. "Have a marvelous day!" He pulled the door shut. The bolt clicked.

Padmere took a deep breath. He looked over to Ghost. "In many concepts of human existence there is something called 'predestination.' All things have been decided in advance. All is inevitable." He licked his lips. "This trial is predestined. There is no hope."

"We are just handed over to this civilian court?"

Padmere scooped up the papers and began to page through them. "The party bringing charges is Brin Pharmaceuticals," he read, "the majority partner invested in the Primates Lab. There is a long list of other investors, but Brin Pharma has control."

"Brin?" asked Ghost. "As in, ComCan Three Brin?"

"Yes."

"Papa is charging the son?"

Padmere flipped through more pages. "We're the only ones charged. According to this, the other ComCans were only following our orders, and are disassociated from all blame." Padmere closed his eyes. "Royals protect their own, and the unscrubs are thrown into the volcano."

Both men were quiet. Then, Padmere pushed back from the table.

"I see our story, and our fate," said Padmere. "Command Captain Bendan has gone to Brin the pater, telling him he needs to charge us to save his boy from censure for not participating in the rescue. Brin Pharma has filed the charges, and whistled up a corrupt judge. Ruhyollah is infamous, he is an assassin for sale to the Corporations. We will be found guilty, then handed back to Bendan for the penalty phase, since civil courts cannot impose sentences on FSF personnel. Bendan will award the maximum sentence, and send us to the penal asteroid. We will be off this station in chains inside two hours. Our appeal is delayed by Bendan's 72 hour hold on message traffic. Once we are out of the jurisdiction under which the trial was held, Federated Central civil jurisdiction, we must make a formal appeal through both civilian and JAG channels from the penal asteroid."

"How long for an appeal?" asked Ghost.

"Years. Three?"

"Brin Pharmaceuticals," mused Ghost. "Would a son of the 35 have a financial interest in Papa's companies?"

"Yes, most certainly. A direct percentage, or stock, or a trust fund."

"B-for-Bastard Brin uses drugs, and *we* get charged." Ghost straightened up, and pulled out his skinsuit auxiliary clipscreen. "We're not going to a penal colony," said Ghost flatly. "You go through those papers. I need to research the legal system."

"How can you do that?"

"My skinsuit is non-standard. Is there a communications transcript in that pile?"

Padmere slumped in his chair. "Whatever." He pushed the pile towards Ghost. "I am not one to deny fate," he said, with a glassy expression. "We are just tiny motes in a kaleidoscope of motes, our destiny inconsequential."

"In that case, Artisan Lieutenant," said Ghost, "may I take the lead?"

With a graceful wave of his hand, Padmere passed control to Ghost.

107: *Ghost*

The conference room door opened with a bang, revealing two Marines in combat dress, armed, with helmets retracted.

"Artisan Lieutenant Padmere, Command Candidate Three Coast, we're your escort to the Conference Room." The Marine's tone was almost apologetic.

Padmere rose and walked out, leaving the papers scattered on the table. Ghost gathered them up and followed.

One Marine took the lead while the other followed behind Ghost. Ghost recognized them both, from the dinner in the Sergeants' Mess.

"ComCan Coast," whispered the Marine behind him. "Scuttlebutt says the trial is fixed."

Ghost nodded.

"Leathernecks are standing by," the Marine said quietly. "They'll make a diversion, pull an alarm or something, and we get you lost in the Station. Be ready to move."

Ghost stopped, and turned to face the Marine. "Get the word out. No actions, no diversions. Nobody does anything. Bendan would take any excuse to bust the entire Marine detachment."

"We knew you'd say that. We got three Marine Juniors who make us believe otherwise. Be ready."

Ghost put a hand on the Marine's arm. "Get ComCan Brin. Don't let him off the station."

"Can do, sir." The Marine began to talk into his communicator.

Padmere and Ghost walked into the ornate Command Conference Room. It was twenty-five feet long, featuring an expansive polished nickel-iron table surrounded by elegant chairs, with lessor-status seats lining the walls. Large digital screens were mounted on three walls.

The Ensign who had delivered the charges was seated in the back. He got up, walked to them, and pointed. "You two sit there, up front."

Padmere drew himself up. "Ensign, a salute?"

The Ensign smiled. "A Command officer saluting an Artisan who is about to be thrown out of my Force? I don't think so." He turned his back on Padmere and walked to a seat in the observers' rows.

Padmere sat closest to the throne-like chair at the head of the table, with Ghost the next one over. The seats were soft and comfortable.

The door opened. Captain Bendan entered, followed by three Command Lieutenants and a Command Ensign. Ghost and Padmere rose and saluted. Bendan ignored them. He went to the back of the room.

Ghost said, "Captain Bendan. As this is a civil trial, may I inquire as to your place in the proceedings?"

Bendan smiled. "I represent the FSF, to ensure a fair hearing."

Padmere laughed. Bendan glowered at him. "Insubordinate shit."

The door opened and a civilian, short, blond hair pulled back in a pony tail and a cute pug nose, wearing a blue tunic over a skinsuit, came in. She carried a box and duffle bag. "Hello 'allo, this the hanging?" She smiled, looking about for appreciation. There was none. "Sorry 'bout that; judicial humor, don't ya know. Got a 230-volt single phase power outlet?"

"Who are you?" spit out Captain Bendan.

"Court Recorder. The judge is getting into his robes."

The Court Recorder extracted some equipment from her box, spotted a wall outlet, read the placard, plugged in and started to initialize her gear.

Another man walked in, clad in an expensive blue business suit and carrying a well-worn valise. His fashionable haircut was mashed down, marring an impeccable blond coiffure.

"Is this the trial?" he asked the air.

The Court Recorder nodded. "Yup. Grab a pew."

"I represent Brin Pharmaceuticals, controlling owner of the Newton Science Station Primates Laboratory," he announced to the room, with an air of confidence and the assumption that his assignment was approved by God, personally. "Who is counsel for the defense?"

"The FSF will not provide counsel," said the Ensign from the back.

"Indeed?" The lawyer smiled. "This shouldn't take long, then." He ignored Padmere and Ghost, sat down, and began pulling papers out of his case.

"Roger-dodger," announced the Court Recorder. She placed a black box, about four inches square, at the head of the table. "Everyone, we have to calibrate. Would each of you look at the receiver and say 'my name is,' state your real name, then say, 'My name is Booster Bob'. That's for a representative sample."

Ghost cocked his head and stared at the lady. The Court Recorder looked at him, and winked.

"Like this: my name is Jasonette the Court Recorder. My name is Booster Bob."

Padmere and Ghost said the required sentences. The lawyer said, "My name is Corporate Lawyer Cochran. My name is Booster Bob."

The Court Recorder looked to the back of the room. "Do any of you have a role in this trial? If there is a possibility you will speak, I must get a level. Without registration, you will not be allowed to speak."

Bendan stood and muttered, "This is ridiculous," followed by, "My name is Command Captain Nikita Bendan. My name is Booster Bob."

One of his group snickered.

The Captain glared at his coterie. One by one they stood and complied with the Court Recorder's request. The Court Recorder pressed a few buttons on the box, nodded approval, then sat in a chair against the wall closest to her equipment.

The door swung open. A short, round, leprechaun of a man strode rapidly into the room, black judicial robes flapping in his wake, gray barrister's wig askew atop red hair, a sheaf of papers clutched in his left hand and a large duffle over his right arm. He saw the court recorder. "What ho, Jasonette!"

The Court Recorder stood. She intoned in a lyric soprano, "All rise. Oyez, oyez—"

The judge plopped his papers on the table. "Oh, *please*, hold the oyezes, I've a headache as it is. Those shuttles are getting worse every year. Sit everyone, sit."

Padmere whispered to Ghost, "This does not look like—"

"I am Judge Murphy. I understand you were expecting someone taller, but Judge Ruhyollah was called to testify before a Senate committee. Jasonette, are you initiated and calibrated or plugged in or whatever it is you do so mysteriously?"

"Yes, Judge."

"Very well. I see Corporate Lawyer Cochran is here for the complainant. I have read the transcript of the incident and the statements of facts. As the defendants have chosen to waive a jury trial and have dispensed with a defense counsel—"

Ghost stood.

The judge raised an eyebrow. "Yes, young man? You are one of the accused?"

"Sir," said Ghost, "Command Candidate Three Coast. We did not waive a jury trial, and were given no opportunity to obtain legal assistance."

"No?" said the judge, elevating the other eyebrow. "I seem to have seen a document…" The judge started shuffling through his papers.

Rising to his feet, from the back of the room Captain Bendan said, "Your Honor. Where jurisdiction is transferred from the Federated Space Forces to civil authorities, the local commander defines the terms of the transfer."

"The local commander would be?" asked the judge.

"I am, your Honor. Command Captain Bendan. I command Station Three and Environs, and represent Federated Forces authority."

"Your Honor," interjected Ghost, "Command Captain Bendan is involved in this case as a principle. He is under Title Ten charges—"

"Objection, Your Honor! Irrelevant," called out Cochran.

The judge gave the attorney an exasperated look. "I need to hear what he has to say before I can judge if it is irrelevant, Derr Cochran. Continue, young man."

"Sir. Captain Bendan interfered with our efforts after we assumed responsibilities as Command. Under Title Ten Twenty-Eight, he committed a felony. Subsequently, he has done everything to restrict our abilities to defend ourselves. He did not allow us to communicate with anyone or send messages. Our clipscreens were confiscated. We were not allowed a defense attorney or to consult with the office of the Judge Advocate General."

Bolting to his feet, Captain Bendan ejaculated, "No! Absolutely false. None of that is true. We provided an opportunity for them to send messages, but they did not submit any."

"Your Honor," began Ghost, "that is—"

Judge Murphy held up a hand. He glanced at the court recorder, then looked thoughtfully towards the recorder box in front of him, and tapped the table with a fingernail. "I will rule on this later."

"Your Honor," said Ghost, "considering the conflict of interest of Captain Bendan, all evidence provided by his subordinates should be considered as from a hostile witness."

"Outrageous!" shouted Captain Bendan.

"Objection," called Cochran. "Unsubstantiated."

"Quiet!" The judge looked down into his bag. "Floggin' Francis on the Fire, where in Eire did I put my—"

The Court Recorder stood, holding an oblong box. "Your Honor, I happen to have a new gavel."

Judge Murphy held out a hand. "Gimmie."

Holding it out, Jasonette said, "You Honor, it did cost…"

The judge snatched the box. "Yes, I know, four stans fifty. That's what, eighteen standards this month? Why don't you open an outlet? You're making a living off me."

"Your Honor, I would not want your courtroom presence handicapped by lack of a gavel."

Judge Murphy carefully opened the box, pulled out its contents and extracted a beautiful ebony gavel from its wrapping tissue. He gripped it, gave an experimental wave, and banged it vigorously on the table.

"Everybody, quiet!" he ordered the quiet room.

Pointing the gavel, he looked Ghost in the eyes. "I don't need some sprout telling me if somebody is hostile or not, I can figure things out for myself." He glared. "This is a bench trial. There is no jury. I make the decision. I have read the case. I have questions, and then I can rule and get back on that cursed shuttle and get home for my bridge night. So, everybody stay quiet and let me get through this."

Lieutenant Padmere blinked a few times, and looked at Ghost. "Doomed," he silently mouthed.

Finding the right paper, the judge read. "Right. The first charge is manslaughter. The charge alleges the victim died because incompetent piloting by the defendants delayed getting care to the victim, which resulted in his death."

Ghost stood. The judge sighed. "Yes," he squinted, reading the name tag on Ghost's skinsuit, "Coast. What do you want to say."

"Derr Judge. Two points. First, I was the pilot. Artisan Lieutenant Padmere should not be included in this charge."

"Denied. Padmere was in command. I know enough about the FSF to know that he bears a share of responsibility. Second point?"

"Sir. The death occurred before we freed the laboratory. We cannot be responsible."

The judge shuffled through the papers. "The victim was formally declared deceased by medical personnel on Station Three, nine minutes after arrival. Motion denied."

Ghost sat. Padmere offered a wry smile. Padmere whispered, "Why bother?"

"All right," said the judge, "evidence of incompetence is alleged by one Command Ensign, ah," he consulted his papers, "Clarke Griswold. Is Command Ensign Griswold available for testimony?"

One of Bendan's coterie stood. "Here, Derr."

"Good, good, come forward, sit down next to Corporate Advocate Cochran, there." The young man came forward and sat. "State your case."

The Ensign, obviously well-rehearsed, held his head high. "Derr, your honor. Shuttle 401 was incompetently piloted. Instead of *pushing* the compartment into Cargo Bay Five, they should have used the shuttle on the other side of the compartment, to *brake*. If they had released the compartment at a higher velocity and positioned the shuttle to brake instead of push, they could have arrived at Station Three twelve point two three minutes sooner. The victim could have been treated, and likely saved."

The judge nodded.

Ghost stood.

The judge grimaced. "Yes," he squinted again at the nametag, "Coast."

"Your Honor, may I question Command Ensign Griswold?"

"Yes, yes, go ahead."

Ghost looked to the other side of the table. "Command Ensign Griswold, have you ever piloted a shuttle?"

The ensign glanced nervously back towards Captain Bendan. "I am a Command officer. Piloting is left to Artisans."

"How, then, did you determine that Shuttle 401's maneuver was wrong?"

The ensign smiled confidently. "I ran a simulation. I often run simulations of ground-to-orbit insertions." He pointed up to one of the wall screens with the air of one who has just successfully sprung a trap. "Here is the simulation of the proper maneuver to dock the laboratory." He whispered into his clipscreen.

The screen flashed, then showed the wheel of Newton Station on a black background. The Primate Laboratory separated. It aligned, went quickly across to Station Three, slowed, and nestled inside Bay Five.

"The simulation is time compressed," said Griswold. "The time log in the lower right corner shows arrival was twelve point two three minutes sooner." He pushed his chair back.

"Wait," said Ghost. "How did you maneuver the compartment?"

"I applied maneuvering factors associated with the thrust available from that class of shuttle."

"Where is the shuttle in that display?"

"It is abstracted by the maneuvering factors. It does not have to be displayed."

"What program did you use for the simulation?"

Captain Bendan stood. "Really, Your Honor, this is—"

The judge waved him silent. "Proceed," he said to Ghost.

"The program?" asked Ghost.

"Station Three Organic ran the simulation."

Ghost turned to the judge. "I would like to call Station Three

Organic to answer a question."

Popping to his feet, Cochran said wearily, "Objection, Your Honor. We all know Organics are not competent to testify in a trial."

"Station Three Organic is providing data as evidence," said Ghost. "I wish to clarify the data."

"Very well, proceed," said Murphy, with some exasperation, "but this will not serve you well if you are wasting our time."

Looking up at the simulation on the screen, Ghost said, "Station Three Organic, Coast, are you monitoring?"

An overhead speaker announced, "Coast, Station Three Organic. Monitoring."

"Station Three Organic, Coast. Re-run the simulation. Include a depiction of the shuttle. Include a depiction of thruster and engine exhaust associated with the maneuver, anything over 100 degrees Celsius over ambient."

The lawyer popped to his feet. "Your Honor, I object! The accused is not asking a question, he is attempting to manipulate the evidence."

With his eyes locked on the screen, Judge Murphy said, "I like simulations. I beat my daughter all the time in *Space Racer*. Let's see it."

A picture of Shuttle 401 appeared on the screen about half way to Station Three, with its nose pointed at Newton Station. Newton Station spun, and the compartment separated and quickly aligned in an attitude to fit into the cargo bay.

Shuttle 401 maneuvered in front of the compartment. The main engines fired; the exhaust plume was shown on the screen. The compartment slowed. The shuttle's main engine exhaust enveloped Station Three. The shuttle passed through the walls of Bay Five as if they did not exist. The compartment came to rest in the center of Bay Five, with the shuttle sticking out through the far wall.

"Your Honor," said Ghost, "the maneuver proposed by Command Ensign Griswold would have destroyed Bay Five."

Captain Bendan stood. He glared at the hapless ensign like Zeus on Mount Olympus preparing to launch a thunderbolt at an incompetent peasant. "Your Honor, that should not be considered conclusive. There are other, better maneuvers that should have been used."

Judge Murphy glanced down at the box on his desk, then shuffled some more of his papers. "I'll take that under advisement. Let's move to 'theft.' It's a bit less technical. Clear-cut, to us non-teckkies." He looked up at Ghost and Padmere. "Artisan Lieutenant Padmere, Command Candidate Coast, did you have permission to take the property of the Brin Corporation and seven other joint owners, valued to the amount of," he looked at his papers, and chuckled, "over a quarter of a billion standards?" He leaned back and locked his gaze on Ghost. "It appears gerbils are more valuable than humans these days, even more than the orangutang. Did you?"

"Your Honor," said, Coast, "a statement of permission was made."

"What!" cried out Captain Bendan. He jumped to his feet. "This is absurd!"

Ghost looked directly into the judge's eyes. "A statement of permission was made by a representative owner of the Brin Corporation. That permission has been removed from the communications transcript, as has other evidence."

"Lies!" shouted Captain Bendan. "He has been lying ever since he mutinied! He's a disgrace, and I won't have it!"

Judge Murphy slammed his gavel down on the table with the force of a pile driver. The crash resounded through the room. The head of the gavel broke off, bounced off the overhead, and rattled to the deck. Half rising from his chair, he said, "I will have order in my courtroom!" He pointed the jagged gavel handle at the Captain. "One more word during these proceedings and I will hold you in contempt. You will be fined and removed."

The judge settled back into his chair. He took a few breaths, then looked ruefully at the gavel's stub.

The Court Recorder reached into her bag, pulled out another oblong box, and put it on the edge of the table. She nudged it towards the judge. Judge Murphy murmured, "Four stans fifty," took it, and unwrapped the new gavel. He looked at Ghost. "A serious charge, concealing evidence. Can you support it?"

"May I call a witness? Command Candidate Three Brin."

Captain Bendan awakened one of his lieutenants with an elbow and a glare. The lieutenant stood. "Judge, as Command Candidates Brin, Ortega, Ka-Shing, and Roddy are not principles in these proceedings, they have departed on a shuttle back to Federated Central."

Ghost interrupted. "Station Three Organic, Coast. Report location of Command Candidate Brin."

"Young man, you are out of order!" said the judge. He banged the new gavel with satisfaction, and again for good measure.

"Coast, Station Three Organic. Command Candidate Brin is outside the Command Conference Room."

Jasonette walked to the door and opened it. Brin was outside, flanked by two Marines in full battle dress, each gripping an elbow.

Captain Bendan stood up, raised an arm, looked at the judge, and… sat down.

Judge Murphy looked at Brin, then at Ghost, then back to Brin, and again to Ghost. He sighed. "You might as well ask your questions."

A Marine dragged Brin into the room. With a nod the Marine departed, wearing a crooked smile.

"Command Candidate Brin," said Ghost, "you are a scion of the Brin family, majority owner of Brin Pharmaceuticals?"

Brin, displaying the look of a fish that has just swallowed a laxative, said, "Yes."

"Your father heads the corporation?"

"He owns Brin Corporation, which owns Brin Pharma."

"As a member of the family, do you have any direct ownership of Brin Corporation stock?"

"Over five thousand shares." That statement seemed to calm Brin.

"That makes you part owner of Brin Corporation?"

"I suppose. Yeah, I'm an owner."

"During the Newton Station Catastrophe, were you aware of any other owners within 100 kilometers of Newton Station?"

"No."

"That's all."

The Judge said, "Cochran, questions?"

The Corporate Lawyer opened his eyes and straightened in his chair. He suppressed a yawn. "No, your Honor."

The judge nodded. Brin squared his shoulders and departed.

As the door shut, Judge Murphy looked at Ghost. "Are you claiming that Command Candidate Brin gave you permission to take the Primate Laboratory to Station Three? There has to be more than a wink and a nod. I don't see any such permission in the transcript of your cockpit communications."

"Sir, the transcript has been edited. Maliciously edited."

Captain Bendan stood up, then sat.

Judge Murphy looked over to the Captain. "Captain Bendan? Is this true? Is this transcript," he pointed to the papers on his desk, "incomplete? Answer the question, I give permission for you to speak."

Bendan stood. "Shuttle 401 was severely damaged during this junior candidate's incompetent piloting. The cockpit voice recorder was damaged. Some parts were unreadable. We have provided what was recovered." With a smug look, Bendan sat.

Judge Murphy looked down at the court recorder's box and pursed his lips.

"Derr Judge," said Ghost, "I have a complete record of the incident. All communications."

There was a stirring from the back of the room.

Judge Murphy said, "Oh? How is this?"

"My skinsuit has non-standard features. I recorded all our communications during the catastrophe."

The lawyer bounced to his feet. "Your Honor! I object! Any such recording could be manipulated by the defendants. It has not been under neutral custody."

Judge Murphy waved him down. "I'll hold a decision on that. Young man, let's hear what you have."

"Your Honor, the first two voices are mine and Artisan Lieutenant Padmere. The question came from Command Candidate Ortega, who was assisting in the cockpit. The last voice is Command Candidate Brin, the only available representative of the owners of the Primate Laboratory within the catastrophe zone."

The judge nodded. "Proceed."

Ghost pulled a hardwire connection out of his suit's electronics pack and plugged it into the table's electronics. "Zoot, play clip one."

The speaker crackled.

"Command, Pilot. There is a catastrophe on Newton Station. The Primate Lab has survivors and requires assistance. I recommend we go to the assistance of the Primate Lab."

"Pilot, Command. Go to the assistance of the Primate Lab."

"Command, Pilot. Acknowledged, go to the assistance of the Primate Lab."

"Hey, Brin. Okay?"

"All yours. Take it away."

There was an immediate uproar from the back of the room. The judge banged his gavel vigorously. "Order! I say order!"

"You Honor," called out Ghost, as the noise settled, "another part was deleted."

The lawyer popped to his feet. The judge glared at him. He sat.

"Let's hear it," Murphy said.

"Zoot, play clip two."

The speaker again came to life.

"Command, Franklin. Whether we get through this or not, I want the record to show that I approve of the decisions made by the Command regarding the impending rescue of the people in the Primate Lab. I commend all personnel on your initiative. We wouldn't have a chance without all of you on Shuttle 401, Station Three, Newton Station. Well done. Everyone here is looking forward to arriving at Station Three. Franklin, out."

Judge Murphy, with a look of disgust, threw his gavel. It cleared the court recorder's box by inches, skittered down the long table, and disappeared off the far edge among the Command officers. "Captain Bendan? Am I to assume this declaration was cut from my transcript because it was also unreadable? Those transmissions identified in the transcript as coming from 'unknown voice' were Senator Franklin?"

"Your Honor, we had no confirmation of the source of those transmissions," said Bendan. "They might have been anyone. They could be voice manipulation by these two," he pointed to Ghost and Padmere, "to cover up their crimes."

"You seriously expect me to believe, as pressed as they were during their *successful* rescue, that these lads were doing *voice manipulation?*" said the judge. "I play bridge with Senator Franklin every month. I damn well ought to recognize his voice. I damn well ought to consider the opinion of one of the greatest leaders of the Federated Space Forces over yours, that is, *Admiral* Franklin's judgment, *Captain* Bendan."

Judge Murphy looked about the table. He held out his hand. The Court Recorder handed him another oblong box.

The judge unwrapped the new gavel and used it to tap the top of the box in front of him. "You might be curious about this little bit of teckkie. It is new, and not just a recorder. It can tell me if the speaker is telling the truth." He glanced at the court recorder, who smiled and nodded. "It's not 100 percent accurate, the boffins say 99 percent, so I am only allowed to use it on an advisory basis." His eyes locked on the Captain across the room. "This box advises me, Command Captain Bendan," he said, pointing his new gavel at the Captain, "there is a 99 percent probability that you are a vicious, conniving, sneaky backstabbing son-of-a-bitch who wouldn't own up to the truth if it was holding a laser to your head. These charges are a farce. I will pass that on as my legal opinion to Admiral Quoun at Station One, along with my legal opinion that he should pursue that Title Ten felony, formally charging you with impeding the rescue effort."

He looked over everyone in the room. "I hereby rule," the judge said firmly, "that Artisan Lieutenant Padmere and Command Candidate Three Coast are Not Guilty, that is, Not Guilty, of any and all charges that have been entered, or may be entered against them, associated with the Catastrophe at Newton Station. Release the defendants. Charges are dismissed, with prejudice. Case dismissed."

He banged the gavel, hard. The head of the gavel flew off, arced across the room, bounced off the overhead, and landed in Captain Bendan's lap.

108: Mike

The sleeping pad in Mike's cell was unyielding. He lay on his back, hands behind his head, eyes closed against the glare from the overhead light.

He might as well keep his eyes closed forever. He had no future.

No word. Nothing about Soak and Sampson. Ella dead, Sherri

dead, exposed to hard vak. LaMancha, gray goosh, in pieces over the office floor. Stepped on. The Lacrosse Shot destroyed. Ella, Sherri, LaMancha, dead, dead, dead.

He had never witnessed a decompression death. There were Vakker stories about people who lasted two minutes in horrible agony. The image of Ella dying haunted him during the nights isolated in this cell. Three nights— or was it four? —with no visitors, meals delivered and removed by a silent guard—he had nothing else to think about.

Yesterday he had stirred enough initiative to consider getting a lawyer. He didn't know any lawyers. Men use lawyers when handshakes couldn't be trusted. The only Vakker turned shyster he knew was so pissed at him he'd volunteer the ammunition for Mike's firing squad. Maybe Bookie could find someone willing to take his case.

He asked a guard if he could make a call. The guard led him to a pay phone. He pointed. "Here you go. Coins in the slot there, or your CID."

"You guys have my stuff. You emptied my pockets before that paralysis crap wore off."

"Hellfire, man, you want a free call? You expect us to pick up expenses of a criminal? I offered you a call. Not my fault you can't pay the freight."

He tried manually entering his CID number. The phone said, "This account is no longer active."

It really didn't make any difference. There wasn't anything to care about anymore.

He blinked. The ceiling was too bright, too white. He closed his eyes. The world had ended, and where Tevil was going to send him, he would have to look up to see the bottom of Hell.

The door rattled and swung open. Two corppers. "On your feet. Arraignment."

Mike swung his feet to the floor. "Can I wash my face first?"

"Move your mass. Marx don't take kindly to waiting."

With a guard ahead and behind, Mike was escorted through a warren of green-painted corridors. The guard behind him started talking. "When you get to the courtroom, sit behind the closest table. No talking with spectators. Some brain-dead Carabinieri let them in a couple of hours ago, dammit. No inciting the crowd."

Crowd?

"Keep your mouth shut and your hands to yourself. Judge comes in, stand. You don't have a mietmaul, so you answer the judge's questions yourself. Stay respectful, or I haul you back to your cell and we try your ass in absentia."

They came to a door. The guard opened it, and shoved him through.

Mike stepped into the courtroom.

And the crowd roared.

There was a shoulder-to-shoulder jam of people in the spectators' section of the courtroom, all standing and cheering Mike's appearance. Fists were raised high, people were waving bar towels, jerkins, shirts removed from skinsuits. Bloggers in the front row leaned out with their cameras, recording his entrance.

"MIKE! MIKE! MIKE! MIKE! MIKE!"

The court recorder turned the volume of his speakers up to maximum. "Oyez, Oyez, Oyez, all persons having business before the Honorable Justice, Judge Vladimir Marx, a stalwart of integrity—" The announcement was swamped by the noise from the crowd.

Judge Marx entered and ascended the dais. He surveyed the crowd. The cheers shifted to boos. He had to shout. "Bailiff! Clear the courtroom!"

The Bailiff looked at the crowd, weighed his chances, and called out, "Seats!"

The volume abated slightly.

"Seats! PLEASE!"

The din stopped. There was a rustle and murmurs of "Excuse me" as the crowd settled into their seats.

The Bailiff wore the same expression as the missionary who converted the cannibals into Jehovah Witnesses just before he was to become the main course. "Your Honor, order has been restored."

"Yes, well…" Marx banged his gavel.

A voice called out, "We're with ya, Mike!"

Marx banged his gavel three times, vigorously. "Any further disruptions and I *will* clear the courtroom! I'll call out a company of Carabinieri!"

The silence was disturbed only by the inevitable coughing. Mike looked over the throng, making eye contact with Vakkers who had supported him over the months by patronizing the Lacrosse Shot, who helped him back from the edge of bankruptcy. He saw members of the AISOO. Steinem, TaxiGal, Diana and ScrewLoose were sitting together and discretely waving to him. Churchill and Aaron gave him a smile, Shengwu met his glimpse with dignity. Bookie flourished a 'thumbs up' and a grin.

Marx's glare assaulted the audience. "Bailiff, call the case."

"You Honor, arraignment C-229, Tevil Corporation versus Citizen Captain Mike. Who stands for the prosecution?"

A slickly-dressed lawyer stood behind the prosecution's table. "Corporate Advocate Arnold, Office of the Planetary Attorney."

"Who stands for the defense?"

Mike looked at the empty chair next to him.

Judge Marx said to the bailiff, "Call the accuser."

Corporate Advocate Arnold stood and said, "Tevil Corporation calls Corporate Lieutenant Capone."

The lieutenant who led the assault on the Lacrosse Shot came out a side door, stepped up to the witness chair, and was sworn in.

"Corporate Lieutenant, relate the events that led you to file against the accused," said Arnold.

Capone consulted his clipscreen. "On Thursday last, 2342 hours, Central Public Safety received an anonymous call reporting a violent altercation in progress between criminals involved in electronics smuggling in the Lacrosse Shot restaurant. We responded immediately, I arrived at the entrance at 2356." He looked up, as if to gauge if he had the audience's attention. "I then heard shots, that is, the discharge of a firearm, from within the restaurant. As firearms are a violation of Dome City regulations, I had probable cause to enter the restaurant to investigate. I discovered the defendant, Citizen Captain Mike, in possession of a firearm. After a warning he was taken into custody."

There was a rumble from the crowd. "Mike wouldn't do that!" "Frame-up! Frame-up!" The voices were suppressed by a blow of Judge Marx's gavel.

"Citizen Captain Mike had used his firearm to disable access to other portions of the facility. Surveillance cameras were also destroyed. I concluded the cameras were broken so Citizen Captain Mike's resistance would not be recorded. I believed he was attempting to delay us so his smuggling confederates could remove cargo in an effort to avoid lawful customs duties. This proved to be correct, as our search later discovered ten cases of silicon-lithium power chips, valued at 60,000 standards, with a forty percent duty owed. Felony smuggling." He looked back to his clipscreen. "The accused did not inform us of anyone occupying outlying spaces, so we employed breaching charges—"

The door in the back of the courtroom flew open with a resounding crash. Mike turned, as did everyone in the audience. In marched one of the smallest adult humans who ever wore a skinsuit covered by a black silk barrister's robe. He was followed by a broad-shouldered man carrying a valise. The two made a parade down to the railing separating the audience from the judges' arena.

"May it please the court, I apologize for my late arrival. I am counsel for the accused."

Judge Marx's expression was sour. "Citizen Advocate Mauz. The court does not have—"

Mauz pulled out an over-sized clipscreen and hit an icon. "You Honor, I now forward to the court the required declarations. May I have a moment with my client while you review the representation?"

Marx grunted.

Taking that for assent, Mauz and his associate passed through the swinging gate in the railing and stepped to Mike's table.

"Mighty? What are you doing here?" asked Mike.

Mauz looked to him sourly, then gestured to his assistant. "Derr Lurch, my good man, here." He patted the empty chair. The huge assistant popped open the briefcase, extracted papers, placed them on the table, and pulled out a small cube. With the press of a button the cube inflated into a booster seat. Mauz deftly jumped up and sat.

"Mighty?"

Mauz's response was testy. "Citizen Captain Chemistry, you son of a bitch."

"What? I haven't seen you since, what, since *Regina*, three years ago?"

"Sulfasalazine."

"What the hell is—"

"*Regina.* Sulfasalazine. You spiked my oatmeal with sulfasalazine. I needn't remind you that the version of sulfasalazine issued by an AutoDoc is neutralized, it is odorless, colorless, tasteless, only it turns the urine bright orange. Your comedy team re-programmed the AutoDoc to say the orange urine was caused by a sexually transmitted disease, and did the same to Amazon. Ha ha, very funny, four foot six making whoopee with six foot four, and suddenly I'm callsign 'Mighty'."

With his hands up in defense, Mike eloquently spluttered, "Hey!"

"Illnesses are entered in the ship's log. I was publicly and permanently humiliated." He paused, glared at him and said, "AutoDoc had prescribed sulfasalazine to you the day before. Double dose."

"Come on, Mighty. I've never taken sulfasalazine, neutralized or not. You think somebody who can reprogram an AutoDoc to give a hacked diagnosis might also reprogram who got issued the drug?"

Mauz looked at him with his head cocked to the side. "I'm listening."

Mike shrugged. "Maybe you ought to check into *Regina's* Zeros & Ones Gang. Every Vakker in this universe knows that gag was one of Filbert's Follies. Ask around." He made a dismissive gesture. "Don't bother. If I owe you for that, I'm going to owe you a lot more if you represent me. I've heard you're the most expensive counselor since Pharaoh sued the contractors when his pyramid collapsed."

"You get what you pay for, you pay for what you get."

Mike leaned back in his chair; his shoulders slumped. "Tevil confiscated my last standard. I can't pay you. See you in fifty years to life."

"I have been engaged to represent you by Derr Panza. I received my retainer yesterday."

Mike sat up. "Who's ... I don't know any Panza. If you were retained yesterday, why didn't you contact me? Why were you late?"

"I wanted to get their accusations on the record. I also had some papers to chase. I will now proceed to tear them a new asshole. This won't take long."

"Good. I hear you bill by the second."

The Court Recorder called out, "The court acknowledges Citizen Advocate Mauz representing Citizen Captain Mike."

Acerbically, Judge Marx asked, "May we now be allowed to proceed, counselor?"

Mauz slid down off his chair and walked towards the dais. "Your Honor, thank you for your accommodation. Before we continue with Corporate Lieutenant Capone's accusations, however, he has yet to establish his credentials. May I?"

Marx looked alert, and a bit nervous. "Proceed."

Mauz walked next to the witness stand. "Corporate Lieutenant Capone. What is your job?"

"I am head of Security and Law Enforcement for First Precinct, Dome City."

"You are an employee of Tevil Corporation?"

"Yes."

"Whose law do you enforce?"

The lieutenant cocked his head and blinked. "I'm not sure I understand your question."

Mauz smiled wickedly. "Let me try again. As an employee of Tevil, your authority is established under the Grant of Planetary Monopoly issued to Tevil Corporation, correct?"

"I suppose."

"That grant establishes the extent of Tevil's legal authority, correct?"

"Yes."

"Tevil's authority, thus your authority, is limited. Areas outside of Tevil's authority are under Federated or Admiralty jurisdiction. For instance, outlying independent mines, such as those at Flatplain, are under Federated law. Is this your understanding?"

Capone squirmed in his chair. "The Feds have law enforcement at Flatplain."

"When I consult Tevil's Grant," Mauz walked over to the table and picked up a thick sheaf of papers, "it tells me that Tevil's authority encompasses permanent orbital structures over 12 gross registered tons, the Lynnium Exotica-179a mining deposit, and..." he paused dramatically "...to within and directly under the confines of Dome City. I checked the Admiralty register. *Ajax* is registered as an active spaceship, a fact that this court has acknowledged when they identify the accused as Citizen *Captain* Mike. Tell me, Lieutenant, is the spaceship *Ajax*, within which is the enterprise known as The Lacrosse Shot, within the boundaries of Dome City?"

The audience roared.

"Order! Silence!" shouted Judge Marx. "Order in the courtroom! Order, or I will clear the court!"

The volume quickly came down, but the atmosphere in the room was now joyous.

Mauz looked up to Marx on his dais, and waved his papers. "Your Honor, spaceship *Ajax* lies outside the boundaries of the authority of Tevil Corporation, and thus outside Corporate Lieutenant Capone's jurisdiction. The landing field, upon which *Ajax* sits, is under Admiralty law. There are no Admiralty laws against possessing a firearm, or discharging it within the confines of an individual's property. Corporate Lieutenant Capone's forced entry into the Lacrosse Shot was unjustified and illegal. In addition, goods are not required to pay duty until they pass the customs boundaries of Dome City, so his search for supposed smuggled goods, and his confiscation of ten cases of chips, was unjustified, illegal, and constitutes theft."

A voice called, "Go get 'em, Mighty Mauz!" Marx banged his gavel and pointed. The overenthusiastic Vakker grinned back.

Mighty picked up his clipscreen and began hitting buttons. "Your Honor. I send to the court several documents. Document One is an injunction issued by the Board of Admiralty Law calling upon Tevil Corporation to drop all charges against my client, and to cease and desist in attempting to apply Corporate authority within Admiralty jurisdiction."

He hit another button. "My second document is a warrant, issued by the Admiralty, calling for the Carabinieri to arrest Corporate Lieutenant Capone and three other unnamed persons who participated in the illegal arrest of my client, on charges of assault, malicious damage of personal property, and manslaughter. In fact, it was Corporate Lieutenant Capone and his confederates that discharged the firearm, broke the cameras, and used oversized breaching charges that resulted in the inexcusable deaths. Photographic and aural records of the event prompted this Admiralty Court action."

Another button. "My third petition is a civil suit against Tevil Corporation, calling for restitution to my client for all damages done to the spaceship *Ajax* and its improvements, at that time resting outside the jurisdiction of Tevil, along with compensation for lost business, loss of good will among his customer community, slanderous assault against his reputation, and restitution for the lives lost. Consistent with the gravity of the offense and its egregious nature, which includes loss of life and extensive property damage, I will also be asking for punitive damages to be paid by Tevil Corporation, to the maximum allowed by law, along with all court costs and lawyer's expenses."

The audience stood and applauded. Then cheered. Marx pounded his gavel. It was not heard; or, if heard, it was ignored.

Eventually, order was restored.

Judge Marx seized his clipscreen. He quickly scrolled through Mighty's documents. He noted the cameras, the newsbloggers whispering into their recorders, the member of the Federation Bar Association in the front row, frowning.

Ajax was outside Tevil's jurisdiction. That was irrefutable. He glanced up at the audience. Any legal maneuvering might get him mobbed.

If there was one thing Marx knew, it was to pick his battlefields. This one was a loser.

He put his clipscreen in a pocket, grabbed his gavel, and gathered his robe around him. "Case-dismissed-court-adjourned." He raced out of the room quicker than an eight-legged dog with its tail between its legs.

There was a roar of approval.

Mike was instantly submerged in a swirl of cheering well-wishers. Derr Lurch reached down and lifted Mighty Mauz to sit on top of the table, where he too could receive the congratulations of the crowd without being trampled. It was a very happy mob of supporters.

Finally, after minutes of joyful uproar, the noise abated, the congratulations completed, and the audience began to thin.

Mike was in shock. He was not sure how he should react. At least he knew what was needed at the moment. He caught Mauz's attention.

"Hey. Mighty," he said. "I owe you."

"Nah," said Mauz. "Don't owe, won't owe. Tevil will pay for your defense, as you say, charged by the second." He raised an eyebrow. "But on damages and punitive I'm working for a percentage of the judgment. I'm going to squeeze Tevil for enough to fund your humble retirement and a decade of my extravagant lifestyle. I figure punitive alone to come in at six figures, maybe seven depending upon how many political chips Tevil is willing to burn."

"You won't hear me objecting."

"Tevil will dump Capone into the volcano. Probably also the rest of the corpper response team, which is actually sad. The recordings suggest they weren't in on the conspiracy. I'd rather have the hides of the people who gave the orders." His expression turned thoughtful. "Ever read OldEarth legal history? An event called the 'Boston Massacre'? Soldiers fired into a mob in self-defense. They were taken to court. A lawyer named Adams defended them; a very unpopular action on his part, but ethically an example of the glory of the law. He was later elected president of the North American amalgamated states. Maybe I could do a little *pro bono publico*, and represent those corppers. Not Capone, who clearly deserves the lava, but the others. Might be entertaining."

Mike took a deep breath, then said, "I'm grateful Panza obtained your services. Really grateful. How do I get in touch with him? Or her? I don't want Panza out of pocket waiting for the settlement. Send your bills to me. I can float a short-term loan until Tevil returns my stuff."

Mauz gave him a twisted smile. "You might get a cash infusion sooner." He pulled out his clipscreen and hit another button. "Document Four: a petition for Tevil Corporation to restore to you ten cases of power chips, valued at 60,000 standards."

"Power chips? I don't own any power chips. They were planted by Tevil, to frame me for smuggling."

Mighty smiled. "If Tevil comes forward and says their frame-up didn't work so they don't want to give you the phony evidence, I will be considerably surprised. Tevil will just write it off. Consider the chips part of your restitution." Mighty grinned. "Use it to cover my fees." Then, Mauz frowned. "That smuggling charge was brainless, unnecessary piling-on. Vakkers have every right to store goods in their ships before paying customs. Someone lacking in intelligence planned this whole thing. They were probably counting on you not having counsel, and Judge Marx greasing their phony charges." Mauz smiled benignly. "They should have consulted me, first."

Mighty winked.

Mike was feeling a little overwhelmed. "Yes. Okay. Sixty thousand stans in chips. Mine. That's … something."

"Shengwu will get you a good price at a reasonable commission."

"Yeah. Shengwu's good. He's supported me, supported Ghost. If anyone deserves the business, it's him." Mike thought for a minute. "After the repairs, anything over counts as Lacrosse Shot profit. Ghost gets his percent." He sighed. "I don't think Soak and Sampson had families."

"Their wills were read yesterday. They named you Executor, and major beneficiary. No other relatives. You are to receive all their belongings. Both had life insurance, if you can get Tevil to pay. Their wills were very touching. They said they may have slept in the Vakker's Hostel but the Lacrosse Shot was home. There were also bequests to their friends, TaxiGal, Crunch, Steinem, Geezer and ScrewLoose."

Mike felt like he had just been punched in the heart.

"Also, someone named Edgar the O. As Executor, you'll have to track him down. With a name like that, he's probably Vakker."

"Sherri." He swallowed hard, "Ella. Did they have families?"

Mauz thumped himself on the forehead with the heel of his hand. "Bloody hell," he said. "Damn. Zing, right past my so-called brain." Mauz pulled out his clipscreen and hit a button.

"What?" asked Mike, looking at him closely. "What?"

"MIKE!"

Mike turned to the familiar voice. He looked up to the entrance doors. Down the aisle, dodging past straggling Vakkers, came Sherri.

And Ella.

Mike stepped over to the aisle and through the gate.

Sherri was in the lead. Ella overtook her and threw herself into Mike's arms.

Mike hugged her, tightly, desperately. His throat choked with unfamiliar emotion. "I thought you were dead," he whispered into her hair. He buried his face into her neck, inhaling the sweet smell of her perfume, her skin. Warm. Sweet. Alive.

He felt a hand on his shoulder. Sherri had an expansive grin on her face. "About time," she chortled. Mike freed an arm and gathered Sherri in. "You, too," he said. "Happy."

"Maxed out overjoyed," said Sherri.

Mike spared a glare for Mauz. "Why didn't you tell me?"

"What, and have you go all mushy during my court performance? Steal my audience? Your mournful looks were part of my strategy."

After a time, Ella leaned back out of the embrace. She displayed a radiant smile.

Mike looked at Ella, then at Sherri, and thought for a moment. "Panza. Sancho Panza. I should have made the connection. LaMancha is good, too, right?"

"You betcha!" said Sherri. "He's not ducking my dissertation."

"How?" said Mike. "I heard the reports. His tank burst. They were walking on him. I heard them say you were dead. Exploded eyeballs."

"Euww," said Sherri, scrunching up her face.

"Let's sit," said Ella. She looked up to Mauz. "Thank you, again."

Mauz smiled. He and Derr Lurch headed out the exit.

After they were seated Mike said, "Tell."

Ella and Sherri looked at each other, then Sherri charged into their story. "We got Soak on the AutoDoc. Nothing we could do. He died before we could get him connected."

Mike nodded. He had already come to terms with Soak's passing.

"The corppers came in the dining room. They shot out the p-door controls. We were trapped in the office."

"You escaped?" asked Mike, like a gob-smacked boxer trying to figure out why the sun was up.

Sherri looked mournful. "Nope. Sorry. We died."

Ella gave Sherri's arm a playful slap. "Sherr-eee."

"Sorry 'bout that," said Sherri, grinning without repentance. "Line from The Three Stooges. I had to explain it to LaMancha. Always wanted to use it."

Ella took over. "We were in the office when they broke all the cameras in the dining room, but they missed Gardenbottie. He was hiding in those upside-down hanging tables. His camera recorded everything. LaMancha linked in. We saw them put the bombs on the doors."

"And?" said Mike.

"Thank goodness for Sampson. He pushed aside the bookcase next to your cot—really, Mike, you sleep on a cot? We're going shopping for a real bed for you." Ella looked him right in the eyes, while Mike looked everywhere but into her eyes. She allowed a small smile. "He'd flown an *Ajax* class before. He knew the location of the Personnel Escape Pod."

Mike's expression cleared. "The PEP. I forgot about the PEP."

"I put LaMancha to sleep," said Sherri, "Sampson carried his tank into the PEP."

"But, I heard, brains on the deck?"

"Ophelia," said Ella. "Sampson went back for her. We tried to stop him. He was kinda crazy, after Soak died, kept saying he should have done something, it was all his fault, he didn't want anyone else to die. The door bomb got them both."

They were quiet for a moment.

Ella took up the tale. "The PEP environmental system activated automatically and sealed us in. During the blowout the bookcase fell and covered the hatch."

Mike shuddered, thinking about how close he had come to selling the PEP. "But, how did you get out? There weren't any skinsuits in the PEP. I cleaned it out."

"No, you left the emergency supplies," said Ella. "We ate for a day and a half on dehydrated rations."

"Cardboard delicately seasoned with Tabasco Sauce, and copper-flavored water," grumbled Sherri. "You should be ashamed to have that in a restaurant." Then she frowned. "The emergency radio. The frequency was jammed at first. That's why LaMancha couldn't get through to medical for Soak."

Mike had a flash of anger. "I'll let Mauz know. They'll pay. Jamming the emergency freq is a felony."

Sherri nodded. "We waited a day to make sure Tevil wasn't listening, then I got on the university ham radio frequency and whistled up Z2ADD. A couple of friends brought over our skinsuits and a vak transport enclosure for LaMancha. Corppers were guarding the Dome City entrance, but not the cargo door with the great big hole. You should see the mess there. The blowout scattered dishes and beer all the way out to Pad 2." Sherri grinned. "We brought LaMancha back to TCU. Professor Ella awarded lab credit for Organic Computing 110, 'Care and Transportation of Mobile Organic Computers'."

"At least you didn't have to bribe them," commented Mike dryly.

Sherri looked up with a guilty expression. "Pizza party, on you, when the Shot's back up." Her expression cleared, and she grinned. "Think of it not as a bribe, but a celebration."

Mike barked out a laugh. He was feeling a little giddy.

Ella continued. "LaMancha managed the trip well. He's in the TCU organic computing lab in Ophelia's old slot. He forwarded Gardenbottie's recordings to Derr Mauz, and the rest is history."

"Excellent," said Mike. "But, how did he grease the palm? He'd need a couple hundred standards to meet Mauz's minimum retainer."

Ella gave Mike a puzzled look. "You haven't looked at LaMancha's accounts?"

"Accounts? LaMancha doesn't have accounts. He was winning some money at chisel, waitshooter bets, had a few scams going. Pence-a-point cash drawer stuff. I figured it was harmless."

Sherri snorted. "You *really* need to get away from the grill more."

"What?"

Ella gave Mike a crooked smile. "He started out with tips from waitshooting. Bets. Some chisel games. Then, the stock market, betting on tram races. He's won FoxxFone Network's 'Fargle O'Clary's Funniest Videos' contest three times. At night, he's been providing data analytic services for Tevil's Medical Insurance subsidiary."

"*LaMancha* works for *Tevil*?"

"Yup," nodded Sherri. "Work-at-home. Tevil is very pleased they don't have to provide him with an office and computer."

"Well, I'll be snicker-doodled. Damn. So, he had enough to get Mauz on board? I'll pay him back."

Sherri scrunched her face and said, "I think LaMancha would be insulted if you tried to pay him back. He feels like, what was his term, it's what *compadres* do."

"But Mighty's bill could run to hundreds," said Mike. "Thousands! Mauz bills until Tevil pays, which won't be soon."

"Not to worry," said Sherri. "LaMancha's cash reserves are over thirty thousand now."

"WHAT! Money thousands? STANDARDS?"

"Yup," said Sherri nonchalantly. "That's just his cash. Lots more's invested. Stocks, bonds, and commodities. He's saving for his own quantum computing machine, the ones that compute using the spin on quantum bits. Not smart like Organics, but *really* fast. Another six million, and the order's in."

Mike leaned back in his seat. He took in the two ladies, so happy in the moment. He felt like he had just risen from the grave.

"Ella, Sherri," he said, "I've been eating prison food for the last hundred years, and you both deserve a treat. Maybe you'll let me take you out now to the Monarch? I'm told it's fantastic."

"Oh, absolutely, yes!" cheered Sherri.

Ella smiled and said, "That would be lovely."

Sherri's FoxxFone buzzed. She pulled it out. "Hello, Sherri Brightly."

"Mike, LaMancha. Ah would be *dee-lighted—*"

109: Marshall

Coast walked into the Commandant's outer office at the Federated Space Academy, passing Mahkinen, the guardian of Captain Marshall's authority and privacy. Petty Officer Mahkinen half rose from her chair. Coast strode by.

Mahkinen hit the intercom. "Captain, Command Candidate Three Coast is—"

Captain Marshall glanced up from his screen to see Coast entering.

"—here to see you."

Marshall stood. His smile showed his relief. "Coast. Welcome back."

"Sir." Coast had an odd expression Captain Marshall couldn't interpret, was it anger, or resolve, or regret?

"Please, let's sit down." Marshall gestured to his conference table.

Coast remained standing.

Marshall came around his desk. "I wanted to express my admiration. Your actions at Newton Station were outstanding." He held out his hand.

Coast put a paper in Marshall's hand. "Resignation."

Marshall drew his hand back, refusing to close his fingers on the paper. It fluttered to the floor.

"The trial. I can see how you could be upset."

Coast's eyes flared. In a controlled voice, he said, "*Could* be? Your Force wanted me in *prison*."

"That whole incident." Marshall shook his head. "Most unfortunate."

"Unfortunate? 'Unfortunate' is taking orders from Clown Captain. Royals barely survive in vak, but they *command?* Arrogant, self-centered, egotistical incompetents."

Marshall ignored the fact that he was included in that insult, partly because, in truth, it was accurate. It was what he was fighting.

Captain Marshall remained calm. "That is one of the problems."

"Bendan would let those kids die before he risked a dent to his precious station. He violated Title Ten; *he broke the law.* He set up a civil trial to bury us in prison. Does the FSF object? Do we get help from FSF JAG, or even a five-stan civvie shyster? I'm supposed to go to prison for *stealing gerbils.* Save kids, accused of *murder.*"

"Please, sit. Let me help make sense of this."

Coast stepped back. His anger retracted; his rage collapsed inward. Shaking his head an emphatic 'no,' he said, "Might not survive next clown captain." He pointed to the paper on the floor. "Resignation."

Marshall refused to look at the paper. "You promised. Vakker's Word."

Coast looked him in the eyes. "Vakker's Word is based on honor. *Both* sides' honor. Is there honor in sending an Artisan and Candidate to prison to cover up a Command officer's crime? That's honor?" Coast looked at the paper on the deck. "Two times I save lives, and Freddy wants to send me to prison. That's honor? Vakkers have honor. Not the corpukes, not the corppers, not Freddy's Space Fuggups." He looked at Marshall with sadness. "Your Navy broke Vakker's Word, not me. Contract broken, *by you.*"

He turned and walked towards the door.

Addressing his back, Marshall said, "There are Marines at the gate."

"Tell them to shoot me."

110: Mahkinen

She had heard nothing from the Captain since Command Candidate Coast departed. The situation might need an intervention.

Mahkinen knocked and entered the Captain's office. He was standing, staring out the window. "Sir, I—"

She saw the paper on the floor. She walked over to pick it up.

"Don't," said Marshall. "Leave it. It stays there. Tell the cleaning crew. No one moves it. No one touches it."

"Sir, I don't understand."

"If I see it, it becomes official, and I have to take official action."

"Yes sir. It doesn't exist." She shifted on her feet. "Sir, I'm sorry, I should have intercepted him before he came in."

Marshall said nothing. He just kept staring out the window.

She started to leave. She had some calls to make to deal with this flapadoodle. She'd get it sorted.

"Don't," said Marshall.

She stopped, and looked back at him.

"Don't," he repeated. "Coast was not here. No instructions to have him picked up. Or anything." The Captain rubbed his face. "Let things settle." He glanced back. "If anyone picks him up, it's official, he's AWOL. If I tell people *not* to pick him up, I undermine disciple and display favoritism. There can be no favoritism in the Fleet Code of Military Justice."

"Yes, sir." She slipped out of the office.

Sometimes the Captain needed some help, whether he liked it or not.

She did not see Marshall's slight smile.

111: Lance Corporal

Coast walked towards Academy Gate 2 like he hadn't a care in the universe.

There were two Marines standing outside the guard shack. They saluted. "Command Candidate Three Coast. G'day, sir."

"Good day." Coast smiled, pulled out his FSF clipscreen and handed it to the private, nodded, smiled again pleasantly, and walked past.

The Marines didn't see him, didn't watch him walk out of the Academy grounds.

Coast walked to the end of the gate access road, turned right and strolled down the far side of the cross street. He passed an apartment's large trash dumpster, stopped, and walked back. He emptied the pockets of his Academy coverall, stripped off the powder blue garment with the third class rank insignia, carefully folded it, and dropped it into the dumpster. He walked on, clad in his gray skinsuit, stared at by children playing hopscotch.

The unseen Command Candidate disappeared from sight behind a building.

The lance corporal scuffed the sole of his brilliant spit-shined boots. He glanced at the private. "Up at Newton, he saved nine kids. Three Marine Juniors."

"Yeah. Word's out. Honorary Marine."

"Clown Captain up at Three, bastard, trying to cover his ass by busting Coast."

"Not right, that."

"Not right."

The Lance Corporal tapped the private's shoulder. "Nobody knows about this. We didn't get any calls, Coast didn't come by, we didn't see any Candidates this trick. You tell nobody, not your poker buddies, not your squad mates, not even the spirit of your long-lost dead grandmother in your sleep. Even a hint gets out, she'll make sure your next orders are to a frozen asteroid guarding a garbage dump, if you should live that long."

"Roger that, Corp."

The lance corporal stared towards where Coast had disappeared. Somehow, he had a feeling of loss, that something of great value had just passed through his hands.

The private said, "I don't think we'll see him again."

"Could have been a good Marine, but."

"He'll end up running some corner of the universe somewhere, maybe a galaxy or two."

The lance corporal gave him a crooked smile. "Yeah?"

112: *Ghost*

It was coming on to dark, a nice evening, warm but not hot, pleasant breeze, billowy paper-white clouds. Ghost put one foot in front of the other, heading … away.

Since the end of the trial, his anger had grown.

First, he had felt empty, like it was less a victory than a lynching averted. Walking out of that room, he had no words for anyone. He ignored the hands thrust out in congratulation, he was numb to the rage on Captain Bendan's face, he disregarded Brin's plea of 'I didn't do it,' and the fear on his bulldog features.

The first tram had taken him to the shuttle boarding lounge. Without thinking, he had walked to the gangway area, picked a shuttle at random, found an empty place, plugged in, and lowered the coffin top.

It was the next scheduled run to New Berne. No one bothered him, all the way down to dirt, hours of blessed privacy. Time to think.

Still confused, he checked into a hotel as Bonzo, a hidden alternate Vakker identity that had escaped Judge Marx's depredations. He slept, ate a room service meal, slept again.

Hours of thinking, a train ride to the Academy, yet when he walked into the Commandant's office he hadn't a clue what he was going to say. He had written his resignation three times, torn up two, half expected to crumple and toss the third. But the injustice of it all, the unfairness, every calamity against which he had struggled over the last months flooded his emotions and made his mouth say words that came from passion rather than thought.

Now, committed to a new path, he must plot a future.

Bonzo had papers as a Class 2 engineer and cargo handler. He'd catch a shuttle to Cargo Four, and find a billet in a Vakker ship outbound for a long trip, five or six punches.

Checking Bonzo's account on the clipscreen he had rigged to be invisible to the Freddies, he saw only a little over sixty stans remaining after the hotel bill. He would have to use the Goddard Mike had given him, for the shuttle fare. A shame. It had almost been like the Goddard was a good luck piece. At Cargo Four he could access his New Kong Bank account holding the money from Queen's Casino Club. A Vakker could go far on 8,995 standards.

The maglev rail station was ahead. Ghost was surprised. He hadn't thought of a destination, only that he needed to walk. His arrival here must be God's work, opening doors, closing doors.

Cross the street, stroll under the entrance arch, he let the escalator lift him to the boarding area. As he passed through the fare door Bonzo's credit balance was decrement by the minimum ticket price. His first success on the way to freedom.

To the left there was a group of four tall, muscular men in business suits, bulges under their coats, haircuts high 'n' tight. Corporate security? No, they had radio earbuds. Federated security. Did the Commandant put out the word he'd bolted from the Academy? He couldn't turn around and leave, it would look suspicious. Show a bland mien. You're just another guy wanting a train ride.

A security suit spotted him and walked purposefully over. Ghost assumed a questioning expression, his head cocked to the side.

The man flashed a badge. "Federated Agent. Please move forward on the platform. Sorry for the inconvenience." The agent looked him over. Probably checking for weapons, or wondering why a Citizen boarding a train would be wearing a skinsuit without carrying luggage.

The agent gave a small nod. Hard to hide a weapon while wearing a skinsuit.

Ghost did not let his relief show. "Certainly. Someone important?"

"Step forward, Derr. Thank you. I appreciate your cooperation."

Ghost walked along the platform a dozen meters and flopped down on a bench. Should he watch the agents, or ignore them? He figured a resident of the capital planet would see plenty of Federated agents pushing people around. Nothing new. He pulled out his clipscreen, rolled out the large screen and clicked it stiff, called up a news feed, and pretended to read.

A train pulled into the station, causing a swirling breeze that caught up dried leaves, adding a crackling sound to the train's soft swish. He got up and walked to the edge of the platform. After a recorded voice told him to 'mind the gap,' the doors opened.

He paused for a second, like a curious citizen, and looked. The Federated Agents were standing in a circle with their backs to the train, with some obviously-important individuals waiting to greet whoever got off. Some well-dressed people left the train, VIPs with a security detail. Good. It would distract attention away from him. Ghost turned to step on the train.

"Derr Coast! Derr Coast!"

That sounded like … He stepped back on to the platform.

A little boy barreled into him. "Derr Coast! Booster Buddy on Patrol!"

For the first time in days Ghost's heart registered joy. "Auggie! Booster Buddy!" He squatted, put a hand around the little boy's shoulders, the other behind his head, and hugged. It was an awkward hug. It felt good.

Auggie took a step back, holding on to Ghost's hand, smiling broadly. "We were coming to see you! Grandpa has to see some Commandant guy so he said we could come by and visit you and maybe have dinner or something. Zowie, we almost missed you!"

"Settle down, Booster Buddy, deep breaths, calm out. Hey, you look great."

"We did it, didn't we! Saved those people at Newton Station! Grandpa says you're a hero!"

Ghost smiled at Auggie's irrepressible enthusiasm. "Nothing would have worked without you. *You* were the key. You did super-zowie, the bravest Booster Buddy ever. I said you'd have a great adventure to tell, didn't I?"

Then Ghost noticed a large suit standing behind Auggie. Auggie noticed, too.

"Hey, Agent Hulk, this is Derr Coast, he's a Booster Buddy too, we were up at Newton Station." Auggie looked at Ghost, and lowered his volume to a not-quite-soft whisper. "Hulk is his code name. We use it to be covert from the bad guys."

Hulk looked Ghost over, gave a nod and a hint of a smile, and stepped back, scanning the platform around them.

Auggie pulled Ghost over to a bench, and they sat.

"Tell me about your adventure," said Ghost.

Auggie's eyes got very wide. "Zowie! Like, we were taking this tour through the Science Station, me and Grandpa and Maxie, and they were showing us all sorts of neat stuff, environmental and a reactor and a cooling system 'cause being in space is like being in a vacuum thermos bottle that keeps hot cocoa hot and how trams move from the rotating section to fixed section, and the huge momentum wheel they use to keep the station spinning and I got one of the techs to sign that off for my Space Station Merit Badge, and everybody was telling Grandpa how much everything cost and he was frowning a lot, then while Grandpa was in the Primate Lab Maxie was flirting with this science nerd who kinda looked like one of the monkeys when BLOWIE! Sirens were going off, real loud! All the air was going out of our compartment, and Maxie grabbed me and shoved me into the Primate Lab, I coulda made it by myself, but lots of people were pushing kids in too so I guess it was okay, then the—" Auggie paused for a breath, "—pressure isolation doors—" he said carefully, after a gasp, "—the p-doors shut, and we were trapped!"

"Wow," said Ghost, as much to express admiration as to force Auggie to pause and take in some O_2, his lips were turning a shade of blue.

"So, Booster Buddy Disaster Emergency Procedures say an 'immediate action' is to establish communications, and the phones weren't working and the clipscreen net was all junky, so I made the Booster Buddy Emergency Call all by myself on my suit comms like you taught me! You answered!"

Ghost nodded. "Exactly the right thing to do."

Auggie's hands were busy helping to tell the story. "And then Grandpa took charge and talked to you, and they released all these monkeys and a ton of gerbils, and they all got in this little room, and Grandpa tied me to a pipe and I put my helmet up, then my O_2 was flashing yellow and I called you and you said I wasn't to worry, and I didn't, and I heard a bang bang but nothing happened, and then BANG BANG BANG BANG! and all the leak balloons went to the corners, I got leak balloons signed off too, and they popped but the holes all 'exceeded capacity' so all the air was gone and all the gravity, no, all the *centrifugal force* went away, that's what I learned for my Space Station Merit Badge."

"Exactly right."

"When the bangs went off, I musta bumped my e-pack. I lost comms."

"No worries. You did everything that needed to be done. You did great."

"You pushed the nose of the shuttle into the lab! Right through the wall! The whole lab shook, I could feel it! I could see you through the shuttle window, you were upside down! I waved, did you see me, I was in the corner? All the air was gone and it was real quiet, because without air there is no way for sound to, to propagate!"

"You certainly have learned a lot."

Auggie nodded happily. "Then you pushed us into the cargo bay, and you wiggled the shuttle and took away a *whole wall*, and I was really happy to be tied to the pipe because I could see all out into space and all the stars and it was like being real high above everything and I felt like I was going to fall ..." Auggie got quieter. "I was a little bit scared, then."

"Everyone is a little bit scared the first time they confront the Deep Dark, even Vakkers tied to a pipe."

"And then these huge doors shut, and we were in the cargo bay!"

A deeper voice next to them spoke. "Then we got air, and opened the hatch, and all the gerbils got out."

Auggie and Ghost looked up and saw Senator Franklin standing next to them, displaying a pleasant, indulgent smile. Ghost stood.

"Aw, Grandpa! I wanted to tell about the gerbils!"

"I'm sorry. I'll let you tell it next time. I'd like a few words with Command Candidate Coast. Agent, ah, Hulk, has agreed to escort you to the Spacers' Memorial. You said you needed it for your Space History Merit Badge."

"Zowie, double roger right! Grandpa, don't tell him about the Booster Buddy surprise! Gotta go, Derr Coast. Booster Buddy on Patrol!"

"Booster Buddy on Patrol," acknowledged Ghost dutifully. Auggie waved back at them as the agent took his hand and led him to the escalator.

"Please, Candidate Coast, let's sit for a moment," said the Admiral.

The joy of seeing Auggie bled away. Ghost sat.

Three agents stood around them at a discrete distance, close enough for protection, far enough for privacy. Several personages stood off in a group, talking among themselves, continually glancing at them.

"I am sorry I was not able to meet your shuttle," said the Admiral. "I wanted to thank you personally for your efforts. You saved Augustus, Maxine, me, the others. My most sincere, most sincere thanks."

"Sir." *If you were so thankful,* thought Ghost, *why did you allow that Clown Captain to lay a trial on me?* Resentfulness flared.

Reading his expression, the Admiral said, "That trial. *Most* regrettable. I learned of the charges too late, or they never would have been filed."

Ghost said nothing.

"I was able to do some things to interrupt the travesty," Franklin said.

Ghost thought back. The replacement judge, the court recorder, the court recorder's box.

"I understand," said the Admiral, "you are being considered at the highest Fleet level for an award."

An award. Captain Bendan displayed a chest full of medals. Command officers spent a lot of bandwidth giving each other awards and fancy medals. Do you really think Command Officers would give an unscrub a medal? That would be a rock-solid admission that Bendan was the felon. Vakkers didn't give awards; they gave respect.

Ghost looked up at the Admiral. "Will *Artisan* Lieutenant Padmere be honored?"

"Yes, Padmere too."

"The other ComCans? Brin?"

"All but Brin. There is an investigation as to how Flipper Juice got in his skinsuit dispenser. He did not contribute to the rescue, and will not be honored. There are award recommendations for others on Newton and Station Three as well. Kenya and Roberts, cargo handlers, someone titled a 'Mag Wrangler,' others."

Ghost clenched his fist out of the Admiral's sight. "Captain Bendan?"

The admiral leaned against the seat back. "Nikita Bendan. There is a case for special handling." He tapped his fingers together. "A powerful man, with powerful connections, well beyond his rank. He has support from several of the 35 Families, Brin Industries, The

Chavez Group, a son who married into Rothchild's, other associations. At the last promotion board, he was selected for Flag rank."

Another reason for me to disappear, thought Ghost.

"The flag nomination is on hold awaiting a determination regarding a certain Title Ten felony charge. I'm not expecting anything out of that, unfortunately, too many rice bowls would be broken if Command officers would actually be held accountable to the law. He'll rally his supporters, cash in political chits, let loose legal lackeys, and the Command Officer's Protective Association will close ranks around him. Odds are, he'll wiggle free." The Senator folded his hands. "There is a consolation. All flag promotions must be confirmed by the Senate Fleet Command Committee. I head the committee."

"You'll stop it?"

The Admiral smiled, as if rebuking him gently for his presumption. "Captain Bendan has been removed from command of Station Three for the duration of the catastrophe investigation. He has been placed on temporary assignment, to write a review of space emergency procedures. That assignment will take at least, oh, say, six months, during which he will remain at his current rank. If he survives Title Ten Twenty-eight, he must be resubmitted for advancement. If the flag nomination is not renewed and passed by the Fleet Selection Board, and confirmed by my committee, he will be at the captains' mandatory retirement age."

Ghost was not sure what to make of that.

"You, on the other hand, with Artisan Lieutenant Padmere and Roddy, Ka-Shing and Ortega, will write a report on the incident, with recommendations. I have come to ask the Commandant for that report in a month's time, no later, for I intend to act on Title Ten in the Chamber. Knowing the ways of bureaucracy, to allow time for chain-of-command reviews and editing, your first draft must be ready by, I think, yesterday."

This forced Ghost to crack a small smile, not at the Admiral's little joke, but at the knowledge he would not be around to write any stupid reports.

"Last, there is the Booster Buddy surprise."

Ghost blinked. "Augustus said—?"

"You need to know. With the acclamation of the Associates of

Space Flight, now being tabulated, but so far with no dissenting votes, you will receive the Beacon of Bravery award. It is the second highest award the society has to confer."

"That, that is … oh."

"You were nominated by *several* Association members. Augustus submitted one. I was very proud of him for that, unselfishly thinking of honoring others. I admit to helping him with the 'Justification for Award' section. The application software was giving him trouble. It would not permit 'very, very, very, very, very brave' and 'very, very, very, very, top-notch Booster Buddy zowie heroic' as grammatically acceptable."

All Ghost could manage in response was another "Oh."

"He originally submitted you for the Banner of Bravery, the top award, based on the magnitude of your accomplishment and how many lives you saved. But the Awards Committee felt it appropriate to reduce the decoration by one level when they discovered, of the scores of lives Augustus mentioned, 123 were gerbils."

Ghost could not help himself. He laughed.

"That is not to say that Enhanced Cognition Gerbil lives are not valued," said the Senator, "Only, by how much? Petitions have been submitted demanding that EC Gerbils be given the same status as citizens. The Junior Booster Buddy ranks are in an uproar."

This was too, too ridiculous.

The Admiral smiled. "There are nine thousand junior Booster Buddies, on the Seventeen Systems and countless stations and facilities, who look to you as a hero, as a role model. Including, if I may single out one Booster Buddy, my grandson, who thinks you are very special. He told me you spent a day in *Lxchu* teaching him the skinsuit. Foregoing all the entertainment available in Queen Galaxy Class to help a little boy overcome the taunts of bullies tells me as much about your character as, say," the Senator flashed a smile, "saving 123 gerbils." He then nodded thoughtfully. "Augustus is proud of his own achievement, but most of his happiness stems from helping you. Teaming with you."

The admiral looked into Ghost's eyes. "There will be an awards ceremony at the next Associates of Space Flight Interplanetary Convention. I hope you will accept the award personally. It will mean a lot to thousands of children. Augustus will also receive an award, not a Beacon, hasn't been a Beacon awarded in fifteen years. The last was to Luther King, you probably know of him. He was Electric Plant Controls Technician when the *Costa Eastlande's* PunchPlane Generator went unstable. He maintained power manually while they evacuated over 900 passengers. He was lost in the explosion."

Ghost nodded. All Vakkers honored Luther King.

The Admiral stood. Ghost joined him on his feet.

Franklin held out his hand. "I must run. I'm meeting with the Commandant. Besides the report, I was planning on mentioning the ceremony. I'm sure he'll be able to arrange your schedule. April."

113: Lance Corporal

It was approaching the end of their watch, the sky darkening with the end of day. The private and lance corporal at Guard Post 2 were happily anticipating shedding their immaculate but stiff uniforms, checking their sidearms in to the armory, a late snack, and then cards or a vid before taps.

The lance corporal looked down the street. Coming into view, under a streetlight, a figure in a skinsuit walked. He nudged the private and gestured with his head.

The private glanced up, then looked more carefully. "There's a sight."

The figure stopped at a dumpster, reached in, and pulled out a neatly folded blue garment.

The lance corporal looked at the private and raised an eyebrow.

With an exaggerated sigh surmounted by a smile he could not contain, the private handed over a one standard coin. "Bad as he was screwed, I figured it was a sure thing."

"Nah. His type, they don't walk when a job needs doing. He would have been back, tonight, tomorrow, a few days. Guaranteed." The lance corporal buffed the coin on his tunic sleeve, admired it at arm's length, then pocketed it with a flourish.

They could see bugs circling around the lamp light, flashing silver wings and lines of black shadow. A deep breath pulled in the damp air. There might be fog before morning.

"I heard he was recruited Over the Drum."

"Heard the same."

"Shame that drum wasn't Fleet Marine."

"Shame."

The man under the street light unfolded the garment with a snap and began brushing it with his hand.

Opening a drawer, the lance corporal pulled out a cloth and bottle of water, and passed them to the private. He added a clipscreen.

"Take these over. He'll need his Academy clipscreen. He can use a wet towel to clean off his bluesies. I wouldn't want to have to report him for passing a Marine Guard Post wearing a dirty uniform."

Volume 1 — THE END

Volume 2 — MISPLACED PERILS — Arrival Imminent

About the Author

In thorough preparation for writing science fiction, Alan Zimm started out as a nuclear engineer/surface line officer in the US Navy. After completing active duty as a Commander, he joined The Johns Hopkins University Applied Physics Laboratory, advancing to Principle Professional Staff and a Section Leader in the Aviation Systems and Advanced Concepts Group. He worked as an Operations Research analyst on many US Navy, Marine, and Army systems. He holds a BS in Physics from UCLA, an MS in Operations Research from the Naval Postgraduate School, and a Doctorate in Public Administration from the University of Southern California. He has taught Naval History at JHU, extensively published in that field, and lectured at APL, The Defense Intelligence College, King's College London, Naval Postgraduate School, the Marine Corps University, the Center for Naval Analyses and other venues. His great failure has been in trying to attract his wife, Deborah, into reading science fiction; daughter Natalie, a licensed Therapist, has often attempted to diagnose his mental aberrations (so far with uncertain results). He was taught to fly at a young age by his father in a Champion high-wing taildragger powered by a 70-horsepower Lycoming engine, that barely got them aloft during hot weather. He is an Honorary Life Member of the US Naval Institute, a member of the Society for Military History, and a Companion of the Naval Order of the United States.

www.ingramcontent.com/pod-product-compliance
Lightning Source LLC
Chambersburg PA
CBHW051134300726
48978CB00011B/275